The
Greatest
Exploration Stories
Ever Told

The Greatest Exploration Stories Ever Told

True Tales of Search and Discovery

EDITED BY
DARREN BROWN

THE LYONS PRESS
Guilford, Connecticut
An imprint of The Globe Pequot Press

The Lyons Press is an imprint of The Globe Pequot Press

Printed in the United States of America

10 9 8 7 6 5 4 3 2 1

Design by Compset, Inc.

Library of Congress Cataloging-in-Publication Data

The greatest exploration stories ever told : true tales of discovery from Marco Polo to Jon Krakauer, from Charles Darwin to Teddy Roosevelt / edited and with an introduction by Darren Brown.
  p. cm.
  ISBN 1-58574-777-7 (hc : alk. paper)
  1. Discoveries in geography—History. 2. Voyages and travel—History. 3. Explorers—History. 4. Adventure and adventurers—History. I. Brown, Darren.
  G80 .G699 2003
  910'.9—dc21   2002154438

Acknowledgments

I would like to thank Tony Lyons and Jay Cassell of The Lyons Press for making this book possible. Thanks also to the staff at the Bozeman Public Library for helping me track down many of the books necessary to put this collection together.

Contents

Introduction

It might have been the death of me and my men. I might have lost everything.... But the adventure, the conquest of an unknown country, the struggle against the impossible, all have a fascination which draws me with irresistible force.

Sven Hedin
My Life as an Explorer

Imagine standing with Henry Stanley on the banks of the upper Congo, racked by fever, worn down by months of hardship and incessant fighting, facing a thousand miles of rapids and tribe after tribe of hostile cannibals, yet bursting with enthusiasm for a chance to shove off into a river without knowing where it might lead. The urge to see what lies around the next bend or over the next hill has been an irresistible lure to explorers for thousands of years. It has helped us define our world and shown over and over the indomitable nature of the human spirit. And although we live in an ever-shrinking world these days, stories of bold, courageous, implacable explorers continue to leave us spellbound.

Many famous expeditions, ones that cost much in suffering, expense, and life's blood, had very little practical meaning. Finding the source of the Nile occupied the western world for centuries, even though it was just a dot on the map. Reaching the North and South Poles was an exercise in endurance, a test of willpower and planning that ended with little more than men hammering flags into barren seas of ice. The search for the Northwest Passage continued long after it was found to be worthless as a trade route. Yet there was still something compelling in the idea of standing where no human had ever stood before, seeing something in a way that no other would ever see it again, surviving where the world thought survival impossible.

One of the most fascinating aspects of exploration is how various discoveries were judged in the scope of history. John Franklin's bungled, amateurish attempts at finding the Northwest Passage left him a national hero in

England, while James Bruce's clever, determined exploration of Abyssinia (present-day Ethiopia), which led him to the source of the Blue Nile and brought to light much new information about Africa, was greeted with derision. He was branded a liar, and his discoveries scoffed at for over a century. Paul Du Chaillu, one of the first westerners to visit the West African interior, was forced to make a second trip to gather additional proof of his claims when he was accused of making up stories about gorilla hunting, cannibals, and pygmies.

In recent years, Ernest Shackleton has probably become the most famous of the polar explorers, despite never reaching either pole or making significant new discoveries, while the names of pioneering polar explorers like Fridtjof Nansen are virtually unknown today. Alexander von Humboldt's popularity in the 19th century dwarfed that of Lewis & Clark, making him one of the most famous men in the western world, but who today remembers what he accomplished—or even his name?

The stories of some amazing explorations have suffered due to language difficult for modern readers to follow, such as those collected in *Hakluyt's Voyages*. Others, like Alexander Mackenzie's Canadian crossing, were hurt by less-than-inspired writing.

On the other hand, many excellent writers made less-daring expeditions much more entertaining. Robert Dunn's journal of Albert Cooke's failed assault on Mt. McKinley is one of the funniest books of exploration ever written. Wilfred Thesiger was a reluctant writer, uninterested in the glory most explorers reveled in, but he wrote a beautiful account of minor explorations through one of the world's last unexplored deserts. Charles Darwin really wasn't an explorer at all, but his *Voyage of the Beagle* remains one of the most interesting books of discovery over 150 years after being written. Mungo Park's journal of his wandering search for the Niger in the late 1700s has stayed almost continuously in print and still makes great reading.

Had better records survived, surely some of the most interesting exploration stories would have come from the ancient world, as men tentatively tested the waters beyond the Mediterranean, or from early China, where the discoveries of intrepid sailors were deliberately suppressed for centuries.

The stories gathered here run the gamut from Henry Stanley's big-budget African expedition to Alexandra David-Neel's quiet trip into Tibet, and span virtually every continent and ocean. Most come from the "Age of Discovery," which saw much of the unknown world explored in a relatively brief period of just a hundred years or so (although it is always debatable whether one can "discover" an area in which thousands of native people are already living).

Modern civilization has left few places on the globe untouched, but these stories will take you back to a wonderful time when this wasn't the case.

—Darren Brown

The
Greatest
Exploration Stories
Ever Told

The Great Khan

BY MARCO POLO

Marco Polo's amazing adventures in the service of Mongol emperor Kublai Khan in the late thirteenth century almost weren't written. After years abroad, he returned home to Venice to take up life as a merchant and was captured during fighting with rival city Genoa. While in prison, he met a writer who recorded his story. Although the book sold well, most readers didn't believe a word of it. It would be centuries before the western world realized how accurate his reporting was.

Polo was a merchant, not an explorer, but his travels represented some of the most extensive explorations of his era. His style of writing is reminiscent of Herodotus, mixing history with personal experience and outrageous hearsay. In the following excerpt from *The Book of Ser Marco Polo*, he describes the lifestyle of "The Great Khan." To Europeans during the latter years of the Middle Ages, the lavishness of what he related must have seemed beyond comprehension.

★ ★ ★ ★ ★

The personal appearance of the Great Khan, Lord of Lords, whose name is Cublay, is such as I shall now tell you. He is of a good stature, neither tall nor short, but of a middle height. He has a becoming amount of flesh, and is very shapely in all his limbs. His complexion is white and red, the eyes black and fine, the nose well formed and well set on. He has four wives, whom he retains permanently as his legitimate consorts; and the eldest of his sons by those four wives ought by rights to be emperor—I mean when his father dies. Those four ladies are called empresses, but each is distinguished also by her proper name. And each of them has a special court of her own, very grand and ample; no one of them having fewer than 300 fair and charming damsels. They have also many pages and eunuchs, and a number of other attendants of both sexes; so that each of these ladies has not fewer than 10,000 persons attached to her court.

When the Emperor desires the society of one of these four consorts, he will sometimes send for the lady to his apartment and sometimes visit her at her own. He has also a great number of concubines, and I will tell you how he obtains them.

You must know that there is a tribe of Tartars called Ungrat, who are noted for their beauty. Now every year a hundred of the most beautiful maidens of this tribe are sent to the Great Khan, who commits them to the charge of certain elderly ladies dwelling in his palace. And these old ladies make the girls sleep with them, in order to ascertain if they have sweet breath (and do not snore), and are sound in all their limbs. Then such of them as are of approved beauty, and are good and sound in all respects, are appointed to attend on the Emperor by turns. Thus six of these damsels take their turn for three days and nights, and wait on him when he is in his chamber and when he is in his bed, to serve him in any way, and to be entirely at his orders. At the end of the three days and nights they are relieved by other six. And so throughout the year, there are reliefs of maidens by six and six, changing every three days and nights.

The Emperor hath, by those four wives of his, twenty-two male children; the eldest of whom was called CHINKIN for the love of the good Chinghis Khan, the first Lord of the Tartars. And this Chinkin, as the Eldest Son of the Khan, was to have reigned after his father's death; but, as it came to pass, he died. He left a son behind him, however, whose name is Temur, and he is to be the Great Khan and Emperor after the death of his Grandfather, as is but right; he being the child of the Great Khan's eldest son. And this Temur is an able and brave man, as he hath already proven on many occasions.

The Great Khan hath also twenty-five other sons by his concubines; and these are good and valiant soldiers, and each of them is a great chief. I tell you moreover that of his children by his four lawful wives there are seven who are kings of vast realms or provinces, and govern them as well; being all able and gallant men, as might be expected. For the Great Khan their sire is, I tell you, the wisest and most accomplished man, the greatest Captain, the best to govern men and rule an Empire, as well as the most valiant, that ever has existed among all the Tribes of Tartars.

You must know that for three months of the year, to wit December, January, and February, the Great Khan resides in the capital city of Cathay, which is called Cambaluc [and which is at the north-eastern extremity of the county]. In that city stands his great Palace, and now I will tell you what it is like.

It is enclosed all round by a great wall forming a square, each side of which is a mile in length; that is to say, the whole compass thereof is four miles. This you may depend on; it is also very thick, and a good ten paces in height, whitewashed and loop-holed all round. At each angle of the wall there is a very fine and rich palace in which the war-harness of the Emperor is kept, such as bows and quivers, saddles and bridles, and bowstrings, and everything needful for an army. Also midway between every two of these Corner Palaces there is another of the like; so that taking the whole compass of the enclosure you find eight vast Palaces stored with the Great Lord's harness of war. And you must understand that each Palace is assigned to only one kind of article; thus one is stored with bows, a second with saddles, a third with bridles, and so on in succession right round.

The great wall hath five gates on its southern face, the middle one being the great gate which is never opened on any occasion except when the Great Khan himself goes forth or enters. Close on either side of this great gate is a smaller one by which all other people pass; and then towards each angle is another great gate, also open to people in general; so that on that side there are five gates in all.

Inside of this wall there is a second, enclosing a space that is somewhat greater in length than in breadth. This enclosure also hath eight places corresponding to those of the outer wall, and stored like them with the Lord's harness of war. This wall also hath five gates on the southern face, corresponding to those in the outer wall, and hath one gate on each of the other faces, as the outer wall hath also. In the middle of the second enclosure is the Lord's Great Palace, and I will tell you what it is like.

You must know that it is the greatest Palace that ever was. [Towards the north it is in contact with the outer wall, whilst towards the south there is a vacant space which the Barons and the soldiers are constantly traversing. The Palace itself] hath no upper story, but is all on the ground floor, only the basement is raised some ten palms above the surrounding soil [and this elevation is retained by a wall of marble raised to the level of the pavement, two paces in width and projecting beyond the base of the Palace so as to form a kind of terrace-walk, by which people can pass round the building, and which is exposed to view, whilst on the outer edge of the wall there is a very fine pillared balustrade; and up to this the people are allowed to come]. The roof is very lofty, and the walls of the Palace are all covered with gold and silver. They are also adorned with representations of dragons [sculptured and gilt], beasts and birds, knights and idols, and sundry other subjects. And on the ceiling too you see nothing but gold and silver and painting. [On each of the four sides there is a great marble staircase leading to the top of the marble wall, and forming the approach to the Palace.]

The Hall of the Palace is so large that it could easily dine 6,000 people; and it is quite a marvel to see how many rooms there are besides. The building is altogether so vast, so rich, and so beautiful, that no man on earth could design anything superior to it. The outside of the roof also is all coloured with vermilion and yellow and green and blue and other hues, which are fixed with a varnish so fine and exquisite that they shine like crystal, and lend a resplendent lustre to the Palace as seen for a great way round. This roof is made too with such strength and solidity that it is fit to last forever.

[On the interior side of the Palace are large buildings with halls and chambers, where the Emperor's private property is placed, such as his treasures of gold, silver, gems, pearls, and gold plate, and in which reside the ladies and concubines. There he occupies himself at his own convenience, and no one else has access.]

Between the two walls of the enclosure which I have described, there are fine parks and beautiful trees bearing a variety of fruits. There are beasts also of sundry kinds, such as white stags and fallow deer, gazelles and roebucks, and fine squirrels of various sorts, with numbers also of the animal that gives the musk, and all manner of other beautiful creatures, insomuch that the whole place is full of them, and no spot remains void except where there is traffic of people going and coming. [The parks are covered with abundant grass; and the roads through them being all paved and raised two cubits above the surface, they never become muddy, nor does the rain lodge on them, but flows off into the meadows, quickening the soil and producing that abundance of herbage.]

From that corner of the enclosure which is towards the north-west there extends a fine Lake, containing foison of fish of different kinds which the Emperor hath caused to be put in there, so that whenever he desires any he can have them at his pleasure. A river enters this lake and issues from it, but there is a grating of iron or brass put up so that the fish cannot escape in that way.

Moreover on the north side of the Palace, about a bow-shot off, there is a hill which has been made by art [from the earth dug out of the lake]; it is a good hundred paces in height and a mile in compass. This hill is entirely covered with trees that never lose their leaves, but remain ever green. And I assure you that wherever a beautiful tree may exist, and the Emperor gets news of it, he sends for it and has it transported bodily with all its roots and the earth attached to them, and planted on that hill of his. No matter how big the tree may be, he gets it carried by his elephants; and in this way he has got together the most beautiful collection of trees in all the world. And he has also caused the whole hill to be covered with the ore of azure, which is very green. And thus not only are the trees all green, but the hill itself is all green likewise; and there is nothing to be seen on it that is not green; and hence it is called the GREEN MOUNT; and in good sooth 'tis named well.

On the top of the hill again there is a fine big palace which is all green inside and out; and thus the hill, and the trees, and the palace form together a charming spectacle; and it is marvellous to see their uniformity of colour! Everybody who sees them is delighted. And the Great Khan had caused this beautiful prospect to be formed for the comfort and solace and delectation of his heart.

You must know that beside the Palace [that we have been describing]; *i.e*, the Great Palace, the Emperor has caused another to be built just like his own in every respect, and this he hath done for his son when he shall reign and Emperor after him. Hence it is made just in the same fashion and of the same size, so that everything can be carried on in the same manner after his own death. [It stands on the other side of the lake from the Great Khan's Palace, and there is a bridge crossing the water from one to the other.] The Prince in question holds now a Seal of Empire, but not with such complete authority as the Great Khan, who remains supreme as long as he lives.

The three months of December, January, and February, during which the Emperor resides at his Capital City, are assigned for hunting and fowling, to the extent of some 40 days' journey round the city; and it is ordained that the larger game taken be sent to the Court. To be more particular: Of all the larger beasts of the chase, such as boars, roebucks, bucks, stags, lions, bears, etc., the greater part of what is taken has to be sent, and feathered game likewise. The animals are gutted and dispatched to the Court on carts. This is done by all the people within 20 or 30 days' journey, and the quantity so dispatched is immense. Those at a greater distance cannot send the game, but they have to send the skins after tanning them, and these are employed in the making of equipments for the Emperor's army.

The Emperor hath numbers of leopards trained to the chase, and hath also a great many lynxes taught in like manner to catch game, and which afford excellent sport. He hath also several great Lions, bigger than those of Babylonia, beasts whose skins are coloured in the most beautiful way, being striped all along the sides with black, red, and white. These are trained to catch boars and wild cattle, bears, wild asses, stags, and other great or fierce beasts. And 'tis a rare sight, I can tell you, to see those lions giving chase to such beasts as I have mentioned! When they are to be so employed the Lions are taken out in a covered cart, and every Lion has a little doggie with him. [They are obliged to approach the game against the wind, otherwise the animals would scent the approach of the Lion and be off].

There are also a great number of eagles, all broken to catch wolves, foxes, deer, and wild goats, and they do catch them in great numbers. But those especially that are trained to wolf-catching are very large and powerful birds, and no wolf is able to get away from them.

The Emperor hath two Barons who are own brothers, one called Baian and the other Mingan; and these two are styled *Chinuchi* (or *Cunichi*), which is as much as to say, "The Keepers of the Mastiff Dogs." Each of these brothers hath 10,000 men under his orders; each body of 10,000 being dressed alike, the one in red and the other in blue, and whenever they accompany the Lord to the chase, they wear his livery, in order to be recognized. Out of each body of 10,000 there are 2,000 men who are each in charge of one or more great mastiffs, so that the whole number of these is very large. And when the Prince goes a-hunting, one of those Barons, with his 10,000 men and something like 5,000 dogs, goes towards the right, whilst the other goes toward, the left with his party in like manner. They move along, all abreast of one another, so that the whole line extends over a full day's journey, and no animal can escape them. Truly it is a glorious sight to see the working of the dogs and the huntsmen on such an occasion! And as the Lord rides a-fowling across the plains, you will see these big hounds coming tearing up, one pack after a bear, another pack after a stag, or some other beast, as it may hap, and running the game down now on this side and now on that, so that it is really a most delightful sport and spectacle.

[The Two Brothers I have mentioned are bound by the tenure of their office to supply the Khan's Court from October to the end of March with 1,000 head of game daily, whether of beasts or birds, and not counting quails; and also with fish to the best of their ability, allowing fish enough for three persons to reckon as equal to one head of game.]

Now I have told you of the Masters of the Hounds and all about them, and next I will tell you how the Lord goes off on an expedition for the space of three months.

After he has stopped at his capital city those three months that I mentioned, to wit, December, January, February, he starts off on the 1st day of March, and travels southward towards the Ocean Sea, a journey of two days. He takes with him full 10,000 falconers, and some 500 gerfalcons besides peregrines, sakers, and other hawks in great numbers; and goshawks also to fly at the water-fowl. But do not suppose that he keeps all these together by him; they are distributed about, hither and thither, one hundred together, or two hundred at the utmost, as he thinks proper. But they are always fowling as they advance, and the most part of the quarry taken is carried to the Emperor. And let me tell you when he goes thus a-fowling with his gerfalcons and other hawks, he is attended by full 10,000 men who are disposed in couples; and these are called *Toscaol*, which is as much as to say, "Watchers." And the name describes their business. They are posted from spot to spot, always in couples, and thus they cover a great deal of ground! Every man of them is provided with a whistle and hood, so as to be able to call in a hawk and hold it in hand. And when the Emperor makes a cast, there is no need that he follow it up, for those men I speak of keep so good a look out that they never lose sight of the birds, and if these have a need of help they are ready to render it.

All the Emperor's hawks, and those of the Barons as well, have a little label attached to the leg to mark them, on which is written the names of the owner and the keeper of the bird. And in this way the hawk, when caught, is at once identified and handed over to its owner. But if not, the bird is carried to a certain Baron, who is styled the *Bularguchi*, which is as much as to say, "The Keeper of Lost Property." And I tell you that whatever may be found without a known owner, whether it be a horse, or a sword, or a hawk, or what not, it is carried to that Baron straightaway, and he takes charge of it. And if the finder neglects to carry his trover to the Baron, the latter punishes him. Likewise the loser of any article goes to the Baron, and if the thing be in his hands it is immediately given up to the owner. Moreover, the said Baron always pitches on the highest spot of the camp, with his banner displayed, in order that those who have lost or found anything may have no difficulty in finding their way to him. Thus nothing can be lost but it shall be incontinently found and restored.

And so the Emperor follows this road that I have mentioned, leading along in the vicinity of the Ocean Sea (which is within two days' journey of his capital city, Cambaluc), and as he goes there is many a fine sight to be seen, and plenty of the very best entertainment in hawking; in fact, there is no sport in the world to equal it!

The Emperor himself is carried upon four elephants in a fine chamber made of timber, lined inside with plates of beaten gold, and outside with lions' skins [for he always travels in this way on his fowling expeditions because he is troubled with gout]. He always keeps beside him a dozen of his choicest gerfalcons, and is attended by several of his Barons, who ride on horseback alongside. And sometimes, as they may be going along, and the Emperor from his chamber is holding discourse with the Barons, one of the latter shall exclaim: "Sire! Look out for Cranes!" Then the Emperor instantly has the top of his chamber thrown open, and having marked the cranes he casts one of his gerfalcons, whichever he pleases; and often the quarry is struck within his view, so that he has the most exquisite sport and diversion, there as he sits in his chamber or lies on his bed; and all the Barons with him get the enjoyment of it likewise! So it is not without reason that I tell you that I do not believe there ever existed in the world or ever will exist, a man with such sport and enjoyment as he has, or with such rare opportunities.

And when he has traveled till he reaches a place called CACHAR MODUN, there he finds his tents pitched, with the tents of his Sons, and his Barons, and those of his Ladies and theirs, so that there shall be full 10,000 tents in all, and all fine and rich ones. And I will tell you how his own quarters are disposed. The tent in which he holds his courts is large enough to give cover easily to a thousand souls. It is pitched with its door to the south, and the Barons and Knights remain in waiting in it, whilst the Lord abides in another close to it on the west side. When he wishes to speak with any one he causes the person to be summoned to that other tent. Immediately behind the great tent there is a fine large chamber where the Lord sleeps; and there are also many other tents and chambers, but they are not in contact with the Great Tent as these are. The two audience tents and the sleeping chamber are constructed in this way. Each of the audience tents has three poles, which are of spice-wood, and are most artfully covered with lions' skins, striped with black and white and red, so that they do not suffer from any weather. All three apartments are also covered outside with similar skins of striped lions, a substance that lasts forever. And inside they are all lined with ermine and sable, these two being the finest and most costly furs in existence. For a robe of sable, large enough to line a mantle, is worth 2,000 bezants of gold, or 1,000 at least, and this kind of skin is called by the Tartars "The King of Furs." The beast itself is about the size of a marten. These two furs of which I speak are applied and inlaid so exquisitely, that it is really something worth seeing. All the tent-ropes are of silk. And in short I may say that those tents, to wit the two audience halls and the sleeping chamber, are so costly that it is not every king could pay for them.

Round about these tents are others, also fine ones and beautifully pitched, in which are the Emperor's ladies, and the ladies of the other princes and officers. And then there are the tents for the hawks and their keepers, so that altogether the number of tents there on the plain is something wonderful. To see the many people that are thronging to and fro on every side and every day there, you would take the camp for a good big city. For you must reckon the Leeches, and the Astrologers, and the Falconers, and all the other attendants on so great a company; and add that everybody there has his whole family with him, for such is their custom.

The Lord remains encamped there until the spring, and all that time he does nothing but go hawking round about among the canebrakes along the lakes and rivers that abound in that region, and across fine plains on which are plenty of cranes and swans, and all sorts of other fowl. The other gentry of the camp also are never done with hunting and hawking, and every day they bring home great store of venison and feathered game of all sorts. Indeed, without having witnessed it, you would never believe what quantities of game are taken, and what marvellous sport and diversion they all have whilst they are in camp there.

There is another thing I should mention; to wit, that for 20 days' journey round the spot nobody is allowed, be he who he may, to keep hawks or hounds, though anywhere else whosoever list may keep them. And furthermore throughout all the Emperor's territories, nobody however audacious dares to hunt any of these four animals, to wit, hare, stag, buck, and roe, from the month of March to the month of October. Anybody who should do so would rue it bitterly. But those people are so obedient to their Lord's command that even if a man were to find one of those animals asleep by a roadside he would not touch it for the world! And thus the game multiplies at such a rate that the whole country swarms with it, and the Emperor gets as much as he could desire. Beyond the term I have mentioned, however, to wit that from March to October, everybody may take these animals as he list.

After the Emperor has tarried in that place, enjoying his sport as I have related, from March to the middle of May, he moves with all his people, and returns straight to his capital city of Cambaluc (which is also the capital of Cathay, as you have been told), but all the while continuing to take his diversion in hunting and hawking as he goes along.

On arriving at this capital of Cambaluc, he stays in his palace there three days and no more; during which time he has great court entertainments and rejoicings, and makes merry with his wives. He then quits his palace at Cambaluc, and proceeds to that city which he has built, as I told you before, and which is called Chandu, where he has that grand park and palace of cane, and where he keeps his gerfalcons in mew. There he spends the summer, to escape the heat, for the situation is a very cool one. After stopping there from the beginning of May to the 28th of August, he takes his departure (that is the time when they sprinkle the white mares' milk as I told you) and returns to his capital Cambaluc. There he stops, as I have told you also, the month of September, to keep his Birthday Feast, and also throughout October, November, December, January, and February, in which last month he keeps the grand feast of the New Year, which they call the White Feast, as you have heard already with all particulars. He then sets out on his march towards the Ocean Sea, hunting and hawking, and continues out from the beginning of March to the middle of May; and then comes back for three days only to the capital, during which he makes merry with his wives, and holds a great court and grand entertainments. In truth, 'tis something astonishing, the magnificence displayed by the Emperor in those three days; and then he starts off again as you know.

Thus his whole year is distributed in the following manner: six months at his chief palace in the royal city of Cambaluc, to wit, *September, October, November, December, January, February*;

Then on the great hunting expedition towards the sea, *March, April, May*;

Then back to his palace at Cambaluc for *three days*;

Then off to the city of Chandu which he heas built, and where the Cane Palace is, where he stays *June, July, August*;

Then back again to his capital city of Cambaluc.

So thus the whole year is spent; six months at the capital, three months in hunting, and three months at the Cane Palace to avoid the heat. And in this way he passes his time with the greatest enjoyment; not to mention occasional journeys in this or that direction at his own pleasure.

Magellan's Voyage Round the World

BY ANTONIO PIGAFETTA

Ferdinand Magellan set out in 1519 with five ships and 270 men to claim glory for Spain and establish trade ties with the so-called Spice Islands of the Far East. Three years later, just 18 sailors and one ship arrived home after completing the first circumnavigation of the globe. This grand achievement was made more impressive by the fact that it remained the only circumnavigation for the next 50 years (when Sir Francis Drake did it).

While Magellan did not survive the voyage, he is generally credited with making it a success. In addition to the normal rigors of sea travel in the 1500s, he had to deal with mutinous crews, finding a passage through the dangerous waters that would become known as the Straits of Magellan on the southern tip of South America, and facing the immense waters of an ocean he would name the Pacific (due to the unusually mild weather he experienced while crossing it).

Thanks to an account of the voyage by one of its participants, Antonio Pigafetta, we are left with a record of much of what happened.

★　★　★　★　★

As there are men whose curiosity would not be satisfied with merely hearing related the marvelous things I have seen, and the difficulties I experienced in the course of the perilous expedition I am about to describe, and who are anxious to know by what means I was enabled to surmount them; and as due credit by such would not be given to the success of a similar undertaking if they were left ignorant of its most minute details, I have deemed it expedient briefly to relate what gave origin to my voyage, and the means by which I was so fortunate as to bring it to a successful termination.

In the year 1519, I was in Spain at the court of Charles V, King of the Romans, in company with Signor Chiericato, then apostolical prothonotary and orator of Pope Leo X of holy memory, who by his merits was raised to the dignity of Bishop and Prince of Teramo. Now as from the books I had read, and from the conversation of the learned men who frequented the house of this prelate, I knew that by navigating the ocean wonderful things were to be seen, I determined to be convinced of them by my own eyes, that I might be enabled to give to others the narrative of my voyage, as well for their amusement as advantage, and at the same time acquire a name which should be handed down to posterity.

An opportunity soon presented itself. I learned that a squadron of five vessels was under equipment at Sevilla, destined for the discovery of the Molucca Islands, whence we derive our spices; and that Fernandez [Ferdinand] Magellan, a Portuguese gentleman, and commander of the order of St. Jago [Santiago] de la Spata, who had already more than once traversed the ocean with great reputation, was nominated Captain General of the expedition. I therefore immediately repaired to Barcelona, to request permission of His Majesty to be one on this voyage, which permission was granted. Thence, provided with letters of recommendation, I went by sea to Malaga, and from that city overland to Sevilla, where I waited three months before the expedition was in readiness to sail. . . .

The Captain General Ferdinand Magellan had resolved on undertaking a long voyage over the ocean, where the winds blow with violence and storms are very frequent. He had also determined on taking a course as yet unexplored by any navigator; but this bold attempt he was cautious of disclosing, lest anyone should strive to dissuade him from it by magnifying the risk he would have to encounter, and this dishearten his crew. To the perils naturally incident on a similar voyage was joined the unfavorable circumstance of the four other vessels he commanded beside his own being under the direction of captains who were inimical to him, merely on account of his being a Portuguese, they themselves being Spaniards. . . .

Monday morning the tenth of August 1519, the squadron having everything requisite on board and a complement of 237 men, its departure [from Seville] was announced by a discharge of artillery, and the foresail was set. . . .

The twentieth of September we sailed from San Lucar, steering toward the southwest, and on the twenty-sixth reached one of the Canary Islands called Teneriffe, situated in 28 degrees of latitude north. We stopped here for three days, at a spot where we could take in wood and water. . . .

On Monday, the third of October, we made sail directly toward the south. We passed between Cape Verd [Verde] and its islands in latitude 14 degrees 30 minutes north. After coasting along the shores of Guinea for several days, we arrived in latitude 8 degrees north, where is a mountain called Sierra Leona. . . .

After we had passed the equinoctial line, we lost sight of the polar star. We then steered south-southwest, making for the Terra di Verzino (Brazil), in latitude 23 degrees 30 minutes south. This land is a continuation of that on which Cape Augustin [St. Augustine] is situated in latitude 8 degrees 30 minutes south.

Here we laid in a good stock of fowls; potatoes; a kind of fruit which resembles the cone of the pine tree (the anana or pineapple), but which is very sweet and of an exquisite flavor; sweet reeds; the flesh of the anta, which resembles that of a cow, etc. We made excellent bargains here. For a hook or a knife we purchased five or six fowls; a comb brought us two geese; and a small looking-glass, or a pair of scissors, as much fish as would serve ten people; the inhabitants for a little bell or a ribbon gave a basket of potatoes, which is the name they give to roots somewhat resembling our turnips, and which are nearly like chestnuts in taste.

Our playing cards were an equally advantageous object of barter; for a king of spades I obtained half a dozen fowls, and the hawker even deemed his bargain an excellent one.

We entered this port [Rio de Janeiro] on Saint Lucy's day, the thirteenth of December. The sun at noon was vertical, and we suffered much more from the heat than on passing the line.

The land of Brazil, which abounds in all kinds of productions, is as extensive as Spain, France, and Italy united. It belongs to Portugal. . . .

We stayed thirteen days at this port; after which, resuming our course, we coasted along this country as far as 34 degrees 40 minutes south, where we found a large river of fresh water. . . .

This river [Rio de la Plata] contains seven small islands. In the largest, called Santa Maria, precious stones are found. It was formerly imagined that this was not a river, but a channel which communicated with the South Sea; but it was shortly found to be truly a river, which at its mouth is 17 leagues across. Here John [Juan Diaz] de Solis, while on a voyage of discovery like us, was with sixty of his crew devoured by cannibals, in whom they placed too great confidence.

Coasting constantly along this land toward the Antarctic Pole, we stopped at two islands, which we found peopled by geese [penguins] and sea wolves [seals] alone. The former are so numerous and so little wild that we caught a sufficient store for the five ships in the space of a single hour. They are black, and seem to be covered alike over every part of the body with short feathers, without having wings with which to fly; in fact they cannot fly, and live entirely on fish. They are so fat that we were obliged to singe them, as we could not pluck their feathers. Their beak is curved like a horn.

The sea wolves are of a different color, and nearly the size of a calf, with a head much like the head of that animal. Their ears are round and short, and their teeth very long. They have no legs, and their paws, which adhere to the body, somewhat resemble our hands, having also small nails. They are, however, web-footed like a duck. Were these animals capable of running, they would be much to be dreaded, for they seem very ferocious. They swim with great swiftness, and subsist on fish.

We experienced a dreadful storm between these islands, during which the lights of Saint Elmo, Saint Nicholas, and Saint Clare were oftentimes perceived at the tops of our masts. Instantly as they disappeared, the fury of the tempest abated.

On leaving these islands to continue our course, we ascended as high as 49 degrees 30 minutes south, where we discovered an excellent port [Port St. Julian], and as winter approached [the month was May], we thought best to take shelter here during the bad weather.

Two months elapsed without our perceiving any inhabitant of the country. One day when the least we expected anything of the kind, a man of gigantic figure presented himself before us. He capered almost naked on the sands, and was singing and dancing, at the same time casting dust on his head. The Captain sent one of our seamen onshore with orders to make similar gestures as a token of friendship and peace, which were well understood, and the giant suffered himself to be quietly led to a small island where the Captain had landed. I likewise went on shore there, with many others. He testified great surprise on seeing us, and holding up his finger, undoubtedly signified to us that he thought us descended from Heaven.

This man was of such immense stature that our heads scarcely reached to his waist. He was of handsome appearance, his face broad and painted red, except a rim of yellow round his eyes and two spots in shape of a heart on his cheeks. His hair, which was thin, appeared lightened with some kind of powder. His coat, or rather his cloak, was made of furs, well sewed together, taken from an animal which, as we had afterward an opportunity of seeing, abounds in this country. This animal [guanaco] has the head and ears of a mule, the body of a camel, the legs of a stag, and the tail of a horse, and like this last animal, it neighs.

This man likewise wore a sort of shoe, make of the same skin. [Amoretti remarks that is was because of this shoe, which made the man's foot resemble the foot of a bear, that Magellan called the people Patagonians.] He held in his left hand a short and massive bow, the string of which, somewhat thicker than that of a lute, was made of the intestines of the same animal. In the other hand he held arrows made of short reeds, with feathers at one end, similar to ours, and at the other, instead of iron, a white-and-black flint stone. With the same stone they likewise form instruments to work wood with.

The Captain General gave him victuals and drink, and among other trifles presented him with a large steel mirror. The giant, who had not the least conception of this trinket, and who saw his likeness now perhaps for the first time, started back in so much fright as to knock down four of our men who happened to stand behind him. We gave him some little bells, a small looking-glass, a comb, and some glass beads; after which he was set on shore, accompanied by four men well armed.

His comrade, who had objected to coming on board the ship, seeing him return, ran to advise his comrades, who, perceiving that our armed men advanced toward them, ranged themselves in file without arms, and almost naked. They immediately began dancing and singing, in the course of which they raised the forefinger to Heaven, to make us comprehend that it was thence they reckoned us to have descended. They at the same time showed us a white powder, in clay pans, and presented it to us, having nothing else to offer us to eat. Our people invited them by signs to come on board our ship, and proffered to carry on board with them whatever they might wish. They accepted the invitation, but the men, who merely carried a bow and arrow, loaded everything on the women as if they had been so many beasts of burden.

The women are not of equal size with the men, but in recompense they are much more lusty. Their breasts, which hang down, are more than a foot in length. They paint, and dress in the same manner as their husbands, but they have a thin skin of some animal with which they cover their nudity. They were, in our contemplation, far from handsome; nevertheless their husbands seemed very jealous.

The women led four of the animals of which I have previously spoken, in a string, but they were young ones. They make use of these young to catch the old ones. They fasten them to a tree, the old ones come to play with them, when from their concealment the men kill them with their arrows. The inhabitants of the country, both men and women, being invited by our people to repair to the vicinage of the ships, divided themselves into two parties, one on each side of the port, and diverted us with an exhibition of the mode of hunting before recited.

Six days afterward, while our people were employed in felling wood for the ships, they saw another giant, dressed like those we had parted with and like them armed with a bow and arrow. On approaching our people he touched his head and body, afterward raising his hands to Heaven, gestures which the men imitated. The Captain General, informed of this circumstance, sent the skiff onshore to conduct him to the islet in the port, on which a house had been erected to serve as a forge, and a magazine for different articles of merchandise.

This man was of higher stature and better made than the others; he was moreover of gentler manners. He danced and sprang so high, and with such might, that his feet sank several inches deep in the sand. He remained with us some days. We taught him to pronounce the name of Jesus, to say the Lord's Prayer, etc., which he did with equal ease with ourselves, but in a much stronger tone of voice. Finally, we baptized him by the name of John. The Captain General made him a present of a shirt, a vest, cloth drawers, a cap, a looking-glass, comb, some little bells, and other trifling things. He returned toward his own people, apparently well contented.

The next day he brought us one of the large animals of which we have made mention, and received other presents to induce him to repeat his gift; but from that day we saw nothing of him, and suspected his companions had killed him on account of his attachment to us.

At the end of a fortnight four other of these men repaired to us. They were without arms, but we afterward found they had concealed them behind some bushes, where they were pointed out to us by two of the party, whom we detained. They were all of them painted, but in a different manner to those we had seen before.

The Captain wished to keep the two youngest, who as well were of the handsomest form, to carry them with us on our voyage, and even take them to Spain; but, aware of the difficulty of securing them by forcible means, he made use of the following artifice.

He presented them a number of knives, mirrors, glass beads, etc., so that both their hands were full. He afterward offered them two of those iron rings used for chaining felons, and when he saw their anxiety to be possessed of them (for they are passionately fond of iron), and moreover that they could not hold them in their hands, he proposed to fasten them to their legs, that they might more easily carry them home, to which they consented. Upon this, our people put on the irons and fastened the rings, by which means they were securely chained.

As soon as they became aware of the treachery used toward them they were violently enraged, and puffed and roared aloud, invoking Setebos, their chief demon, to come to their assistance.

Not content with having these men, the Captain was anxious of securing their wives also, in order to transport a race of giants to Europe. With this view he ordered the two others to be arrested, to oblige them to conduct our people to the spot where they were. Nine of our strongest men were scarcely able to cast them to the ground and bind them, and still even one of them succeeded in freeing himself, while the other exerted himself so much that he received a slight wound in the head from one of the men; but they were in the end obliged to show our people the way to the abode of the wives of our two prisoners. These women, on learning what had happened to their husbands, made such loud outcries as to be heard at a great distance.

Johan Carvajo, the pilot, who was at the head of our people, as night was drawing on, did not choose to bring away at that time the women to whose house he had been conducted, but remained there till morning, keeping a good guard. In the meantime came there two other men, who without expressing any dissatisfaction or surprise continued all night in the hut; but soon as dawn began to break, upon saying a few words, in an instant everyone took flight, man, woman, and child, the children even scampering away with greater speed than the rest. They abandoned their hut to us, and all that it contained. In the meantime one of the men drove off to a distance the little animals which they used in hunting, while another, concealed behind a bush, wounded one of our men in the thigh, who died immediately.

Though our people fired on the runaways, they were unable to hit any, on account of their not escaping in a straight line, but leaping from one side to another, and getting on as swiftly as horses at a full gallop. Our people burned the hut of these savages, and buried their dead companion.

Savage as they are, these Indians are yet not without their medicaments. When they have a pain in the stomach, for example, in lieu of an operative medicine they thrust an arrow pretty deeply down the throat, to excite a vomit, and throw up a matter of greenish color, mixed with blood. The green is occasioned by a sort of thistle, on which they feed. If they have the headache, they make a gash in their forehead, and do the same with the other parts of the body where they experience pain, in order to draw from the affected part a considerable quantity of blood. Their theory, as explained to us by one of those we had taken, is on a par with their practice. Pain, they say, proceeds from the reluctance of the blood to abide any longer in the part where it is felt; by releasing it, consequently, the pain is removed.

Their hair is cut circularly like that of monks, but is longer, and supported round the head by a cotton string, in which they place their arrows when they go hunting. When the weather is very cold, they tie their private parts closely to the body. It appears that their religion is limited to adoring the Devil. They pretend that when one of them is on the point of death, ten or twelve demons appear dancing and singing around him. One of these, who makes a greater noise than the rest, is termed Setebos, the inferior imps are called Cheleule; they are painted like the people of the country. Our giant pretends to have once seen a devil, with horns, and hair of such length as to cover his feet; he cast out flames, added he, from his mouth and his posteriors.

These people, as I have already noticed, clothe themselves in the skin of an animal, and with the same kind of skin do they cover their huts, which they transport whither suits them best, having no fixed place of abode, but wandering from spot to spot like gypsies. They generally live upon raw meat, and a sweet root called *capac*. They are great feeders; the two we took daily consumed a basketful of bread each, and drank half a pail of water at a draught. They eat mice raw, and without even slaying them. Our Captain gave these people the name of Patagonians.

We spent five months in this port, to which we gave the denomination of St. Julian, and met with no accidents onshore during the whole of our stay, save what I have noticed.

Scarcely had we anchored in this port before the four captains of the other vessels plotted to murder the Captain General. These traitors were Juan of Carthagena, *vehador* of the squadron; Lewis de Mendoza, the treasurer; Antonio Cocca, the paymaster; and Gaspar de Casada. The plot was discovered, the first was flayed alive, and the second was stabbed to the heart. Gaspar de Casada was forgiven, but a few days after, he meditated treason anew. The Captain General then—who dared not take his life, as he was created a captain by the Emperor himself—drove him from the squadron, and left him in the country of the Pantagonians, together with a priest, his accomplice. [When Gomez, who commanded the San Antonio, deserted the squadron in the strait and returned to St. Julian, he took them both on board again, and carried them back to Spain.]

Another mishap befell part of the squadron while we remained at this station. The ship St. Jago [Santiago] which had been detached to survey the coast, was cast upon rocks; nevertheless, as if by a miracle, the whole of the crew were saved. Two seamen came overland to the port where we were to acquaint us of this disaster, and the Captain General sent men to the spot immediately, with some sacks of biscuit.

The crew stopped two months near the place where the vessel was stranded, to collect the wreck and merchandise which the sea successively cast onshore; and during all this time means of subsistence was transported them overland, although 100 miles distant from the port of St. Julian, and by a very bad and fatiguing road, through thickets and briers, among which the bearers of provision were obliged to pass the whole night without any other beverage than what they obtained from the ice they found, and which they were able with difficulty to break.

As for us, we fared tolerably in this port, though certain shellfish of great length, some of which contained pearls, but of very small size, were not edible. We found ostriches [rheas] here, foxes, rabbits much smaller than ours, and sparrows. The trees yield frankincense.

We planted a cross on the summit of a neighboring mountain, which we termed Monte Christo, and took possession of the country in the name of the King of Spain.

We at length left this port (the twenty-first of August) and keeping along the coast, in latitude 50 degrees 40 minutes south, discovered a river of fresh water [the Santa Cruz], into which we entered. The whole squadron nearly experienced shipwreck here, owing to the furious winds with which it was assailed, and which occasioned a very rough sea; but God and the *corpora sancta* [the lights which shone on the summits of the masts] brought us succor and saved us from harm.

We spent two months here, to stock our vessels with wood and water. We laid in provision also of a species of fish nearly 2 feet in length and covered with scales; it was tolerable eating, but we were unable to take a sufficient number of them. Before we quitted this spot our Captain ordered all of us to make confession, and, like good Christians, to receive the communion.

Continuing our course toward the south, on the twenty-first of October, in latitude 52 degrees, we discovered a strait which we denominated the strait of the Eleven Thousand Virgins, in honor of the day. This strait, as will appear in the sequel, is 440 miles, or 110 maritime leagues, in length; it is half a league in breadth, sometimes more, sometimes less, and terminates in another sea, which we denominated the Pacific Ocean. This strait is enclosed between lofty mountains covered with snow, and it is likewise very deep, so that we were unable to anchor except quite close to shore, where was from 25 to 30 fathoms of water.

The whole of the crew were so firmly persuaded that this strait had no western outlet that we should not, but for the deep science of the Captain

General, have ventured on its exploration. This man, as skillful as he was intrepid, knew that he would have to pass by a strait very little known, but which he had seen laid down on a chart of Martin de Boheme [Martin Behaim], a most excellent cosmographer, in the treasury of the King of Portugal.

As soon as we entered on this water, imagined to be only a bay, the Captain sent forward two vessels, the *Sant' Antonio*, and *La Concepción* [*Concepción*] to examine where it terminated, or whither it led, while we in the *Trinidad* and the *Vittoria* awaited them in the mouth of it.

At night came on a terrible hurricane, which lasted six and thirty hours, and forced us to quit our anchors and leave our vessels to the mercy of the winds and waves in the gulf.

The two other vessels, equally buffeted, were unable to double a cape in order to rejoin us; so that by abandoning themselves to the gale, which drove them constantly toward what they conceived to be the bottom of a bay, they were apprehensive momentarily of being driven onshore. But at the instant they gave themselves up for lost, they saw a small opening, which they took for an inlet of the bay. Into this they entered, and perceiving that this channel was not closed, they threaded it, and found themselves in another, through which they pursued their course to another strait leading into a third bay still larger than the preceding. Then, in lieu of following up their exploration, they deemed it most prudent to return and render account of what they had observed to the Captain General.

Two days passed without the two vessels returning, sent to examine the bottom of the bay, so that we reckoned they had been swallowed up during the tempest; and seeing smoke on shore, we conjectured that those who had had the good fortune to escape had kindled those fires to inform us of their existence and distress.

But while in this painful incertitude as to their fate, we saw them advancing toward us under full sail, and their flags flying; and when sufficiently near, heard the report of their bombards and their loud exclamations of joy. We repeated the salutation, and when we learnt from them that they had seen the prolongation of the bay, or, better speaking, the strait, we made toward them, to continue our voyage in this course, if possible.

When we had entered into the third bay, which I have before noticed, we saw two openings, or channels, the one running to the southeast, the other to the southwest. The Captain General sent the two vessels, the *Sant' Antonio* and *La Concepción* to the southeast, to examine whether or not this channel terminated in an open sea. The first set sail immediately, under press of canvas, not choosing to wait for the second, which the pilot wished to leave behind, as he had no intention to avail himself of the darkness of the night to retrace his course, and return to Spain by the same way we came.

This pilot was Emanuel Gómez, who hated Magellan, for the sole reason that when he came to Spain to lay his project before the Emperor of proceeding to the Moluccas by a western passage, Gómez himself had requested, and was on the point of obtaining, some caravels for an expedition of which he would have had the command. This expedition had for its object to make new discoveries; but the arrival of Magellan prevented his request from being complied with, and he could only obtain the subaltern situation of his serving under a Portuguese. In the course of the night he conspired with the other Spaniards on board the ship. They put in irons, and even wounded, the captain, Alvaro de Meschita, the cousin german of the Captain General, and carried him thus to Spain. They reckoned likewise on transporting thither one of the two giants we had taken, and who was on board their ship; but we learnt on our return that he died on approaching the equinoctial line, unable to bear the heat of the tropical regions.

The vessel, *La Concepción*, which could not keep up with the *Sant' Antonio*, continued to cruise in the channel to await its return, but in vain.

We, with the other two vessels, entered the remaining channel, on the southwest, and continuing our course, came to a river which we called Sardine River, on account of the vast number of the fish of this denomination we found in it. We anchored here to wait for the two other ships, and remained in the river four days; but in the interim we dispatched a boat, well manned, to reconnoiter the cape of this channel, which promised to terminate in another sea. On the third day the sailors sent on this expedition returned and announced their having seen the cape where the strait ended, and with it a great sea—that is to say, the ocean. We wept for joy. This cape was denominated Il Capo Deseado (The Wished-for Cape; Cape of Good Hope) for in truth we had longed wished to see it.

We returned to join the two other vessels of the squadron, and found *La Concepción* alone. On inquiring of the pilot, Johan Serano, what had become of the other vessel, we learnt that he conceived it to be lost, as he had not once seen it since he entered the channel. The Captain General then ordered it to be sought for everywhere, but especially in the channel into which it had penetrated. He sent back the *Vittoria* to the mouth of the strait, with directions if they should not find it, to hoist a standard on some eminent spot at the foot of which, in a small pot, should be placed a letter pointing out the course the

Captain General would take in order to enable the missing ship to follow the squadron. This mode of communication, in case of a division, was concerted at the instant of our departure.

Two other signals were hoisted in the same manner on eminent sites in the first bay, and on a small island of the third bay, on which we saw a number of sea wolves and birds. The Captain General, with *La Concepción*, awaited the return of the *Vittoria* near the River of Sardines, and erected a cross on a small island, at the foot of two mountains covered with snow, where the river had its source.

Had we not discovered this strait leading from one sea to the other, it was the intention of the Captain General to continue his course toward the south, as high as 75 degrees, where in summer there is no night, or very little, as in winter there is scarcely any day. While we were in the strait, in the month of October, there were but three hours' night.

The shore in this strait, which on the left turns to the southeast, is low. We called it the Strait of the Patagonians [Strait of Magellan]. At every half-league it contains a safe port, with excellent water, cedar wood, sardines, and a great abundance of shellfish. There were here also some vegetables, part of them of bitter taste but others fit to eat, especially a species of sweet celery, which grows on the margin of springs and which, for want of other, served us for food.

In short, I do not think the world contains a better strait than this. . . .

On Wednesday, the twenty-eighth of November, we left the strait and entered the ocean to which we afterward gave the denomination of Pacific, and in which we sailed the space of three months and twenty days, without tasting any fresh provisions. The biscuit we were eating no longer deserved the name of bread; it was nothing but dust, and worms which had consumed the substance; and what is more, it smelled intolerably, being impregnated with the urine of mice. The water we were obliged to drink was equally putrid and offensive.

We were even so far reduced, that we might not die of hunger, to eat pieces of the leather with which the main yard was covered to prevent it from wearing the rope. These pieces of leather, constantly exposed to the water, sun, and wind, were so hard that they required being soaked four or five days in the sea in order to render them supple; after this we broiled them to eat. Frequently indeed we were obliged to subsist on sawdust, and even mice, a food so disgusting, were sought after with such avidity that they sold for half a ducat apiece.

Nor was this all. Our greatest misfortune was being attacked by a malady in which the gums swelled so as to hide the teeth, as well in the upper as the lower jaw, whence those affected were thus incapable of chewing their food. Nineteen of our number died of this complaint [scurvy], among whom was the Patagonian giant, and a Brazilian whom we had brought with us from his own country. Besides those who died, we had from 25 to 30 sailors ill, who suffered dreadful pains in their arms, legs, and other parts of the body; but these all of them recovered. As for myself, I cannot be too grateful to God for the continued health I enjoyed; though surrounded with sick, I experienced not the slightest illness.

In the course of these three months and twenty days we traversed nearly 4,000 leagues in the ocean denominated by us Pacific, on account of our not having experienced throughout the whole of this period any the least tempestuous weather. We did not either in this whole length of time discover any land, except two desert islands; on these we saw nothing but birds and trees, for which reason we named them Las Islas Desdichados [The Unfortunate Islands]. We found no bottom along their shores, and saw no fish but sharks. The two islands are 200 leagues apart. The first lies in latitude 15 degrees south, the second in latitude 9 degrees.

From the run of our ship, as estimated by the log, we traversed a space of from 60 to 70 leagues a day; and if God and His Holy Mother had not granted us a fortunate voyage, we should all have perished of hunger in so vast a sea. I do not think that anyone in the future will venture upon a similar voyage.

If on leaving the straits we had continued a western course under the same parallel, we should have made the tour of the world; and without seeing any land should have returned by Wished-for Cape [Cape of Good Hope] to the cape of the Eleven Thousand Virgins, both of which are in latitude 52 degrees south.

The Antarctic has not the same stars as the Arctic Pole; but here are seen two clusters of small nebulous stars which look like small clouds, and are but little distant the one from the other. [These are now called the Magellanic Clouds]. In midst of these clusters of small stars two are distinguished very large and very brilliant, but of which the motion is scarcely apparent. These indicate the Antarctic Pole.

Though the needle declined somewhat from the North Pole, it yet oscillated toward it, but not with equal force as in the Northern Hemisphere. When out a sea, the Captain General directed the course the pilots should steer, and inquired how they pointed. They unanimously replied they bore in that direction he ordered them. He then informed them that their course was wrong, and directed them to correct the needle, because, being in the Southern, it had not an equal power to designate the true north as in the Northern Hemisphere.

When in midst of the ocean, we discovered in the west five stars of great brilliancy, in form of a cross.

We steered northwest by west till we reached the equinoctial line in 122 degrees of longitude, west of the line of demarcation [laid down by Pope Alexander VI]. This line is 30 degrees west of the meridian, and 3 degrees west of Cape Verde. . . .

After we had crossed the line we steered west by north. We then ran 200 leagues toward the west; when, changing our course again, we ran west by south until in the latitude of 13 degrees north. We trusted by this course to reach Cape Gatticara, which cosmographers have placed in this latitude; but they are mistaken, this cape lying 12 degrees more toward the north. They must, however, be excused the error in their plan, as they have not like us had the advantage of visiting these parts.

When we had run 70 leagues in this direction and were in latitude 12 degrees north, longitude 146 degrees, on Wednesday, the sixth of March, we discovered in the northwest a small island, and afterward two others in the southwest. A first was more lofty and larger than the other two.

The Captain General meant to stop at the largest to victual and refresh, but this was rendered impossible, as the islanders came on board our ships and stole first one thing and then another, without our being able to prevent them. They invited us to take in our sails and come on shore, and even had the address the steal the skiff which hung astern of our vessel.

Exasperated at length, our Captain landed with forty men, burnt forty or fifty of their houses and several of their boats, and killed seven of the people. By acting thus he recovered his skills but he did not deem it prudent to stop any longer after such acts of hostility. We therefore continued our course in the same direction as before. . . . [Although the expedition had only this brief encounter, Pigafetta felt able to describe in some detail the manners and customs of these natives. In the course of his remarks he states, "The inhabitants of these islands are poor, but very dexterous, and above all at thieving; for this reason we gave the name of De los Ladrones to the islands." The group which received this uncomplimentary name was later called the Marianas, by which name these islands are still known.]

The sixteenth of March, at sunrise we found ourselves near an elevated land 300 leagues from the island De los Ladrones. We soon discovered it to be an island. It is called Zamal [Samar]. Behind this island is another not inhabited, and we afterward learnt that its name is Humunu. Here the Captain General resolved on landing the next day to take in water in greater security, and take some rest after so long and tedious a voyage. Here likewise he caused two tents to be erected for the sick, and ordered a sow to be killed. . . .

Perceiving around us a number of islands on the fifth Sunday of Lent, which also is the feast of St. Lazarus, we called the archipelago by the name of that saint.

(These islands are now called the Philippines. Magellan made contact with the natives, who proved friendly, and he stayed in the area to trade and explore. Unfortunately, he also became involved in local politics among the tribes as he tried to spread Christianity and exert Spanish sovereignty.—Editor)

On Sunday, the seventh of April, we entered the port of Zubu [Cebu]. We passed several villages, in which we saw houses built upon trees. When near the town, the Captain ordered all our colors to be hoisted and all our sails to be taken in; and a general salute was fired, which caused great alarm among the islanders.

The Captain then sent one of his pupils, with the interpreter, as ambassador to the King of Cebu. On arriving at the town the found the King surrounded by an immense concourse of people alarmed at the noise occasioned by the discharge of our bombards. The interpreter began with removing the apprehension of the monarch, informing him that this was a custom with us, and meant as a mark of respect toward him, and as a token of friendship and peace. Upon this assurance the fears of all were dissipated.

The King inquired by his Minister what brought us to his island, and what we wanted. The interpreter answered that his master, who commanded the squadron, was a captain in the service of the greatest monarch upon earth, and that the object of his voyage was to proceed to Malucho [the Moluccas]; but that the King of Massana, at whose island we had touched, having spoken very highly of him, he had come hither to pay him his respects, and at the same time to take in provisions and give merchandise in exchange.

The King replied he was welcome, but at the same time he advised him that all vessels which might enter his port in view of trading were subject previously to pay duties. In proof of the truth of which he added that four days had not yet elapsed since his having received port duties for a junk from Ciam [Siam], which had come thither to take in slaves and gold; he moreover sent for a Moorish [Mohammedan] merchant, who came from Siam with the same view, to bear witness to what he stated.

The interpreter answered that his master, being the captain of so great a king, could not consent to pay duty to any monarch upon earth; that if the King of Cebu wished for peace, he brought peace with him, but if he wished to be hostile, he was prepared for war.

The merchant from Siam then, approaching the King, said to him in his own language, "*Cata rajah chita*"—that is to say, "Take care, Sire, of that." "These people," added he, for he taught us Portuguese, "are those who conquered Calicut, Malacca, and all Upper India."

The interpreter, who comprehended what the Moor said, then remarked that his monarch was one vastly more powerful than the King of Portugal, to whom the Siamese alluded, as well by sea as by land; that it was the King of Spain, the Emperor of the whole Christian world; and that if he preferred to have him for an enemy rather than a friend he would have sent a sufficient number of men and vessels entirely to destroy his island.

The Moor confirmed what the interpreter said. The King then, finding himself embarrassed, said he would advise with his Ministers, and return an answer the next day. In the meantime he ordered a breakfast, consisting of several dishes, to be set before the deputy of the Captain General and the interpreter, all the dishes consisting of meat served up in porcelain.

After breakfast our deputies returned and reported what had taken place. The King of Massana, who next to that of Cebu was the most powerful monarch of these islands, went on shore to announce to the King the friendly intentions of our Captain General with respect to him. . . .

Tuesday, in the morning, the King of Massana came on board our vessel, in company with the Moorish merchant, and after saluting the Captain on the part of the King of Cebu, told him he was authorized to communicate that the King was busied in collecting all the provisions he could to make a present to him, and that in the afternoon he would send his nephew with some of his Ministers to confirm a treaty of peace. The Captain thanked the deputation, and at the same time exhibited to them a man armed cap-à-pie, observing in case of a necessity to fight, we should all of us be armed in the same manner.

The Moor was terribly frightened at sight of a man armed in this manner; but the Captain tranquilized him with the assurance that our arms were as advantageous to our friends as fatal to our enemies; and that we were able as readily to disperse all the enemies of our sovereign and our faith as to wipe the sweat from our brows.

The Captain made use of this lofty and threatening tone purposely, that the Moor might make report of it to the King. . . .

[When the treaty with the King of Cebu had been concluded, European goods were carried ashore and placed in a house that had been turned over to the Spaniards for this purpose.]

On Friday, we opened our warehouse and exhibited our different merchandise, which excited much admiration among the islanders. For brass, iron, and other weighty articles, they gave us gold in exchange. Our trinkets, and articles of a lighter kind, were bartered for rice, hogs, goats, and other edibles. For 14 pounds of iron we received 10 pieces of gold, of the value of a ducat and a half. The Captain General forbade too great an anxiety for receiving gold, without which order every sailor would have parted with all he had to obtain this metal, which would have ruined our commerce forever.

Contiguous to the island Cebu is another called Matan [Mactan], which has a port of the same name, in which our vessels laid at anchor. The chief village of this island is likewise called Mactan, over which Zula and Cilapulapu presided as chiefs. In this island the village of Bulaia with situated, which we burnt.

On Friday, the twenty-sixth of April, Zula, one of the chiefs, sent one of his sons with two goats to the Captain General and observed that if he did not send him the whole of what he had promised, the blame was not to be imputed to himself, but to the other chief, Cilapulapu, who would not acknowledge the authority of the King of Spain. He further stated that if the Captain General would only send to his assistance the following night a boat with some armed men, he would engage to beat and entirely subjugate his rival.

On receiving this message the Captain General determined on going himself with these boats. We entreated him not to hazard his person on this adventure, but he answered that as a good pastor he ought not to be far away from his flock.

At midnight we left the ship, 60 in number, armed with helmets and cuirasses. The Christian King, the Prince, his nephew, and several chiefs of Cebu, with a number of armed men, followed us in twenty or thirty balangays. We reached Mactan three hours before day. The Captain would not then begin the attack; but he sent the Moor on shore to inform Cilapulapu and his people that if he would acknowledge the sovereignty of the King of Spain, obey the Christian King of Cebu, and pay the tribute he demanded, they should be looked upon as friends. Otherwise they should experience the strength of our lances.

The islanders, nothing intimidated, replied they had lances as well as we, although they were only sticks of bamboo pointed at the end, and staves hardened in the fire. They merely requested that they might not be attacked in the night, as they expected reinforcements, and should then be better able to cope with us. This they said designedly to induce us to attack them immediately, in hope that thus we should fall in the dikes they had dug between the sea and their houses.

We accordingly waited until daylight, when we jumped into the water up to our thighs, the boats not being able to approach near enough to land, on account of the rocks and shallows. The number which landed was 49 only, as 11 were left in charge of the boats. We were obliged to wade some distance through the water before we reached the shore.

We found the islanders, 1,500 in number, formed into three battalions, who immediately upon our landing fell upon us, making horrible shouts. Two of these battalions attacked us in flank, and the third in front.

Our Captain divided his company into two platoons. The musketeers and crossbowmen fired from a distance the space of half an hour without making the least impression on the enemy; for though the balls and arrows penetrated their bucklers made of thin wood, and even wounded them at times in their arms, this did not make them halt, as the wounds failed of occasioning them instant death, as they expected; on the contrary, it only made them more bold and furious.

Moreover, trusting to the superiority of their numbers, they showered on us such clouds of bamboo lances, staves hardened in the fire, stones, and even dirt, that it was with difficulty we defended ourselves. Some even threw spears headed with iron at our Captain General, who to intimidate and cause them to disperse, ordered away a party of our men to set fire to their houses, which they immediately effected.

The sight of the flames served only to increase their exasperation. Some of them even ran to the village which was set on fire, and in which twenty or thirty houses were consumed, and killed two of our men on the spot. They seemed momently to increase in number and impetuosity. A poisoned arrow struck the Captain in the leg, who on this ordered a retreat in slow and regular order; but the majority of our men took to flight precipitately, so that only 7 or 8 remained about the Captain.

The Indians, perceiving their blows were ineffectual when aimed at our body or head, on account of our armor, and noticing at the same time that our legs were uncovered, directed against these their arrows, javelins, and stones, and these in such abundance that we could not guard against them. The bombards we had in our boats were of no utility, as the levelness of the strand would not admit the boats' being brought sufficiently close inshore.

We retreated gradually, still continuing to fight, and were now at a bowshot from the islanders, and in the water up to our knees, when they renewed their attack with fury, throwing at us the same lance five or six times over as they picked it up on advancing. As they knew our Captain, they chiefly aimed at him, so that his helmet was twice struck from his head. Still he did not give himself up to despair, and we continued in a very small number fighting by his side.

This combat, so unequal, lasted more than an hour.

An islander at length succeeding in thrusting the end of his lance through the bars of the helmet, and wounding the Captain in the forehead, who, irritated on the occasion, immediately ran the assailant through the body with his lance, the lance remaining in the wound. He now attempted to draw his sword, but was unable, owing to his right arm being grievously wounded. The Indians, who perceived this, pressed in crowds upon him, and one of them having given him a violent cut with a sword on the left leg, he fell on his face. On this they immediately fell upon him.

Thus perished our guide, our light, and our support. On falling, and seeing himself surrounded by the enemy, he turned toward us several times, as if to know whether we had been able to save ourselves. As there was not one of those who remained with him but was wounded, and as we were consequently in no condition either to afford him succor or revenge his death, we instantly made for our boats, which were on the point of putting off. To our Captain indeed did we owe our deliverance, as the instant he fell, all the islanders rushed toward the spot where he lay.

The Christian King had it in his power to render us assistance, and this he would not doubt have done; but the Captain General, far from foreseeing what was about to happen when he landed with his people, had ordered him not to leave his balangay, but merely to remain a spectator of our manner of fighting. His Majesty bitterly bewailed his fate on seeing him fall.

But the glory of Magellan will survive him. He was adorned with every virtue; in the midst of the greatest adversity he constantly possessed an immovable firmness. At sea he subjected himself to the same privations as his men. Better skilled than anyone in the knowledge of nautical charts, he was a perfect master of navigation, as he proved in making the tour of the world, an attempt on which none before him had ventured.

Noche Triste

BY WILLIAM PRESCOTT

The exploration of Central and South America by the Spanish conquistadors is more a story of conquest and cupidity than discovery. But there is no doubt they forged through vast territories new to Europeans at great personal risk, conquering the Aztec and Inca Empires with amazingly small armies. One of their best techniques was to take the local emperors hostage and force them to bend to their will—usually a strange combination of Christian fervor and greed for gold.

In the following story, taken from William Prescott's excellent *The Conquest of Mexico*, this method backfired for conquistador Hernán Cortés. He took the mighty Aztec leader Montezuma prisoner, but could not quell the ill-will of the people. Montezuma was eventually stoned to death by an angry mob while trying to convince his subjects to listen to Cortes. In one of the bloodiest scenes to occur during the long conquest, Cortes is then forced to flee the Aztec capital to save his men from total annihilation. Much like Xenophon's March of the Ten Thousand through the Middle East in ancient times, Cortés' retreat is not really a direct exploration of anything. Yet it remains one of the most important events in the exploration of Mexico.

★   ★   ★   ★   ★

There was no longer any question as to the expediency of evacuating the capital. The only doubt was as to the time of doing so, and the route. The Spanish commander called a council of officers to deliberate on these matters. It was his purpose to retreat on Tlascala, and in that capital to decide according to circumstances on his future operations. After some discussion, they agreed on the causeway of Tlacopan as the avenue by which to leave the city. It would, indeed, take them back by a circuitous route, considerably longer than either of those by which they had approached

30

the capital. But, for that reason, it would be less likely to be guarded, as least suspected; and the causeway itself, being shorter than either of the other entrances, would sooner place the army in comparative security on the main land.

There was some difference of opinion in respect to the hour of departure. The day-time, it was argued by some, would be preferable, since it would enable them to see the nature and extent of their danger, and to provide against it. Darkness would be much more likely to embarrass their own movements than those of the enemy, who were familiar with the ground. A thousand impediments would occur in the night, which might prevent their acting in concert, or obeying, or even ascertaining, the orders of the commander. But, on the other hand, it was urged, that the night presented many obvious advantages in dealing with a foe who rarely carried his hostilities beyond the day. The late active operations of the Spaniards had thrown the Mexicans off their guard, and it was improbable they would anticipate so speedy a departure of their enemies. With celerity and caution, they might succeed, therefore, in making their escape from the town, possibly over the causeway, before their retreat should be discovered; and, could they once get beyond that pass of peril, they felt little apprehension for the rest.

These views were fortified it is said, by the counsels of a soldier named Botello, who professed the mysterious science of judicial astrology. He had gained credit with the army by some predictions which had been verified by the events; those lucky hits which made chance pass for calculations with the credulous multitude. This man recommended to his countrymen by all means to evacuate the place in the night, as the hour most propitious to them, although he should perish in it. The event proved the astrologer better acquainted with his own horoscope than with that of others.

It is possible Botello's predictions had some weight in determining the opinion of Cortés. Superstition was the feature of the age, and the Spanish general, as we have seen, had a full measure of its bigotry. Seasons of gloom, moreover, dispose the mind to a ready acquiescence in the marvellous. It is, however, quite as probable that he made use of the astrologer's opinion, finding it coincided with his own, to influence that of his men and inspire them with higher confidence. At all events, it was decided to abandon the city that very night.

The general's first care was to provide for the safe transportation of the treasure. Many of the common soldiers had converted their share of the prize, as we have seen, into gold chains, collars, or other ornaments, which they easily carried about on their persons. But the royal fifth, together with that of Cortés himself, and much of the rich booty of the principal cavaliers, had been converted into bars and wedges of solid gold and deposited in one of the strong apartments of the palace. Cortés delivered the share belonging to the Crown to the royal officers, assigning them one of the strongest horses, and a guard of Castilian soldiers, to transport it. Still, much of the treasure, belonging both to the Crown and to individuals, was necessarily abandoned, from the want of adequate means of conveyance. The metal lay scattered in shining heaps along the floor, exciting the cupidity of the soldiers. "Take what you will of it," said Cortés to his men. "Better you should have it, than these Mexican hounds. Be careful not to overload yourselves. He travels safest in the dark night who travels lightest." His own more wary followers took heed to this counsel, helping themselves to a few articles of least bulk, though, it might be, of greatest value. But the troops of Narvaez, pining for riches, of which they had heard so much, and hitherto seen so little, showed no such discretion. To them it seemed as if the very mines of Mexico were turned up before them, and, rushing on the treacherous spoil, they greedily loaded themselves with as much of it, not merely as they could accommodate about their persons, but as they could stow away in wallets, boxes, or any other mode of conveyance at their disposal.

Cortés next arranged the order of march. The van, composed of two hundred Spanish foot, he placed under the command of the valiant Gonzalo de Sandoval, supported by Diego de Ordaz, Francisco de Lujo, and about twenty other cavaliers. The rear-guard, constituting the strength of the infantry, was instructed to Pedro de Alvarado, and Velasquez de Leon. The general himself took charge of the "battle," or centre, in which went the baggage, some of the heavy guns, most of which, however, remained in the rear, the treasure, and the prisoners. These consisted of a son and two daughters of Montezuma, Cacama, the deposed lord of Tezcuco, and several other nobles, whom Cortés retained as important pledges in his future negotiations with the enemy. The Tlascalans were distributed pretty equally among the three divisions; and Cortés had under his immediate command a hundred picked soldiers, his own veterans most attached to his service, who, with Christóval de Olid, Francisco de Morla, Alonso de Avila, and two or three other cavaliers, formed a select corps, to act wherever occasion might require.

The general had already superintended the construction of a portable bridge to be laid over the open canals in the causeway. This was given in charge to an officer named Magarino, with forty soldiers under his orders, all pledged to defend the passage to the last extremity. The bride was to be taken up when the entire army had crossed one of the breaches, and transported to the next. There were three of these openings in the causeway, and most fortunate would it have been for the expedition, if the foresight of the commander had provided the same number of bridges. But the labor would have been great, and time was short.

At midnight the troops were under arms, in readiness for the march. Mass was performed by Father Olmedo, who invoked the protection of the Almighty through the awful perils of the night. The gates were thrown open, and, on the first of July, 1520, the Spaniards for the last time sallied forth from the walls of the ancient fortress, the scene of so much suffering and such indomitable courage.

The night was cloudy, and a drizzling rain, which fell without intermission, added to the obscurity. The great square before the palace was deserted, as indeed, it had been since the fall of Montezuma. Steadily, and as noiselessly as possible, the Spaniards held their way along the great street of Tlacopan, which so lately had resounded to the tumult of battle. All was now hushed in silence; and they were only reminded of the past by the occasional presence of some solitary corpse, or a dark heap of the slain, which too plainly told where the strife had been hottest. As they passed along the lanes and alleys which opened into the great street, or looked down the canals, whose polished surface gleamed with a sort of ebon lustre through the obscurity of night, they easily fancied that they discerned the shadowy forms of their foe lurking in ambush, and ready to spring on them. But it was only fancy; and the city slept undisturbed even by the prolonged echoes of the tramp of the horses, and the hoarse rumbling of the artillery and baggage trains. At length, a lighter space beyond the dusky line of buildings showed the van of the army that it was emerging on the open causeway. They might well have congratulated themselves on having thus escaped the dangers of an assault in the city itself, and that a brief time would place them in comparative safety on the opposite shore.—But the Mexicans were not all asleep.

As the Spaniards drew near the spot where the street opened on the causeway, and were preparing to lay the portable bridge across the uncovered breach, which now met their eyes, several Indian sentinels, who had been stationed at his, as at the other approaches to the city, took the alarm, and fled, rousing their countrymen by their cries. The priests, keeping their night watch on the summit of the *teocallis*, instantly caught the tidings and sounded their shells, while the huge drum in the desolate temple of the war-god sent forth those solemn tones, which, heard only in seasons of calamity, vibrated through every corner of the capital. The Spaniards saw that no time was to be lost. The bridge was brought forward and fitted with all possible expedition. Sandoval was the first to try its strength, and, riding across, was followed by his little body of chivalry, his infantry, and Tlascalan allies, who formed the first division of this army. Then came Cortés and his squadrons, with the baggage, ammunition wagons, and a part of the artillery. But before they had time to defile across the narrow passage, a gathering sound was heard, like that of a mighty forest agitated by the winds. It grew louder and louder, while on the dark waters of the lake was heard a splashing noise, as of many oars. Then came a few stones and arrows striking at random among the hurrying troops. They fell every moment faster and more furious, till they thickened into a terrible tempest, while the very heavens were rent with the yells and war-cries of myriads of combatants, who seemed all at once to be swarming over land and lake!

The Spaniards pushed steadily on through this arrowy sleet, though the barbarians, dashing their canoes against the sides of the causeway, clambered up and broke in upon their ranks. But the Christians, anxious only to make their escape, declined all combat except for self-preservation. The cavaliers, spurring forward their steeds, shook off their assailants, and rode over prostrate bodies, while the men on foot with their good swords or the butts of their pieces drove them headlong again down the sides of the dike.

But the advance of several thousand men, marching, probably, on a front of not more than fifteen or twenty abreast, necessarily required much time, and the leading files had already reached the second breach in the causeway before those in the rear had entirely traversed the first. Here they halted; as they had no means of effecting a passage, smarting all the while under unintermitting volleys from the enemy, who were clustered thick on the waters around this second opening. Sorely distressed, the van-guard sent repeated messages to the rear to demand the portable bridge. At length the last of the army had crossed, and Magarino and his sturdy followers endeavored to raise the ponderous framework. But it stuck fast in the sides of the dike. In vain they strained every nerve. The weight of so many men and horses, and above all of the heavy artillery, had wedged the timbers so firmly in the stones and earth, that it was beyond their power to dislodge them. Still they labored amidst a torrent of missiles, until, many of them slain, and all wounded, they were obliged to abandon the attempt.

The tidings soon spread from man to man, and no sooner was their dreadful import comprehended, than a cry of despair arose, which for a moment drowned all the noise of conflict. All means of retreat were cut off. Scarcely hope was left. The only hope was in such desperate exertions as each could make for himself. Order and subordination were at an end. Intense danger produced intense selfishness. Each thought only of his own life. Pressing forward, he trampled down the weak and the wounded, heedless whether it were friend or foe. The leading files, urged on by the rear, were crowded on the brink of the gulf. Sandoval, Ordaz, and the other cavaliers dashed into the water. Some succeeded in swimming their horses across. Others failed, and some, who reached the opposite bank, being overturned in the ascent, rolled headlong with their steeds into the lake. The infantry followed pell-mell, heaped promiscuously on one another, frequently pierced by the shafts, or struck down by the war-clubs of the Aztecs; while many an unfortunate victim was dragged half-stunned on board their canoes, to be reserved for a protracted, but more dreadful, death.

The carnage raged fearfully along the length of the causeway. Its shadowy bulk presented a mark of sufficient distinctness for the enemy's missiles, which often prostrated their own countrymen in the blind fury of the tempest. Those nearest the dike, running their canoes alongside, with a force that shattered them to pieces, leaped on the land, and grappled with the Christians, until both came rolling down the side of the causeway together. But the Aztec fell among his friends, while his antagonist was borne away in triumph to the sacrifice. The struggle was long and deadly. The Mexicans were recognised by their white cotton tunics, which showed faint through the darkness. Above the combatants rose a wild and discordant clamor, in which horrid shouts of vengeance were mingled with groans of agony, with invocations of the saints and the blessed Virgin, and with the screams of women; for there were several women, both natives and Spaniards, who had accompanied the Christian camp. Among these, one named Maria de Estrada is particularly noticed for the courage she displayed, battling with broadsword and target like the stanchest of the warriors.

The opening in the causeway, meanwhile, was filled up with the wreck of matter which had been forced into it, ammunition wagons, heavy guns, bales of rich stuffs scattered over the waters, chests of solid ingots, and bodies of men and horses, till over this dismal ruin a passage was gradually formed, by which those in the rear were enabled to clamber to the other side. Cortés, it is said, found a place that was fordable, where, halting, with the water up to his saddle-girths, he endeavored to check the confusion, and lead his followers by a safer path to the opposite bank. But his voice was lost in the wild uproar, and finally, hurrying on with the tide, he pressed forwards with a few trusty cavaliers, who remained near his person, to the van; but not before he had seen his favorite page, Juan de Salazar, struck down, a corpse, by his side. Here he found Sandoval and his companions, halting before the third and last breach, endeavoring to cheer on their followers to surmount it. But their resolution faltered. It was wide and deep; though the passage was not so closely beset by the enemy as the preceding ones. The cavaliers again set the example by plunging into the water. Horse and foot followed as they could, some swimming, others with dying grasp clinging to the manes and tails of the struggling animals. Those fared best, as the general had predicted, who traveled lightest; and many were the unfortunate wretches, who, weighed down by the fatal gold which they loved so well, were buried with it in the salt floods of the lake. Cortés, with his gallant comrades, Olid, Morla, Sandoval, and some few others, still kept in the advance, leading his broken remnant off the fatal causeway. The din of battle lessened in the distance; when the rumor reached them, that the rearguard would be wholly overwhelmed without speedy relief. It seemed almost an act of desperation; but the generous hearts of the Spanish cavaliers did not stop to calculate danger, when the cry for succor reached them. Turning their horses' bridles, they galloped back to the theatre of action, worked their way through the press, swam the canal, and placed themselves in the thick of the *mêlée* on the opposite bank.

The first grey of the morning was now coming over the waters. It showed the hideous confusion of the scene which had been shrouded in the obscurity of the night. The dark masses of combatants, stretching along the dike, were seen struggling for mastery, until the very causeway on which they stood appeared to tremble, and reel to and fro, as if shaken by an earthquake; while the bosom of the lake, as far as the eye could reach, was darkened by canoes crowded with warriors, whose spears and bludgeons, armed with blades of "volcanic glass," gleamed in the morning light.

The cavaliers found Alvarado unhorsed, and defending himself with a poor handful of followers against an overwhelming tide of the enemy. His good steed, which had borne him through many a hard fight, had fallen under him. He was himself wounded in several places, and was striving in vain to rally his scattered column, which was driven to the verge of the canal by the fury of the enemy, then in possession of the whole rear of the causeway, where they were reinforced every hour by fresh combatants from the city. The artillery in the earlier part of the engagement had not been idle, and its iron shower, sweeping along the dike, had mowed down the assailants by hundreds. But nothing could resist their impetuosity. The front ranks, pushed on by those behind, were at length forced up to the pieces, and, pouring over them like a torrent, overthrew men and guns in one general ruin. The resolute charge of the Spanish cavaliers, who had now arrived, created a temporary check, and gave time for their countrymen to make a feeble rally. But they were speedily borne down by the returning flood. Cortés and his companions were compelled to plunge again into the lake—though all did not escape. Alvarado stood on the brink for a moment, hesitating what to do. Unhorsed as he was, to throw himself into the water, in the face of the hostile canoes that now swarmed around the opening, afforded but a desperate chance of safety. He had but a second for thought. He was a man of powerful frame, and despair gave him unnatural energy. Setting his long lance firmly on the wreck which strewed the bottom of the lake, he sprang forward with all his might, and cleared the wide gap at a leap! Aztecs and Tlascalans gazed in stupid amazement, exclaiming, as they beheld the incredible feat, "This is truly the *Tonatiuh*—the child of the Sun!" The breadth of the opening is not given. But it was so great, that the valorous captain Diaz, who well remembered the place, says the leap was impossible to any man. Other contemporaries, however, do not discredit the story. It was, beyond doubt, matter of popular belief at the time; it is to this day familiarly known to every inhabitant of the capital; and the name of the *Salto de Alvarado*, "Alvarado's Leap," given to the spot, still commemorates an exploit which rivaled those of the demi-gods of Grecian fable.

Cortés and his companions now rode forward to the front, where the troops, in a loose, disorderly manner, were marching off the fatal causeway. A few only of the enemy hung on their rear, or annoyed them by occasional flights of arrows from the lake. The attention of the Aztecs was diverted to the rich spoil that strewed the battleground; fortunately for the Spaniards, who, had their enemy pursued with the same ferocity with which he had fought, would, in their crippled condition, have been cut off, probably to a man. But little molested, therefore, they were allowed to defile through the adjacent village, or suburbs, it might be called, of Popotla.

The Spanish commander there dismounted from his jaded steed, and, sitting down on the steps of an Indian temple, gazed mournfully on the broken files as they passed before him. What a spectacle did they present! The cavalry, most of them dismounted, were mingled with the infantry, who dragged their feeble limbs along with difficulty; their shattered mail and tattered garments dripping with the salty ooze, showing through their rents many a bruise and ghastly wound; their bright arms soiled, their proud crests and banners gone, the baggage, artillery, all, in short, that constitutes the pride and panoply of glorious war, forever lost. Cortés, as he looked wistfully on their thinned and disordered ranks, sought in vain for many a familiar face, and missed more than one dear companion who had stood side by side with him through all the perils of the Conquest. Though accustomed to control his emotions, or, at least, to conceal them, the sights was too much for him. He covered his face with his hands, and the tears, which trickled down, revealed too plainly the anguish of his soul.

He found some consolation, however, in the sight of several of the cavaliers on whom he most relied. Alvarado, Sandoval, Olid, Ordaz, Avila, were yet safe. He had the inexpressible satisfaction, also, of learning the safety of the Indian interpreter, Marina, so dear to him, and so important to the army. She had been committed, with a daughter of a Tlascalan chief, to several of that nation. She was fortunately placed in the van, and her faithful escort had carried her securely through all the dangers of the night. Aguilar, the other interpreter, had also escaped. And it was with no less satisfaction, that Cortés learned the safety of the ship builder, Martin López. The general's solicitude for the fate of this man, so indispensable, as he proved, to the success of his subsequent operations, showed that, amidst all his affliction, his indomitable spirit was looking forward to the hour of vengeance.

Meanwhile, the advancing column had reached the neighboring city of Tlacopan (Tacuba), once the capital of an independent principality. There it halted in the great street, as if bewildered and altogether uncertain what course to take; like a herd of panic-stricken deer, who, flying from the hunters, with the cry of hound and horn still ringing in their ears, look wildly around for some glen or copse in which to plunge for concealment. Cortés, who had hastily mounted and rode on to the front again, saw the danger of remaining in a populous place, where the inhabitants might sorely annoy the troops from the *azoteas*, with little risk to themselves. Pushing forward, therefore, he soon led them into the country. There he endeavored to reform his disorganized battalions, and bring them to something like order.

Hard by, at no great distance on the left, rose an eminence, looking toward a chain of mountains which fences in the Valley on the west. It was called the Hill of Otoncalpolco, and sometimes the Hill of Montezuma. It was crowned with an Indian *teocalli*, with its large outworks of stone covering an ample space, and by its strong position, which commanded the neighboring plain, promised a good place of refuge for the exhausted troops. But the men, disheartened and stupefied by their late reverses, seemed for the moment incapable of further exertion; and the place was held by a body of armed Indians. Cortés saw the necessity of dislodging them, if he would save the remains of his army from entire destruction. The event showed he still held a control over their wills stronger than circumstances themselves. Cheering them on, and supported by his gallant cavaliers, he succeeded in infusing into the most sluggish something of his own intrepid temper, and led them up the ascent in face of the enemy. But the latter made slight resistance, and after a few feeble volleys of missiles which did little injury, left the ground to the assailants.

It was covered by a building of considerable size, and furnished ample accommodations for the diminished numbers of the Spaniards. They found there some provisions; and more, it is said, were brought to them, in the course of the day, from some friendly Otomie villages in the neighborhood. There was, also, a quantity of fuel in the courts, destined to the use of the temple. With this they made fires to dry their drenched garments, and busily employed themselves in dressing one another's wounds, stiff and extremely painful from exposure and long exertion. Thus refreshed, the weary soldiers threw themselves down on the floor and courts of the temple, and soon found the temporary oblivion—which Nature seldom denies even in the greatest extremity of suffering.

There was one eye in that assembly, however, which we may well believe did not so speedily close. For what agitating thoughts must have crowded on the mind of their commander, as he beheld his poor remnant of followers thus huddled together in this miserable bivouac! And this was all that survived of the brilliant array with which but a few weeks since he had entered the capital of Mexico! Where now were his dreams of conquest and empire? And what was he but a luckless adventurer, at whom the finger of scorn would be uplifted as a madman? Whichever way he turned, the horizon was almost equally gloomy, with scarcely one light spot to cheer him. He had still a weary journey before him, through perilous and unknown paths, with guides of whose fidelity he could not be assured. And how could he rely on his reception at Tlascala, the place of his destination; the land of his ancient enemies; where, formerly as a foe, and now as a friend, he had brought desolation to every family within its borders?

Yet these agitating and gloomy reflections, which might have crushed a common mind, had no power over that of Cortés; or rather, they only served to renew his energies, and quicken his perceptions, as the war of the elements purifies and gives elasticity to the atmosphere. He looked with an unblenching eye on his past reverses; but, confident in his own resources, he saw a light through the gloom which others could not. Even in the shattered relics which lay around him, resembling in their haggard aspect and wild attire a horde of famished outlaws, he discerned the materials out of which to reconstruct his ruined fortunes. In the very hour of discomfiture and general despondency, there is no doubt that his heroic spirit was meditating the plan of operations which he afterwards pursued with such dauntless constancy.

The loss sustained by the Spaniards on this fatal night, like every other event in the history of the Conquest, is reported with the greatest discrepancy. If we believe Cortés' own letter, it did not exceed one hundred and fifty Spaniards, and two thousand Indians. But the general's bulletins, while they do full justice to the difficulties to be overcome, and the importance of the results, are less scrupulous in stating the extent either of his means or of his losses.

Thoan Cano, one of the cavaliers present, estimates the slain at eleven hundred and seventy Spaniards and eight thousand allies. But this is a greater number than we have allowed for the whole army. Perhaps we may come nearest the truth by taking the computation of Gomara, who was the chaplain of Cortés, and who had free access, doubtless, not only to the general's papers but to other authentic sources of information. According to him, the number of Christians killed and missing was four hundred and fifty, and that of natives four thousand. This, with the loss sustained in the conflicts of the previous week, may have reduced the former to something more than a third and the latter to a fourth, or perhaps fifth, of the original force with which they entered the capital. The brunt of the action fell on the rear-guard, few of whom escaped. It was formed chiefly of the soldiers of Narvaez, who fell the victims, in some measure, of their cupidity. Forty-six of the cavalry were cut off, which with previous losses reduced the number in this branch of the service to twenty-three, and some of these in very poor condition. The greater parts of the treasure, the baggage, the general's papers, including his accounts, and a minute diary of transactions since leaving Cuba—which, to posterity at least, would have been of more worth than the gold—had been swallowed up by the waters. The ammunition, the beautiful little train of artillery, with which Cortés had entered the city, were all gone. Not a musket even remained, the men having thrown them away, eager to disencumber themselves of all that might retard their escape on that disastrous night. Nothing, in short, of their military apparatus was left, but their swords, their crippled cavalry, and a few damaged crossbows, to assert the superiority of the European over the barbarian.

The prisoners, including, as already noticed, the children of Montezuma and the cacique of Tezcuco, all perished by the hands of their ignorant countrymen, it is said, in the indiscriminate fury of the assault. There were, also, some persons of consideration among the Spaniards, whose names were inscribed on the same bloody roll of slaughter. Such was Francisco de Morla, who fell by the side of Cortés, on returning with him to the rescue. But the greatest loss was that of Juan Velasquez de Leon, who with Alvarado, had command of the rear. It was the post of danger on that night, and he fell, bravely defending it at an early part of the retreat. He was an excellent officer, possessed of many knightly qualities, though somewhat haughty in his bearing, being one of the best connected cavaliers in the army. The near relation of the governor of Cuba, he looked coldly, at first, on the pretentions of Cortés; but whether from a conviction that the latter had been wronged, or from personal preference, he afterwards attached himself zealously to his leader's interests. The general requited this with a generous confidence, assigning him, as we have seen, a separate and independent command, where misconduct, or even a mistake, would have been fatal to the expedition. Velasquez proved himself worthy of the trust; and there was no cavalier in the army, with the exception, perhaps, of Sandoval and Alvarado, whose loss would have been so deeply deplored by the commander. Such were the disastrous results of this terrible passage of the causeway; more disastrous than those occasioned by any other reverse which has stained the Spanish arms in the New World; and which have branded the night on which it happened, in the national annals, with the name of the *noche triste*, "the sad or melancholy night."

Stuck on the Great Barrier Reef

BY CAPTAIN JAMES COOK

Historians still debate which explorer was the first to see which piece of land or ocean, but there is little doubt that Captain Cook was among the first to see quite a bit of the unknown world. His three voyages, which started in the late 1760s and lasted through the 1770s, were not successful in their goals of finding a great southern continent north of the polar ice or in finding a Northwest Passage from the Pacific Ocean, but they did much to advance geographic knowledge of the day.

Cook was murdered in Hawaii during his third voyage after sailing as far north as Alaska. The natives thought him a god and treated the crew with great kindness, but eventually the welcome wore out and problems arose. Cook's method of dealing with trouble was invariably to take the local chief hostage until hostilities were settled, but on this occasion he miscalculated the anger of the native mob and was stabbed and stoned to death on the beach when he turned to give orders to his ship while retreating. His body was ripped to pieces, but most of it was returned several days later for proper burial.

This excerpt from his famous journals is taken from the voyage of the *Endeavor*, when the ship encountered the Great Barrier Reef off the coast of Australia. Nothing had prepared them for navigating this dangerous stretch of water, and the near death of the entire crew is written about so calmly that it is hard to believe they are alone and halfway around the world, stuck fast off a previously unknown coast. It was during this trip that they discovered the dingo and kangaroo, whose name resulted from a misunderstanding of the aborigine language.

★   ★   ★   ★   ★

Hitherto we had safely navigated this dangerous coast, where the sea in all parts conceals shoals that suddenly project from the shore, and rocks that rise abruptly like a pyramid from the bottom, for an extent of two-and-twenty degrees of latitude, more than one thousand three hundred miles; and therefore hitherto none of the names which distinguish the several parts of the country that we saw, are memorials of distress; but here we become acquainted with misfortune, and we therefore called the point which we had just seen farthest to the northward, CAPE TRIBULATION.

This capes lies in latitude 16° 6' S., and longitude 214° 39' W. We steered along the shore N. by W., at the distance of between three and four leagues, having from fourteen to twelve, and ten fathom water; in the offing we saw two islands, which lie in latitude 16° S., and about six or seven leagues from the main. At six in the evening the northernmost land in sight bore N. by W. ½ W. and two low woody islands, which some of us took to be rocks above water, bore N. ½ W. At this time we shortened sail, and hauled off shore E.N.E. and N.E. by E. close upon a wind; for it was my design to stretch off all night, as well to avoid the danger we saw ahead, as to see whether any islands lay in the offing, especially as we were now near the latitude assigned to the islands which were discovered by Quiros, and which some geographers, for what reason I know not, have thought it fit to join to this land. We had the advantage of a fine breeze, and a clear moonlight night, and in standing off from six till near nine o'clock, we deepened our water from fourteen to twenty-one fathom; but while we were at supper, it suddenly shoaled, and we fell into twelve, ten, and either fathom, within the space of a few minutes; I immediately ordered everybody to their station, and all was ready to put about and come to an anchor, but meeting at the next cast of the lead with deep water again, we concluded that we had gone over the tail of the shoals which we had seen at sunset, and that all danger was past; before ten we had twenty and one-and-twenty fathom, and this depth continuing, the gentlemen left the deck in great tranquility, and went to bed; but a few minutes before eleven, the water shallowed at once from twenty to seventeen fathom; and the before the lead could be cast again, the ship struck, and remained immovable, except by the heaving of the surge that beat her against the crags of the rock upon which she lay. In a few moments everybody was upon the deck, with countenances which sufficiently expressed the horrors of our situation. We had stood off the shore three hours and a half, with a pleasant breeze, and therefore knew that we could not be very near it, and we had too much reason to conclude that we were upon a rock of coral, which is more fatal than any other, because the points of it are sharp, and every part of the surface so rough, as to grind away whatever is rubbed against it, even with the gentlest motion. In this situation all the sails were immediately taken in, and the boats hoisted out to examine the depth of water round the ship; we soon discovered that our fears had not aggravated our misfortune and that the vessel had been lifted over a ledge of the rock, and lay in a hollow within it; in some places there was from three to four fathom, and in others not so many feet. The ship lay with her head to the N.E., and at the distance of about thirty yards on the starboard side, the water deepened to eight, ten, and twelve fathom. As soon as the long-boat was out, we struck our yards and topmasts, and carried out the stream anchor on the starboard bow, got the coasting-anchor and cable into the boat, and were going to carry it out the same way; but upon sounding a second time round the ship, the water was found to be deepest astern; the anchor, therefore, was carried out from the starboard quarter instead of the starboard bow—that is, from the stern instead of the head—and having taken ground, our utmost force was applied to the capstan, hoping that if the anchor did not come home, the ship would be got off; but, to our great misfortune and disappointment, we could not move her; during all this time she continued to beat with great violence against the rock, so that it was with the utmost difficulty that we kept upon our legs; and to complete the scene of distress, we saw by the light of the moon the sheathing-boards from the bottom of the vessel floating away all round her, and at last her false keel, so that every movement was making way for the sea to rush in which was to swallow us up. We had now no chance but to lighten her, and we had lost the opportunity of doing that to the greatest advantage, for unhappily we went on shore just at high water, and by this time it had considerably fallen, so that after she should be lightened so as to draw as much less water as the water had sunk, we should be but in the same situation as at first; and the only alleviation of this circumstances was, that as the tide ebbed the ship settled to the rocks, and was not beaten against them with so much violence. We had indeed some hope from the next tide, but it was doubtful whether she would hold together so long, especially as the rock kept grating her bottom under the starboard bow with such force as to be heard in the fore storeroom. This, however, was no time to indulge conjecture, nor was any effort remitted in despair of success; that no time might be lost, the water was immediately started in the hold, and pumped up; six of our guns, being all we had upon the deck, our iron and stone baliast, casks, hoop-staves, oil-jars, decayed stores, and many other things that lay in the way of heavier materials, were thrown overboard with the utmost expedition, everyone exerting himself with an alacrity almost approaching to cheerfulness, without the least repining or discontent; yet the men were so far impressed with a sense of their situation, that not an oath was heard among them, the habit of profaneness, however strong, being instantly subdued by the dread of incurring guilt when death seemed to be so near.

While we were thus employed day broke upon us, and we saw the land at about eight leagues distance, without any island in the intermediate space, upon which, if the ship should have gone to pieces, we might have been set ashore by the boats, and from which they might have taken us by different turns to the main; the wind, however, gradually died away and early in the forenoon it was a dead calm; if it had blown hard the ship must inevitably have been destroyed. At eleven in the forenoon we expected high water, and anchors were got out, and everything made ready for another effort to heave her off if she should float, but to our inexpressible surprise and concern, she did not float by a foot and a half, though we had lightened her near fifty ton; so much did the day-tide fall short of that in the night. We now proceeded to lighten her still more, and threw overboard everything that it was possible for us to spare; hitherto she had not admitted much water, but, as the tide fell, it rushed in so fast, that two pumps, incessantly worked, could scarcely keep her free. At two o'-clock she lay heeling two or three streaks to starboard, and the pinnace, which lay under her bows, touched the ground; we had now no hope but from the tide at midnight, and to prepare for it we carried out our two bower-anchors, one on the starboard quarter, and the other right astern, got the blocks and tackle which were to give us a purchase upon the cables in order, and brought the falls, or ends of them, in abaft, straining them tight, that the next effort might operate upon the ship, and by shortening the length of the cable between that and the anchors, draw her off the ledge upon which she rested, towards the deep water. About five o'clock in the afternoon, we observed the tide begin to rise, but we observed at the same time that the leak increased to a most alarming degree, so that two more pumps were manned, but unhappily only one of them would work. Three of the pumps, however, were kept going, and at nine o'clock the ship righted; but the leak had gained upon us so considerably, that it was imagined she must go to the bottom as soon as she ceased to be supported by the rock. This was a dreadful circumstance, so that we anticipated the floating of the ship not as an earnest of deliverance, but as an event that would probably precipitate our destruction. We well knew that our boats were not capable of carrying us all on shore, and that when the dreadful crisis should arrive, as all command and subordination would be at an end, a contest for preference would probably ensue, that would increase even the horrors of shipwreck, and terminate in the destruction of us all by the hands of each other; yet we knew that if any should be left on board to perish in the waves, they would probably suffer less upon the whole than those who should get on shore, without any lasting or effectual defense against the natives in a country where even nets and fire-arms would scarcely furnish them with food; and where, if they should find the means of subsistence, they must be condemned to languish out the remainder of life in a desolate wilderness, without the possession, or even hope, of any domestic comfort, and cut off from all commerce with mankind, except the naked savages who prowled the desert, and who perhaps were some of the most rude and uncivilised upon the earth.

To those only who have waited in a state of such suspense, death has approached in all his terrors; and as the dreadful moment that was to determine our fate came on, everyone saw his own sensations pictured in the countenances of his companions; however, the capstan and windlass were manned with as many hands as could be spared from the pumps, and the ship floating about twenty minutes after ten o'clock, the effort was made, and she was heaved into deep water. It was some comfort to find that she did not now admit more water than she had done upon the rock; and though, by the gaining of the leak upon the pumps, there was no less than three feet nine inches water in the hold, yet the men did not relinquish their labour, and we held the water as it were at bay; but having now endured excessive fatigue of body and agitation of mind for more than four-and-twenty hours, and having but little hope of succeeding at last, they began to flag; none of them could work at the pump more than five or six minutes together, and then, being totally exhausted, they threw themselves down upon the deck, though a stream of water was running over it from the pumps, between three and four inches deep; when those who succeeded them had worked their spell, and were exhausted in their turn, they threw themselves down in the same manner, and the others started up again, and renewed their labour; thus relieving each other till an accident was very near putting an end to their efforts at once. The planking which lines the inside of the ship's bottom is called the ceiling, and between this and the outside planking there is a space of about eighteen inches; the man who till this time had attended the well to take the depth of water, had taken it only to the ceiling, and gave the measure accordingly; but he being now relieved, the person who came in his stead reckoned the depth to the outside planking, by which it appeared in a few minutes to have gained upon the pumps eighteen inches, the difference between the planking without and within. Upon this, even the bravest was upon the point of giving up his labour with his hope, and in a few minutes everything would have been involved in all the confusion of despair. But this accident, however dreadful in its first consequences, was eventually the cause of our preservation; the mistake was soon detected, and the sudden joy which every man felt upon finding his situation better than his fears had suggested, operated like a charm, and seemed to possess him with a strong belief that scarcely any real danger remained. New confidence and new hope, however founded, inspired new vigour; and though our state was the same as when the men first began to slacken in their labour

through weariness and despondency, they now renewed their efforts with such
alacrity and spirit, that before eight o'clock in the morning the leak was so far
from having gained upon the pumps, that the pumps had gained considerably
upon the leak. Everybody now talked of getting the ship into some harbour as
a thing not to be doubted, and as hands could be spared from the pumps, they
were employed in getting up the anchors; the stream-anchor and best bower
we had taken on board; but it was found impossible to save the little bower, and
therefore it was cut away at a whole cable; we lost also the cable of the stream-
anchor among the rocks; but in our situation these were trifles which scarcely
attracted our notice. Our next business was to get up the fore-topmast and
fore-yard, and warp the ship to the south-east, and at eleven, having now a
breeze from the sea, we once more got under sail and stood for land.

It was, however, impossible long to continue the labour by which the
pumps had been made to gain upon the leak; and as the exact situation of it
could not be discovered, we had no hope of stopping it within. In this situation
Mr. Monkhouse, one of my midshipmen, came to me, and proposed an expedient that he had once seen used on board a merchant-ship, which had sprung
a leak that admitted above four feet water an hour, and which, by this expedient, was brought safely from Virginia to London; the master having such confidence in it, that he took her out of harbour, knowing her condition, and did
not think it worthwhile to wait till the leak could be otherwise stopped. To this
man, therefore, the care of the expedient, which is called fothering the ship,
was immediately committed, four or five of the people being appointed to assist him, and he performed it in this manner. He took a lower studdingsail, and
having mixed together a quantity of oakum and wool, chopped pretty small, he
stitched it down in handfuls upon the sail, as lightly as possible, and over this he
spread the dung of our sheep and other filth; but horse dung, if we had it,
would have been better. When the sail was thus prepared, it was hauled under
the ship's bottom by ropes, which kept it extended, and when it came under
the leak, the suction which carried in the water, carried in the oakum and
wool from the surface of the sail, which in other parts the water was not sufficiently agitated to wash off. By the success of this expedient our leak was so far
reduced, that instead of gaining upon three pumps, it was easily kept under
with one. This was a new source of confidence and comfort; the people could
scarcely have expressed more joy if they had been already in port; and their
views were so far from being limited to running the ship ashore in some harbour, either of an island or the main, and building a vessel out of her materials
to carry us to the East Indies, which had so lately been the utmost object of
our hope, that nothing was now thought of but ranging along the shore in

search of a convenient place to repair the damage she had sustained and then prosecuting the voyage upon the same plan as if nothing had happened. Upon this occasion I must observe, both in justice and gratitude to the ship's company, and the gentlemen on board, that although in the midst of our distress everyone seemed to have a just sense of his danger, yet no passionate exclamations or frantic gestures were to be heard or seen; everyone appeared to have the perfect possession of his mind; and everyone exerted himself to the uttermost, with a quiet and patient perseverance, equally distant from the tumultuous violence of terror, and the gloomy inactivity of despair. In the meantime, having light airs at E.S.E., we got up the main-top-mast and main-yard, and kept edging in for the land, till about six o'clock in the evening, when we came to an anchor in seventeen fathom water, at the distance of seven leagues from the shore, and one from the ledge of rocks upon which we had struck.

This ledge or shoal lies in latitude 15° 45' S., and between six and seven leagues from the main. It is not, however, the only shoal on this part of the coast, especially to the northward; and at this time we saw one to the southward, the tail of which we passed over, when we had uneven soundings about two hours before we struck. A part of this shoal is always above water, and has the appearance of white sand; a part also of that upon which we had lain is dry at low water, and in that place consists of sandstones; but all the rest of it is a coral rock.

While we lay at anchor for the night, we found that the ship made about fifteen inches water an hour, from which no immediate danger was to be apprehended; and at six o'clock in the morning, we weighed and stood to the N.W., still edging in for the land with a gentle breeze at S.S.E. At nine we passed close without two small islands that lie in latitude 15° 41' S., and about four leagues from the main; to reach these islands had, in the height of our distress, been the object of our hope, or perhaps rather of our wishes, and therefore I called them HOPE ISLANDS. At noon we were about three leagues from the land, and in latitude 15° 37' S.; the northernmost part of the main in sight bore N. 30 W.; and HOPE ISLANDS extended from S. 30 E. to S. 40 E. In this situation we had twelve fathom water, and several sand-banks without us. At this time the leak had not increased; but that we might be prepared for all events, we got the sail ready for another fothering. In the afternoon, having a gentle breeze at S.E. by E., I sent out the master with two boats, as well to sound ahead of the ship, as to look out for a harbour where we might repair our defects, and put the ship in a proper trim. At three o'clock, we saw an opening that had the appearance of a harbour, and stood off and on while the boats examined it; but they soon found that there was not depth of water in it sufficient for the ship. When it was near sunset, there being many shoals about us, we anchored in four fathom, at the distance of about two miles from the shore, the land extending from N. ½ E. to S. by E. ½ E. The pinnace was still out with one of the mates; but at nine o'clock she returned, and reported, that about two leagues to leeward she had discovered just such a harbour as we wanted, in which there was a sufficient rise of water, and every other convenience that could be desired, either for laying the ship ashore, or heaving her down.

In consequence of this information, I weighed at six o'clock in the morning, and having sent two boats ahead, to lie upon the shoals that we saw in our way, we ran down to the place; but notwithstanding our precaution, we were once in three fathom water. As soon as these shoals were passed, I sent the boats to lie in the channel that led to the harbour, and by this time it began to blow. It was happy for us that a place of refuge was at hand; for we soon found that the ship would not work, having twice missed stays; our situation, however, though it might have been much worse, was not without danger; we were entangled among shoals, and I had great reason to fear being driven to leeward, before the boats could place themselves so as to prescribe our course. I therefore anchored in four fathom, about a mile from the shore, and then made the signal for the boats to come on board. When this was done, I went myself and buoyed the channel, which I found very narrow; the harbour also I found smaller than I expected, but most excellently adapted to our purpose; and it is remarkable, that in the whole course of our voyage we had seen no place which, in our present circumstances, could have afforded us the same relief. At noon, our latitude was 15° 26' S. During all the rest of this day, and the whole night, it blew too fresh for us to venture from our anchor and run into the harbour; and for our farther security, we got down the topgallant yards, unbent the mainsail and some of the small sails; got down the fore-topgallant-mast, and the jib-boom, and spritsail, with a view to lighten the ship forwards as much as possible, in order to come at her leak, which we supposed to be somewhere in that part; for in all the joy of our unexpected deliverance, we had not forgot that at this time there was nothing but a lock of wool between us and destruction. The gale continuing, we kept our station all the 15th. On the 16th, it was somewhat more moderate; and about six o'clock in the morning, we hove the cable short, with a design to get under sail, but were obliged to desist, and veer it out again. It was remarkable that the sea-breeze, which blew fresh when we anchored, continued to do so almost every day while we stayed here; it was calm only when we were upon the rock, except once; and even the gale that afterwards wafted us to shore, would then certainly have beaten us to pieces. In the evening of the preceding day, we had observed a fire near the beach over against us; and as it would be necessary for us to stay some time in this place, we were not without hope of making an acquaintance with the people. We saw more fires upon the hills today, and with our glasses discovered four Indians going along the shore, who stopped and made two fires; but for what purpose it was impossible we should guess.

The scurvy now began to make its appearance among us, with many formidable symptoms. Our poor Indian, Tupia, who had some time before complained that his gums were sore and swelled, and who had taken plentifully of our lemon juice by the surgeon's direction, now had livid spots upon his legs, and other indubitable testimonies that the disease had made a rapid progress, notwithstanding all our remedies, among which the bark had been liberally administered. Mr. Green, our astronomer, was also declining; and these, among other circumstances, embittered the delay which prevented our going ashore.

In the morning of the 17th, though the wind was still fresh, we ventured to weigh, and push in for the harbour; but in doing this we twice ran the ship aground; the first time she went off without any trouble, but the second time she stuck fast. We now got down the fore-yard, fore-top-masts, and booms, and taking them overboard, made a raft of them alongside of the ship. The tide was happily rising, and about one o'clock in the afternoon she floated. We soon warped her into the harbour, and having moored her alongside of a steep beach to the south, we got the anchors, cables, and all the hawsers on shore before night.

In the morning of Monday the 18th, a stage was made from the ship to the shore, which was so bold that she floated at twenty feet distance; two tents were also set up, one for the sick, and the other for stores and provisions, which were landed in the course of the day. We also landed all the empty water-casks, and part of the stores. As soon as the tent for the sick was got ready for their reception, they were sent ashore to the number of eight or nine, and the boat was dispatched to haul the seine, in hopes of procuring some fish for their refreshment; but she returned without success. In the meantime, I climbed one of the highest hills among those that overlooked the harbour, which afforded by no means a comfortable prospect; the lowland near the river is wholly overrun with mangroves, among which the salt-water flows every tide; and the highland appeared to be everywhere stony and barren. In the meantime, Mr. Banks had also taken a walk up the country, and met with the frames of several old Indian houses, and places where they had dressed shell-fish; but they seemed not to have been frequented for some months. Tupia, who had employed himself in angling, and lived entirely upon what he caught, recovered in a surprising degree; but Mr. Green still continued to be extremely ill.

The next morning I got the four remaining guns out of the hold, and mounted them upon the quarter-deck; I also got a spare anchor and anchor-stock ashore, and the remaining part of the stores and ballast that were in the hold; set up the smith's forge, and employed the armourer and his mate to make nails and other necessities for the repair of the ship. In the afternoon, all the officers' stores and the ground tier of water were got out; so that nothing remained in the fore and main hold, but the coals, and a small quantity of stone ballast. This day Mr. Banks crossed the river to take a view of the country on the other side; he found it to consist principally of sand hills, where he saw some Indian houses, which appeared to have been very lately inhabited. In this walk, he met with vast flocks of pigeons and crows; of the pigeons, which were exceedingly beautiful, he shot several; but the crows, which were exactly like those in England, were so shy that he could not get within reach of them.

On the 20th, we landed the powder, and got out the stone ballast and wood, which brought the ship's draught of water to eight feet ten inches forward, and thirteen feet abaft; and this, I thought, with the difference that would be made by trimming the coals aft, would be sufficient; for I found that the water rose and fell perpendicularly eight feet at the spring-tides; but as soon as the coals were trimmed from over the leak, we could hear the water rush in a little abaft the foremast, about three feet from the keel; this determined me to clear the hold entirely. This evening Mr. Banks observed that in many parts of the inlet there were large quantities of pumice stones, which lay at a considerable distance above high-water mark; whither they might have been carried either by the freshes or extraordinarily high tides, for there could be no doubt but that they came from the sea.

The next morning we went early to work, and by four o'clock in the afternoon had got out all the coals, cast the moorings loose, and warped the ship a little higher in the harbour, to a place which I thought most convenient for laying her ashore, in order to stop the leak. Her draught of water forward was now seven feet nine inches, and abaft thirteen feet six inches. At eight o'clock, its being high-water, I hauled her bow close ashore; but kept her stern afloat, because I was afraid of neaping her; it was however necessary to lay the whole of her as near the ground as possible.

At two 'clock in the morning of the 22nd, the tide left her, and gave us an opportunity to examine the leak, which we found to be at her floor heads, a little before the starboard fore-chains. In this place the rocks had made their way through four planks, and even into the timbers; three more planks were much damaged, and the appearance of these breaches was very extraordinary; there was not a splinter to be seen, but all was as smooth as if the whole had been cut away by an instrument; the timbers in this place were happily very close, and if they had not, it would have been absolutely impossible to have saved the ship. But after all, her preservation depended upon a circumstance still more remarkable; one of the holes, which was big enough to have sunk us, if we had had eight pumps instead of four, and been able to keep them incessantly going, was in great measure plugged up by a fragment of the rock, which, after having made the wound, was left sticking in it; so that the water, which at first had gained upon our pumps, was what came in at the interstices, between the stone and the edges of the hold that received it. We found also several pieces of the fothering, which had made their way between the timbers, and in a great measure stopped those parts of the leak which the stone had left open. Upon further examination, we found that, besides the leak, considerable damage had been done to the bottom; great part of the sheathing was gone from under the larboard bow; a considerable part of the false keel was also wanting; and these indeed we had seen swim away in fragments from the vessel, while she lay beating against the rock; the remainder of it was in so shattered a condition that it had better have been gone; and the fore foot and main keel were also damaged, but not so as to produce any immediate danger; what damage she might have received abaft could not yet be exactly known, but we had reason to think it was not much, as but little water made its way into her bottom, while the tide kept below the leak which has already been described. By nine o'clock in the morning the carpenters got to work upon her, while the smiths were busy in making bolts and nails. In the meantime, some of the people were sent on the other side of the water to shoot pigeons for the sick, who at their return reported that they had seen an animal as large as a greyhound, of a slender make, a mouse colour, and extremely swift; they discovered also many Indian houses, and a fine stream of fresh water.

The next morning, I sent a boat to haul the seine; but at noon it returned with only three fish, and yet we saw them in plenty leaping about the harbour. This day the carpenter finished the repairs that were necessary on the starboard side; and at nine o'clock in the evening, we heeled the ship the other way, and hauled her off about two feet for fear of neaping. This day almost everybody had seen the animal which the pigeon-shooters had brought an account of the day before; and one of the seamen, who had been rambling in the woods, told us at his return, that he verily believed he had seen the devil; we naturally inquired in what form he had appeared, and his answer was in so singular a style that I shall set down his own words: "He was," says John, "as large as a one-gallon keg, and very like it; he had horns and wings, yet he crept so slowly through the grass, that if I had not been *afeard* I might have touched him." This formidable apparition we afterwards discovered to have been a bat; and the bats here must be acknowledged to have a frightful appearance, for they are nearly black, and full as large as a partridge; they have indeed no horns, but the fancy of a man who thought he saw the devil might easily supply that defect.

Early on the 24th, the carpenters began to repair the sheathing under the larboard bow, where we found two planks cut about half through; and in the meantime I sent a party of men, under the direction of Mr. Gore, in search of refreshments for the sick; this party returned about noon, with a few palm cabbages, and a bunch or two of wild plantain; the plantains were the smallest I had ever seen, and the pulp, though it was well tasted, was full of small stones. As I was walking this morning at a little distance from the ship, I saw, myself, one of the animals which had been so often described; it was of a light mouse color, and in size and shape very much resembling a greyhound; it had a long tail also, which it carried like a greyhound; and I should have taken it for a wild dog, if, instead of running, it had not leapt like a hare or deer; its legs were said to be very slender, and the print of its foot to be like that of a goat; but where I saw it, the grass was so high that the legs were concealed, and the ground was too hard to receive the track. Mr. Banks also had an imperfect view of this animal, and was of the opinion that its species was hitherto unknown.

After the ship was hauled ashore, all the water that came into her of course went backwards; so that although she was dry forwards, she had nine feet water abaft; as in this part therefore her bottom could not be examined on the inside, I took the advantage of the tide being out this evening to get the master and two of the men to go under her, and examine her whole larboard side without. They found the sheathing gone about the floor heads abreast of the mainmast, and a part of a plank a little damaged; but all agreed that she had received no other material injury. The loss of her sheathing alone was a great misfortune, as the worm would now be let into her bottom, which might expose us to great inconvenience and danger; but as I knew no remedy for the mischief but heaving her down, which would be a work of immense labour and long time, if practicable at all in our present situation, I was obliged to be content. The carpenters, however, continued to work under her bottom in the evening till they were prevented by the tide; the morning tide did not ebb out far enough to permit them to work at all, for we had only one tolerable high and low tide in four-and-twenty hours, as indeed we had experienced when we lay upon the rock. The position of the ship, which threw the water in her abaft, was very near depriving the world of all the knowledge which Mr. Banks had endured so much labour, and so many risks, to procure; for her had removed the curious collection of plants which he had made during the whole voyage, into the bread-room, which lies in the after-part of the ship, as a place of the greatest security; and nobody having thought of the danger to which laying her head so much higher than the stern would expose them, they were this day found under water. Most of them however were, by indefatigable care and attention, restored to a state of preservation, but some were entirely spoilt and destroyed.

The 25th was employed in filling water and overhauling the rigging; and at low water the carpenters finished the repairs under the larboard bow, and every other place which the tide would permit them to come at; some casks were then lashed under her bows to facilitate her floating; and at night, when it was high water, we endeavoured to heave her off, but without success, for some of the casks that were lashed to her gave way.

The morning of the 26th was employed in getting more casks ready for the same purpose, and in the afternoon we lashed no fewer than eight-and-thirty under the ship's bottom, but to our great mortification these also proved ineffectual, and we found ourselves reduced to the necessity of waiting till the next spring-tide.

This day, some of our gentleman, who had made an excursion into the woods, brought home the leaves of a plant, which was thought to be the same that in the West Indies is called cocco; but upon trial, the roots proved too acrid to be eaten; the leaves however were little inferior to spinage. In the place where these plants were gathered, grew plenty of the cabbage trees which have occasionally been mentioned before, a kind of wild plantain, the fruit of which was so full of stones as scarcely to be eatable; another fruit was also found about the size of a small golden pippen, but flatter, and of a deep purple color; when first gathered from the tree, it was very hard and disagreeable, but after being kept a few days became soft, and tasted very much like an indifferent damson.

The next morning we began to move some of the weight from the after-part of the ship forward, to ease her; in the meantime the armourer continued to work at the forge, the carpenter was busy in calking the ship, and the men employed in filling water and overhauling the rigging; in the forenoon I went myself in the pinnace up the harbour, and made several hauls with the seine, but caught only between twenty and thirty fish, which were given to the sick and convalescent.

On the 28th, Mr. Banks went with some of the seamen up the country, to show them the plant which in the West Indies is called Indian kale, and which served us for greens. Tupia had much meliorated the root of the coccos, by giving them a long dressing in his country oven; but they were so small that we did not think them an object for the ship. In their walk they found one tree which had been notched for the convenience of climbing it, in the same manner with those we had seen in Botany Bay; they saw also many nests of white ants, which resemble those of the East Indies, the most pernicious insects in the world. The nests were of a pyramidical figure, from a few inches to six feet high, and very much resembled the stones in England which are said to be monuments of the Druids. Mr. Gore, who was also this day four or five miles up the country, reported that he had seen the footsteps of men, and tracked animals of three or four different sorts, but had not been fortunate enough to see either man or beast.

At two o'clock in the morning of the 29th , I observed, in conjunction with Mr. Green, an emersion of Jupiter's first satellite, the time here was 2', 18', 53", which gave the longitude of this place 214° 42' 30"W.; its latitude is 15° 26' S. At break of day, I sent the boat out again with the seine, and in the afternoon it returned with as much fish as enabled me to give every man a pound and a half. One of my midshipmen, an American, who was this day abroad with his gun, reported that he had seen a wolf, exactly like those which he had been used to seeing in his own country, and that he had shot at it, but did not kill it. [This was probably a "dingo" or native dog, the *Warragul* of the aborigines, (*Canis Australasia,* Dem.) as no species of the wolf is found throughout the country. The dingo is remarkable for its extreme tenacity of life, some singular instances of which are related by Mr. Bennett, in his "Wanderings in New South Wales"; which may account for the bad success of the American marksman.]

The next morning, encouraged by the success of the day before, I sent the boat again to haul the seine, and another party to gather greens; I sent also some of the young gentlemen to take a plan of the harbour, and went myself upon a hill, which lies over the south point, to take a view of the sea. At this time it was low water, and I saw, with great concern, innumerable sandbanks and shoals lying all along the coast in every direction. The innermost lay about three or four miles from the shore, the outermost extended as far as I could see with my glass, and many of them did but just rise above water. There was some appearance of a passage to the northward, and I had no hope of getting clear but in that direction, for, as the wind blows constantly from the S.E., it would have been difficult, if not impossible, to return back to the southward.

Mr. Gore reported, that he had this day seen two animals like dogs, of a straw colour, that they ran like a hare, and were about the same size. In the afternoon, the people returned from hauling the seine, with still better success than before, for I was now able to distribute two pounds and a half to each man; the greens that had been gathered I ordered to be boiled among the pease, and they made an excellent mess, which, with two copious supplies of fish, afforded us unspeakable refreshment.

The next day, July the 1st, being Sunday, everybody had liberty to go ashore, except one from each mess, who were again sent out with the seine. The seine was again equally successful, and the people who went up the country gave an account of having seen several animals, though none of them was to be caught. They saw a fire also about a mile up the river, and Mr. Gore, the second lieutenant, picked up the husk of a cocoa-nut, which had been cast upon the beach, and was full of barnacles; this probably might come from some island to windward, perhaps from the Terra del Espirito Santo of Quiros, as we were now in the latitude where it is said to lie. [Captain King remarks upon this passage: "From the prevailing winds, it would appear more likely to have drifted from New Caledonia, which island was at that time unknown to Cook; the fresh appearance of the cocoa-nut seen by us (at Cape Cleveland) renders, however, even this conclusion doubtful. Captain Flinders also found one as far to the south as Shoalwater Bay".] This day the thermometer in the shade rose to 87, which was higher than it had been on any day since we came upon this coast.

Early the next morning, I sent the master in the pinnace out of the harbour, to sound about the shoals in the offing, and look for channel to the northward; at this time we had a breeze from the land, which continued till about nine o'clock, and was the first we had since our coming into the river. At low water we lashed some empty casks under the ship's bows, having some hope that, as the tides were rising, she would float the next high water. We still continued to fish with great success, and at high water we again attempted to heave the ship off, but our utmost efforts were still ineffectual.

The next day at noon, the master returned, and reported, that he had found a passage out to sea between the shoals and described its situation. The shoals, he said, consisted of coral rocks, many of which were dry at low water, and upon one of which he had been ashore. He found here some cockles of so enormous a size, that one of them was more than two men could eat, and a great variety of other shell-fish, of which he brought us a plentiful supply; in the evening, he had also landed in a bay about three leagues to the northward of our station, where he disturbed some of the natives who were at supper; they all fled with the greatest precipitation at his approach, leaving some fresh sea eggs, and a fire ready kindled behind them, but there was neither house nor hovel near the place. We observed, that although the shoals that lie just within sight of the coast abound with shell-fish, which may be easily caught at low water, yet we saw no such shells about the fireplaces on shore. This day an alligator was seen to swim about the ship for some time, and at high water we made another effort to float her, which happily succeeded; we found however that by lying so long with her head aground and her stern afloat, she had sprung a plank between decks, abreast of the main chains, so that it was become necessary to lay her ashore again.

The next morning was employed in trimming her upon an even keel, and in the afternoon, having warped her over, and waited for high-water, we laid her ashore on the sandbank on the south side of the river, for the damage she had received already from the great descent of the ground made me afraid to lay her broadside to the shore in the same place from which we had just floated her. I was now very desirous to make another trial to come at her bottom, where the sheathing had been rubbed off; but although she had scarcely four feet water under her when the tide was out, yet that part was not dry.

On the 5th, I got one of the carpenter's crew, a man in whom I could confide, to go down again to the ship's bottom, and examine the place. He reported, that three streaks of the sheathing about eight feet long, were wanting, and that the main plank had been a little rubbed; this account perfectly agreed with the report of the master, and others, who had been under her bottom before; I had the comfort however to find the carpenter of opinion that this would be of little consequence, and therefore the other damage being repaired, she was again floated at high-water, and moored alongside the beach, where the stores had been deposited; we then went to work to take the stores on board, and put her in a condition for the sea. This day, Mr. Banks crossed to the other side of the harbour, where, as he walked along a sandy beach, he found innumerable fruits, and many of them such as no plants which he had discovered in this country produced; among others were some cocoa-nuts, which Tupia said had been opened by some kind of crab, which from his description we judged to be the same that the Dutch call *Bears Krabbe*, and which we had not seen in these seas. All the vegetable substances which he found in this place were encrusted with marine productions, and covered with barnacles; a sure sign that they must have come far by sea, and, as the trade-wind blows right upon the shore, probably from Terra del Espirito Santo, which has been mentioned already.

The next morning, Mr. Banks, with Lieutenant Gore, and three men, set out in a small boat up the river, with a view to spend two or three days in an excursion, to examine the country, and kill some of the animals which had been so often seen at a distance.

On the 7th, I sent the master again out to sound about the shoals, the account which he had brought me of the channel being by no means satisfactory; and we spent the remainder of his day and the morning of the next, in fishing, and other necessary occupations.

About four o'clock in the afternoon, Mr. Banks and his party returned, and gave us an account of their expedition. Having proceeded about three leagues among swamps and mangroves, they went up into the country, which they found to differ but little from what they had seen before; they pursued their course therefore up the river, which at length was contracted into a narrow channel, and was bounded, not by swamps and mangroves, but by steep banks, that were covered with trees of a most beautiful verdure, among which was that which in the West Indies is called Mohoe, or the bark-tree, the *Hibiscus tiliaceus*; the land within was in general low, and had a thick covering of long grass; the soil seemed to be such as promised great fertility, to any who should plant and improve it. In the course of the day, Tupia saw an animal, which, by his description, Mr. Banks judged to be a wolf; they also saw three other animals, but could neither catch nor kill one of them, and a kind of bat, as large as a partridge, but this also eluded all their diligence and skill. At night, they took up their lodging close to the banks of the river, and made a fire, but the mosquitoes swarmed about them in such numbers, that their quarters were almost untenable; they followed them into the smoke, and almost into the fire, which, hot as the climate was, they could better endure than the stings of these insects, which were an intolerable torment. The fire, the flies, and the want of a better bed than the ground, rendered the night extremely uncomfortable, so that they passed it, not in sleep, but in restless wishes for the return of day. With the first dawn they set out in search of game, and in a walk of many miles they saw four animals of the same kind, two of which Mr. Banks's greyhound fairly chased, but they threw him out at a great distance, by leaping over the long thick grass, which prevented his running; this animal was observed, not to run upon four legs, but to bound or hop forward on two, like the *Jerboa*, or *Mus Jaculus*. About noon, they returned to the boat, and again proceeded up the river, which was soon contracted into a fresh-water brook, where, however, the tide rose to a considerable height; as evening approached, it became low-water, and it was then so shallow that they were obliged to get out of the boat and drag her along, till they could find a place in which they might, with some hope of rest, pass the night. Such a place at length offered, and while they were getting the things out of the boat, they observed a smoke at the distance of about a furlong; as they did not doubt but that some of the natives, with whom they had so long and earnestly desired to become personally acquainted, were about the fire, three of the party went immediately towards it, hoping that so small a number would not put them to flight; when they came up to the place, however, they found it deserted, and therefore they conjectured, that before they had discovered the Indians, the Indians had discovered them. They found the fire still burning, in the hollow of an old tree that was become touchwood, and several branches of trees newly broken down, with which children appeared to have been playing; they observed also many footsteps upon the sand, below high-water mark, which were certain indications that the Indians had been recently upon the spot. Several houses were found at a little distance, and some ovens dug in the ground, in the same manner as those of Otaheite, in which victuals appeared to have been dressed since the morning, and scattered about them lay some shells of a kind of clam, and some fragments of roots, the refuse of the meal. After regretting their disappointment, they repaired to their quarters, which was a broad sandbank, under the shelter of a bush. The beds were plantain leaves, which they spread upon the sand, and which were as soft as a mattress; their cloaks served them for bedclothes, and some bunches of grass for pillows; with these accommodations they hoped to pass a better night than the last, especially as, to their great comfort, not a mosquito was to be seen. Here then they lay down, and such is the force of habit, they resigned themselves to sleep, without once reflecting upon the probability and danger of being found by the Indians in that situation. If this appears strange, let us for a moment reflect, that every danger and every calamity, after a time, becomes familiar, and loses its effect upon the mind. If it were possible that a man should first be made acquainted with his mortality, or even with the inevitable debility and infirmities of old age, when his understanding had arrived at its full strength, and life was endeared by the enjoyments of youth, and vigour, and health, with what an agony of terror and distress would the intelligence be received! Yet, being gradually acquainted with these mournful truths, by insensible degrees, we scarce know when, they lose all their force, and we think no more of the approach of old age and death, than these wanderers of an unknown desert did of a less obvious and certain evil—the approach of the native savages, at a time when they must have fallen an easy prey to their malice or their fears. And it is remarkable, that the greater part of those who have been condemned to suffer a violent death, have slept the night immediately preceding their execution, though there is perhaps no instance of a person accused of a capital crime having slept the first night of his confinement. Thus is the evil of life in some degree a remedy for itself, and though every man at twenty deprecates fourscore, almost every man is as tenacious of life at fourscore as at twenty; and if he does not suffer under any painful disorder, loses as little of the comforts that remain by reflecting that he is upon the brink of the grave, where the earth already crumbles under his feet, as he did of the pleasures of his better days, when his dissolution, though certain, was supposed to be at a distance.

Our travelers having slept, without once awakening till the morning, examined the river, and finding the tide favoured their return, and the country promised nothing worthy of a farther search, they re-embarked in their boat, and made the best of their way to the ship.

A Bloody Banquet

James Bruce traveled to Ethiopia in 1769 in search of the source of the Blue Nile. By most accounts, he was a giant of a man, conceited, a skilled horseman, and well acquainted with the weaponry of the day, but he also exhibited an amazing knack for the diplomacy necessary to travel through the morass of primitive African politics—the first obstacle of any white explorer on the Dark Continent. He spent much more time placating the leading warlords of Abyssinia than he did exploring, but his adroit handling of his relationship with one of the most powerful, Ras Michael, allowed him to see many things no other European had ever even imagined.

The book he wrote about his amazing adventures and the fantastic behavior of the natives he encountered was ridiculed as fantasy, and for the remainder of his life his account was scoffed at. Another century would pass before the essential truth of what he had written was substantiated. Bruce's tone and attitude in *Travels to Discover the Source of the Nile* are often irritating, but he could also be quite entertaining and witty—as he is in these episodes.

★ ★ ★ ★ ★

Consistent with the plan of this work, which is to describe the manners of the several nations through which I passed, good and bad, as I observed them, I cannot avoid giving some account of this Polyphemus banquet, as far as decency will permit me; it is part of the history of a barbarous people; whatever I might wish, I cannot decline it.

In the capital, where one is safe from surprise at all times, or in the country or villages, when the rains have become so constant that the vallies will not bear a horse to pass them, or that men cannot venture far from home through fear of being surrounded and swept away by temporary torrents, occasioned by sudden showers on the mountains; in a word, when a man can say he is safe at home, and the spear and shield are hung up in the hall, a number of people of the best fashion in the villages, of both sexes, courtiers in the palace, or citizens in the town, meet together to dine between twelve and one o'clock.

A long table is set in the middle of a large room, and benches beside it for a number of guests who are invited. Tables and benches the Portuguese introduced amongst them; but bull hides, spread upon the ground, served them before, as they do in camp and country now. A cow or bull, one or more, as the company is numerous, is brought close to the door, and his feet are strongly tied. The skin that hangs down under his chin and throat, which I think we call the dew-lap in England, is cut only so deep as to arrive at the fat, of which it totally consists, and, by the separation of a few small blood vessels, six or seven drops of blood only fall upon the ground. They have no stone, bench, nor altar upon which these cruel assassins lay the animal's head in this operation. I should beg his pardon indeed for calling him an assassin, as he is not so merciful as to aim at the life, but, on the contrary, to keep the beast alive till he be totally eaten up. Having satisfied the Mosaical law, according to his conception, by pouring those six or seven drops upon the ground, two or more of them fall to work; on the back of the beast, and on each side of the spine, they cut skindeep, then putting their fingers between the flesh and the skin, they begin to strip the hide of the animal halfway down his ribs, and so on to the buttock, cutting the skin wherever it hinders them commodiously to strip the poor animal bare. All the flesh on the buttocks is cut off then, and in solid, square pieces, without bones or much effusion of blood, and the prodigious noise the animal makes is a signal for the company to sit down to table.

There are then laid before every guest, instead of plates, round cakes, if I may so call them, about twice as big as a pan-cake, and something thicker and tougher. It is unleavened bread of a sourish taste, far from being disagreeable, and very easily digested, made of a grain called teff. It is of different colours, from black to the colour of the whitest wheat-bread. Three or four of these cakes are generally put uppermost, for the food of the person opposite to whose seat they are placed. Beneath these are four or five of ordinary bread, and of a blackish kind. These serve the master to wipe his fingers upon; and afterwards the servant for bread for his dinner.

Two or three servants then come, each with a square piece of beef in their bare hands, laying it upon the cakes of teff, placed like dishes down the table, without cloth or anything else beneath them. By this time all the guests have knives in their hands, and their men have the large crooked ones, which they put to all sorts of uses during the time of war. The women have small clasped knives, such as the worst of the kind made at Birmingham, sold for a penny each.

The company are so ranged that one man sits between two women; the man with his long knife cuts a thin piece, which would be thought a good beef-steak in England, while you see the motion of the fibres yet perfectly distinct, and alive in the flesh. No man in Abyssinia, of any fashion whatever, feeds himself, or touches his own meat. The women take the steak and cut it lengthways like strings, about the thickness of your little fingers, then crossways into square pieces, something smaller than dice. This they lay upon a piece of the teff bread, strongly powdered with black pepper, or Cayenne pepper, and fossile-salt; they then wrap it up in the teff bread like a cartridge.

In the meantime, the man having put up his knife, with each hand resting upon his neighbour's knee, his body stooping, his head low and forward, and mouth open, very like an idiot, turns to the one whose cartridge is first ready, who stuffs the whole of it into his mouth, which is so full that he is in constant danger of being choked. This is a mark of grandeur. The greater the man would seem to be, the larger piece he takes in his mouth; and the more noise he makes in chewing it, the more polite he is thought to be. They have, indeed, a proverb that says, "Beggars and thieves only eat small pieces, or without making a noise." Having dispatched this morsel, which he does very expeditiously, his next female neighbour holds forth another cartridge, which goes the same way, and so on till he is satisfied. He never drinks till he has finished eating; and, before he begins, in gratitude to the fair ones who fed him, he makes up two small rolls of the same kind and form; each of his neighbours opens her mouth at the same time, while with each hand he puts her portion into her mouth. He then falls to drinking out of a large, handsome horn; the ladies eat till they are satisfied, and then all drink together, "Vive la Joye et la Jeunesse!" A great deal of mirth and joke goes round, very seldom with any mixture of acrimony or ill-humour.

All this time the unfortunate victim at the door is bleeding indeed, but bleeding little. As long as they can cut off the flesh from his bones, they do not meddle with the thighs, or the parts where the great arteries are. At last they fall upon the thighs likewise; and soon after the animal, bleeding to death, becomes so tough that the cannibals, who have the rest of it to eat, find very hard work to separate the flesh from the bones with their teeth like dogs.

In the meantime, those within are very much elevated; love lights all its fires, and everything is permitted with absolute freedom. There is no coyness, no delays, no need of appointments or retirement to gratify their wishes; there are no rooms but one, in which they sacrifice both to Bacchus and to

Venus. The two men nearest the vacuum a pair have made on the bench by leaving their seats, hold their upper garment like a screen before the two that have left the bench; and, if we may judge by sound, they seem to think it as great a shame to make love in silence as to eat.—Replaced in their seats again, the company drink the happy couple's health; and their example is followed at different ends of the table, as each couple is disposed. All this passes without remark or scandal, not a licentious word is uttered, nor the most distant joke upon the transaction.

Interview with the King's Ladies

A few days after this I had a message from the palace. I found the king sitting alone, apparently much chagrined, and in ill-humour. He asked me in a very peevish manner, "If I was not yet gone?" To which I answered, "Your Majesty know that it is impossible for me to go a step from Sennaar without assistance from you." He again asked me, in the same tone as before, "How could I think of coming that way?" I said, "Nobody imagined in Abyssinia, but that he was able to give a stranger safe conduct through his own dominions." He made no reply, but nodded a sign for me to depart; which I immediately did, and so finished this short, but disagreeable, interview.

About four o'clock the same afternoon I was again sent for to the palace, when the king told me that several of his wives were ill, and desired that I would give them my advice, which I promised to do without difficulty, as all acquaintance with the fair sex had hitherto been much to my advantage. I must confess, however, that calling these the fair sex is not preserving a precision in terms. I was admitted into a large, square apartment, very ill-lighted, in which were about fifty women, all perfectly black, without any covering but a very narrow piece of cotton rag about their waists. While I was musing whether or not these all might be queens, or whether there was any queen among them, one of them took me by the hand and led me rudely enough into another apartment. This was much better lighted than the first. Upon a large bench, or sofa, covered with blue Surat cloth, sat three persons cloathed from the neck to the feet with blue cotton shirts.

One of these, who, I found, was the favourite, was about six feet high, and corpulent beyond all proportion. She seemed to me, next to the elephant and rhinoceros, the largest living creature I had met with.—Her features were perfectly like those of a Negro; a ring of gold passed through her under lip, and weighed it down, till, like a flap, it covered her chin, and left her teeth bare, which were very small and fine.—The inside of her lip she had made black with antimony. Her ears reached down to her shoulders, and had the appearance of wings; she had in each of them a large ring of gold, somewhat smaller than a man's little finger, and about five inches in diameter. The weight of these had drawn down the hole where her ear was pierced so much, that three fingers might easily pass above the ring. She had a gold necklace, like what we used to call *esclavage*, of several rows, one below another, to which were hung rows of sequins pierced. She had on her ancles two manacles of gold, larger than any I had ever seen upon the feet of felons, with which I could not conceive it was possible for her to walk, but afterwards I found they were hollow.—The others were dressed pretty much in the same manner; only there was one that had chains, which came from her ears to the outside of each nostril, where they were fastened. There was also a ring put through the gristle of her nose, and which hung down to the opening of her mouth. I think she must have breathed with great difficulty. It had altogether something of the appearance of a horse's bridle. Upon my coming near them, the eldest put her hand to her mouth, and kissed it, saying, at the same time, in very vulgar Arabic, "Kifhalek howaja? (how do you do, merchant).—I never in my life was more pleased with distant salutations than at this time. I answered, "Peace be among you! I am a physician, and not a merchant."

I shall not entertain the reader with the multitude of their complaints; being a lady's physician, discretion and silence are my first duties. It is sufficient to say, that there was not one part of their whole bodies, inside and outside, in which some of them had not ailments. The three queens insisted upon being blooded, which desire I complied with, as it was an operation that required short attendance; but, upon producing the lancets, their hearts failed them. They then all cried out for the Tabange, which, in Arabic, means a pistol; but what they meant by this word was, the cupping instrument, which goes off with a spring like the snap of a pistol. I had two of these with me, but not at that time in my pocket. I sent my servant home, however, to bring one, and, that same evening, performed the operation upon the three queens with great success. The room was overflowing with an effusion of royal blood, and the whole ended with their insisting upon my giving them the instrument itself, which I was obliged to do, after cupping two of their slaves before them, who had no complaints, merely to shew them how the operation was to be performed.

Another night I was obliged to attend them, and gave the queens, and two or three of the great ladies, vomits. I will spare my reader the recital of so nauseous a scene. The ipecacuanha had great effect, and warm water was drunk very copiously. The patients were numerous, and the floor of the room received all evacuations. It was most prodigiously hot, and the horrid, black figures, moaning and groaning with sickness all around me, gave me, I think, some slight idea of the punishment in the world below. My mortifications, however, did not stop here. I observed that, on coming into their presence, the queens were all covered with cotton shirts; but no sooner did their complaints make part of our conversation, than, to my utmost surprise, each of them, in her turn, stript herself entirely naked, laying her cotton shirt loosely on her lap, as she sat cross-legged like a tailor. The custom of going naked in these warm countries abolishes all delicacy concerning it. I could not but observe that the breasts of each of them reached the length of their knees.

This exceeding confidence on their part, they thought, merited some consideration on mine; and it was not without great astonishment that I heard the queen desire to see me in the like dishabille in which she had spontaneously put herself. The whole court of female attendants flocked to the spectacle. Refusal, or resistance, were in vain. I was surrounded with fifty or sixty women, all equal in stature and strength to myself. The whole of my cloathing was, like theirs, a long loose shirt of blue Surat cotton cloth, reaching from the neck down to the feet. The only terms I could possibly, and that with great difficulty, make for myself were, that they should be contented to strip me no farther than the shoulders and breast. Upon seeing the whiteness of my skin, they gave all a loud cry in token of dislike, and shuddered, seeming to consider it rather the effects of disease than natural. I think in my life I never felt so disagreeably. I have been in more than one battle, but surely I would joyfully have taken my chance again in any of them to have been freed from that examination. I could not help likewise reflecting, that, if the king had come in during this exhibition, the consequence would either have been impaling, or stripping off that skin whose colour they were so curious about; though I can solemnly declare there was not an idea in my breast, since ever I had the honour of seeing these royal beauties, that could have given his majesty of Sennaar the smallest reason for jealousy; and I believe the same may be said of the sentiments of the ladies in what regarded me. Ours was a mutual passion, but dangerous to no one concerned. I returned home with very different sensations from those I had felt after an interview with the beautiful Aiscach of Teawa. Indeed, it was impossible to be more chagrined at, or more disgusted with, my present situation than I was, and the more so, that my delivery from it appeared to be very distant, and the circumstances were more and more unfavourable every day.

An Alligator-Infested River

BY WILLIAM BARTRAM

It would be difficult to call the naturalist William Bartram an explorer in the traditional sense, but his account of five years of nearly constant travel in south-eastern North America in the 1790s certainly qualifies as one of the most important books in American history. His quirky and poetical descriptions of plants, animals, and Native Americans inspired poets like Coleridge and Wordsworth, and even influenced contemporary novels like *Cold Mountain*.

This episode of travel on a river in Florida shows Bartram's abiding desire to explore new areas alone—regardless of the dangers.

*   *   *   *   *

Being desirous of continuing my travels and observations higher up the river, and having an invitation from a gentleman who was agent for, and resident at, a large plantation, the property of an English gentleman, about sixty miles higher up, I resolved to pursue my researches to that place; and having engaged in my service a young Indian, nephew to the white captain, he agreed to assist me in working my vessel up as high as a certain bluff, where I was, by agreement, to land him, on the West or Indian shore, whence he designed to go in quest of the camp of the White Trader, his relation.

Provisions and all necessities being procured, and the morning pleasant, we went on board and stood up the river. We passed for several miles on the left, by islands of high swamp land, exceedingly fertile, their banks for a good distance from the water, much higher than the interior part, and sufficiently so to build upon, and be out of the reach of inundations. They consist of a loose black mould, with a mixture of sand, shells, and dissolved vegetables. The opposite Indian coast is a perpendicular bluff, ten or twelve feet high, consisting of a black sandy earth, mixed with a large proportion of shells, chiefly various species of fresh water cochleae and mytuli. Near the river, on this high shore, grew corypha palma, magnolia grandiflora, live oak, callicarpa, myrica cerifera, hibiscus spinifex, and the beautiful evergreen shrub called wild lime or tallow nut. This last shrub grows six or eight feet high, many erect stems spring from a root; the leaves are lanceolate and entire, two or three inches in length and one in breadth, of a deep green colour, and polished; at the foot of each leaf grows a stiff sharp thorn; the flowers are small and in clusters, of a greenish yellow colour, and sweet scented; they are succeeded by a large oval fruit, of the shape and size of an ordinary plum, of a fine yellow colour when ripe; a soft sweet pulp covers a nut which has a thin shell, enclosing a white kernel somewhat of the consistence and taste of the sweet almond, but more oily and very much like hard tallow, which induced my father, when he first observed it, to call it the tallow-nut.

At the upper end of this bluff is a fine orange grove. Here my Indian companion requested me to set him on shore, being already tired of rowing under a fervid sun, and having for some time intimated a dislike to his situation. I readily complied with his desire, knowing the impossibility of compelling an Indian against his own inclinations, or even prevailing upon him by reasonable arguments, when labour is in the question. Before my vessel reached the shore, he sprang out of her and landed, when uttering a shrill and terrible whoop, he bounded off like a roebuck, and I lost sight of him. I at first apprehended, that as he took his gun with him, he intended to hunt for some game and return to me in the evening. The day being excessively hot and sultry, I concluded to take up my quarters here until the next morning.

The Indian not returning this morning, I set sail alone. The coasts on each side had much the same appearance as already described. The palm-trees here seem to be of a different species from the cabbage tree; their straight trunks are sixty, eighty, or ninety feet high, with a beautiful taper, of a bright ash colour, until within six or seven feet of the top, where it is a fine green colour, crowned with an orb of rich green plumed leaves; I have measured the stem of these plumes fifteen feet in length, besides the plume, which is nearly of the same length.

The little lake, which is an expansion of the river, now appeared in view; on the east side are extensive marshes, and on the other high forests and orange groves, and then a bay, lined with vast cypress swamps, both coasts gradually approaching each other, to the opening of the river again, which is in this place about three hundred yards wide. Evening now drawing on, I was anxious to reach some high bank of the river, where I intended to lodge; and agreeably to my wishes, I soon after discovered, on the west shore, a little promontory, at the turning of the river, contracting it here to about one hundred and fifty yards in width. This promontory is a peninsula, containing about three acres of high ground, and is one entire orange grove, with a few live oaks, magnolias, and palms. Upon doubling the point, I arrived at the landing, which is a circular harbour, at the foot of the bluff, the top of which is about twelve feet high; the back of it is a large cypress swamp, that spreads each way, the right wing forming the west coast of the little lake, and the left stretching up the river many miles, and encompassing a vast space of low grassy marshes. From this promontory, looking eastward across the river, I beheld a landscape of low country, unparalleled as I think; on the left is the east coast of the little lake, which I had just passed; and from the orange bluff at the lower end, the high forests begin, and increase in breadth from the shore of the lake, making a circular sweep to the right, and contain many hundred thousand acres of meadow; and this grand sweep of high forests encircles, as I apprehend, at least twenty miles of these green fields, interspersed with hommocks or islets of evergreen trees, where the sovereign magnolia and lordly palm stand conspicuous. The islets are high shelly knolls, on the side of creeks or branches of the river, which wind about and drain off the superabundant waters that cover these meadows during the winter season.

The evening was temperately cool and calm. The crocodiles began to roar and appear in uncommon numbers along the shores and in the river. I fixed my camp in an open plain, near the utmost projection of the promontory, under the shelter of a large live oak, which stood on the highest part of the ground, and but a few yards from my boat. From this open, high situation, I had a free prospect of the river, which was a matter of no trivial consideration to me, having good reason to dread the subtle attacks of the alligators, who were crowding around my harbour. Having collected a good quantity of wood for the purpose of keeping up a light and smoke during the night, I began to think of preparing my supper, when, upon examining my stores, I found but a scanty provision. I thereupon determined, as the most expeditious way of supplying my necessities, to take my bob and try for some trout. About one hundred yards above my harbour began a cove or bay of the river, out of which opened a large lagoon. The mouth or entrance from the river to it was narrow, but the waters soon after spread and formed a little lake, extending into the marshes; its entrance and shores within I observed to be verged with floating lawns of the pistia and nymphea and other aquatic plants; these I knew were excellent haunts for trout.

The verges and islets of the lagoon were equally embellished with flowering plants and shrubs; the laughing coots with wings half spread were tripping over the little coves, and hiding themselves in the tufts of grass; young broods of the painted summer teal, skimming the still surface of the waters, and following the watchful parent unconscious of danger, were frequently surprised by the voracious trout; and he, in turn, as often by the subtle greedy alligator. Behold him rushing forth from the flags and reeds. His enormous body swells. His plaited tail brandished high, floats upon the lake. The waters like a cataract descend from his opening jaws. Clouds of smoke issue from his dilated nostrils. The earth trembles with his thunder. When immediately from the opposite coast of the lagoon, emerges from the deep his rival champion. They suddenly dart upon each other. The boiling surface of the lake marks their rapid course, and a terrific conflict commences. They now sink to the bottom folded together in horrid wreaths. The water becomes thick and discoloured. Again they rise, their jaws clap together, re-echoing through the deep surrounding forests. Again they sink, when the contest ends at the muddy bottom of the lake, and the vanquished makes a hazardous escape, hiding himself in the muddy turbulent waters and sedge on a distant shore. The proud victor exulting returns to the place of action. The shores and forests resound his dreadful roar, together with the triumphing shouts of the plaited tribes around, witnesses of the horrid combat.

My apprehensions were highly alarmed after being a spectator of so dreadful a battle. It was obvious that every delay would but tend to increase my dangers and difficulties, as the sun was near setting, and the alligators gathered around my harbour from all quarters. From these considerations I concluded to be expeditious in my trip to the lagoon, in order to take some fish. Not thinking it prudent to take my fusee with me, lest I might lose it overboard in case of a battle, which I had every reason to dread before my return, I therefore furnished myself with a club for my defense, went on board, and penetrating the first line of those which surrounded my harbour, they gave way; but being pursued by several very large ones, I kept strictly on the watch, and paddled with all my might towards the entrance of the lagoon, hoping to be sheltered there from the multitude of my assailants; but ere I had halfway reached the place, I was attacked on all sides, several endeavouring to overset the canoe. My situation now became precarious to the last degree; two very large ones attacked me closely, at the same instant, rushing up with their heads and parts of their bodies above the water, roaring terribly and belching floods of water over me. They struck their jaws together so close to my ears, as almost to stun me, and I expected every moment to be dragged out of the boat and instantly devoured. But I applied my weapons so effectually about me, though at random, that I was so successful as to beat them off a little; when, finding that they designed to renew the battle, I made for the shore, as the only means left me for my preservation; for, by keeping close to it, I should have my enemies on one side of me only, whereas I was before surrounded by them; and there was a probability, if pushed to the last extremity, of saving myself, by jumping out of the canoe on shore, as it is easy to outwalk them on land, although comparatively as swift as lightning in the water. I found this last expedient alone could fully answer my expectations, for as soon as I gained the shore, they drew off and kept aloof. This was a happy relief, as my confidence was, in some degree, recovered by it. On recollecting myself, I discovered that I had almost reached the entrance of the lagoon, and determined to venture in, if possible, to take a few fish, and then return to my harbour, while daylight continued; for I could now, with caution and resolution, make my way with safety along shore; and indeed there was no other way to regain my camp, without leaving my boat and making my retreat though the marshes and reeds, which, if I could even effect, would have been in a manner throwing myself away, for then there would have been no hopes of ever recovering my bark, and returning in safety to any settlements of men. I accordingly proceeded, and made good my entrance into the lagoon, though not without opposition from the alligators, who formed a line across the entrance, but did not pursue me into it nor was I molested by any there, though there were some very large ones in a cove at the upper end. I soon caught more trout than I had present occasion for, and the air was too hot and sultry to admit of their being kept for many hours, even though salted or barbecued. I now prepared for my return to camp, which I succeeded in with but little trouble, by keeping close to the shore; yet I was opposed upon re-entering the river out of the lagoon, and pursued near to my landing (though not closely attacked) particularly by an old daring one, about twelve feet in length, who kept close after me; and when I stepped on shore and turned about, in order to draw up my canoe, he rushed up near my feet, and lay there for some time, looking me in the face, his head and shoulders out of water. I resolved he should pay for his temerity, and having a heavy load in my fusee, I ran to my camp, and returning with my piece, found him with his foot on the gunwale of the boat, in search of fish. On my coming up he withdrew sullenly and slowly into the water, but soon returned and placed himself in his former position, looking at me, and seeming neither fearful nor any way disturbed. I soon dispatched him by lodging the contents of my gun in his head, and then proceeded to cleanse and prepare my fish for supper; and accordingly took them out of the boat, laid them down on the sand close to the water, and began to scale them; when, raising my head, I saw before me, through the clear water, the head and shoulders of a very large alligator, moving slowly towards me. I instantly stepped back, when, with a sweep of his tail, he brushed off several of my fish. It was certainly most providential that I looked up at that instant, as the monster would probably, in less than a minute, have seized and dragged me into the river. This incredible boldness of the animal disturbed me greatly, supposing there could now be no reasonable safety for me during the night, but by keeping continually on the watch; I therefore, as soon as I had prepared the fish, proceeded to secure myself and effects in the best manner I could. In the first place, I hauled my bark upon the shore, almost clear out of the water, to prevent their oversetting or sinking her; after this, every moveable was taken out and carried to my camp, which was but a few yards off; then ranging some dry wood in such order as was the most convenient, I cleared the ground round it, that there might be no impediment in my way, in case of an attack in the night, either from the water or the land; for I discovered by this time, that this small isthmus, from its remote situation and fruitfulness, was resorted to by bears and wolves. Having prepared myself in the best manner I could, I charged my gun, and proceeded to reconnoitre my camp and the adjacent grounds; when I discovered that the peninsula and grove, at the distance of about two hundred yards from my encampment, on the land side, were invested by a cypress swamp, covered with water, which below was joined to the shore of the little lake, and above to the marshes surrounding the lagoon; so that I was confined to an islet exceedingly circumscribed, and I found there was no other retreat for me, in case of an attack, but by either ascending one of the large oaks, or pushing off with my boat.

It was by this time dusk, and the alligators had nearly ceased their roar, when I was again alarmed by a tumultuous noise that seemed to be in my harbour, and therefore engaged my immediate attention. Returning to my camp, I found it undisturbed, and then continued on to the extreme point of the promontory, where I saw a scene, new and surprising, which at first threw my senses into such a tumult, that it was some time before I could comprehend what was the matter; however, I soon accounted for the prodigious assemblage of crocodiles at this place, which exceeded every thing of the kind I had ever heard of.

How shall I express myself so as to convey an adequate idea of it to the reader, and at the same time avoid raising suspicions of my veracity? Should I say, that the river (in this place) from shore to shore, and perhaps near half a mile above, and below me, appeared to be one solid bank of fish, of various kinds, pushing through this narrow pass of St. Juan's into the little lake, on their return down the river, and that the alligators were in such incredible numbers, and so close together from shore to shore, that it would have been easy to have walked across on their heads, had the animals been harmless? What expressions can sufficiently declare the shocking scene that for some minutes continued, whilst this mighty army of fish were forcing the pass? During this attempt, thousands, I may say hundreds of thousands, of them were caught and swallowed by the devouring alligators. I have seen an alligator take up out of the water several great fish at a time, and just squeeze them betwixt his jaws, while the tails of the great trout flapped about his eyes and lips, ere he had swallowed them. The horrid noise of their closing jaws, their plunging amidst the broken banks of fish, and rising with their prey some feet upright above the water, the floods of water and blood rushing out of their mouths, and the clouds of vapour issuing from their wide nostrils, were truly frightful. This scene continued at intervals during the night, as the fish came to the pass. After this sight, shocking and tremendous as it was, I found myself somewhat easier and more reconciled to my situation; being convinced that their extraordinary assemblage here was owing to the annual feast of fish; and that they were so well employed in their own element, that I had little occasion to fear their paying me a visit.

It being now almost night, I returned to my camp, where I had left my fish broiling, and my kettle of rice stewing; and having with me oil, pepper, and salt, and excellent oranges hanging in abundance over my head (a valuable substitute for vinegar), I sat down and regaled myself cheerfully. Having finished my repast, I rekindled my fire for light, and whilst I was revising the notes of my past day's journey, I was suddenly roused with a noise behind me toward the main land. I sprang up on my feet, and listening, I distinctly heard some creature wading the water of the isthmus. I seized my gun and went cautiously from my camp, directing my steps toward the noise; when I had advanced about thirty yards, I halted behind a coppice of orange trees, and soon perceived two very large bears, which had made their way through the water, and had landed in the grove, about one hundred yards distance from me, and were advancing towards me. I waited until they were within thirty yards of me, they there began to snuff and look towards my camp; I snapped my piece, but it flashed, on which they both turned about and galloped off, plunging through the water and swamp, never halting, as I suppose, until they reached fast land, as I could hear them leaping and plunging a long time. They did not presume to return again, nor was I molested by any other creature, except being occasionally awakened by the whooping of owls, screaming of bitterns, or the wood-rats running amongst the leaves.

The wood-rat is a very curious animal. It is not half the size of the domestic rat; of a dark brown or black colour; its tail slender and shorter in proportion, and covered thinly with short hair. It is singular with respect to its ingenuity and great labour in the construction of its habitation, which is a conical pyramid about three or four feet high, constructed with dry branches, which it collects with great labour and perseverance, and piles up without any apparent order; yet they are so interwoven with one another, that it would take a bear or wild-cat some time to pull one of their castles to pieces, and allow the animals sufficient time to secure a retreat with their young.

The noise of the crocodiles kept me awake the greater part of the night; but when I arose in the morning, contrary to my expectations, there was perfect peace; very few of them to be seen, and those were asleep on the shore. Yet I was not able to suppress my fears and apprehensions of being attacked by them in future; and indeed yesterday's combat with them, notwithstanding I came off in a manner victorious, or at least made a safe retreat, had left sufficient impression on my mind to damp my courage; and it seemed too much for one of my strength, being alone in a very small boat, to encounter such collected danger. To pursue my voyage up the river, and be obliged every evening to pass such dangerous defiles, appeared to me as perilous as running the gauntlet betwixt two rows of Indians armed with knives and fire-brands. I however resolved to continue my voyage one day longer, if I possibly could with safety, and then return down the river, should I find the like difficulties to oppose. Accordingly, I got everything on board, charged my gun, and set sail, cautiously, along shore. As I passed by Battle lagoon, I began to tremble and keep a good look-out; when suddenly a huge alligator rushed out of the reeds, and with a tremendous roar came up, and darted as swift as an arrow under my boat, emerging upright on my lee quarter, with open jaws, and belching water and smoke that fell upon me like rain in a hurricane. I laid soundly about his head with my club, and beat him off; and after plunging and darting about my boat, he went off on a straight line through the water, seemingly with the rapidity of lightning, and entered the cape of the lagoon. I now employed my time to the very best advantage in paddling close along shore, but could not forbear looking now and then behind me, and presently perceived one of them coming up again. The water of the river hereabouts was shoal and very clear; the monster came up with the usual roar and menaces, and passed close by the side of my boat, when I could distinctly see a young brood of alligators, to the number of one hundred or more, following after her in a long train. They kept close together in a column, without straggling off to the one side or the other; the young appeared to be of an equal size, about 15 inches in length, almost black, with pale yellow transverse waved clouds or blotches, much like rattlesnakes in color. I now lost sight of my enemy again.

Still keeping close along shore, on turning a point or projection of the river bank, at once I beheld a great number of hillocks or small pyramids, resembling hay-cocks, ranged like an encampment along the bank. They stood fifteen or twenty yards distant from the water, on a high marsh, about four feet perpendicular above the water. I knew them to be the nests of the crocodile, having had a description of them before; and now expected a furious and general attack, as I saw several large crocodiles swimming abreast of these buildings. These nests being so great a curiosity to me, I was determined at all events immediately to land and examine them. Accordingly, I ran my bark on shore at one of their landing places, which was a sort of nick or little dock, from which ascended a sloping path or road up to the edge of the meadow, where their nests were; most of them were deserted, and the great thick whitish egg-shells lay broken and scattered upon the ground round about them.

The nests or hillocks are of the form of an obtuse cone, four feet high and four or five feet in diameter at their bases; they are constructed with mud, grass and herbage. At first they lay a floor of this kind of tempered mortar on the ground, upon which they deposit a layer of eggs, and upon this a stratum of mortar, seven or eight inches in thickness, and then another layer of eggs; and in this manner one stratum upon another, nearly to the top. I believe they commonly lay from one to two hundred eggs in a nest; these are hatched, I suppose, by the heat of the sun; and perhaps the vegetable substances mixed with the earth, being acted upon by the sun, may cause a small degree of fermentation, and so increase the heat in those hillocks. The ground for several acres about those nests shewed evident marks of a continual resort of alligators; the grass was everywhere beaten down, hardly a blade or straw was left standing; whereas, all about, at a distance, it was five or six feet high, and as thick as it could grow together. The female, as I imagine, carefully watches her own nest of eggs until they are all hatched; or perhaps while she is attending her own brood, she takes under her care and protection as many as she can get at one time, either from her own particular nest or others; but certain it is, that the young are not left to shift for themselves; for I have had frequent opportunities of seeing the female alligator leading about the shores her train of young ones, just as a hen does her brood of chickens; and she is equally assiduous and courageous in defending the young, which are under her care, and providing for their subsistence; and when she is basking upon the warm banks, with her brood around her, you may hear the young ones continually whining and barking like young puppies. I believe but few of the brood live to the years of full growth and magnitude, as the old feed on the young as long as they can make prey of them.

The alligator when full grown is a very large and terrible creature, and of prodigious strength, activity, and swiftness in the water. I have seen them twenty feet in length, and some are supposed to be twenty-two or twenty-three feet. Their body is as large as that of a horse; their shape exactly resembles that of a lizard, except their tail, which is flat or cuneiform, being compressed on each side, and gradually diminishing from the abdomen to the extremity, which, with the whole body is covered with horny plates or squammae, impenetrable when on the body of the live animal, even to a rifle ball, except about their head and just behind their fore-legs or arms, where it is said they are only vulnerable. The head of a full grown one is about three feet, and the mouth opens nearly the same length; their eyes are small in proportion, and seem sunk deep in the head, by means of the prominency of the brows; the nostrils are large, inflated, and prominent on the top, so that the head in the water resembles, at a distance, a great chunk of wood floating about. Only the upper jaw moves, which they raise perpendicular, so as to form a right angle with the lower one. In the fore-part of the upper jaw, on each side, just under the nostrils, are two very large, thick, strong teeth or tusks, not very sharp, but rather the shape of a cone; these are as white as the finest polished ivory, and are not covered by any skin or lips, and always in sight, which gives the creature a frightful appearance; in the lower jaws are holes opposite to these teeth, to receive them; when they clap their jaws together it causes a surprising noise, like that which is made by forcing a heavy plank with violence upon the ground, and may be heard at a great distance.

But what is yet more surprising to a stranger, is the incredibly loud and terrifying roar, which they are capable of making, especially in the spring season, their breeding time. It most resembles very heavy distant thunder, not only shaking the air and waters, but causing the earth to tremble; and when hundreds and thousands are roaring at the same time, you can scarcely be persuaded, but that the whole globe is violently and dangerously agitated.

An old champion, who is perhaps absolute sovereign of a little lake or lagoon (when fifty fewer than himself are obliged to content themselves with swelling and roaring in little cover round about) darts forth from the reedy coverts all at once, on the surface of the waters, in a right line; at first seemingly as rapid as lightning, but gradually more slowly until he arrives at the centre of the lake, when he stops. He now swells himself by drawing in wind and water through his mouth, which causes a loud sonorous rattling in the throat for near a minute, but it is immediately forced out again through his mouth and nostrils, with a loud noise, brandishing his tail in the air, and the vapour ascending from his nostrils like smoke. At other times, when swollen to an extent ready to burst, his head and tail lifted up, he spins or twirls round on the surface of the water. He acts his part like an Indian chief when rehearsing his feats of war; and then retiring, the exhibition is continued by others who dare to step forth, and strive to excel each other, to gain the attention of the favourite female.

Having gratified my curiosity at this general breeding-place and nursery of the crocodiles, I continued my voyage up the river without being greatly disturbed by them.

The Search for the Niger River

Mungo Park's matter-of-fact account of his wanderings—and incredible suffering—while searching for the Niger River in the 1790s was a bestseller in
England, making the young, unknown Scottish doctor a national celebrity. His
book, *Travels in the Interior Districts of Africa*, remains in print to this day and is
still a great read. Like many early European explorers in Africa, Park's journey
was mostly a tale of mere survival and brutal treatment at the hands of local
despots. He was robbed of nearly all his possessions, taken prisoner for a time,
and often wandered alone—begging his meals and suffering illness and disaster
at nearly every turn. Yet he still found the Niger, solving one of the leading geographical mysteries of his day.

Back in Scotland, Park chafed at the mundane life of a doctor, longing
to head back to Africa despite his earlier tribulations. His second trip to further
explore the Niger met with nearly total disaster, with most of the Europeans
who had signed on for the journey dying before they even reached the great
river. Park would eventually die on this expedition as well, a victim of his own
thirst for adventure.

The following story relates a small portion of his suffering at the hands
of the Moors while being held captive during his first journey.

★   ★   ★   ★   ★

April 7th. About four o'clock in the afternoon, a whirlwind passed
through the camp, with such violence that it overturned three tents,
and blew down one side of my hut. These whirlwinds come from
the Great Desert, and, at this season of the year, are so common, that
I have seen five or six of them at one time. They carry up quantities of sand to
an amazing height, which resembles, at a distance, so many moving pillars of
smoke.

The scorching heat of the sun, upon a dry and sandy country, makes the air insufferably hot. Ali having robbed me of my thermometer, I had no means of forming a comparative judgment; but in the middle of the day, when the beams of the vertical sun are seconded by the scorching wind from the Desert, the ground is frequently heated to such a degree, as not to be borne by the naked foot; even the Negro slaves, will not run from one tent to another, without their sandals. At this time of the day, the Moors lie stretched at length in their tents, either asleep, or unwilling to move; and I have often felt the wind so hot, that I could not hold my hand in the current of air which came through the crevices of my hut, without feeling sensible pain.

April 8th. This day the wind blew from the south-west, and in the night there was a heavy shower of rain, accompanied with thunder and lightning.

April 10th. In the evening the Tabala, or large drum, was beat, to announce a wedding, which was held at one of the neighbouring tents. A great number of people of both sexes assembled, but without the mirth and hilarity which take place at a Negro wedding; here there was neither singing nor dancing; nor any other amusement that I could perceive. A woman was beating the drum, and the other women joining at times, like a chorus, by setting up a shrill scream; and at the same time, moving their tongues from one side of the mouth to the other, with great celerity. I was soon tired, and had returned into my hut, where I was sitting almost asleep, when an old woman entered, with a wooden bowl in her hand, and signified that she had brought me a present from the bride. Before I could recover from the surprise which this message created, the woman discharged the contents of the bowl full in my face. Finding that it was the same sort of holy water, with which, among the Hottentots, a priest is said to sprinkle a new married couple, I began to suspect that the old lady was actuated by mischief, or malice; but she gave me seriously to understand, that it was a nuptial benediction from the bride's own person; and which, on such occasions, is always received by the young unmarried Moors as a mark of distinguishing favour. This being the case, I wiped my face, and sent my acknowledgments to the lady. The wedding drum continued to beat, and the women to sing, or rather whistle, all night. About nine in the morning, the bride was brought in state from her mother's tent (a present from the husband), some bearing up the poles, others holding by the strings; and in this manner they marched, whistling as formerly, until they came to the place appointed for her residence, where they pitched the tent. The husband followed, with a number of men leading four bullocks, which they tied to the tent strings; and having killed another, and distributed the beef among the people, the ceremony was concluded.

One whole month had now elapsed since I was led into captivity; during which time, each returning day brought me fresh distress. I watched the lingering course of the sun with anxiety, and blessed his evening beams as they shed a yellow lustre along the sandy floor of my hut; for it was then that my oppressors left me, and allowed me to pass the sultry night in solitude and reflection.

About midnight, a bowl of kouskous with some salt and water was brought for me and my two attendants; this was our common fare, and it was all that was allowed us, to allay the cravings of hunger, and support nature for the whole of the following day; for it is to be observed, that this was the Mahomedan Lent; and as the Moors keep the fast with a religious strictness, they thought it proper to compel me, though a Christian, to a similar observance. Time, however, somewhat reconciled me to my situation: I found that I could bear hunger and thirst better that I expected; and at length, I endeavoured to beguile the tedious hours, by learning to write Arabic. The people who came to see me, soon made me acquainted with the characters; and I discovered, that by engaging their attention in this way, they were not so troublesome as otherwise they would have been; indeed, when I observed any person whose countenance I thought bore malice towards me, I made it a rule to ask him, either to write in the sand himself, or to decipher what I had already written; and the pride of shewing his superior attainments, generally induced him to comply with my request.

April 14th. As Queen Fatima had not yet arrived, Ali proposed to go to the north, and bring her back with him; but as the place was two days' journey from Benowm, it was necessary to have some refreshment on the road; and Ali, suspicious of those about him, was so afraid of being poisoned, that he would never eat anything but what was dressed under his own immediate inspection. A fine bullock was therefore killed, and the flesh being cut up into thin slices, was dried in the sun; and this, with two bags of dry kouskous, formed his travelling provisions.

Previous to his departure, the black people of the town of Benowm came, according to their annual custom, to shew their arms, and bring their stipulated tribute of corn and cloth. They were but badly armed; twenty-two with muskets, forty or fifty with bows and arrows; and nearly the same number of men and boys, with spears only; they arranged themselves before the tent, where they waited until their arms were examined, and some little disputes settled.

About midnight on the 16th, Ali departed quietly from Benowm, accompanied by a few attendants. He was expected to return in the course of nine or ten days.

April 18th. Two days after the departure of Ali, a Shereef arrived with salt, and some other articles, from Walet, the capital of the kingdom of Biroo. As there was no tent appropriated for him, he took up his abode in the same hut with me. He seemed to be a well-informed man, and his acquaintance both with the Arabic and Bambarra tongues, enabled him to travel, with ease and safety, through a number of kingdoms; for though his place of residence was Walet, he had visited Houssa, and had lived some years at Tombuctoo. Upon my inquiring so particularly about the distance from Walet to Tomboctoo, he asked me if I intended to travel that way; and being answered in the affirmative, he shook his head, and said, *it would not do*; for that Christians were looked upon there as the devil's children, and enemies to the Prophet. From him I learned the following particulars; that Houssa was the largest town he had ever seen; that Walet was larger than Tombuctoo; but being remote from the Niger, and its trade consisting chiefly of salt, it was not so much resorted to by strangers; that between Benown and Walet was ten days' journey; but the road did not lead through any remarkable towns, and travellers supported themselves by purchasing milk from the Arabs, who keep their herds by the watering places; two of the days' journies, was over a sandy country, without water. From Walet to Tombuctoo, was eleven days more; but water was more plentiful, and the journey was usually performed upon bullocks. He said there were many Jews at Tombuctoo, but they all spoke Arabic, and used the same prayers as the Moors. He frequently pointed his hand to the south-east quarter, or rather the east by south; observing, that Tombuctoo was situated in that direction; and though I made him repeat this information, again and again, I never found him to vary more than half a point, which was to the southward.

April 24th. This morning Shereef Sidi Mahomed Moora Abdalla, a native of Morocco, arrived with five bullocks loaded with salt. He had formerly resided some months at Gibraltar, which he had picked up as much English, as enabled him to make himself understood. He informed me, that he had been five months in coming from Santa Cruz; but that great part of the time had been spent in trading. When I requested him to enumerate the days employed in travelling from Morocco to Benowm, he gave them as follows—to Swera, three days; to Agadier, three; to Jiniken, ten; to Wadenoon, four; to Lakeneig, five; to Zeeriwin-zeriman, five; to Tisheet, ten; to Benowm, ten; in all fifty days, but travellers usually rest a long while at Jiniken and Tisheet; at the latter of which places they dig the rock salt, which is so great an article of commerce with the Negroes.

In conversing with these Shereefs, and the different strangers that resorted to the camp, I passed my time with rather less uneasiness than formerly. On the other hand, as the dressing of my victuals was now left entirely to the care of Ali's slaves over whom I had not the smallest control, I found myself but ill supplied, worse even than in the fast month; for two successive nights, they neglected to send us our accustomed meal, and though my boy went to a small Negro town near the camp, and begged with great diligence from hut to hut, he could only procure a few handfuls of ground nuts, which he readily shared with me. Hunger, at first, is certainly a very painful sensation; but when it has continued for some time, this pain is succeeded by languor and debility; in which case, a draught of water, by keeping the stomach distended, will greatly exhilarate the spirits, and remove for a short time every sort of uneasiness. Johnson and Demba were very much dejected. They lay stretched upon the sand, in a sort of torpid slumber; and even when the kouskous arrived, I found some difficulty in awakening them. I felt no inclination to sleep, but was affected with a deep convulsive respiration, like constant sighing; and, what alarmed me still more, a dimness of sight, and a tendency to faint when I attempted to sit up. These symptoms did not go off until some time after I had received nourishment.

We had been for some days in daily expectation of Ali's return from Saheel (or the north country) with his wife Fatima. In the meanwhile Mansong, King of Bambarra, as I have related in Chapter VIII, had sent for Ali for a party of horse to assist in storming Gedingooma. With this demand Ali had not only refused to comply, but had treated the messengers with great haughtiness and contempt; upon which Mansong gave up all thoughts of taking the town, and prepared to chastize Ali for his contumacy.

Things were in this situation when, on the 29th of April, a messenger arrived at Benowm with the disagreeable intelligence that the Bambarra army was approaching the frontiers of Ludamar. This threw the whole country into confusion; and in the afternoon Ali's son with about twenty horsemen arrived at Benowm. He ordered all the cattle to be driven away immediately, all the tents to be struck, and the people to hold themselves in readiness to depart at daylight the next morning.

April 30th. At daybreak the whole camp was in motion. The baggage was carried upon bullocks, the two tent poles being placed one on each side, and the different articles of the tent distributed in like manner; the tent cloth was thrown over all, and upon this was commonly placed one or two women; for the Moorish women are very bad walkers. The king's favourite concubines rode upon camels, with a saddle of a particular construction, and a canopy to shelter them from the sun. We proceeded to the northward until noon, when the king's son ordered the whole company, except two tents, to enter a thick low wood, which was upon our right. I was sent along with the two tents, and arrived in the evening at a Negro town called Farani: here we pitched the tents in an open place, at no great distance from the town.

The hurry and confusion which attended this decampment, prevented the slaves from dressing the usual quantity of victuals; and lest their dry provisions should be exhausted before they reached their place of destination (for as yet none but Ali and the chief men knew whither we were going), they thought proper to make me observe this day as a day of fasting.

May 1st. As I had some reason to suspect that this day was also to be considered as a fast, I went in the morning to the Negro town of Farani, and begged some provisions from the Dooti, who readily supplied my wants, and desired me to come to his house every day during my stay in the neighbourhood. These hospitable people are looked upon by Moors as an abject race of slaves, and are treated accordingly. Two of Ali's household slaves, a man and a woman, who had come along with the two tents, went this morning to water the cattle from the town wells, at which there began to be a great scarcity. When the Negro women observed the cattle approaching, they took up their pitchers and ran with all possible haste toward the town, but before they could enter the gate, they were stopped by the slaves, who compelled them to bring back the water they had drawn for their own families, and empty it into the troughs for the cattle. When this was exhausted, they were ordered to draw water until such time as the cattle had all drunk; and the woman slave actually broke two wooden bowls over the heads of the black girls, because they were somewhat dilatory in obeying her commands.

May 3rd. We departed from the vicinity of Farani, and after a circuitous route through the woods, arrived at Ali's camp in the afternoon. This encampment was larger than that of Benowm, and was situated in the middle of a thick wood about two miles distant from a Negro town, called Bubaker. I immediately waited upon Ali, in order to pay my respects to Queen Fatima, who had come with him from Saheel. He seemed much pleased with my coming; shook hands with me, and informed his wife that I was the Christian. She was a woman of the Arab cast, with long black hair, and remarkably corpulent. She appeared at first rather shocked at the thought of having a Christian so near her; but when I had (by means of a Negro boy, who spoke the Mandingo and Arabic tongues) answered a great many questions, which her curiosity suggested, respecting the country of the Christians, she seemed more at ease, and presented me with a bowl of milk, which I considered as a very favourable omen.

The heat was now almost insufferable; all nature seemed sinking under it. The distant country presented to the eye a dreary expanse of sand, with a few stunted trees and prickly bushes, in the shade of which the hungry cattle licked up the withered grass, while the camels and goats picked off the scanty foliage. The scarcity of water was greater here than at Benowm. Day and night the wells were crowded with cattle, lowing and fighting with each other to come at the trough; excessive thirst made many of them furious; others, being too weak to contend for the water, endeavoured to quench their thirst by devouring the black mud from the gutters near the wells; which they did with great avidity, though it was commonly fatal to them.

This great scarcity of water was felt severely by all the people of the camp, and by none more than myself; for though Ali allowed me a skin for containing water, and Fatima, one or twice, gave me a small supply, when I was in distress, yet such was the barbarous disposition of the Moors at the wells, that, when my boy attempted to fill the skin, he commonly received a sound drubbing for his presumption. Everyone was astonished that the slave of a Christian should attempt to draw water from wells which had been dug by the followers of the Prophet. This treatment, at length, so frightened the boy, that I believe he would sooner have perished with thirst, than attempted again to fill the skin; he therefore contended himself with begging water from the Negro slaves that attended the camp; and I followed his example, but with very indifferent success; for though I let no opportunity slip, and was very urgent in my solicitations, both to the Moors and the Negroes, I was but ill supplied, and frequently passed the night in the situation of *Tantalus*. No sooner had I shut my eyes, than fancy would convey me to the streams and rivers of my native land; there, as I wandered along the verdant brink, I surveyed the clear stream with transport, and hastened to swallow the delightful draught; but alas! Disappointment awakened me; and I found myself a lonely captive, perishing of thirst amidst the wilds of Africa!

One night, having solicited in vain for water at the camp, and being quite feverish, I resolved to try my fortune at the wells, which were about half a mile distant from the camp. Accordingly, I set out about midnight, and, being guided by the lowing of the cattle, soon arrived at the place; where I found the Moors were busy drawing water. I requested permission to drink, but was driven away, with outrageous abuse. Passing, however, from one well to another, I came at last to one where there was only an old man and two boys. I made the same request to this man, and he immediately drew me up a bucket of water; but, as I was about to take hold of it, he recollected that I was a Christian, and fearing that his bucket might be polluted by my lips, he dashed the water into the trough, and told me to drink from thence. Though this trough was none of the largest, and three cows were already drinking in it, I resolved to come for my share; and kneeling down, thrust my head between two of the cows, and drank with great pleasure, until the water was nearly exhausted; and the cows began to contend with each other for the last mouthful.

Exploring the Marias

BY MERIWETHER LEWIS

Lewis & Clark's journey to the Pacific probably enjoys more fame today than at any time in American history. And there are certainly more books available about their trip than any other American exploration, from ten-volume journal sets with the original grammar and spelling intact to well-written, popular accounts like *Undaunted Courage*, by Stephen Ambrose. Despite how easy it is to find an account of Lewis & Clark's journey these days, it would be difficult to assemble a collection of great exploration stories without including something from their famous journals, as their trip has had such a lasting impact on our national consciousness.

This selection, from the version of the journals edited by Elliott Coues, involves their only real encounter with hostile Indians. It occurred during the return trip, while Lewis and a few of his men were exploring the Marias River in north-central Montana.

★   ★   ★   ★   ★

Monday, July 21st, 1806. At sunrise we proceeded along the northern side of the river for a short distance, when finding the ravines too steep, we crossed to the south; but after continuing for three miles, returned to the north, and took our course through the plains, at some distance from the river. After making 15 miles, we came to the forks of the river, the largest branch of which bears S. 75° W. [about 30 miles] to the mountains, while the course of the other is N. 40° W. We halted for dinner; and believing, on examination, that the northern branch came from the mountains and would probably lead us to the most northern extent of Maria's river, we proceeded, though at a distance over the plains, till we struck it eight miles from the junction. This river [*i.e.*, the North Fork, now called Cut-bank river] is about 30 yards wide; the water clear, but shallow and unfit for navigation. It is closely confined between cliffs of freestone; the adjacent country is broken and poor. We crossed to the south side and proceeded [up this fork N.25° W] for five miles, till we camped under a cliff where, not seeing any timber, we made a fire of buffalo dung, and passed the night.

July 22ⁿᵈ. We went on [up the west side of Cut-bank river]; but as the ground was now steep and unequal, and the horses' feet were very sore, we were obliged to proceed slowly. The river was still confined by freestone cliffs, till at seven miles [N. 30° W. from camp] the country opens, is less covered with gravel, and has some bottoms, though destitute of timber or underbrush. The river here makes a considerable bend to the northwest, so that we crossed the plains [S. 80°W.] for 11 miles, when we again crosed the river [from south to north]. Here we halted for dinner; and having no wood, made a fire of the dung of the buffalo, with which we cooked the last of our meat, except a piece of spoiled buffalo. Our course [N. 80° W.] then lay across a level, beautiful plain, with wide bottoms near the bank of the river. The banks are three or four feet high, but are not overflowed. After [thus] crossing for ten miles a bend of the river toward the south, we saw, for the first time during the day, a clump of cottonwood trees in an extensive bottom; and [having recrossed the river from its north to its south side] halted there for the night.

This place is about ten miles below the foot of the Rocky mountains; and being now able to trace distinctly that the point at which the river issued from those mountains was to the south of west, we concluded that we had reached its most northern point; and as we have ceased to hope that any branches of Maria's river extend as far north as the 50ᵗʰ degree of latitude, we deemed it useless to proceed further, and rely chiefly on Milk and White-earth rivers for the desired boundary. We therefore determined to remain here two days, for the purpose of making the necessary observations and resting our horses.

July 23ʳᵈ. Drewyer was sent to examine the bearings of the river, till its entrance into the mountains, which he found to be at the distance of ten miles, in a direction S. 50° W. He had seen also the remains of a camp of 11 leathern lodges, recently abandoned, which induced us to suppose that the Minnetarees of Fort de Prairie are somewhere in this neighborhood—a suspicion which was confirmed by the return of the hunters, who had seen no game of any kind. As these Indians have probably followed the buffalo toward the main branch of Maria's river, we shall not strike it [this game] above the north branch.

The course of the mountains continues from southeast to northwest; in which last direction from us the front range appears to terminate abruptly at the distance of 35 miles. Those which are to the southwest and more distinctly in view, are of an irregular form, composed chiefly of clay, with a very small mixture of rock, without timber; and though low are yet partially covered with snow to their bases. The river itself has nearly doubled the volume of water which it possessed, when we first saw it below, a circumstance to be ascribed, no doubt, to the great evaporation and absorption of water in its passage through these open plains. The rock in this neighborhood is of a white color and a fine grit, and lies in horizontal strata in the bluffs of the river. We attempted to take some fish, but could procure only a single trout. We had, therefore, nothing to eat except the grease which we pressed from our tainted meat and [with which we] formed a mush of cows, reserving one meal more of the same kind for tomorrow. We have seen near this place a number of the whistling squirrel [*Spermophilus coumbianus?*] common in the country watered by the Columbia, but which we observed here for the first time in the plains of the Missouri. The cottonwood of this place is similar to that of the Columbia. Our observations this evening were prevented by clouds. The weather was clear for a short time in the morning.

July 24th, but the sky soon clouded over, and it rained during the rest of the day. We were therefore obliged to remain one day longer for the purpose of completing our observations. Our situation now became unpleasant from the rain, the coldness of the air, and the total absence of game; for the hunters could find nothing of a large kind, and we were obliged to subsist on a few pigeons and a kettle of mush made of the remainder of our bread of cows. This supplied us with one more meal in the morning.

July 25th, when, finding that the cold and rainy weather would still detain us here, two of the men were dispatched to hunt. They returned in the evening with a fine buck, on which we fared sumptuously. In their excursion they had gone [southward] as far as the main branch of Maria's river, at the distance of ten miles, through an open extensive valley, in which were scattered a great number of lodges lately evacuated.

July 26th. The weather was still cloudy, so that no observation could be made; and what added to our disappointment, Captain Lewis's chronometer stopped yesterday from some unknown cause, though when set in motion again it went as usual. We now despaired of taking the longitude of this place; and as our staying any longer might endanger our return to the United States during the present season, we therefore waited till nine o'clock, in hopes of a change of weather; but seeing no prospect of that kind, we mounted our horses, and leaving with reluctance our position, which we now named Camp Disappointment, directed our course across the open plains, in a direction nearly southeast. At 12 miles' distance [having crossed Willow creek at two miles from camp] we reached [Two Medicine Lodge river] a branch of Maria's river, about 65 yards wide, which we crossed, and continued along its southern side for two miles, where it is joined by another branch [Badger river], nearly equal in size from the southwest, and far more clear than the north branch, which is turbid, though the beds of both are composed of pebbles. We now decided on pursuing this river [resulting from the confluence of Badger with Two Medicine Lodge] to its junction with that [North] fork of Maria's river which we had ascended, then cross the country obliquely to Tansy [Teton] river, and descend that stream to its confluence with Maria's river. We therefore crossed and descended the river; and at one mile below the junction, halted to let the horses graze in a fertile bottom, in which were some Indian lodges that appeared to have been inhabited during the past winter. We here discern more timber than the country in general possesses; for, besides an undergrowth of rose, honeysuckle, and red berry bushes, and a small quantity of willow timber, the three species of cottonwood, the narrow-leaved, the broad-leaved, and the species known to the Columbia, though here seen for the first time on the Missouri, are all united at this place. Game appears in greater abundance. We saw a few antelopes and wolves, and killed a buck, besides which we saw also two of the small burrowing-foxes [*Vulpes velox*] of the plains, about the size of the common domestic cat, and of a reddish-brown color, except the [tip of the] tail, which is black.

At the distance of three miles we ascended the hills close to the riverside, while Drewyer pursued the valley of the river on the opposite side. But scarcely had Captain Lewis reached the high plain when he saw, about a mile on his left, a collection of about 30 horses. He immediately halted, and by the aid of his spy-glass discovered that one-half of the horses were saddled, and that on the eminence above the horses several Indians were looking down the river, probably at Drewyer. This was a most unwelcome sight. Their probable numbers rendered any contest with them of doubtful issue; to attempt to escape would only invite pursuit, and our horses were so bad that we must certainly be overtaken; besides which, Drewyer could not yet be aware that the Indians were near, and if we ran he would most probably be sacrificed. We therefore determined to make the most of our situation, and advance toward them in a friendly manner. The flag which we had brought in case of any such accident was therefore displayed, and we continued slowly our march toward them. Their whole attention was so engaged by Drewyer that they did not immediately discover us. As soon as they did see us, they appeared to be much alarmed and ran about in confusion; some of them came down the hill and drove their horses within gunshot of the eminence, to which they then returned, as if to await our arrival. When we came within a quarter of a mile, one of the Indians mounted and rode at full speed to receive us; but when within a hundred paces of us, he halted. Captain Lewis, who had alighted to receive him, held out his hand and beckoned to him to approach; he only looked at us for some time, and then, without saying a word, returned to his companions with as much haste as he had advanced. The whole party now descended the hill and rode toward us. As yet we saw only eight, but presumed that there must be more behind us, as there were several horses saddled. We however advanced, and Captain Lewis now told his two men that he believed these were the Minnetarees of Fort de Prairie, who, from their infamous character, would in all probability attempt to rob us; but being determined to die rather than lose his papers and instruments, he intended to resist to the last extremity, and advised them to do the same, and to be on the alert should there be any disposition to attack us. When the two parties came within a hundred yards of each other, all the Indians, except one, halted. Captain Lewis therefore ordered his men to halt while he advanced, and after shaking hands with the Indian, went on and did the same with the others in the rear, while the Indian himself shook hands with the two men. They all now came up; and after alighting, the Indians asked to smoke with us. Captain Lewis, who was very anxious for Drewyer's safety, told them that the man who had gone down the river had the pipe, and requested that as they had seen him, one of them would accompany R. Fields, to bring him back. To this they assented, and Fields went with a young man in search of Drewyer.

Captain Lewis now asked them by signs if they were the Minnetarees of the North, and was sorry to learn by their answer that his suspicion was too true. He then inquired if there was any chief among them. They pointed out three; but though he did not believe them, yet it was thought best to please them, and he therefore gave to one a flag, to another a medal, and to a third a handkerchief. They appeared to be well satisfied with these presents, and now recovered from the agitation into which our first interview had thrown them; for they were really more alarmed than ourselves at the meeting. In our turn, however, we became equally satisfied on finding that they were not joined by any more of their companions; for we consider ourselves quite a match for either Indians, particularly as these have but two guns, the rest being armed with only eye-dogs [or eye-daggs, Lewis L 127—a sort of war-hatchet] and bows and arrows. As it was growing late Captain Lewis proposed that they should camp together near the river; for he was glad to see them and had a great deal to say to them. They assented; and being soon joined by Drewyer, we proceeded toward the river, and after descending a very steep bluff, 250 feet high, camped in a small bottom.

Here the Indians formed a large semicircular tent of dressed buffalo-skins, in which the two parties assembled; and by the means of Drewyer, the evening was spent in conversation with the Indians. They informed us that they were a part of a large band which at present were camped on the main branch of Maria's river, near the foot of the Rocky mountains, at the distance of a day and half's journey from this place. Another large band were hunting buffalo near the Broken mountains, from which they would proceed in a few days to the north of Maria's river. With the first of these there was a white man. They added that from this place to the establishment on the Saskashawan at which they trade is only six days' easy march—that is, such a day's journey as can be made with their women and children; so that we computed the distance at 150 miles. There they carry the skins of wolves and beavers, to exchange for guns, ammunition, blankets, spirituous liquors, and other articles of Indian traffic. Captain Lewis in turn informed them that he had come from a great distance up the large river which runs toward the rising sun; that he had been as far as the great lake where the sun sets; that he had seen many nations, the greater part of whom were at war with each other, but by his mediation were restored to peace; that all had been invited to come and trade with him west of the mountains; that he was now on his way home, but had left his companions at the falls, and come in search of the Minnetarees, in hopes of inducing them to live at peace with their neighbors, and to visit the trading-houses which would be formed at the entrance of Maria's river. They said that they were anxious to be at peace with the Tushepaws; but those people had lately killed a number of their relations, as they proved by showing several of the party who had their hair cut as a sign of mourning. They were equally willing, they added, to come down and trade with us. Captain Lewis therefore proposed that they should send some of their young men to invite all their band to meet us at the mouth of Maria's river, the rest of the party to go with us to that place, where he hoped to find his men; offering them ten horses and some tobacco in case they would accompany us. To this they made no reply. Finding them very fond of the pipe, Captain Lewis, who was desirous of keeping a constant watch during the night, smoked with them until a late hour. As soon as they were all asleep, he woke R. Fields, and ordering him to rouse us all in case any Indians left the camp, as they would probably attempt to steal our horses, he lay down by the side of Drewyer in the tent with all the Indians, while the Fieldses were stretched near the fire at the mouth of it.

Sunday, July 27th. At sunrise, the Indians got up and crowded around the fire near which J. Fields, who was then on watch, had carelessly left his rifle, near the head of his brother, who was still asleep. One of the Indians slipped behind him, and unperceived, took his brother's and his own rifle, while at the same time two others seized those of Drewyer and Captain Lewis. As soon as Fields turned, he saw the Indian running off with the rifles; instantly calling his brother, they pursued him for 50 or 60 yards; just at they overtook him, in the scuffle for the rifles R. Fields stabbed him through the heart with his knife. The Indian ran about fifteen steps and fell dead. They now ran back with their rifles to the camp. The moment the fellow touched his gun, Drewyer, who was awake, jumped up and wrested it from him. The noise awoke Captain Lewis, who instantly started from the ground and reached for his gun; but finding it gone, drew a pistol from his belt, and turning saw the Indian running off with it. He followed him and ordered him to lay it down, which he did just as the two Fieldses came up, and were taking aim to shoot him; when Captain Lewis ordered them not to fire, as the Indian did not appear to intend any mischief. He dropped the gun and was going slowly off when Drewyer came out and asked permission to kill him; but this Captain Lewis forbade, as he had not yet attempted to shoot us. But finding that the Indians were now endeavoring to drive off all the horses, he ordered [all] three of us to follow the main party, who were chasing the horses up the river, and fire instantly upon the thieves; while he, without taking time to run for his shot-pouch, pursued the fellow who had stolen his gun and another Indian, who were driving away the horses on the left of the camp. He pressed them so closely that they left twelve of their horses, but continued to drive off one of our own. At the distance of 300 paces they entered a steep niche in the river-bluffs, when Captain Lewis, being too much out of breath to pursue them any further, called out, as he had done several times before, that unless they gave up the horse he would shoot them. As he raised his gun one of the Indians jumped behind a rock and spoke to the other, who stopped at the distance of thirty paces. Captain Lewis shot him in the belly. He fell on his knees and right elbow: but raising himself a little, fired, and then crawled behind a rock. The shot had nearly been fatal, for Captain Lewis, who was bareheaded, felt the wind of the ball very distinctly. Not having his shot-pouch, he could not reload his rifle; and having only a single load for his pistol, he thought it most prudent not to attack the Indians, and therefore retired slowly to the camp. He was met by Drewyer, who, hearing the report of the guns, had come to his assistance, leaving the Fieldses to pursue the Indians. Captain Lewis ordered him to call out to them to desist from the pursuit, as we could take the horses of the Indians in place of our own; but they were at too great a distance to hear him. He therefore returned to the camp; and whilst he was saddling the horses, the Fieldses returned with four of our own, having followed the Indians until two of them swam the river and two others ascended the hills, so that the horses became dispersed.

We, however, were rather gainers by this contest, for we took four of the Indian horses, and lost only one of our own. Besides which, we found in the camp four shields, two bows with quivers, and one of the guns, which we took with us, as also the flag which we had presented to the Indians, but left the medal round the neck of the dead man, in order that they might be informed who we were. The rest of their baggage, except some buffalo-meat, we left; and as there was no time to be lost, we mounted our horses, and after ascending the river-hills, took our course through the beautiful level plains, in a direction a little to the south of east. We had no doubt but that we should be immediately pursued by a much larger party, and that as soon as intelligence was given to the band near the Broken mountains, they would hasten to the mouth of Maria's river to intercept us. We hoped, however, to be there before them, so as to form a junction with our friends. We therefore pushed our horses as fast as we possibly could; fortunately for us, the Indian horses were very good, the plains perfectly level, without many stones or prickly pears, and in fine order for traveling after the late rains. At eight miles from our camp we passed a stream 40 yards wide, to which, from the occurrence of the morning, we gave the name of Battle river. At three o'clock we reached Rose [or Tansy] river, five miles above where we had formerly passed it; and having now come by estimate 63 miles, halted for an hour and a half to refresh our horses. We then pursued our journey 17 miles farther, when, as night came on, we killed a buffalo, and again stopped for two hours. The sky was now overclouded, but as the moon gave light enough to show us the route, we continued through immense herds of buffalo for 20 miles, and then, almost exhausted with fatigue, halted at two in the morning,

July 28th, to rest ourselves and the horses. At daylight we awoke sore and scarcely able to stand; but as our own lives as well as those of our companions depended on our pressing forward, we mounted our horses and set out. The men were desirous of crossing the Missouri at Grog spring, where Rose river approaches so near the river, and passing down the southwest side of it, thus avoiding the country at the junction of the two rivers, through which the enemy would most probably pursue us. But as this circuitous route would consume the whole day, and the Indians might in the meantime attack the canoes at the point [*i.e.* mouth of Maria's river], Captain Lewis told his party it was now their duty to risk their lives for their friends and companions; that he would proceed immediately to the point to give the alarm to the canoes; and if they had not yet arrived he would raft the Missouri, and after hiding the baggage, ascend the river on foot through the woods till he met them. He told them also that it was his determination, in case they were attacked in crossing the plains, to tie the bridles of the horses and stand together till they either routed their enemies, or sold their lives as dearly as possible.

To this they all assented, and we therefore continued our route to the eastward, till at the distance of twelve miles we came near the Missouri, where we heard a noise which seemed like the report of a gun. We therefore quickened our pace for eight miles farther, and about five miles from Grog spring heard distinctly the noise of several rifles from the river. We hurried to the bank, and saw with exquisite satisfaction our friends coming down the river.

John Franklin: The Man
Who Ate His Boots

BY FERGUS FLEMING

John Franklin was one of a series of English explorers sent to find the elusive Northwest Passage that would connect East to West. His first attempt to sail through the ice above Canada proved fruitless and he was forced to turn back. Despite his failure, he became a hero in England.

On the expedition detailed here, Franklin tried to follow the route Alexander Mackenzie took overland through Canada to the Arctic Sea, hoping to connect the dots on the map to show where a passage could be made. Unfortunately, the journey was poorly planned and poorly led and soon became a struggle for survival. This well-researched account is taken from *Barrow's Boys*, by Fergus Fleming, an interesting and entertaining look at English exploration in the nineteenth century.

The story begins after the expedition spends a discontented winter in northern Canada in 1821, waiting to continue their journey to the Arctic Ocean—already knowing they will face starvation and death.

★ ★ ★ ★ ★

Once moving, the expedition's squabbles faded, but were soon replaced by other problems. The Indian guides, who knew the region little better than Franklin himself, proved useless. Crossing a frozen lake they directed him to its west shore, then, suddenly remembering an important feature in the landscape, they sent him to the northeast. The ocean was now distant, now near. "Our reliance on the information of the guides, which had been for some time shaken, was now quite at an end," Franklin wrote on 14 July, having climbed a hill to get a view of the promised sea to find "a plain similar to that we had just left, terminated by another range of trap hills, between whose tops the summits of some distant blue mountains appeared." Richardson, however, always more willing to trust the natives, walked another three miles that evening and spied the sought-after Arctic Ocean. To his disappointment but no great surprise, it was covered with ice. He brought his news back to camp as the sun's last rays fell on the surrounding peaks.

They had crossed the line dividing Indian territory from Eskimo and Akaitcho's men were becoming increasingly nervous, especially when they reached Bloody Falls to find an Eskimo encampment still in place. But its occupants had already fled at the Indians' approach, leaving their dogs, tents and food behind. If Franklin needed a reminder that food was scarce, the Eskimo camp provided it. The dried salmon was putrid and covered with maggots. Hung out to dry on wooden frames was their future sustenance: A number of small birds and two mice. Apart from one elderly cripple and his wife, who had been unable to evacuate and who prodded feebly at the intruders with a brass-tipped spear, the Eskimos kept their distance. Occasionally they could be spotted hovering singly at a safe distance, but despite all attempts to draw them into conversation they could not be tempted nearer.

Even this, however, was too much for the Indians. They left for home on 18 July, according to the agreement Akaitcho had made with Franklin. The following day Wentzel also left, leaving Franklin with fifteen men: the two interpreters, St. Germain and Adam, plus thirteen others whose names were Augustus, Junius, Michel Teroahauté, Joseph Benoit, Credit, Registe Vaillant, Jean Baptiste Belanger and Solomon Belanger, Gabriel Beauparlant, Fontano, Ignace Perrault, Joseph Peltier and François Samandré. Of these, St. Germain and Adam wanted to go with Wentzel, arguing not unreasonably that their services were no longer needed now that the Indians had gone. However, much as Franklin would have liked to rid himself of the trouble-makers, they were the best hunters in the party. He put them under twenty-four-hour watch until Wentzel and the Indians were a safe distance upriver.

To every man who left, Franklin gave strict instructions that depots of food were to be left at various points inland and, in particular, that a large supply of dried meat was to be cached at Fort Enterprise. This last was of vital importance because Franklin feared that should he fail to reach Repulse Bay—and it was looking increasingly likely that he would—he would nevertheless have gone sufficiently far to be cut off from the Coppermine by winter ice. Therefore he would have to travel overland through the uncharted territory of the Barren Lands to Fort Enterprise, relying for food on whatever could be shot or trapped *en route*. As the ground was almost certainly empty at that time of the year they would be near starving-point by the time they reached base and thus it was imperative that Fort Enterprise be well stocked.

Franklin drummed this fact into Wentzel. Then, a few days later, he set off for the coast in three bark canoes containing fourteen days' provisions and a group of voyageurs who were terrified of the sea—they had never seen it— who were equally terrified of the Eskimos they might meet on land, who had limited hunting skills and who were appalled at the prospect of hunger. "It is of no use to speak to a Canadian voyageur of going upon short allowance," wrote Richardson. "They prefer running the risk of going entirely without hereafter, that they may have a present belly full, and if it is not given to them they will steal it and in their opinion it is no disgrace to be caught pilfering provisions." Several men, he noted, had "secreted and distributed among themselves a bag of small shot. They hope thus to be enabled . . . privately to procure ducks and geese and to avoid the necessity of sharing them with the officers." These words, which appeared in Richardson's journal on Thursday 19 July 1821, were followed with supreme lack of concern by a one-page description of the starry flounder.

The three canoes reached open sea—Richardson had either miscon-strued the state of the ice or it had opened since—and scuttled eastwards. They followed the coastline along every creek and indentation for 555 miles before Franklin called a halt. During this time storms had arisen which broke fifteen timbers in one canoe, nearly separated the struts from the bark in another and had the voyageurs gibbering with terror. Despite frequent landings they had amassed only a bare sufficiency of food—for which Franklin blamed the bale-ful influence of St. Germain and Adam. "We now strongly suspected that their recent want of success in hunting had proceeded from an intentional relax-ation in their efforts to kill deer in order that the want of provisions might compel us to put a period to our voyage."

On 18 August, Franklin walked overland to mark his farthest point east—the aptly named Point Turnagain. Then, on 22 August 1821, the very day, unknown to him, that Parry had sailed into Repulse Bay, he turned back for Fort Enterprise. As he had feared, Franklin had explored himself into a corner. The seas were too rough to reach the Coppermine, and the deer had already begun to move south for the winter. He therefore made for the mouth of what he called Hood's River, a spot they had visited on their outward journey, which seemed to lead in the direction of Fort Enterprise and where they had sighted plenty of game. This would be the short side of a triangle that would lead them back to their winter base with its stores of dried meat.

The voyage to Hood's River took three days, during which Franklin was pleased to see that the voyageurs were at last exerting themselves, driven by the prospect of being once more in their element. On landing, he ordered the large, seagoing canoes broken up to build two smaller, portable versions that could be carried overland and launched whenever one of Canada's unpredictable rivers blocked their path.

The voyageurs were overjoyed to be on land again. But they were less happy when Franklin forbade them dinner. The deer had migrated south and those that remained were too shy to be shot. Pemmican was limited. That evening, the first of many, they went without dinner.

The canoes were hard to carry. They blew about in the wind and scraped against sharp rocks which also ripped the men's moccasins to shreds. The going was treacherous, and as Richardson remarked, "If anyone had broken a limb here, his fate would have been melancholy indeed, we could neither have remained with him, nor carried him on with us." Had they had the opportunity to escape, the voyageurs would have fled *en masse*. But they had nowhere to go.

The expedition's woes started in earnest in September with the premature arrival of winter. Confined to their tent by a howling storm, they ate their last piece of pemmican on 4 September. Three days later, when the weather had lessened, they resumed their march. Before they even started Franklin fainted from a combination of hunger and exposure. That same day the voyageurs dropped one of the canoes, rendering it useless (this was a greater disaster than at first realized as the remaining canoe had been accidentally built too small and was therefore unable to cross a river of any size without being lashed to its larger counterpart). Franklin had strong suspicions that the canoe had been dropped on purpose, but making the best of things, he used the remains as firewood to heat the last of their supplies—a tin of soup.

From now on they had nothing to eat save what could be had from the land. The game had not altogether disappeared. They were able to shoot the occasional deer but it was not enough to satisfy their hunger, and even when they made a kill they were so overburdened that although they got a good meal at the time they could not carry the excess with them. The voyageurs, whose standard ration was eight pounds of meat a day, and who were carrying some ninety pounds apiece, were hardest hit. One can blame them for their stupidity, but little else, when they secretly threw away the expedition's weighty fishing nets. The loss infuriated Franklin. But by now even he was willing to jettison articles. In a belated purge, he deposited Richardson's natural history specimens, most of the expedition's scientific instruments and the hefty manuals which were required for their operation.

As the winter worsened the game became scarce, then it vanished altogether. They were driven to eating lichen from the rocks, an acrid and barely nutritious growth which induced severe diarrhoea. Many of them could stomach no more than a few mouthfuls. In a sleight of hand worthy of the finest restaurant, they dubbed it *tripes de roche*.

On 14 September, while crossing a river, the canoe overturned. With it went Franklin's journal. Solomon Belanger was stranded in mid-river, up to his waist in freezing water for several minutes until he was rescued. "He was instantly stripped," wrote Richardson, "and being rolled up in blankets, two men undressed themselves and went to bed with him—but it was some hours before he recovered his warmth and sensation."

The following day they were lucky enough to shoot a deer. But that, apart from another deer on 25 September and a single partridge on 29 October, was to be their only game for another two months. During that period they lived off *tripes de roches*, augmented by a few scraps of deer skin from which the hair had first been singed. Occasionally, if they were lucky, they might find the remains of a wolf kill left over from the previous season. Although lacking any meat, the bones could be made edible by heating them in the fire. Anything that could be eaten was eaten, right down to their spare shoes which, having been either roasted or boiled, were "greedily devoured." In fact, their shoes were probably the most palatable item on the menu. The *tripes de roche* caused diarrhoea, and the charred bones were so acrid, even when made into soup, that their mouths became ulcerated. The few sections of putrid spinal marrow which they managed to suck from the backbones of dead deer took the skin off their lips.

The expedition began to break up, both physically and mentally. The line elongated and split as the stronger members forged ahead, and the weaker dropped behind. Back led the way, with some of the fitter voyageurs. But while Richardson was able to keep pace in the centre, Franklin and Hood fell back to the rear. Hood, racked by diarrhoea from the *tripes de roche*, which seemed to affect him more than the others, was fading fast.

The voyageurs, meanwhile, were well nigh uncontrollable. On 23 September Richardson recorded with despair that "The canoe was broken today and left behind, notwithstanding every remonstrance. The men had become desperate and were perfectly regardless of the commands of the officers." Only with the greatest difficulty could they be persuaded not to drop everything and made a mad dash for Fort Enterprise. That they did not do so owed less to the officers' commands than the fact that they did not know where Fort Enterprise was.

The men's belief that Franklin knew where he was going was all that kept them even vaguely obedient. But the truth was that Franklin did not really know where he was. The countryside was hilly and unfamiliar. The magnetic deviation for this area was unknown, making it impossible to adjust their compass readings with any degree of accuracy. And in weather conditions that ranged from thick snow, through thick rain, to thick mist, they were unable to take their bearings from the sun. When they did catch a brief glimpse of the sun and adjusted their course accordingly, it merely sowed the suspicion that Franklin was lost.

A mutiny would have been inevitable had they not reached on 26 September a river which, from its size and course, could only have been the Coppermine. From his calculations Franklin reckoned Fort Enterprise was only forty miles away. The news cheered everyone, as did the discovery of a deer carcase whose meat, though putrid, was cooked and eaten on the spot. When this failed to satisfy, the intestines were scraped up and thrown into the pot. The chance discovery of a number of cranberry and blackberry bushes added further to their joy. But even so, wrote Richardson, "nothing could allay our inordinate appetites."

After the euphoria came disappointment. They may well have been forty miles from Fort Enterprise but in order to reach it they first had to cross the swiftly flowing Coppermine which was here 120 yards wide. They could possibly have managed it had they had even one canoe. But they had none. "They bitterly execrated their folly and impatience in breaking up the canoe," Richardson wrote, "and the remainder of the day was spent in wandering slowly along the river, looking in vain for a fordable place and inventing schemes for crossing, no sooner devised than abandoned."

The voyageurs, in the depths of despondency, all but gave up. They became "careless and disobedient, they had ceased to dread punishment or hope for reward." At length, however, they rallied round to construct a raft from the meagre willow trees which grew along the river's bank. It was a poor vessel, the wood being green and heavy with sap. At best it could carry only one man. And it was quite unnavigable, the available trees being neither thick enough to make a paddle nor long enough to make a pole capable of reaching the bottom. However, if it could make just the initial trip, carrying a line to the opposite bank, then the expedition could be ferried across one by one. But the raft never reached the opposite bank. Driven back by adverse winds it went no further then the voyageurs, waist-deep in freezing water, could push it.

Then Richardson stepped forward. If the raft could make no headway maybe a swimmer could. Back was scouting ahead with his hunters. Richardson was the strongest officer left. Tying the line around his waist he launched himself into the river. For a man who was already reduced to skin and bone, and who suffered accordingly from degrees of cold that would normally have been disregarded, to willingly immerse himself in temperatures of less than 38° F was an act of enormous bravery. Sadly, his courage achieved nothing. Only a short distance from the bank Richardson's arms became so numb that he could not move them. Turning on his back, he kicked on with his legs. He had almost reached the other side when his legs too gave out and he sank to the riverbed. Seeing him go under, the others hauled on the line and drew him back to safety. When they dragged him ashore he was unable to move and could barely speak. Following his muttered instructions they placed him beside a fire and waited for sensation to reappear. Several hours later he was finally strong enough to crawl into a tent. But the whole of his left side was paralysed and although feeling was gradually restored his left arm and leg did not regain their full strength for another five months. To make matters worse he had stepped on a knife just before diving into the river and had cut his foot to the bone.

In any other circumstance Richardson would have been carried as an invalid for the rest of the journey. But hunger allowed neither invalids nor carriers. They were all in the same state. Richardson's body, when stripped of clothes, was a horrible mirror to the others of how far they had sunk. "I cannot describe," wrote Franklin, "what everyone felt at beholding the skeleton which the doctor's debilitated frame exhibited." The voyageurs were aghast. "Ah! Que nous sommes maigres!" they exclaimed simultaneously.

Ironically, it was St. Germain, the voyageurs' discontented ringleader, who came up with a solution. He volunteered to make a canoe from willow branches and the canvas in which their bedding was wrapped. It took him two days to complete the task, during which time the whole party almost disintegrated. The voyageurs, utterly downcast by Richardson's failure, reconciled themselves to death. The refused to gather *tripes de roche*, declaring they would rather die than waste their last hours harvesting such a revolting crop. Junius wandered off, presumably to find his own way home, and was never seen again.

Of the officers, Richardson was lame, Franklin was prostrate, Hood was so thin that he hardly cast a shadow and even the redoubtable Back could not stand without a stick. It was left to John Hepburn, the hero-seaman of the expedition, to gather a few scraps of lichen for his commanders. Their weakness can be gauged by Franklin's attempt on 3 October to visit St. Germain at this canoe-building site. The voyageur was working in a grove of willows three-quarters of a mile distant. Franklin returned after three hours having been unable to reach his objective. They were now so famished that they did not care whether they ate or not. "The sensation of hunger is no longer felt by us," Richardson recorded. Yet the memory of food lingered obstinately in their minds—"we are scarcely able to converse upon any other subject than the pleasures of eating."

St. Germain finished his slight, one-man canoe on 4 October. They "assembled in anxious expectation" as he set out and cheered as he carried a line to the other side. One by one they hauled themselves across, the canoe sinking lower with each crossing until the last men were in water to their knees. Their heaviest bundle, the spare clothes and bedding, was soaked through when it arrived.

They had crossed the Coppermine and had only forty miles to travel before they reached Fort Enterprise. At their previous rate of about six miles per day, salvation was only a week's march away. As they struggled forwards, however, it became obvious that even a week was too much for some. Far behind everybody else the two weakest voyageurs, Credit and Vaillant, collapsed. When Richardson tracked back to see what had happened, Vaillant was "unable to rise and scarcely capable of replying to my questions." He died that day. Credit was never found.

Franklin split his party into two. Back, still hobbling on a stick, was sent ahead with Solomon Belanger, Beauparlant, and St. Germain to contact Akaitcho's Indians at Fort Enterprise and to bring supplies to the men who lagged behind. But once Back had gone, Richardson put forward another proposal; he himself was lame and Hood was so weak as to be incapable, why not leave the two of them, with Hepburn to act as nursemaid, while Franklin went ahead to intercept Back's supplies? Without the drag of its two weakest members, ran Richardson's reasoning, Franklin's party would have a better chance of survival. "I was distressed beyond description at the thought of leaving them in such a dangerous situation, and for a long time combated their proposal;" Franklin wrote, "but they strenuously urged that this step afforded the only chance of safety for the party, and I reluctantly acceded to it."

Franklin went only four and a half miles before he had a crisis. Two voyageurs—Michel, and Jean Baptiste Belanger—declared themselves too weak to continue and asked permission to return to Richardson's camp. The voyageurs were by now in tatters, literally, having thrown aside their tent and cut the canvas into a manageable blanket. Franklin waved them off wearily. A little later another man, Perrault, burst into tears, declared he could go no further, and asked permission to follow Michel and Belanger. Once again Franklin consented. No snow had fallen, the tracks were still clear, and Perrault would have no difficulty finding his way back. A fourth voyageur, Fontano, was sent with him, having become so slow and weak that he was seriously jeopardizing the chances of the others. "I cannot describe my anguish," Franklin wrote, "on the occasion of separating from another companion under circumstances so distressing. There was, however, no alternative. The extreme debility of the party put the carrying him quite out of the question, as he himself admitted."

Franklin heaved himself and his remaining five voyageurs forward to Fort Enterprise. There was no game to be shot even had Adam, his hunter, found any or been strong enough to lift his gun. The Barren Lands were truly barren. "There was no tripes de roche," Franklin regretted, so "we drank tea and ate some of our shoes for supper."

They reached Fort Enterprise on 12 October. It was empty. There were no supplies, there was no store of dried meat, there were no Indians. What they found was a note from Back saying that he had been there two days earlier and was going in search of Akaitcho, God willing that he and his three companions should survive so far. Believing that the white men were doomed, Akaitcho had taken his men hunting.

The only food available was *tripes de roche*, and the detritus of last year's stay; bones from the ash heap, and a pile of skins which the Indians had used as bedding. This, Franklin decided optimistically, "would support us tolerably well for a while." Two days later, while they were feeding the floorboards into the fire—the one point in Fort Enterprise's favour was its availability of wood— The door burst open to reveal Solomon Belanger, one of Back's voyageurs. Belanger was covered in a thin coating of ice, and could barely speak. He did, however, have the strength to give Franklin a letter. Back had seen no Indians and requested further instructions.

Once again Franklin split his party. Sending Belanger back with the message that Back was to change course for Fort Providence in the hope of intercepting the Indians as they made their way back to the winter quarters, he decided to set off upriver himself in the same direction with Augustus and Benoit. Pelticr and Samandré, meanwhile, would stay at the fort to look after Adam, whose legs had swollen so much he could not walk.

Two days into the trek, Franklin's snowshoes fell irreparably to pieces, forcing him to return to Fort Enterprise while Augustus and Benoit struggled on. Over the following week snowstorms blew around Fort Enterprise while the four men within sank into a hunger-induced stupor. Adam and Samandré lay in bed, sobbing quietly. Franklin and Peltier, slightly stronger than the others, did their best to collect food and firewood, but they moved like zombies. "We perceived our strength decline every day," Franklin wrote, " and every exertion began to be irksome. When we were once seated the greatest effort was necessary in order to rise, and we frequently had to lift each other from our seats." But they were cheered by the thought that either Back, or the two voyageurs, would surely have caught up with the Indians by 26 October. It could only be a matter of days before help arrived.

It was now four weeks since any of them had tasted meat.

Michel reached Richardson's camp on 9 October 1821. He was alone. He explained that he and Belanger had split up on the march back and as he had not yet arrived he assumed he must have got lost. Of Perrault and Fontano he said nothing save that the former had given him his rifle and ammunition before he left, with which he had been able to shoot a partridge and a hare.

What doubts they may have had about Michel's story were swept away when he produced the food. To Richardson it was as good as a miracle from the Almighty, "and we looked upon Michel as the instrument he had chosen to preserve all our lives." They pampered him as much as they were able. When he complained of cold Richardson gave him one of the two shirts he was wearing; Hood offered to share his buffalo hide blanket.

Two days later Michel was once again the Almighty's instrument of salvation. While out hunting he found a wolf that had been killed by a deer. They devoured the strange-tasting meat with unbounded gratitude. But as the days wore on, with no sign of Belanger, who they now presumed dead, Michel became surly and evasive. He disappeared for short periods, declining to say where he had been. He brought back no more meat and refused to gather *tripes de roche*. At night he did not sleep in the tent, preferring to lie in the open. By the 16th he was threatening to leave them.

Puzzled by his behaviour, and equally puzzled as to why Franklin had sent no supplies, Richardson and Hood decided that if Michel would hunt for four days, they would let him go forward with Hepburn to see what was happening at Fort Enterprise. At this his attitude became even stranger. He would not hunt. "It is no use," he said, "there are no animals, you had better kill and eat me." Later he began to rave against Europeans, claiming they had eaten his uncle.

Richardson's account of those days is the only version available. It was written later, following consultation with Franklin, and does not say when the first doubt formed in Richardson's mind. It does, however, reveal what both officers agreed must have happened. On the way from Franklin to Richardson, Michel had killed Belanger. Being surprised by Perrault, who was last seen carrying his gun and heading for the smoke of Michel's camp-fire, he had killed him too. Fontano had suffered the same fate. During subsequent days Michel had used the three corpses as a private larder, visiting it whenever he felt hungry. The "wolf" meat he had brought back was almost certainly human flesh. Possibly he planned the same fate for Richardson, Hood and Hepburn.

On 20 October, Richardson was scrabbling together a few handfuls of frozen lichen. Hepburn was chopping willows for a fire. Michel, who refused to do anything, remained at the tent arguing with Hood. A few minutes after noon there was a shot. Richardson and Hepburn hurried back to find Hood dead. A bullet had entered the back of his skull and emerged neatly through his forehead. It had been fired at such close range that his nightcap was still smouldering. Michel greeted them with a gun in his hand.

Michel's explanation ran as follows; there were two guns in camp, long one and a short one. Hood was cleaning the long one, and had asked Michel to fetch the short one from the tent; while Michel was doing so the long gun went off, whether by accident or by design he did not know. Suicide, accident, or murder? Richardson was no detective, but it was obvious what had happened. The long gun was of the outdated type which Britain sold to native soldiers. It was so long that it was near impossible for a man to press its barrel against his head and simultaneously pull the trigger. It was even more difficult for a man to shoot himself in the back of the head with such a weapon. And for a man to do such a thing while holding in one hand a copy of Bickersteth's *Scripture Helps* was beyond the realms of likelihood.

Michel protested his innocence and having a gun in his hand, was listened to with attention. From that point, he was never unarmed and refused to let Hepburn and Richardson be on their own. If either opened their mouths he leaped forwards, waving his gun and demanding to know if they accused him of Hood's murder. The two Britons were at the mercy of a deranged man. Hepburn had a gun, and Richardson a small pistol. Both were too weak to cope with physical violence. Michel, on the other hand, was not only healthy but carried a gun, two pistols, a bayonet, and a knife. "He also," wrote Richardson, "for the first time, assumed such a tone of superiority in addressing me, as evinced that he considered us to be completely in his power." Which they were.

On 21 October Michel tried to lure Richardson into joining him on a hunting expedition. Richardson wisely refused. They set out for Fort Enterprise on 23 October, cajoling the madman in their midst with a semblance of purpose. Michel responded to the routine, but all the time he was reeling inwardly between guilt, self-justification and despair. Despair won. That day, for the first time, he announced his intention to gather *tripes de roche*. He told the other two to go ahead and he would catch them up later.

Alone at last, Richardson and Hepburn conferred. They agreed that Michel had definitely murdered Hood and has probably murdered Belanger too. Hepburn offered to shoot Michel but Richardson decided the duty was his. "Had my own life alone been threatened," he wrote, "I would not have purchased it by such a measure; but I considered myself as entrusted also with the protection of Hepburn's, a man, who, by his humane attentions and devotedness, had so endeared himself to me, that I felt more anxiety for his safety than for my own." When Michel caught up with them, Richardson took his pistol and shot him in the head. "His principles," intoned Richardson, "unsupported by a belief in the divine truths of Christianity, were unable to withstand the pressure of severe distress." Then they set out for Fort Enterprise.

"It is impossible to describe our sensations," Richardson wrote, "when on attaining the eminence that overlooks [Fort Enterprise] we beheld the smoke issuing from one of the chimneys." During their journey he and Hepburn had lived off nothing but *tripes de roche* and Hood's hide blanket. Richardson was now so weak that he fell down twenty times covering a distance of only 100 yards. However, the prospect of salvation gave them strength and on the evening of 29 October they flung open the door of Fort Enterprise.

"No words can convey an idea of the filth and wretchedness that met our eyes." Richardson wrote. The floor had been pulled up, the partitions had been demolished and the skin off the windows was gone. Of the four men present—Franklin, Samandré, Adam and Peltier—only Peltier seemed able to move. He had risen, expecting them to be an Indian relief party. Now he sank back in despair. Accustomed as Hepburn and Richardson were to the sight of each other's emaciated frames, "the ghastly countenances, dilated eye-balls, and sepulchral voices of Captain Franklin and those with him were more than we could at first bear."

Richardson and Hepburn had been expecting Franklin to help them. Now they found themselves having to help him. Despite their weakness they were both far stronger than any man in the building and from that day they undertook the chores of chopping wood and carrying it home. They also went hunting, but were too enfeebled to hold the gun steady on the rare occasions when they encountered game. Franklin, meanwhile, dragged in deer skins from the pile which had been discarded the previous winter. The pile was thirty yards away. Franklin managed to bring back three skins in a day. There were about twenty-six skins in all, thin, rotten things, riddled with warble-fly grubs. The explorers devoured them avidly, right down to the warble grubs which they squeezed out of the hide with their fingernails. They tasted "as fine as gooseberries."

Contrarily, while Peltier had previously been one of the healthiest in the group, he now collapsed, and Adam showed signs of renewed life. Richardson diagnosed Adam's swollen limbs as the result of protein-deficiency oedema and incised his abdomen, scrotum, and legs, whereby "a large quantity of water flowing out he obtained some ease." But there was nothing he could do for Peltier or Samandré. They both died on the night of 1 November.

Richardson and Hepburn now began to flag. On 3 November Richardson noted that Hepburn's limbs were beginning to swell—"his strength as well as mine is declining rapidly." That day they ate the last of the bones.

On 5 November Adam began to wander, leaping to his feet and seizing his gun with the promise of a good day's hunting and food for all, before subsiding into a dejection so deep that he could not even be persuaded to eat. The others were little better off. They tried not to talk about their situation, chatting instead about "common and light subjects." But as Franklin wrote, "our minds exhibited symptoms of weakness, evinced by a kind of unreasonable pettishness with each other. Each of us thought the other weaker in intellect than himself, and more in need of advice and assistance. So trifling a circumstance as a change of place, recommended by one as being more warm and comfortable, and refused by the other, from a dread of motion, frequently called forth fretful expressions, which were no sooner uttered than atoned for, to be repeated, perhaps, in the course of a few minutes."

They were all so thin that it even hurt to sleep. Their bones ached against the floorboards but they put up with it because the pain of turning to a more comfortable position was even greater. To this was added initially the pain of constant hunger. But once the pangs had eased—after three or four days— they usually enjoyed a few hours in which they dreamed of limitless food.

On 7 November Richardson and Hepburn were in the storehouse, trying to separate logs from the frozen pile stored there the previous winter, when they heard a shot. Three of Akaitcho's Indians were outside. They had been contacted by Back two days previously and on hearing his tale, and on taking in his shrivelled appearance—he too was pathetically reduced, and had lost one man from his party—they had immediately set out with emergency rations comprising fat, some dried venison, and a few deer tongues.

Sending the youngest of them back for further supplies, the remaining Indians swiftly took control. They cleared Fort Enterprise of its corpses, swept out the wet, blackened filth of charred bones and singed hair that covered the floor, and built up a crackling fire. The ease with which they did all this stunned Richardson. "We could scarcely," he wrote, "by any effort of reasoning, efface from our minds the idea that they possessed a supernatural degree of strength."

Then came the feeding. Despite Richardson's injunction to "be moderate!" they all suffered severely from overeating. Richardson, who should have known better, devoured the food as extravagantly as the others. For days afterwards—weeks, in Richardson's case—they suffered from distention and indigestion. The passing of a stool caused immense pain. Only Adam, who had to be spoon-fed, escaped the effects of sudden indulgence.

The Indians treated the survivors "with the same tenderness they would have bestowed on their own infants." They persuaded them to wash and to shave their beards which had not been touched since they left the coast and which had grown to a "hideous length." On learning that the Europeans had eaten too much meat they strung lines across the river and came back with four large trout. In every respect they could not have been more solicitous.

But hardly had salvation arrived than it departed. On 13 November the Indians vanished, leaving behind them a handful of pemmican per man. For a while Franklin feared his men would have to revert to their old diet, save that instead of deer skins they now had fish skins. It transpired, however, that the Indians, fearing their messenger had not reached base, had left on a twenty-four-hour march to fetch more supplies from Akaitcho's camp. The Indians reappeared on the morning of 15 November, having walked through a stormy and snow-filled night with two of their wives and Benoit, one of the voyageurs who had accompanied Back. Once again the survivors were faced with an abundance of food, but this time they measured their pace. On 16 November, a sunny Thursday, they left Fort Enterprise for good.

They reached Fort Providence on 11 December, where they were at last reunited with Back. Then began the recriminations. Why had no food been left at Fort Enterprise? In his defence Akaitcho stated that three of his best hunters had drowned and that he had been unable to obtain ammunition from Fort Providence. But he was quite open about the reason for the lack of provisions; he had believed that Franklin's journey was insanity and that none of the expedition would be seen again.

Wentzel the interpreter was equally to blame, having been repeatedly instructed to make sure sufficient food was left behind. But he drew attention away from his failings with an open attack on Franklin and Richardson. The whole party had acted "imprudently, injudiciously and showed in one particular instance an unpardonable want of restraint." Richardson was a murderer who should be brought to trial, he said.

Wentzel was right, in a way. There was nothing to prove that Richardson's story was true. For all anyone knew he and Hepburn might have killed all four voyageurs and Hood, and eaten them. "To tell the truth, Wentzel," Back had written, "things have taken place, which *must* not be known." In classic conspiracy fashion, Wentzel also stated that when he had joined the mission Franklin and his officers had been all over him. When the business was finished he *must* come to London for reunion, they had said, nothing could make them happier. But when the business *was* finished, the same men had advised him to stay in the Arctic for a few more years. It would be in his best interests, they had told him. There should have been some sort of investigation. Had Franklin lost a ship instead of an officer he would be facing a court martial. But Hood was not a ship, and the only witnesses to those fateful days were sticking to their story. In the end both parties dropped their accusations and the matter was swept aside.

The easiest target was of course Akaitcho. But Franklin could not bring himself to attack him. The Indian chief had shown them great kindness and sympathy during their rescue. Moreover, thanks to the usual administrative disputes, he had not yet been paid for any of his troubles. Akaitcho shrugged this off. "The world goes badly," he told Franklin. "All are poor; you are poor; the traders appear to be poor, I and my party are poor likewise; and since the goods have not come in, we cannot have them. I do not regret having supplied you with provisions, for a Copper Indian can never permit white men to suffer from want of food on his lands without flying to their aid."

Franklin reached York Factory on 14 July 1822, where Governor George Simpson took a quiet delight in their failure. "They do not feel themselves at liberty to enter into the particulars of their disastrous enterprize," he wrote on the 16th , "and I fear they have not fully achieved the object of their mission." This was putting it mildly. Franklin had travelled 5,500 miles across land and water, had lost eleven of his twenty-strong party, and had returned with the news that he had mapped a miniscule portion of a coastline that everyone already knew existed. Almost every stage of the journey had been mismanaged, and by his decision to press eastwards at any cost, further than his supplies could last, Franklin was directly responsible for the deaths of his men.

But when the story broke, nobody considered Franklin's failings. To do so would have called in question the wisdom of those who sent him. Only Douglas Clavering voiced the worries of his fellow explorers: "Was the undertaking worth the suffering his party endured?" he wrote to a friend. The answer was no. But what did the public care? Franklin was a hero. He was the man who had eaten his boots.

Among the Fuegians

BY CHARLES DARWIN

Everyone knows the name of Charles Darwin as one of the originators of the theory of evolution. While he developed his thoughts on the subject over many years, no single period was more important than his time on the *Beagle* as it sailed to the southern oceans in the 1830s. The purpose of the voyage was to survey the southern coasts of South America, and Darwin was hired on as a naturalist. Despite his continual seasickness and his clashes with the ship's captain, he was able to study a wide range of habitats and native plants and animals.

The book he wrote following the trip, *The Voyage of the Beagle,* has long been recognized as one of the best books of natural history ever written. It also contained frank and entertaining accounts of native tribes met along the way, like the one here, which describes the primitive and often exasperating Fuegians who populated the desolate region around Cape Horn. The *Beagle* took several Fuegians aboard during its travels through the area, including a man known as "Jemmy Button."

★   ★   ★   ★   ★

January 15th, 1833—The Beagle anchored in Goeree Roads. Captain Fitz Roy having resolved to settle the Fuegians, according to their wishes, in Ponsonby Sound, four boats were equipped to carry them there through the Beagle Channel. This channel, which was discovered by Captain Fitz Roy during the last voyage, is a most remarkable feature in the geography of this, or indeed of any other country; it may be compared to the valley of Lochness in Scotland, with its chain of lakes and friths. It is about one hundred and twenty miles long, with an average breadth, not subject to any very great variation, of about two miles; and it is throughout the greater part so perfectly straight, that the view, bounded on each side by a line of mountains, gradually becomes indistinct in the long distance. It crosses the southern part of Tierra del Fuego in an east and west line, and in the middle is joined at right angles on the south side by an irregular channel, which has been called Ponsonby Sound. This is the residence of Jemmy Button's tribe and family.

19th.—Three whale boats and the yawl, with a party of twenty-eight, started under the command of Captain Fitz Roy. In the afternoon we entered the eastern mouth of the channel, and shortly afterwards found a snug little cove concealed by some surrounding islets. Here we pitched our tents and lighted our fires. Nothing could look more comfortable than this scene. The glassy water of the little harbour, with the branches of the trees hanging over the rocky beach, the boats at anchor, the tents supported by the crossed oars, and the smoke curling up the wooded valley, formed a picture of quiet retirement. The next day (20th) we smoothly glided onwards in our little fleet, and came to a more inhabited district. Few if any of these natives could ever have seen a white man; certainly nothing could exceed their astonishment at the apparition of the four boats. Fires were lighted on every point (hence the name of Tierra del Fuego, or the land of fire), both to attract our attention and to spread far and wide the news. Some of the men ran for miles along the shore. I shall never forget how wild and savage one group appeared; suddenly four or five men came to the edge of an overhanging cliff; they were absolutely naked, and their long hair streamed about their faces; they held rugged staffs in their hands, and, springing from the ground, they waved their arms round their heads, and sent forth the most hideous yells.

At dinner-time we landed among a party of Fuegians. At first they were not inclined to be friendly; for until the Captain pulled in ahead of the other boats, they kept their slings in their hands. We soon, however, delighted them by trifling presents, such as tying red tape round their heads. They liked our biscuit; but one of the savages touched with his finger some of the meat preserved in tin cases which I was eating, and feeling it soft and cold, showed as much disgust at it, as I should have done at putrid blubber. Jemmy was thoroughly ashamed of his countrymen, and declared his own tribe were quite different, in which he was woefully mistaken. It was as easy to please as it was difficult to satisfy these savages. Young and old, men and children, never ceased repeating the word "yammer-schooner," which means "give me." After pointing to almost every object, one after the other, even to the buttons on our coats, and saying their favourite word in as many intonations as possible, they would then use it in a neuter sense, and vacantly repeat "yammer-schooner." After yammerschoonering for any article very eagerly, they would by a simple artifice point to their young women or little children, as much as to say, "If you will not give it to me, surely you will to such as these."

At night we endeavoured in vain to find an uninhabited cove; and at last were obliged to bivouac not far from a party of natives. They were very inoffensive as long as they were few in numbers, but in the morning (21st) being joined by the others they showed symptoms of hostility, and we thought that we should have come to a skirmish. An European labours under great disadvantages when treating with savages like these, who have not the least idea of the power of fire-arms. In the very act of levelling his musket he appears to the savage far inferior to a man armed with a bow and arrow, a spear, or even a sling. Nor is it easy to teach them our superiority except by striking a fatal blow. Like wild beasts, they do not appear to compare numbers; for each individual, if attacked, instead of retiring, will endeavour to dash your brains out with a stone, as certainly as a tiger under similar circumstances would tear you. Captain Fitz Roy on one occasion being very anxious, for good reasons, to frighten away a small party, first flourished a cutlass near them, at which they only laughed; he then twice fired his pistol close to a native. The man both times looked astounded, and carefully but quickly rubbed his head; he then stared awhile, and gabbled to his companions, but he never seemed to think of running away. We can hardly put ourselves in the position of these savages, and understand their actions. In the case of this Fuegian, the possibility of such as sound as the report of a gun close to his ear could never have entered his mind. He perhaps literally did not for a second know whether it was a sound or a blow, and therefore very naturally rubbed his head. In a similar manner, when a savage sees a mark struck by a bullet, it may be some time before he is able at all to understand how it is effected; for the fact of a body being invisible from its velocity would be to him an idea totally inconceivable. Moreover, the extreme force of a bullet, that it penetrates a hard substance without tearing it, may convince the savage that it has no force at all. Certainly I believe that many savages of the lowest grade, such as these of Tierra del Fuego, have seen objects struck, and even small animals killed by the musket, without being in the least aware how deadly an instrument it is.

22nd.—After having passed an unmolested night, in what would appear to be neutral territory between Jemmy's tribe and the people whom we saw yesterday, we sailed pleasantly along. I do not know anything which shows more clearly the hostile state of the different tribes, than these wide border or neutral tracts. Although Jemmy Button well knew the force of our party, he was, at first, unwilling to land amidst the hostile tribe nearest his own. He often told us how the savage Oens men "when the leaf red," crossed the mountains from the eastern coast of Tierra del Fuego, and made inroads on the natives of this part of the country. It was most curious to watch him when thus talking, and see his eyes gleaming and his whole face assume a new and wild expression. As we proceeded along the Beagle Channel, the scenery assumed a peculiar and very magnificent character; but the effect was much lessened from the lowness of the point of view in a boat, and from looking along the valley, and thus losing all the beauty of a succession of ridges. The mountains were here about three thousand feet high, and terminated in sharp and jagged points. They rose in one unbroken sweep from the water's edge, and were covered to the height of fourteen or fifteen hundred feet by the dusky-coloured forest. It was most curious to observe, as far as the eye could range, how level and truly horizontal the line on the mountain side was, at which trees ceased to grow; it precisely resembled the high-water mark of drift-weed on a sea-beach.

At night we slept close to the junction of Ponsonby Sound with the Beagle Channel. A small family of Fuegians, who were living in the cove, were quiet and inoffensive, and soon joined our party round a blazing fire. We were well clothed, and though sitting close to the fire were far from too warm; yet these naked savages, though further off, were observed, to our great surprise, to be streaming with perspiration at undergoing such a roasting. They seemed, however, very well pleased, and all joined in the chorus of the seamen's songs; but the manner in which they were invariably a little behind-hand was quite ludicrous.

During the night the news had spread, and early in the morning (23rd) a fresh party arrived, belonging to the Tekenika, or Jemmy's tribe. Several of them had run so fast that their noses were bleeding, and their mouths frothed from the rapidity with which they talked; and with their naked bodies all be-daubed with black, white, and red, they looked like so many demoniacs who had been fighting. We then proceeded (accompanied by twelve canoes, each holding four or five people) down Ponsonby Sound to the spot where poor Jemmy expected to find his mother and relatives. He had already heard that his father was dead; but as he had had a "dream in his head" to that effect, he did not seem to care much about it, and repeatedly comforted himself with the very natural reflection—"Me no help it." He was not able to learn any particulars regarding his father's death, as his relations would not speak about it.

Jemmy was now in a district well known to him, and guided the boats to a quiet pretty cove named Woollya, surrounded by islets, every one of which and every point had its proper native name. We found here a family of Jemmy's tribe, but not his relations; we made friends with them, and in the evening they sent a canoe to inform Jemmy's mother and brothers. The cover was bordered by some acres of good sloping land, not covered (as elsewhere) either by peat or by forest-trees. Captain Fitz Roy originally intended, as before stated, to have taken York Minister and Fuegia to their own tribe on the west coast; but as they expressed a wish to remain here, and as the spot was singularly favourable, Captain Fitz Roy determined to settle here the whole party, including Matthews, the missionary. Five days were spent in building for them three large wigwams, in landing their goods, in digging two gardens, and sowing seeds.

The next morning after our arrival (the 24th) the Fuegians began to pour in, and Jemmy's mother and brothers arrived. Jemmy recognized the stentorian voice of one of his brothers at a prodigious distance. The meeting was less interesting that that between a horse, turned out into a field, when he joins an old companion. There was no demonstration of affection; they simply stared for a short time at each other; and the mother immediately went to look after her canoe. We heard, however, through York that the mother has been inconsolable for the loss of Jemmy, and had searched everywhere for him, thinking that he might have been left after having been taken in the boat. The women took much notice of and were very kind to Fuegia. We had already perceived that Jemmy had almost forgotten his own language. I should think there was scarcely another human being with so small a stock of language, for his English was very imperfect. It was laughable, but almost pitiable, to hear him speak to his wild brother in English, and then ask him in Spanish ("no sabe?") whether he did not understand him.

Everything went on peaceably during the three next days, whilst the gardens were digging and wigwams building. We estimated the number of natives at about one hundred and twenty. The women worked hard, whilst the men lounged about all day long, watching us. They asked for everything they saw, and stole what they could. They were delighted at our dancing and singing, and were particularly interested at seeing us wash in a neighbouring brook; they did not pay much attention to anything else, not even our boats. Of all things which York saw, during his absence from his country, nothing seems more to have astonished him than an ostrich, near Maldonado; breathless with astonishment, he came running to Mr. Bynoe, with whom he was out walking—"Oh, Mr. Bynoe, oh, bird all same horse!" Much as our white skins surprised the natives, by Mr. Low's account a negro-cook to a sealing vessel, did so more effectually; and the poor fellow was so mobbed and shouted at that he would never go on shore again. Everything went on so quietly, that some of the officers and myself took long walks in the surrounding hills and woods. Suddenly, however, on the 27th, every woman and child disappeared. We were all uneasy at this, as neither York nor Jemmy could make out the cause. It was thought by some that they had been frightened by our cleaning and firing off our muskets on the previous evening; but others, that it was owing to offence taken by an old savage, who, when told to keep further off, had coolly spit in the sentry's face, and had then, by gestures acted over a sleeping Fuegian, plainly showed, as it was said, that he should like to cut up and eat our man. Captain Fitz Roy, to avoid the chance of an encounter, which would have been fatal to so many of the Fuegians, thought it advisable for us to sleep at a cove a few miles distant. Matthews, with his usual quiet fortitude (remarkable in a man apparently possessing little energy of character), determined to stay with the Fuegians, who evinced no alarm for themselves; and so we left them to pass their first awful night.

On our return in the morning (28th) we were delighted to find all quiet, and the men employed in their canoes spearing fish. Captain Fitz Roy determined to send the yawl and one whale-boat back to the ship; and to proceed with the two other boats, one under his own command (in which he most kindly allowed me to accompany him), and one under Mr. Hammond, to survey the western parts of the Beagle Channel, and afterwards to return and visit the settlement. The day to our astonishment was overpoweringly hot, so that our skins were scorched; and with this beautiful weather, the view in the middle of the Beagle Channel was very remarkable. Looking towards either hand, no object intercepted the vanishing points of this long canal between the mountains. The circumstance of its being an arm of the sea was rendered very evident by several huge whales spouting in different directions. On one occasion I saw two of these monsters, probably male and female, slowly swimming one after the other, within less than a stone's throw of the shore, over which the beech-tree extended its branches.

We sailed on till it was dark, and then pitched our tents in a quiet creek. The greatest luxury was to find for our beds a beach of pebbles, for they were dry and yielded to the body. Peaty soil is damp; rock is uneven and hard; sand gets into one's meat, when cooked and eaten boat-fashion; but when lying in our blanket-bags, on a good bed of smooth pebbles, we passed most comfortable nights.

It was my watch until one o'clock. There is something very solemn in these scenes. At no time does the consciousness in what a remote corner of the world you are then standing, come so strongly before the mind. Everything tends to this effect; the stillness of the night is interrupted only by the heavy breathing of the seamen beneath the tents, and sometimes by the cry of a night-bird. The occasional barking of a dog, heard in the distance, reminds one that it is the land of the savage.

January 29th.—Early in the morning we arrived at the point where the Beagle Channel divides into two arms; and we entered the northern one. The scenery here becomes even grander than before. The lofty mountains on the north side compose the granitic axis, or backbone of the country, and boldly rise to a height of between three and four thousand feet, with one peak above six thousand feet. They are covered by a wide mantle of perpetual snow, and numerous cascades pour their waters, through the woods, into the narrow channel below. In many parts, magnificent glaciers extend from the mountain side to the water's edge. It is scarcely possible to imagine anything more beautiful than the beryl-like blue of these glaciers, and especially as contrasted with the dead white of the upper expanse of snow. The fragments which had fallen from the glacier into the water were floating away, and the channel with its icebergs presented, for the space of a mile, a miniature likeness of the Polar Sea. The boats being hauled on shore at our dinner-hour, we were admiring from the distance of half a mile a perpendicular cliff of ice, and were wishing that some more fragments would fall. At last, down came a mass with a roaring noise, and immediately we saw the smooth outline of a wave travelling towards us. The men ran down as quickly as they could to the boats; for the chance of their being dashed to pieces was evident. One of the seamen just caught hold of the bows, as the curling breaker reached it; he was knocked over and over, but not hurt; and the boats, thought thrice lifted on high and let fall again, received no damage. This was most fortunate for us, for we were a hundred miles distant from the ship, and we should have been left without provisions or fire-arms. I had previously observed that some large fragments of rock on the beach had been lately displaced; but until seeing this wave, I did not understand the cause. One side of the creek was formed by a spur of mica-slate; the head by a cliff of ice about forty feet high; and the other side by a promontory fifty feet high, built up of huge rounded fragments of granite and mica-slate, out of which old trees were growing. This promontory was evidently a moraine, heaped up at a period when the glacier had greater dimensions.

When we reached the western mouth of this northern branch of the Beagle Channel, we sailed amongst many unknown desolate islands, and the weather was wretchedly bad. We met with no natives. The coast was almost everywhere so steep, that we had several times to pull many miles before we could find space enough to pitch our two tents; one night we slept on large round boulders, with putrefying seaweed between them; and when the tide rose, we had to get up and move our blanket-bags. The farthest point westward, which we reached was Stewart Island, a distance of about one hundred and fifty miles from our ship. We then returned into the Beagle Channel by the southern arm, and thence proceeded, with no adventure, back to Ponsonby Sound.

February 6ᵗʰ.—We arrived at Woollya. Matthews gave so bad an account of the conduct of the Fuegians, that Captain Fitz Roy determined to take him back to the Beagle; and ultimately he was left at New Zealand, where his brother was a missionary. From the time of our leaving, a regular system of plunder commenced; fresh parties of the natives kept arriving; York and Jemmy lost many things, and Matthews almost everything which had not been concealed underground. Every article seemed to have been torn up and divided by the natives. Matthews described the watch he was obliged always to keep as most harassing; night and day he was surrounded by the natives, who tried to tire him out by making an incessant noise close to his head. One day an old man, whom Matthews asked to leave his wigwam, immediately returned with a large stone in his hand; another day a whole party came armed with stones and stakes, and some of the younger men and Jemmy's brother were crying; Matthews met them with presents. Another party showed by signs that they wished to strip him naked and pluck all the hairs out of his face and body. I think we arrived just in time to save his life. Jemmy's relatives had been so vain and foolish, that they had showed to strangers their plunder, and their manner of obtaining it. It was quite melancholy leaving the three Fuegians with their savage countrymen, but it was a great comfort that they had no personal fears. York, being a powerful resolute man, was pretty sure to get on well, together with his wife Fuegia. Poor Jemmy looked rather disconsolate, and would then, I have little doubt, have been glad to have returned with us. His own brother had stolen many things from him; and as he remarked, "What fashion call that:" he abused his countrymen, "all bad men, no sabe (know) nothing," and though I had never heard him swear before, "damned fools." Our three Fuegians, though they had been only three years with civilized men, would, I am sure, have been glad to have retained their new habits; but this was obviously impossible. I fear it is more than doubtful, whether their visit will have been of any use to them.

In the evening, with Matthews on board, we made sail back to the ship, not by the Beagle Channel, but by the southern coast. The boats were heavily laden and the sea rough, and we had a dangerous passage. By the evening of the 7ᵗʰ we were on board the Beagle after an absence of twenty days, during which time we had gone three hundred miles in the open boats. On the 11ᵗʰ, Captain Fitz Roy paid a visit by himself to the Fuegians and found them going on well; and that they had lost very few more things.

On the last day of February in the succeeding year (1834), the Beagle anchored in a beautiful little cove at the eastern entrance of the Beagle Channel. Captain Fitz Roy determined on the bold, and as it proved successful, attempt to beat against the westerly winds by the same route, which we had followed in the boats to the settlement at Woollya. We did not see many natives until we were near Ponsonby Sound, where we were followed by ten or twelve canoes. The natives did not at all understand the reason of our tacking, and, instead of meeting us at each track, vainly strove to follow us in our zigzag course. I was amused at finding what a difference the circumstance of being quite superior in force made, in the interest of beholding these savages. While in the boats I got to hate the very sound of their voices, so much trouble did they give us. The first and last word was "yammer schooner." When, entering some quiet little cove, we have looked round and thought to pass a quiet night, the odious word "yammerschooner" has shrilly sounded from some gloomy nook, and then the little signal-smoke has curled up to spread the news far and wide. On leaving some place we have said to each other, "Thank Heaven, we have at last fairly left these wretches!" when one more faint hallo from an all-powerful voice, heard at a prodigious distance, would reach our ears, and clearly could we distinguish—"yammerschooner." But now, the more Fuegians the merrier; and very merry work it was. Both parties laughing, wondering, gaping at each other; we pitying them, for giving us good fish and crabs for rags, etc; they grasping at the chance of finding people so foolish as to exchange such splendid ornaments for a good supper. It was most amusing to see the undisguised smiles of satisfaction with which one young woman with her face painted black, tied several bits of scarlet cloth round her head with rushes. Her husband, who enjoyed the universal privilege in this country of possessing two wives, evidently became jealous of all the attention paid to his young wife; and, after a consultation with his naked beauties, was paddled away by them.

Some of the Fuegians plainly showed that they had a fair notion of barter. I gave one man a large nail (a most valuable present) without making any signs for a return; but he immediately picked out two fish, and handed them up on the point of his spear. If any present was designed for one canoe, and it fell near another, it was invariably given to the right owner. The Fuegian boy, whom Mr. Low had on board, showed, by going into the most violent passion, that he quite understood the reproach of being called a liar, which in truth he was. We were this time, as on all former occasions, much surprised at the little notice, or rather none whatever, which was taken of many things, the use of which must have been evident to the natives. Simple circumstances—such as the beauty of scarlet cloth or blue beads, the absence of women, our care in washing ourselves—excited their admiration far more than any grand or complicated object, such as our ship. Bougainville has well remarked concerning these people, that they treat the "chefs-d'oeuvre de l'industrie humaine, comme ils traitent les loix de la nature et ses phénomènes."

On the 5th of March, we anchored in a cove at Woollya, but we saw not a soul there. We were alarmed at this, for the natives in Ponsonby Sound showed by gestures, that there had been fighting; and we afterwards heard that the dreaded Oens men had made a descent. Soon a canoe, with a little flag flying, was seen approaching, with one of the men in it washing the paint off his face. This man was poor Jemmy—now a thin, haggard savage, with long disordered hair, and naked, except a bit of blanket round his waist. We did not recognize him till he was close to us, for he was ashamed of himself, and turned his back to the ship. We had left him plump, fat, clean, and well-dressed—I never saw so complete and grievous a change. As soon, however, as he was clothed, and the first flurry was over, things wore a good appearance. He dined with Captain Fitz Roy, and ate his dinner as tidily as formerly. He told us that he had "too much" (meaning enough) to eat, that he was not cold, that his relations were very good people, and that he did not wish to go back to England; in the evening we found out the cause of this great change in Jemmy's feelings, in the arrival of his young and nice-looking wife. With his usual good feeling, he brought two beautiful otter-skins for two of his best friends, and some spear-heads and arrows made with his own hands for the Captain. He said he had built a canoe for himself, and he boasted that he could talk a little of his own language! But it is a most singular fact, that he appears to have taught all his tribe some English; an old man spontaneously announced "Jemmy Button's wife." Jemmy had lost all his property. He told us that York Minister had built a large canoe, and with his wife Fuegia had several months since gone to his own country, and had taken farewell by an act of consummate villainy; he persuaded Jemmy and his mother to come with him, and then on the way deserted them by night, stealing every article of their property.

Jemmy went to sleep on shore, and in the morning returned, and remained on board till the ship got under way, which frightened his wife, who continued crying violently till he got into his canoe. He returned loaded with valuable property. Every soul on board was heartily sorry to shake hands with him for the last time. I do not now doubt that he will be as happy as, perhaps happier than, if he had never left his own country. Everyone must sincerely hope that Captain Fitz Roy's noble hope may be fulfilled, of being rewarded for the many generous sacrifices which he made for these Fuegians, by some shipwrecked sailor being protected by the descendants of Jemmy Button and his tribe! When Jemmy reached shore, he lighted a signal fire, and the smoke curled up, bidding us a last and long farewell, as the ship stood on her course into the open sea.

The perfect equality among the individuals composing the Fuegian tribes must for a long time retard their civilization. As we see those animals, whose instinct compels them to live in society and obey a chief, are most capable of improvement, so is it with the races of mankind. Whether we look at it as a cause or a consequence, the more civilized always have the most artificial governments. For instance, the inhabitants of Otaheite, who, when first discovered, were governed by hereditary kings, had arrived at a far higher grade than another branch of the same people, the New Zealanders,—who, although benefited by being compelled to turn their attention to agriculture, were republicans in the most absolute sense. In Tierra del Fuego, until some chief shall arise with power sufficient to secure any acquired advantage, such as the domesticated animals, it seems scarcely possible that the political state of the country can be improved. At present, even a piece of cloth given to one is torn into shreds and distributed; and no one individual becomes richer than another. On the other hand, it is difficult to understand how a chief can arise till there is property of some sort by which he might manifest his superiority and increase his power.

I believe, in this extreme part of South America, man exists in a lower state of improvement than in any other part of the world. The South Sea Islanders, of the two races inhabiting the Pacific, are comparatively civilized. The Esquimau in his subterranean hut, enjoys some of the comforts of life, and in his canoe, when fully equipped, manifests much skill. Some of the tribes of Southern Africa, prowling about in search of roots, and living concealed on the wild and acrid plains, are sufficiently wretched. The Australian, in the simplicity of the arts of life, comes nearest the Fuegian; he can, however, boast of his boomerang, his spear and throwing-stick, his method of climbing trees, of tracking animals, and of hunting. Although the Australian may be superior in acquirements, it by no means follows that he is likewise superior in mental capacity; indeed, from what I saw of the Fuegians when on board, and from what I have read of the Australians, I should think the case was exactly the reverse.

Climbing Fremont Peak

BY JOHN CHARLES FREMONT

Although his star has now faded, John Charles Fremont was one of the most famous men in America in the mid- to late 1800s, chiefly due to his four major surveys of western travel routes. The government reports he filed detailing a beautiful, uninhabited territory just waiting for white settlers were widely read by the public and inspired many families to try their fortune in the Far West.

His first major expedition in 1842 was to explore new routes from the Mississippi to South Pass, Wyoming, where settlers crossed the Rocky Mountains. Famous scout Kit Carson accompanied the expedition as guide. A side trip during this journey led Fremont to climb what would be named Fremont Peak in the rugged Wind River Range of Wyoming. Although he mistakenly thought it the highest peak in the Rockies, it was still a major mountaineering accomplishment at the time, and his enthusiasm for the pristine, wild country was infectious.

★　★　★　★　★

1 0th.—The air at sunrise is clear and pure, and the morning extremely cold, but beautiful. A lofty snowy peak of the mountain is glittering in the first rays of the sun, which have not yet reached us. The long mountain wall to the east, rising two thousand feet abruptly from the plain, behind which we see the peaks, is still dark, and cuts clear against the glowing sky. A fog, just risen from the river, lies along the base of the mountain. A little before sunrise, the thermometer was at 35°, and at sunrise 33°. Water froze last night, and fires are very comfortable. The scenery becomes hourly more interesting and grand, and the view here is truly magnificent; but, indeed, it needs something to repay the long prairie journey of a thousand miles. The sun has shot above the wall, and makes a magical change. The whole valley is glowing and bright, and all the mountain peaks are gleaming like silver. Though these

snow mountains are not the Alps, they have their own character of grandeur and magnificence, and doubtless will find pens and pencils to do them justice. In the scene before us, we feel how much wood improves a view. The pines on the mountains seemed to give it much additional beauty. I was agreeably disappointed in the character of the streams on this side of the ridge. Instead of the creeks, which description had led me to expect, I find bold, broad streams, with three or four feet water, and a rapid current. The fork on which we are encamped is upwards of a hundred feet wide, timbered with groves or thickets of the low willow. We were now approaching the loftiest part of the Wind River chain; and I left the valley a few miles from our encampment, intending to penetrate the mountains as far as possible with the whole party. We were soon involved in very broken ground, among low ridges covered with fragments of granite. Winding our way up a long ravine, we came unexpectedly in view of a most beautiful lake, set like a gem in the mountains. The sheet of water lay transversely across the direction we had been pursuing; and, descending the steep, rocky ridge, where it was necessary to lead our horses, we followed its banks to the southern extremity. Here a view of the utmost magnificence and grandeur burst upon our eyes. With nothing between us and their feet to lessen the effect of the whole height, a grand bed of snow-capped mountains rose before us, pile upon pile, glowing in the bright light of an August day. Immediately below them lay the lake, between two ridges, covered with dark pines, which swept down from the main chain to the spot where we stood. Here, where the lake glittered in the open sunlight, its banks of yellow sand and the light foliage of aspen groves contrasted well with the gloomy pines. "Never before," said Mr. Preuss, "in this country or in Europe, have I seen such grand, magnificent rocks." I was so much pleased with the beauty of the place, that I determined to make the main camp here, where our animals would find good pasturage, and explore the mountains with a small party of men. Proceeding a little further, we came suddenly upon the outlet of the lake, where it found its way through a narrow passage between low hills. Dark pines which overhung the stream, and masses of rock, where the water foamed along, gave it much romantic beauty. Where we crossed, which was immediately at the outlet, it is two hundred and fifty feet wide, and so deep that with difficulty we were able to ford it. Its bed was an accumulation of rocks, boulders, and broad slabs, and large angular fragments, among which the animals fell repeatedly.

The current was very swift, and the water cold, and of a crystal purity. In crossing this stream, I met with a great misfortune in having my barometer broken. It was the only one. A great part of the interest of the journey for me was in the exploration of these mountains, of which so much had been said

that was doubtful and contradictory; and now their snowy peaks rose majesti-
cally before me, and the only means of giving them authentically to science,
the object of my anxious solicitude by night and day, was destroyed. We had
brought this barometer in safety a thousand miles, and broke it almost among
the snow of the mountains. The loss was felt by the whole camp—all had seen
my anxiety, and aided me in preserving it. The height of these mountains, considered by many hunters and traders the highest in the whole range, had been a
theme of constant discussion among them; and all had looked forward with
pleasure to the moment when the instrument, which they believed to be as
true as the sun, should stand upon the summits, and decide their disputes. Their
grief was only inferior to my own.

The lake is about three miles long, and of very irregular width, and
apparently great depth, and is the headwater of the third New Fork a tributary to Green river, the Colorado of the west. In the narrative I have called it
Mountain lake. I encamped on the north side, about three hundred and fifty
yards from the outlet. This was the most western point at which I obtained astronomical observations, by which this place, called Bernier's encampment, is
made in 110° 08' 03" west longitude from Greenwich, and latitude 43° 49'
49". The mountain peaks, as laid down, were fixed by bearings from this and
other astronomical points. We had no other compass than the small ones used
in sketching the country; but from an azimuth, in which one of them was
used, the variation of the compass is 18° east. The correction made in our
field work by the astronomical observations indicates that this is a very correct observation.

As soon as the camp was formed, I set about endeavoring to repair my
barometer. As I have already said, this was a standard cistern barometer, of
Troughton's construction. The glass cistern had been broken about midway;
but as the instrument had been kept in a proper position, no air had found its
way into the tube, the end of which had always remained covered. I had with
me a number of vials of tolerably thick glass, some of which were of the same
diameter as the cistern, and I spent the day in slowly working on these, endeavoring to cut them of the requisite length; but, as my instrument was a very
rough file, I invariably broke them. A groove was cut in one of the trees, where
the barometer was placed during the night, to be out of the way of any possible danger, and in the morning I commenced again. Among the powder-
horns in the camp, I found one which was very transparent, so that its contents
could be almost as plainly seen as through glass. This I boiled and stretched on
a piece of wood to the requisite diameter, and scraped it very thin, in order to
increase to the utmost its transparency. I then secured it firmly in its place on

the instrument, with strong glue made from a buffalo, and filled it with mercury, properly heated. A piece of skin, which had covered one of the vials, furnished a good pocket, which was well secured with strong thread and glue, and then the brass cover was screwed to its place. The instrument was left some time to dry; and when I reversed it, a few hours after, I had the satisfaction to find it in perfect order; its indications being about the same as on the other side of the lake before it had been broken. Our success in this little incident diffused pleasure throughout the camp; and we immediately set about our preparations for ascending the mountains.

As will be seen on reference to a map, on this short mountain chain are the head-waters of four great rivers on the continent, namely the Colorado, Columbia, Missouri, and Platte rivers. I had been my design, after ascending the mountains, to continue our route on the western side of the range, crossing through a pass at the northwestern end of the chain, about thirty miles from our present camp, return along the eastern slope, across the head of the Yellowstone river, and join on the line to our station of August 7, immediately at the foot of the ridge. In this way, I should be enabled to include the whole chain, and its numerous waters, in my survey; but various considerations induced me, very reluctantly, to abandon this plan.

I was desirous to keep strictly within the scope of my instructions, and it would have required ten or fifteen additional days for the accomplishment of this object; our animals had become very much worn out with the length of the journey; game was very scarce; and though it does not appear in the course of the narrative (as I have avoided dwelling upon trifling incidents not connected with the objects of the expedition), the spirits of the men had been much exhausted by the hardships and privations to which they had been subjected. Our provisions had wellnigh all disappeared. Bread had been long out of the question; and of all our stock, we had remaining two or three pounds of coffee, and a small quantity of macaroni, which had been husbanded with great care for the mountain expedition we were about to undertake. Our daily meal consisted of dry buffalo meat, cooked in tallow; and, as we had not dried this with Indian skill, part of it was spoiled; and what remained of good, was as hard as wood, having much the taste and appearance of so many pieces of bark. Even of this, our stock was rapidly diminishing in a camp which was capable of consuming two buffaloes in every twenty-four hours. These animals had entirely disappeared; and it was not probable that we should fall in with them again until we returned to the Sweet Water.

Our arrangements for the ascent were rapidly completed. We were in hostile country, which rendered the greatest vigilance and circumspection necessary. The pass at the north end of the mountain was greatly infested by Black-feet, and immediately opposite was one of their forts, on the edge of a little thicket, two or three hundred feet from our encampment. We were posted in a grove of beech, on the margin of the lake, and a few hundred feet long, with a narrow *prairillon* on the inner side, bordered by the rocky ridge. In the upper end of this grove we cleared a circular space about forty feet in diameter, and, with the felled timber, and interwoven branches, surrounded it with a breast-work five feet in height. A gap was left for a gate on the inner side, by which the animals were to be driven in and secured, while the men slept around the little work. It was half hidden by the foliage, and garrisoned by twelve resolute men, would have set at defiance any band of savages which might chance to discover them in the interval of our absence. Fifteen of the best mules, with fourteen men, were selected for the mountain party. Our provisions consisted of dried meat for two days, with our little stock of coffee and some macaroni. In addition to the barometer and thermometer, I took with me a sextant and spyglass, and we had of course our compasses. In charge of the camp I left Bernier, one of my most trustworthy men, who possessed the most determined courage.

12th.—Early in the morning we left the camp, fifteen in number, well armed, of course, and mounted on our best mules. A pack-animal carried our provisions, with a coffeepot and kettle, and three or four tin cups. Every man had a blanket strapped over his saddle, to serve for his bed, and the instruments were carried by turns on their backs. We entered directly on rough and rocky ground; and, just after crossing the ridge, had the good fortune to shoot an antelope. We heard the roar, and had a glimpse of a waterfall as we rode along, and, crossing in our way two fine streams, tributary to the Colorado, in about two hours' ride we reached the top of the first row or range of the mountains. Here, again, a view of the most romantic beauty met our eyes. It seemed as if, from the vast expanse of uninteresting prairie we had passed over, Nature had collected all her beauties together in one chosen place. We were overlooking a deep valley, which was entirely occupied by three lakes, and from the brink to the surrounding ridges rose precipitously five hundred and a thousand feet, covered with the dark green of the balsam pine, relieved on the border of the lake with the light foliage of the aspen. They all communicated with each other, and the green of the waters, common to mountain lakes of great depth, showed that it would be impossible to cross them. The surprise manifested by our guides when these impassable obstacles suddenly barred our progress, proved that they were among the hidden treasures of the place, unknown even to the wandering trappers of the region. Descending the hill, we proceeded to make our way along the margin to the southern extremity. A narrow strip of angular fragments of rock sometimes afforded a rough pathway for our mules, but generally we rode along the shelving side, occasionally scrambling up, at a considerable risk of tumbling back into the lake.

The slope was frequently 60°; the pines grew densely together, and the ground was covered with the branches and trunks of trees. The air was fragrant with the odor of the pines; and I realized this delightful morning the pleasure of breathing that mountain air which makes a constant theme of the hunter's praise, and which now made us feel as if we had all been drinking some exhilarating gas. The depths of this unexplored forest were a place to delight the heart of a botanist. There was a rich undergrowth of plants, and numerous gay-colored flowers in brilliant bloom. We reached the outlet at length, where some freshly-barked willows that lay in the water showed that beaver had been recently at work. There were some small brown squirrels jumping about in the pines, and a couple of large mallard ducks swimming about in the stream.

The hills on this southern end were low, and the lake looked like a mimic sea, as the waves broke on the sandy beach in the force of a strong breeze. There was a pretty open spot, with fine grass for our mules; and we made our noon halt on the beach, under the shade of some large hemlocks. We resumed our journey after a halt of about an hour making our way up a ridge on the western side of the lake. In search of smoother ground, we rode a little inland; and, passing through groves of aspen, soon found ourselves again among the pines. Emerging from these, we struck the summit of the ridge above the upper end of the lake.

We had reached a very elevated point, and in the valley below, and among the hills, were a number of lakes of different levels, some two or three hundred feet above others, with which they communicated by foaming torrents. Even to our great height the roar of the cataracts came up, and we could see them leaping down in lines of snowy foam. From this scene of busy waters, we turned abruptly into the stillness of a forest, where we rode among the open bolls of the pines, over a lawn of verdant grass, having strikingly the air of cultivated grounds. This led us, after a time, among masses of rock which had no vegetable earth but in hollows and crevices though still the pine forest continued. Towards evening we reached a defile, or rather a hole in the mountains, entirely shut in by dark pine-covered rocks.

A small stream, with scarcely perceptible current, flowed through a level bottom of perhaps eighty yards width, where the grass was saturated with water. Into this the mules were turned, and were neither hobbled nor picketed during the night, as the fine pasturage took away all intention to stray; and we made our bivouac in the pines. The surrounding masses were all of granite.

While supper was being prepared, I set out on an excursion in the neighborhood, accompanied by one of my men. We wandered about among the crags and ravines until dark, richly repaid for our walk by a fine collection of plants, many of them in full bloom. Ascending a peak to find the place of our camp, we saw that the little defile in which we lay communicated with the long green valley of some stream, which, here locked up in the mountains, far away to the south, found its way in a dense forest to the plains.

Looking along its upward course, it seemed to conduct, by a smooth gradual slope, directly towards the peak, which, from long consultation as we approached the mountain, we had decided to be the highest of the range. Pleased with the discovery of so fine a road for the next day, we hastened down to the camp, where we arrived just in time for supper. Our table-service was rather scant; and we held the meat in our hands, and clean rocks made good plates, on which we spread our macaroni. Among all the strange places on which we had occasion to encamp during our long journey, none has left so vivid an impression on my mind as the camp of this evening. The disorder of the masses which surrounded us—the little hole through which we saw the stars over head—the dark pines where we slept—and the rocks lit up with the glow of our fires, made a night-picture of very wild beauty.

13th.—The morning was bright and pleasant, just cool enough to make exercise agreeable, and we soon entered the defile I had seen the preceding day. It was smoothly carpeted with soft grass, and scattered over with groups of flowers, of which yellow was the predominant color. Sometimes we were forced, by an occasional difficult pass, to pick our way on a narrow ledge along the side of the defile, and the mules were frequently on their knees; but these obstructions were rare, and we journeyed on in the sweet morning air, delighted at our good fortune in having found such a beautiful entrance to the mountains. This road continued for about three miles, when we suddenly reached its termination in one of the grand views which, at every turn, meet the traveler in this magnificent region. Here the defile up which we had traveled opened out into a small lawn, where, in a little lake, the stream had its source.

There were some fine *asters* in bloom, but all the flowering plants appeared to seek the shelter of the rocks, and to be of lower growth than below, as if they loved the warmth of the soil, and kept out of the way of the winds. Immediately at our feet, a precipitous descent led to a confusion of defiles, and before us rose the mountains, as we have represented them in the annexed view. It is not by the splendor of far off views, which have lent such a glory to the Alps, that these impress the mind; but by a gigantic disorder of enormous masses, and a savage sublimity of naked rock, in wonderful contrast with innumerable green spots of a rich floral beauty, shut up in their stern recesses. Their wildness seems well suited to the character of the people who inhabit the country.

I determined to leave our animals here, and make the rest of our way on foot. The peak appeared so near, that there was no doubt of our returning before night; and a few men were left in charge of the mules, with our provisions and blankets. We took with us nothing but our arms and instruments, and, as the day had become warm, the greater part left our coats. Having made an early dinner, we started again. We were soon involved in the most ragged precipices, nearing the central chain very slowly, and rising but little. The first ridge hid a succession of others; and when, with great fatigue and difficulty, we had climbed up five hundred feet, it was but to make an equal descent on the other side; all these intervening places were filled with small deep lakes, which met the eye in every direction, descending from one level to another, sometimes under bridges formed by huge fragments of granite, beneath which was heard the roar of the water. These constantly obstructed our path, forcing us to make long détours; frequently obliged to retrace our steps, and frequently falling among the rocks. Maxwell was precipitated towards the face of a precipice, and saved himself from going over by throwing himself flat on the ground. We clambered on, always expecting, with every ridge that we crossed, to reach the foot of the peaks, and always disappointed, until about four o'clock, when, pretty well worn out, we reached the shore of a little lake, in which was a rocky island. We remained here a short time to rest, and continued on around the lake, which had in some places a beach of white sand, and in others was bound with rocks, over which the way was difficult and dangerous, as the water from innumerable springs made them very slippery.

By the time we had reached the farther side of the lake, we found ourselves all exceedingly fatigued, and, much to the satisfaction of the whole party, we encamped. The spot we had chosen was a broad flat rock, in some measure protected from the winds by the surrounding crags, and the trunks of fallen trees afforded us bright fires. Nearby was a foaming torrent, which tumbled into the little lake about one hundred and fifty feet below us, and which, by way of distinction, we have called Island lake. We had reached the upper limit of the piney region; as, above this point, no tree was to be seen, and patches of snow lay everywhere around us, on the cold sides of the rocks. The flora of the region we had traversed since leaving our mules was extremely rich, and, among the characteristic plants, the scarlet flowers of the *dodecatheon dentatum* everywhere met the eye, in great abundance. A small green ravine, on the edge of which we were encamped, was filled with a profusion of alpine plants, in brilliant bloom. From barometrical observations, made during our three days' sojourn at this place, its elevation above the Gulf of Mexico is 10,000 feet. During the day, we had seen no sign of animal life; but among the rocks here, we heard what was supposed to be the bleat of a young goat, which we searched for with hungry activity, and found to proceed from a small animal of a gray color, with short ears and no tail—probably the Siberian squirrel. We saw a considerable number of them, and, with the exception of a small bird like a sparrow, it is the only inhabitant of this elevated part of the mountains. On our return, we saw, below this lake, large flocks of the mountain goat. We had nothing to eat to-night. Lajeunesse, with several others, took their guns, and sallied out in search of a goat; but returned unsuccessful. At sunset, the barometer stood at 20.522, the attached thermometer 50°. Here we had the misfortune to break our thermometer, having now only that attached to the barometer. I was taken ill shortly after we had encamped, and continued so until late in the night, with violent headache and vomiting. This was probably caused by the excessive fatigue I had undergone, and want of food, and perhaps, also, in some measure, by the rarity of the air. The night was cold, as a violent gale from the north had sprung up at sunset, which entirely blew away the heat of the fires. The cold, and our granite beds, had not been favorable to sleep, and we were glad to see the face of the sun in the morning. Not being delayed by any preparation for breakfast, we set out immediately.

On every side, as we advanced, was heard the roar of waters, and of a torrent, which we followed up a short distance, until it expanded into a lake about one mile in length. On the northern side of the lake was a bank of ice, or rather of snow covered with a crust of ice. Carson had been our guide into the mountains, and, agreeably to his advice, we left this little valley and took to the ridges again, which we found extremely broken, and where we were again involved among precipices. Here were ice fields; among which we were all dispersed, seeking each the best path to ascend the peak. Mr. Preuss attempted to walk along the upper edge of one of these fields, which sloped away at an angle of about twenty degrees; but his feet slipped from under him, and he went plunging down the plain. A few hundred feet below, at the bottom, were some fragments of sharp rock, on which he landed; and though he turned a couple of somersets, fortunately received no injury beyond a few bruises. Two of the men, Clement Lambert and Descoteaux, had been taken ill, and lay down on the rocks, a short distance below; and at this point I was attacked with headache and giddiness, accompanied by vomiting, as on the day before. Finding myself unable to proceed, I sent the barometer over to Mr. Preuss, who was in a gap two or three hundred yards distant, desiring him to reach the peak if possible, and take an observation there. He found himself unable to proceed further in that direction, and took an observation, where the barometer stood at 19.401 attached thermometer 50° in the gap. Carson, who had gone over to him, succeeded in reaching one of the snowy summits of the main ridge, whence he saw the peak towards which all our efforts had been directed, towering eight or ten hundred feet into the air above him. In the meantime, finding myself grow rather worse than better, and doubtful how far my strength would carry me, I sent Basil Lajeunesse, with four men, back to the place where the mules had been left.

We were now better acquainted with the topography of the country, and I directed him to bring back with him, if it were in any way possible, four or five mules, with provisions and blankets. With me were Maxwell and Ayer; and after we had remained nearly an hour on the rock, it became so unpleasantly cold, though the day was bright, that we set out on our return to the camp, at which we all arrived safely, straggling in one after the other. I continued ill during the afternoon, but became better towards sundown, when my recovery was completed by the appearance of Basil and four men, all mounted. The men who had gone with him had been too much fatigued to return, and were relieved by those in charge of the horses; but in his powers of endurance Basil resembled more a mountain-goat than a man. They brought blankets and provisions, and we all enjoyed our dried meat and a cup of good coffee. We rolled ourselves up in our blankets, and, with our feet turned to a blazing fire, slept soundly until morning.

15th.—It had been supposed that we had finished with the mountains; and the evening before it had been arranged that Carson should set out at daylight, and return to breakfast at the Camp of the Mules, taking with him all but four or five men, who were to stay with me and bring back the mules and instruments. Accordingly, at the break of day they set out. With Mr. Preuss and myself remained Basil Lajeunesse, Clement Lambert, Janisse, and Descoteaux. When we had secured strength for the day by a hearty breakfast, we covered what remained, which was enough for one meal, with rocks, in order that it might be safe from any marauding bird, and, saddling our mules, turned our faces once more towards the peaks. This time we determined to proceed quietly and cautiously, deliberately resolved to accomplish our object if it were within the compass of human means. We were of opinion that a long defile which lay to the left of yesterday's route would lead us to the foot of the main peak. Our mules had been refreshed by the fine grass in the little ravine at the Island camp, and we intended to ride up the defile as far as possible, in order to husband our strength for the main ascent. Though this was a fine passage, still it was a defile of the most rugged mountains known, and we had many a rough and steep slippery place to cross before reaching the end. In this place the sun rarely shone; snow lay along the border of the small stream which flowed through it, and occasional icy passages made the footing of the mules very insecure, and the rocks and ground were moist with the trickling waters in this spring of mighty rivers. We soon had the satisfaction to find ourselves riding along the huge wall which forms the central summits of the chain. There at last it rose by our sides, a nearly perpendicular wall of granite, terminating 2,000 to 3,000 feet above our heads in a serrated line of broken, jagged cones. We rode on until we came almost immediately below the main peak, which I denominated the Snow peak, as it exhibited more snow to the eye than any of the neighboring summits. Here were three small lakes of a green color, each, perhaps, of a thousand yards in diameter, and apparently very deep. These lay in a kind of chasm; and, according to the barometer, we had attained but a few hundred feet above the Island lake. The barometer here stood at 20.450, attached thermometer 70°.

We managed to get our mules up to a little bench about a hundred feet above the lakes, where there was a patch of good grass, and turned them loose to graze. During our rough ride to this place, they had exhibited a wonderful surefootedness. Parts of the defile were filled with angular, sharp fragments of rock, three or four and eight or ten feet cube; and among those they had worked their way, leaping from one narrow point to another, rarely making a false step, and giving us no occasion to dismount. Having divested ourselves of every unnecessary encumbrance, we commenced the ascent. This time, like experienced travelers, we did not press ourselves, but climbed leisurely, sitting down so soon as we found breath beginning to fail. At intervals we reached places where a number of springs gushed from the rocks, and about 1,800 feet above the lakes came to the snow line. From this point our progress was uninterrupted climbing. Hitherto I had worn a pair of thick moccasins, with soles of *parflèche*, but here I put on a light, thin pair, which I had brought for the purpose, as now the use of our toes became necessary to a further advance. I availed myself of a sort of comb of the mountain, which stood against the wall like a buttress, and which the wind and the solar radiation, joined to the steepness of the smooth rock, had kept almost entirely free from snow. Up this I made my way rapidly. Our cautious method of advancing at the outset had spared my strength; and, with the exception of a slight disposition to headache, I felt no remains of yesterday's illness. In a few minutes we reached a point where the buttress was overhanging, and there was no other way of surmounting the difficulty than by passing around one side of it, which was the face of a vertical precipice of several hundred feet.

Putting hands and feet in the crevices between the blocks, I succeeded in getting over it, and, when I reached the top, found my companions in a small valley below. Descending to them, we continued climbing, and in a short time reached the crest. I sprang upon the summit, and another step would have precipitated me into an immense snow-field five hundred feet below. To the edge of this field was a sheer icy precipice; and then, with a gradual fall, the field sloped off for about a mile, until it struck the foot of another lower ridge. I stood on a narrow crest, about three feet in width, with an inclination of about 20° N. 51° E. As soon as I had gratified the first feelings of curiosity, I descended, and each man ascended in his turn; for I would only allow one at a time to mount the unstable and precarious slab, which it seemed a breath would hurl into the abyss below. We mounted the barometer in the snow of the summit, and, fixing a ramrod in a crevice, unfurled the national flag to wave in the breeze where never a flag waved before. During our morning's ascent, we had met no sign of animal life, except the small sparrow-like bird already mentioned. A stillness the most profound and a terrible solitude forced themselves constantly on the mind as the great features of the place. Here, on the summit, where the stillness was absolute, unbroken by any sound, and solitude complete, we thought ourselves beyond the region of animated life; but while we were sitting on the rock, a solitary bee (*bromus, the humble-bee*) came winging his flight from the eastern valley, and lit on the knee of one of the men.

It was a strange place, the ice rock and the highest peak of the Rocky mountains, for a lover of warm sunshine and flowers; and we pleased ourselves with the idea that he was the first of his species to cross the mountain barrier—a solitary pioneer to foretell the advance of civilization. I believe that a moment's thought would have made us let him continue his way unharmed; but we carried out the law of this country, where all animated nature seems at war; and, seizing him immediately, put him in at least a fit place—in the leaves of a large book, among the flowers we had collected on our way. The barometer stood at 18.293, the attached thermometer at 44°, giving for the elevation of this summit 13,570 feet above the Gulf of Mexico, which may be called the highest flight of the bee. It is certainly the highest known flight of that insect. From the description given by Mackenzie of the mountains where he crossed them, with that of a French officer still farther to the north, and Colonel Long's measurements to the south, joined to the opinion of the oldest traders of the country, it is presumed that this is the highest peak of the Rocky mountains. The day was sunny and bright, but a slight shining mist hung over the lower plains, which interfered with our view of the surrounding country. On one side we overlooked innumerable lakes and streams, the spring of the

Colorado of the Gulf of California; and on the other was the Wind River valley, where were the heads of the Yellowstone branch of the Missouri; far to the north, we could just discover the snowy heads of the *Trois Tetons*, where were the sources of the Missouri and Columbia rivers; and at the southern extremity of the ridge, the peaks were plainly visible, among which were some of the springs of the Nebraska or Platte river. Around us, the whole scene had one main, striking feature, which was that of terrible convulsion. Parallel to its length, the ridge was split into chasms and fissures; between which rose the thin lofty walls, terminated with slender minarets and columns. According to the barometer, the little crest of the wall on which we stood was three thousand five hundred and seventy feet above that place, and two thousand seven hundred and eighty above the little lakes at the bottom, immediately at our feet. Our camp at the Two Hills (an astronomical station) bore south 3° east, which, with a bearing afterwards obtained from a fixed position, enabled us to locate the peak. The bearing of the *Trois Tetons* was north 50° west, and the direction of the central ridge of the Wind River mountains south 39° east. The summit rock was gneiss, succeeded by sienitic gneiss. Sienite and feldspar succeeded in our descent to the snow line, where we found a feldspathic granite. I had remarked that the noise produced by the explosion of our pistols had the usual degree of loudness, but was not in the least prolonged, expiring almost instantaneously.

Having now made what observations our means afforded, we proceeded to descend. We had accomplished an object of laudable ambition, and beyond the strict order of our instructions. We had climbed the loftiest peak of the Rocky mountains, and looked down upon the snow a thousand feet below; and, standing where never human foot had stood before, felt the exultation of first explorers. It was about two o'clock when we left the summit, and when we reached the bottom, the sun had already sunk behind the wall, and the day was drawing to a close. It would have been pleasant to have lingered here and on the summit longer; but we hurried away as rapidly as the ground would permit, for it was an object to regain our party as soon as possible, not knowing what accident the next hour might bring forth.

We reached our deposit of provisions at nightfall. Here was not the inn which await the tired traveler on his return from Mont Blanc, or the orange groves of South America, with their refreshing juices and soft fragrant air; but we found our little *cache* of dried meat and coffee undisturbed. Though the moon was bright, the road was full of precipices, and the fatigue of the day had been great. We therefore abandoned the idea of rejoining our friends, and lay down on the rock, and, in spit of the cold, slept soundly.

The Strain Expedition

BY J.T. HEADY

For better or worse, it is often exploring disasters that makes the most compelling reading. One of the most bizarre disasters occurred in 1853, when Lt. Isaac Strain was attempting to lead a small party of American soldiers over the Isthmus of Darien in Central America in an early search for a canal route to link the Atlantic and Pacific Oceans.

The location was based on an Irish adventurer's book, in which he claimed to have crossed the jungle from coast to coast in just three or four relatively easy miles. British capitalists, backed by several governments, including England and America, then sent a professional engineer to survey the supposed route. He returned and published his own book, complete with a mapped route, claiming it was indeed a light journey. He even claimed to have marked the route with blazes on trees. Unfortunately, neither of the men had gone more than a mile or two inland. One simply perpetuated the lie of the other, causing the deaths of several men on the exploring expedition that followed.

Based on these two accounts, the British sent a team in from the Pacific while America sent Strain and company in from the Atlantic. The British team traveled through over 25 miles of dense jungle before retreating just in time to save themselves. The Americans, hale and hearty and outfitted with just ten days of provisions, did not retreat. As they penetrated into the heart of the jungle, they realized that something was amiss, but decided to forge ahead anyway, as they assumed the Pacific was not far off. Soon, their clothes were in tatters, most were ill, and their provisions were gone. The jungle climate had also rusted their firearms, making them next to useless for procuring game. With the main party too ill and exhausted to travel, Strain and three companions set off to complete the trip and bring back help for the others.

★　★　★　★　★

I will now transfer the course of the narrative to the proceedings of the advanced party, which left the main body on the 13th of February.

Breakfastless, but full of hope, the four adventurers set out, and after making a détour in the forest to avoid undergrowth, again struck the river, where the walking was good. Truxton's camp was in sight, and Strain hailed it to bid the party keep the bank. Following this bank until it became scarped and impassable, they took to the forest, and although still attempting to keep the river in sight, were at length forced from it by the denseness of the undergrowth. After an hour's journey they saw the river again close upon their right, and supposing that it was a sudden bend, regained the bank, which was clear and sloping, and followed it for nearly a quarter of a mile, when they found by their old trail that it was the same ground they had already passed over, the river having made a turn upon itself. This was very discouraging at the outset; and hearing the voices of the main body ahead, already following on, and unwilling to discourage them in their march, Strain struck into the forest, and making a wide détour, regained the river, and by rapid traveling left them far behind.

About noon they halted for an hour to allow Mr. Avery to rest, but, with that exception, marched steadily during the day, and made about fifteen miles on the course of the river. At dark they encamped, and kindling a fire to intimidate wild beasts and keep off alligators, laid down to sleep. With so small a party, and traveling rapidly, they did not think it worthwhile to appoint a watch.

The next morning (14th) at earliest dawn, they were afoot. Having obtained no food the day before, there was no delay in cooking and eating. Writing by the dim dawn the note, formerly alluded to, to Truxton, Strain gave the order to march, and the four pushed on. They were, however, soon forced from the river by the undergrowth, and after a march of about two hours, found themselves in a dense thicket, where it was necessary to cut every foot of the way for some two hundred yards. During the time they occupied in making this distance they rarely if ever touched the earth, so matted and close were the standing and fallen branches and bushes. It was painful work, and not without danger; but they cut and floundered through. Emerging into the more open forest, they found themselves in an almost impassable swamp. Struggling through this as they best could, they saw a large body of water, and Strain, in attempting to approach it, became so effectually *bogged*, that it was with great difficulty he extricated himself. The order to countermarch was then given, and after incredible labor they reached the river about noon, and at a point only about 200 yards below the camp from which they had set out some seven hours before. This was disheartening, but they pushed on for two hours longer, when they halted for an hour's rest.

Strain now felt quite discouraged; for, at this rate, the party would perish before it could get through. He determined, therefore, again to try a raft, and finding on the beach some driftwood sufficiently dry to float, he halted at four o'clock and commenced collecting timbers, cutting cross-pieces, and getting vines for lashings. This was slow work, as they had nothing with which to cut the hard logs—that were in some cases imbedded in the earth—except the *machete* (a sore of cutlass of good steel and highly tempered). Still, by working hard, they had by dark collected enough logs to float two or three men. They then began to look around for some food, not having tasted *a mouthful since the night previous to leaving the main body*, two days before. Having obtained a few acid nuts, they made a fire, spread their blankets, and were soon fast asleep on a hard clay bank, with a brilliant full-moon shining down upon them.

At daylight they were hard at work upon the raft, and by ten o'clock had logs enough lashed together to support two persons. Wilson and Strain then got upon it, and pushing off, slowly floated down the river; while Mr. Avery and Golden followed along the bank.

At noon another large log was secured and lashed to the raft with strips of canvas torn from Strain's haversack, and the whole party embarked. But the weight was too heavy, and the crazy structure sank until the water was knee-deep above it. They, however, kept on, but in a short time struck a rapid current which swept them upon a sunken snag. In a moment the logs parted and one broke entirely loose. All was consternation, when Strain cried, "*Silence!*" and sitting down on one log, threw either leg over those each side and kept them together. For a few minutes there was great danger of losing all their arms, and even their lives; and nothing but the presence of mind and coolness of every man saved the raft from entire destruction and in deep water, while, owing to their debility and the weight of their accoutrements, swimming was out of the question.

Landing below, where the current was not so strong, they repaired the raft, and floated sluggishly on till nearly sunset, when they struck upon a shoal. Unable to force the raft over this, they were compelled to take it to pieces and float it down, log by log, to a shelving clay beach, where they could reconstruct it. While getting the raft over they discovered a species of clams—said to be nearly identical with the "Little Neck clams" of New York—one hundred and twenty of which made quite a supper, after their hard day's work. While sitting on the bank they saw a shark, some five feet long, attempting to swim over the shoal; but all attempts to get his body for food proved abortive.

The next day, by nine o'clock, the raft was repaired, and the four again embarked; Strain with neither pantaloons nor drawers—nothing on, in fact, but a shirt—bare-legged, sat exposed to the full rays of a tropical sun, and with the rest not much better protected, drifted lazily down the sluggish, tortuous current. At noon, however, they struck another snag. While working hard to extricate themselves, a heavy rain shower came up, which drenched them thoroughly. Soon after another snag was struck, which caused a delay of two hours. Near sunset they came upon a shoal, and swinging off met a swift current, and were dragged by its force under some overhanging branches, which swept Mr. Avery and Golden off into deep water, while Strain, with Wilson, whose leg was nearly broken, hung on, and were carried upon a snag in deep water. In endeavoring to cut loose, they lost a machete. But Golden, finding his leg not broken, plunged to the bottom, and fortunately recovered it. At length, getting loose, they paddled ashore, and as it was already nearly dark, they encamped for the night. Mr. Avery had all the matches upon his person when he swam ashore, consequently they were wet, and no fire could be obtained. This was the more disagreeable, as their clothes and blankets were all soaked with water. Although the weather was mild, they seldom suffered more; for the cold wet blankets chilled them through and through. Weary and exhausted, they could get no sleep. Wilson and Golden lay growling at each other all night.

In the morning they woke thoroughly chilled and sore from the effects of sleeping on the hard clay bank and in wet clothes. They had determined to abandon the raft, as the snags and shoals were too frequent; and spreading their blankets in the sun, remained in camp till they were dried. They employed the time, however, in cutting down a large tree with hard nuts, the kernels of which being extracted supplied them with four days' provisions, that is, the means of sustaining life, for their hardness and tastelessness hardly entitled them to the name of food. While thus occupied, they discovered a saw-fish, about two feet long, working his way up the shallow river, apparently to enjoy the warmth of the sun. Strain shot him with a revolver, and then jumping upon him succeeded in capturing him. Divided among the four, he was but a scanty breakfast, but the meat was sweet and palatable. They started at half past twelve from "Saw-fish Camp," but after making two or three miles were obliged to encamp, as both Mr. Avery and Strain suffered extremely from sore legs. Exposed as they had been to the sun on the raft for two days, Strain's, which were utterly unprotected, were burnt to a blister in many places, while the undergrowth and vines scratched and irritated them to such a degree, that it produced a fever, which was followed by a chill. This looked discouraging enough, especially as they saw no more indications of approaching the Pacific than two weeks before. The bright hopes with which the men had set out began to fade, and they lay stretched about the bank, saying but little, but looking moody and despondent. Strain spent the long afternoon pacing slowly up and down the lofty beach, pondering over the condition of his men, and vainly endeavoring to come to some conclusion respecting the future. However, with steel and powder, they succeeded in obtaining a fire, which, sending its bright light through the forest, imparted a little more cheerfulness to the scene.

At half past seven next morning they set out, and moved slowly down the left bank. Hearing a heavy report, they thought it was a gun from the main body, and were much surprised at the rapid progress it had made. About ten, after marching some three miles, they halted on a shingle beach, where Mr. Avery was taken extremely ill with severe vomiting and retching. While halting another gun was heard, supposed to be from the main party, which Strain answered, hoping that they might come up, as he intended to leave Mr. Avery with them and push on. At sunset, Mr. Avery showing no signs of recovery, they went into Camp No. 6. Fish were abundant in the stream, but they had no hook to catch them with, and so made their supper on hard nuts.

The next day (Sunday) Avery was better; but convinced that he would embarrass the march, Strain was anxious to leave him with the main party, and fired signals to bring them up, but received no answer. [Truxton's party at this time were lying in the camp where they had halted on the first night after Strain had left them, and the supposed guns were falling trees.]

The next day they started early, but Avery's knee pained him severely. At times, exhausted with pain, he would cry out, "Oh, Captain, hold on! Hold on!" Strain would then stop and wait for him to limp up, but never went back. The necessities of the case were too stern to admit of a backward movement. Thus painfully marching—around swamps, through thickets, still on, toward an ocean that seemed infinitely removed—the half-naked, half-starved group cut their toilsome, disheartened way. At half past four they encamped on a shingle beach, having made about eight miles.

The following morning they started early, but were compelled to halt frequently for Avery, who would be left far behind, his extreme suffering causing faintness and sickness at stomach. He, however, bore up nobly; and, as Strain in his report says, "He comported himself in the most manly manner; and few men, I believe, even when marching for their own lives and the lives of others, could have done better than he, with boils on all parts of his person, and five on one knee." Strain killed a fine wild turkey during the day, which gave them a good supper, though, when divided among four hungry men, the portion that each received appeared small. They also found an abundance of acid palm-nuts.

Next day the marching was more open and easy, and they were fortunate enough to find clams. About 5:15 P.M. they encamped on a wet sand-beach. In cutting down some guinea-grass to protect them from dampness, Strain narrowly escaped being bitten by a large snake of the adder species; his machete cleaving the reptile just as he was about to strike. Every night a stick was set on shore to see if there were any signs of tide. The eagerness with which this was inspected every morning showed the longing of the men for this indication of the proximity of the ocean. In the morning they thought they discovered a slight fall in the water, but found afterward that they were mistaken.

The day following (February 22) the marching a part of the time was tolerably easy, but Wilson and Golden began to show signs of debility. Strain, nearly naked, went ahead and cleared a way with his cutlass. On finding the bushes too thick, he would plunge into them head foremost to break them down, trampling them underfoot for those behind. During the day he killed another adder coiled to strike, but did not tell his men of it, least they should become alarmed. Golden carrying no fire-arms, was often ordered forward to cut a patch, but to-day he gave out completely, and when given the cutlass and directed to go to work with it, he laid the instrument down on the ground, then stretched himself beside it, and wept like a child. Destitution and toil were telling on him. He was a fine, splendid-looking young man; only twenty-two years of age, and brave as a lion; but this was a form of evil he had never dreamed of.

The next morning they proceeded on their journey through the woods and along the banks until 1 P.M., making about five miles, when they halted, as Strain had a most painful boil on his right instep, which prevented him from marching or wearing any boot. He was, moreover, suffering severely from a fall into a deep ravine the day before. Near the camp, where the river runs S.S.W., a small stream (the Uporganti) comes in from the N.E. This encouraged the belief that they might still be upon the Iglesias, as a small stream is shown on the map, coming into that river four miles from its mouth, and another about eleven miles above. About four o'clock, as they lay stretched around on the bank of the river, they were startled by a heavy booming sound, like that of a gun, which they thought at once came from Darien Harbor, the "El Dorado" of the expedition. The delusion for a moment made every heart bound.

In the morning (February 24) Strain made a moccasin from a leather legging which formerly belonged to Truxton, who had proposed to boil it down and eat it. The former, however, prevented him, saying they might yet need it for moccasins. So it turned out, and but for this very insignificant circumstance, it is very doubtful whether Strain could ever had got through at all, and consequently the whole party would have perished. On such simple suggestions, growing out of the knowledge of a backwoods life, the fate of scores of men often depends. Slinging his spare boot to his blanket for future service, Strain gave the order to march at half past six, fondly hoping to reach Darien Harbor before night, but having traveled with great pain some eight miles, and seeing no signs of tidewater, at five o'clock encamped on a sand-bank. Having passed during the day two or three rapids with some ten or twelve feet fall, they consoled themselves with the reflection that this accounted for the absence of tides. During the day Strain killed a bird about the size of a partridge, which they ate raw. I find the following recorded in the journal: "*Saturday, February 25.* Slept well last night, the camp being free from mosquitoes. Set out at 8 A.M. and found bad walking all day, both in the forest and on the beaches which we met. In the former we had to cut our way, while the beaches were so steep that we had sometimes to cut steps to crawl along, and even then we were in constant danger of falling into the river, which I did on one occasion.

"Encamped about 6 P.M. on a mud bank, having made about six miles. During the day's march we found about thirty-two clams, which, divided, gave us something to support life, as the acid nut-skins are less ripe than some miles above, while their kernels are so hard as to be almost inedible in the existing state of our teeth, which have been deprived of their enamel by the use of the acid.

"Saw several turkeys, but could obtain none, owing to the state of our fire-arms, which had become almost useless. My carbine, which was the best in the party, being loaded with difficulty, and requiring two men to fire it, one to take aim and pull the trigger, and the other to pull the cock back and let it go at the word, invariably destroying the aim; under these circumstances I am not ashamed to say that I fired several times at turkeys without success.

"About sunset we saw a wild hog, weighing some 300 pounds, which came rushing toward us as if intending to attack, but paused about twenty yards distant. Considering the ferocity of this animal, and the state of our fire-arms, I should have hesitated in attacking him had we not be so pressed for food; but it was a matter of life and death in either case. I took deliberate aim at his body behind the shoulders, and, with the assistance of Wilson fired my carbine, wounding him severely. I feared firing at his head, lest I should miss him altogether. After receiving the ball he paused a moment, as if uncertain whether to attack, after which he rushed off rapidly some fifty yards, when he was seized with a coughing fit, and slackened his pace to a walk. Handing my carbine to Wilson to reload, I followed him into the jungle, but soon lost him in the darkness of the forest. I am inclined to believe that this animal was not the peccary or wild hog of tropical climate, but one of the domesticated species, which, either in his own generation or that of his progenitors had become wild, because I do not think the peccary ever grows so large. His color was black, with white spots. I passed an almost sleepless night in regretting that we had not obtained him, for at this time food was our only thought, except to push through and obtain assistance for those behind."

The next morning (Sunday) they started early, but the long absence of food had so debilitated them that the marching was slow and difficult. They could make but short distances without being compelled to halt for a long rest. This tattered, skeleton group of four, stretched silent and sad in the forest beside that mysterious, unknown river, presented a most piteous spectacle. It is very doubtful whether the men ever would have started again but for the orders of their commander. As they staggered up to a jungle, Strain, after exhausting himself in clearing a path, would order the men to take their turn; but so feeble and dispirited were they, that often nothing but threats of the severest flogging could rouse them to make another effort for their lives. At length their attention was arrested by the cry of a wild animal. It proved to be the howling of a monkey, and the men, elated at the prospect of food, cried out, "*There's a monkey, Captain, shoot him!*" "Cut away," replied Strain, thinking that the noise would excite its curiosity to come nearer. He was right, for the creature kept leaping from tree to tree, until at length it sat crouched on a limb directly above Strain, who was lying upon his back on the ground.

His carbine being damaged, he took the Sharpe's rifle belonging to Avery, and shooting nearly perpendicularly, sent a ball through the monkey's neck. The rifle, however, being loaded with stronger powder than usual, recoiled, cutting Strain's eyebrow and seriously endangering the eye itself. The monkey, after receiving the wound, made off. Strain, though bleeding profusely, fired again. His distrust of the rifle, however, distracted his aim, when he drew a pistol and shot the creature through the heart. She fell over dead, but her tail would not uncoil, and she hung suspended from the limb. Strain then turned to take care of his eye, saying to the men, "If you want that monkey, you must cut down the tree." Though tired and feeble, they attacked it with a will, and notwithstanding the trunk was three feet in circumference, and they had only a cutlass to work with, soon had it down. This monkey was a prize. She was soon cut up, and portions of her crammed into a tin kettle, which was placed over a blazing fire. Each one took turns at the pot, and they kept it up till midnight, when the animal was nearly all devoured. Weighing some twenty pounds, she gave about *five pounds to a man*. The starved men, however, were not satisfied and demanded that the skin should be cooked. But this Strain, with the foresight which again and again saved his little band, refused to give in, saying he should yet need it for lashings in making a raft.

This feast was on Sunday night, and the next morning at ten o'clock they pushed on; but the thick undergrowth was almost impassable, and after cutting for seven hours, making only three quarters of a mile per hour, they encamped on a damp clay bank.

During the day they crossed several deep ravines, down the steep banks of which they were compelled to slide, and then cut steps in the opposite sides, up which to climb to the top.

The course of march was generally southerly. The journal at this place remarks, that then, and for some time previous, "our bodies were literally covered with wood ticks, and we were obliged to pick them off morning and evening."

During the march Strain shot three small hawks, upon which they made their scanty supper. They suffered severely from mosquitoes during the night, but at eight in the morning were again afoot; and proceeding about two miles over some hills, discovered a considerable river (the Iglesia), entering from the northeast. After making in all about six miles, they encamped at six in the evening. Their only food this day consisted entirely of acid nuts, which were gradually wearing away the teeth.

Having suffered less than usual from mosquitoes, Strain roused his little party at daybreak, and by six o'clock they were again cutting their slow and almost interminable path to the Pacific. After making some six miles they encamped on a bank of rock and indurated clay. During the day they had nothing whatever to eat, and when they halted the whole party was thoroughly worn out. They were too tired even to kindle a fire, but lay down in the darkness and slept on the cheerless bank of the stream. Strain now began to think of another raft, as all were so thoroughly debilitated, and so covered with boils, sores, and scratches that they could not much longer cut their way through the jungle.

Mr. Avery was almost disabled, while the men were becoming daily more and more discouraged. Golden—who was a fine, hale young man when he left the *Cyane*—was fearfully attenuated, and his spirit so utterly broken, that when ordered to do the least work he would lie down and weep bitterly. For several days Strain could make him march only by threatening to tie him up and flog him; then his dread of physical pain overcame for the time being his debility. Had he not resorted to this expedient, he would have been obliged to leave him to perish, or remain and perish with him. Strain had once or twice thrown out a hint of his intention to build another raft; but found the two men violently opposed to it, as the danger they had incurred on the last completely intimidated them. But finding the river bends deeper, free from rapids, and comparatively free from snags, he determined to carry out his design at all hazards, especially as he felt convinced that the condition of his foot would not permit him to march more than two or three days longer. The constant irritation, produced by constant with bushes and vines, was rapidly extending the inflammation from the ankle, down the instep and up the leg. At first the men were disheartened; but when told that they need not get on the raft, but might keep along shore in sight, while he and Mr. Avery managed it, they were better contented.

That night being unmolested by mosquitoes they had a quiet rest, and though without food, began early in the morning to collect sticks for the raft; but the general debility, and want of proper tools and lashings, made their progress very slow, and it was sunset before they had enough brought together and lashed to float two persons. In the evening Mr. Avery and Strain obtained some hard nuts and a small quantity of palmetto, which was all the food they had eaten for two days.

Says Strain in his journal: "This was the second time during the expedition that I really felt voracious; and before obtaining the nuts and palmetto, I found myself casting my eyes around me to see if there was nothing that had been overlooked that could allay my hunger. Without a fire, which at this time we never lighted unless we had meat to cook, as we wished to economize our ammunition, we laid down and slept near our raft."

The next day Strain and Avery got on the raft, and the two floated slowly down the stream, while Golden and Wilson forced their way along the shore. Thus, two on the raft and two on the shore, they proceeded day after day—an occasional halloo, to ascertain each other's whereabouts, alone relieving the monotony of the hours. In making the bends sharp paddling was necessary, which, in their debilitated condition, was very exhausting. The second day they found a dead iguana, with the head eaten off. This they cooked and divided among them. The two men roasted the skin and chewed that. This miserable raft consisted of six half-decayed, broken trunks of trees lashed together with monkey skins and vines. Strain, half-naked, and with his legs dangling in the water, sat on the forward end to steer, while his companion occupied the hinder part to assist. Now a tree in the distance chock full of white cranes, and again a panther gazing on them with a bewildered stare, or young tigers, were the only objects that relieved the noiseless and apparently endless solitude. To pass away the time, Strain one day made Avery tell his history; at another time he would narrate from Don Quixote some amusing story. At length starvation produced the same singular effect on them that it did on Truxton and Maury, and they would spend hours in describing all the good dinners they had ever eaten. For the last two or three days, when most reduced, Strain said that he occupied almost the whole time in arranging a magnificent dinner. Every luxury or curious dish that he had ever seen or heard of composed it, and he wore away the hours in going round his imaginary table, arranging and changing the several dishes. He could not force his mind from the contemplation of this, so wholly had one idea—food—taken possession of it. The animal nature, deprived of its support, was evidently closing with resistless force over the soul, and in a few days more would completely force it from its crumbling, falling tenement. On the 4th of March, however, as they sat on shore eating a portion of a dead, tainted lizard, Strain heard a sudden roaring behind, and on looking up stream saw a rapid which they had just passed in smooth water. He knew at once that they must have floated over it at high tide, which now ebbing revealed the rift. It was clear they had at last reached tide-water. This was Strain's birthday, and he was looking out for some good luck. He, however, did not mention his discovery to the men, lest there might be some mistake. But they soon discovered it themselves, and cried out in transport, "*Oh, Captain, here is tide! Here is tide!*" That night Strain could not sleep until the time for flood-tide again arrived, and at eleven o'clock he took a fire-brand and went down to the shore to see how it was going. The doubt was over—then had reached the swellings of the Pacific, and hope was rekindled in every bosom.

The time after this passed wearily. When it was flood-tide they lashed to the shore, and as the ebb commenced cut loose and slowly drifted downstream. At every turn they strained eagerly forward, hoping to get some look-out, or see some signs of civilization; but the same unbroken wilderness shut them in. Having ascertained how high the tide rose, Avery would take the Hudson River as a gauge, and prove conclusively that there was no great occasion for hope, as they were yet probably at least a hundred and fifty miles from the sea.

Anxious to get forward, they could not spend time to hunt; and a half dozen kernels of the palm nut, hard as ivory, would often constitute a meal. At length, on the 9th, Strain saw that food must be obtained, or the men would sink and die without making farther progress. He therefore put Golden in his place with Avery on the raft, and taking Wilson with him struck into the woods to forage. Only *four cartridges* were left to them; and as Strain turned away with the rifle, Avery exclaimed, "*For God's sake, Strain, don't shoot at anything less than a turkey—remember there are only four cartridges left!*" After beating about for some time, still finding nothing, he came upon a partridge sitting on a limb. The temptation was too strong to be resisted, and he drew up and killed it. His conscience smote him the moment he had done so, as on that single cartridge might yet hang the lives of all the party. At length, however, he came upon a grove of palm nuts. By tightening his cartridge belt around him, and filling his flannel shirt above it with nuts, he soon had all he could carry, and turned back to the river. But the two got entangled in a swamp, and were wholly exhausted before they could extricate themselves. Wilson then began to beg for the partridge; but Strain told him it was for the party, and must be divided equally. The man at length fell down, and said he could and would go no farther without that partridge. Strain then threw it to him, saying, "Take it," and sat down on a log to see him devour it. The starving wretch tore it asunder; but still feeling that his commander needed it as much as he did, said, "*Captain, do you want the blood?*" "No," replied the latter. "*Do you want the entrails?*" "No." He then flung him a piece of the bird, and gorged the rest. At length they reached the river, and kept down the bank. About three o'clock, Strain was startled by Wilson's exclaiming, "*My God, Sir, there is the raft!*" and sure enough, there it was, deserted, and floating quietly in the middle of the river, awaiting the action of the tide (it was then slack water) to determine its course.

The sight of that abandoned structure at first struck like an ice-bolt to the heart of both, but a single glance showed Strain that the blankets, spare arms, etc., had been taken away, and another, that about eight feet of rope, which had been used to lash the logs, was left untouched, while one of the paddles still remained. He concluded at once that the party had either obtained assistance and left the raft—in which case they would not require, and would probably neglect, the lashings—or that they had been murdered by Indians, who had left the raft adrift for the purpose of entrapping the remainder. In answer to Wilson's anxious inquires, he frankly told him his conjectures. "Well, Sir," replied Wilson, "if there be Indians about, you have three cartridges left, and are certain of three men, and I think with my machete I can give an account of two more." This was the ring of the true mettle, and pleased Strain much. While awaiting the progress of the raft, which drifted slowly toward their side of the river, they passed their leisure time in eating nuts. Finally, seeing it foul of some driftwood about one hundred yards below, they after some difficulty got upon it, and proceeded with the current down the river. Strain, however, first made a thorough examination, to see if there was any blood or other evidence of a struggle upon it, or a note from Mr. Avery which might unravel the mystery.

After drifting half an hour they saw a clearing on the left bank; and soon after, in passing the mouth of a small stream on the same side, discovered two canoes approaching rapidly from below.

Not feeling assured that the three paddlers were not Indians, who might prove hostile, as they were colored and spoke loudly in a dialect which, at a distance, he could not understand, Strain determined to keep them at arms' length until assured of their peaceable intentions. He accordingly hailed when they came without rifle shot, and asked who they were and where they were going. They replied, in Spanish, that they were friends, had just taken off his companions, and brought a letter to himself. True to his naval principles, never to let an enemy approach too near without declaring his intentions, Strain sat across the log and hailed as though he trod the deck of a man-of-war. These two skeletons on a mass of driftwood thus demanding explanations, were very much like a shipwrecked mariner lashed to a spar bidding a vessel stand off till she showed her colors. When convinced, however, of the peaceable intentions of the natives, they gladly abandoned the raft and entered the canoe. Finding that the boatmen had tobacco and a pipe, Strain immediately borrowed them, and for the first time since the 4th of February, enjoyed the luxury of a smoke.

It was just dark when they reached the village of Yavisa. The excitement was over—the immediate necessity of effort past, and Strain's over-tasked nature gave way. He could no longer walk, and was helped by two men to the house of the Sub-Alcade, where he met Mr. Avery and Golden. When the commander of the United States Darien Exploring Expedition entered the Alcade's house, his uniform consisted of a blue flannel shirt, one boot, and a Panama hat, neither of which articles was in a very good condition.

★   ★   ★   ★   ★

As they continued to ascend they saw small crosses along the banks, erected, according to previous arrangement, by the main party as they descended, to point out to Strain their progress when he should return with assistance. But the signs soon ceased, and although they passed numerous return camps, there was no symbol from which it could be inferred that they had the remotest hope of relief from below. Worn-out belts and cartouche boxes, found in camps on the river, showed that the party was dispensing with all unnecessary weight, while piece of leather cut from the latter gave evidence that boots and shoes were nearly worn out. Quills and feathers of the loathsome buzzard were scattered along, revealed the character of food to which stern necessity had at last driven them. In the afternoon they arrived at the camp from whence Strain had taken leave of the party, and found that it had been revisited by them, the evidence of which was the remains of a fire and some cartouche boxes which had been discarded. About sunset they encamped on a sloping bank, and passed a night of torture, owing to the myriads of mosquitoes which infested the camp.

This was a sad night for Strain. From the examination of to-day's camp it was evident his command had given him up for lost, and commenced the desperate undertaking of finding their way back to the Atlantic shore. The prospect now grew painfully alarming. Strain could not sleep, but agitated, anxious, and feverish, sat up all night fanning himself. The noble-hearted Bennett kept him company nearly the whole night, and cheered him with promise of assistance to the last. He told him that a fearful and trying day was before him on the morrow—alluding to the revelations which the camps of the men would make. He requested him also to get a pair of boots of one of the men, and try by degrees to wear them; for, said he, no one can tell how distant the party might be, and when we ascend as high as the boats can go, the natives, you know, will refuse to advance, and, in all probability, the English seamen also, as they have a mortal dread of the Indians. And as Strain turned inquiringly toward him, he added, "*And, you know, when all shall turn back, you and I must shoulder our haversacks and take to the woods alone, till we find your men.*" This noble self-devotion of a stranger and foreigner—this grand, high purpose to cast his lot in with the distressed commander, and save his party, or perish with them—reveals one of those lofty, elevated characters which shed lustre on the race.

At early daylight, when the sand-flies relieved the night-guard of mosquitoes, they rose to prepare for a day of labor and excitement, as Strain had every reason to believe he should overtake the main body of his party before night. As they were now nearly in the heart of the Isthmus, and might possibly meet Indians, a regular order of sailing was adopted, and the canoes followed each other in close order.

Strain led the van, accompanied by a canoe containing three natives, who, sailing close along the edge of the shore, examined each camp and searched the riverbank step by step. At about nine o'clock, Strain was startled by the cry from the Padron:

"*Here is a dead body!*"

For a moment he was intimidated, and shrank back as if smitten with a death-chill, and was on the point of asking someone to land and examine it in his place. He did not know which of his friends or comrades he might find stark upon the beach, and for a moment wished to escape the horrible spectacle. Reflection, however, soon convinced him that it was a necessity which must be met, perhaps even till he had counted up, one by one, all of his command, and, nerving himself for the worst, he shoved his canoe ashore. Birds of rapine and beasts of prey had left little more than the skeleton, but a glance at the linen shirt under the blue uniform of the party showed at once that it was an officer. Upon a closer inspection of the bones and skull, he discerned that it was the remains of Mr. Polanco, the junior Granadian commissioner. The outline of a grave was below, which induced the officers and men who accompanied him to believe that the body had been buried and afterward disinterred by wild beasts; but Strain read the history of the recent tragic events more accurately.

The grave was too short for Mr. Polanco; besides, there was not sufficient evidence that the ground had been torn up, while the clothing, flattened over the bones, showed plainly that they had never been covered with earth. He felt, therefore, rather than knew, that Mr. Castilla, his companion, lay beneath, and that he, faithful in death as he had been faithful and docile in life, had laid down and died upon his grave. Where he lay there they interred him, sacredly gathering together even the finger bones; and placing a cross over the joint remains of these unfortunate, educated, and talented young men, before whom but a few weeks previous a bright future appeared to be opening, they continued their journey saddened and subdued by the melancholy spectacle.

The English officers could not witness it, but turned away sick and sad. It was not till after they had left the spot, that Strain mentioned his convictions concerning the grave, lest someone might propose a delay for the purpose of examining it. The dead were beyond reach of human assistance and human sympathy, but to those who remained of this party delay might be death.

At about 10 A.M., a tree was met extending entirely across the river, which had to be cut in two before a passage could be effected. Cheerfully and heartily the English seamen went to work; but the natives, for a long time, hung back, and, after a consultation, declared that they would go no farther.

Grieved and distressed beyond measure by the fearful sight he had just witnessed, and feeling that the skill and dexterity of the natives were becoming every hour more essential to his success, Strain was thoroughly enraged by this despicable conduct. He entreated, upbraided, and threatened by turns, and gave them to understand that, even should they escape alive from his own party of armed and determined men, whose success depended in a great degree upon their assistance, the grape and cannister of the howitzer in the boat below would prevent their reaching Yavisa. He wound up his harangue by swearing, with the most solemn oath known to those barbarians—viz, *by the soul of God*—that, even if they should escape these dangers, he would devote the remainder of his life to their punishment. Sorrow and anger combined gave an impressiveness to the solemn oath—especially as he presented a six-barreled revolver to their breasts, declaring that at least *six* of them should never return. After a short and frightened consultation, they agreed to continue on the remainder of that day. Although Strain hoped confidently that the party would be overtaken before night, he did not accept of these conditions, as he was determined that they should never abandon to a fearful death men whose lives were of so much more value than their own, especially as they had embarked in the enterprise, and by their promises induced him to consume time which was beyond price.

For some hours, early in the afternoon, they lost sight of the return camps, and the English party, officers as well as men, became apprehensive that the party had abandoned the river. But on this subject Strain felt no anxiety, as he knew that they would not dare to leave the stream, which was their only guide and the only certain source from which they could obtain water. Nearly the whole of this day they fired their muskets and shouted at short intervals, in order to attract attention should they be pursuing their march in the forest, where it was generally more free from undergrowth than close to the river bank. Late in the afternoon a log across the river compelled them to leave the canoes, which were forced over by the united strength of the party. Here a stench induced Strain to believe that one of his unfortunate companions had been left in the forest; but, after a brief search in the bushes, not finding anything, he pushed on—feeling that, even if his suspicions were true, the poor creature was beyond human relief, and it was those who suffered and yet lived that demanded his utmost efforts. Soon after passing this barrier ashes were discovered, which the Padron, in his scout canoe, pronounced to be less than four days old. When Strain announced this intelligence to the party, three cheers were given by the English seamen, that made the forest ring, and they sprang to their paddles with such energy that the water foamed away from the prows of their canoes as they bounded onward.

Signs of disorganization, however, now became more alarming, and the evidence of extreme debility and starvation more apparent. Buzzard's quills, haversacks, fragments of clothing strewed along, together with the want of order in the camps, and their close proximity, attested that the little band had well-nigh reached the end of their march. With every fresh symptom of extreme destitution, Strain became more painfully agitated, for the dreadful fear that they had been compelled to resort to cannibalism haunted him, and made him tremble to proceed. But nerving himself to the worst, and keeping his forebodings to himself, he pushed on, and soon after announced a camp less than three days old. This was responded to by a loud cheer and a discharge of fire-arms. Even the natives began to feel the excitement, and bent to their paddles with lustier strokes. They had not proceeded far before another camp was found, the ashes of which were declared to be warm; and then the excitement reached the highest pitch. Shout after shout went up, shot after shot rang through the forest, and a common enthusiasm and ardor inspired every breast.

At about sunset the natives, who were ahead in the scout canoe, announced a smoke in sight, and immediately after making a turn in the river Strain discovered five men standing on the shelving beach just out of the wood. He immediately discharged his musket to warn them of his approach, lest the effect of too sudden joy might be fatal; and then cheer after cheer echoed and re-echoed through the forest, as each canoe in succession swept round the point and caught sight of the motionless forms in the distance.

When Strain saw but five men his heart sank with dread, and he exclaimed, "*My God, is that all?*" but the next moment a faint cheer from the forest in the rear announced that others still remained alive. His canoe swept with a bound to the shore; but before its prow grated upon it he was on the land. His first inquiry of Maury was, "*How many men have you lost?*" "*Five,*" replied Maury. "*I know,*" responded Strain, "*of four, who is the other?*" "*Lombard,*" said Maury. By this time Truxton had staggered up, and flinging his arms around Strain, exclaimed, "*Oh Strain, did I do right to turn back?*" Joy at his sudden release from the terrible death that awaited him, relief from suffering and suspense, were forgotten in the single question of duty. "*Did I do right?*" was the only thought, the only question. How that involuntary exclamation honors him—exalts him above all eulogy! *Duty* had governed him from first to last; *duty* occupied him even in the extreme suffering of starvation. So long as we can have such officers to command our ships, our navy will retain her old renown, and whether flying or struck, our flag will still be covered with glory.

One of the men, named M'Ginness, threw his arms around Strain, and bursting into tears, exclaimed, "Oh, Captain! Poor Boggs is breaking his heart to see you." As Bennett, the noble Irishman, jumped ashore, and saw the hideous spectacle of scarred and almost naked skeletons, he seized each one by the hand, while the tears poured like rain down his cheeks. The Scotch surgeon gazed around him a moment, apparently bewildered, then leaping back into the boat, seized a bottle of port wine under each arm, and hastening from one to the other, said, "*Take a little of this, my poor fellow; take a little of this!*"

But this spectacle was nothing to that which awaited them at camp. Several of the poor men there had heard the shouts of deliverance, but the joyful intelligence could not impart strength to their wasted frames. There they lay—lacerated, ulcerated frames of men half-covered with rags. Each turned his eye as the commander approached, but none could get up. Strain first came upon Vermilyea, stretched on his back and emaciated to such a dreadful degree that he did not know him. "*How do you do, Captain? We are glad to see you back again. We were afraid you were lost.*" Strain, with a breaking heart, gazed on him a moment, when the poor man asked, "*Won't you shake hands with me, Captain?*" "*Yes,*" replied the former. "*I beg pardon, Captain, but I can't get up.*" Strain then kneeled down beside him and tried to cheer him, saying he had brought along provisions, a doctor, and every thing he needed, and he hoped to see him on his feet again soon. "*I am afraid, Captain,*" he faintly replied, "*I shall never march anymore.*" Alas! it proved too true. As Strain rose to his feet, he saw a figure sitting a little way off on the ground doubled up against his knees, his pantaloons off up to this thighs, while a part of a shirt, and a palm-leaf hat with but half a rim completed his costume. He was ghastly and frightful to look upon. As he caught Strain's eye he touched the fragment of his hat brim, and endeavored to smile. The contortions which the effort gave to his almost black and emaciated face rendered him still more horrible. "*Who are you?*" asked Strain. "*Henwood,*" he replied and again attempted to touch his hat in true naval discipline. "*We were getting very uneasy about you, Sir,*" he added; "*very glad to see you back.*" Strain, horrified and struck almost dumb at the spectacle, replied mechanically, "Well, Henwood, how are you getting along?" "Oh, very well, Sir; but we were very uneasy about you. We are very glad to see you back, because, if you had not come up to-night, *there's me, Harris, Miller, and poor Boggs, who could not have gone on tomorrow, Sir.*" The appellation "*poor*" was applied to Boggs, because he was an officer. The posture of this young man, his emaciated, half-naked appearance, the resigned manner in which he spoke of his fate, together with the ghastly attempt at a smile, combined to render him one of the most strange and frightful spectacles the human form ever presents. Beside him sat another in the same condition, who to Strain's inquiries answered in the same manner. Truxton had by this time reached camp again, and exhausted, lay down. Strain advanced a little farther to where Boggs—his old schoolmate and fellow officer—was lying on a ragged counterpane which he had carried instead of a blanket. The poor man had at last yielded to despair, and the presence of his friend failed to rouse him. Strain knelt over him and exclaimed, "Good God! My dear fellow don't think of dying. I have brought plenty of provisions, medicine, doctor, etc. We will soon be on the Pacific. Cheer up, and we will take many a good glass of wine together yet in Springfield!" Finding that he could not rally him, he spoke of the lady to whom he was engaged, of her anxiety and welfare, in order to rekindle hope and effort. "*I don't think I shall die yet,*" replied the sufferer, in a low and feeble voice, "but it is fortunate you came up as you *did, for they had decided to leave me tomorrow.*" The perfect composure and resignation which reigned in that ghastly group, gave tenfold impressiveness to the scene. But no description can convey any adequate impression of its true character. The British officers were shocked beyond measure, and the surgeon declared that though he had seen much of suffering, in hospitals and elsewhere, he never before dreamed that men could live and march in such a state of emaciation and destitution.

To the Secret City of Harar

BY SIR RICHARD FRANCIS BURTON

Burton was one of the most talented European explorers during the Golden Age of Exploration in the 1800s. His insatiable desire for knowledge and his mastery over nearly 30 languages allowed him to make observations that would have been impossible for the average explorer, who cared little about understanding local customs or cultures. He was also brave, smart, an expert swordsman, and contentious—perhaps to a fault.

While serving in the English army in India, Burton made a trip to the forbidden city of Mecca in the disguise of an Arab pilgrim, which led him to more ambitious projects, starting with an exploration of Somalia. He would later lead an expedition to find the source of the Nile, accompanied by John Hanning Speke, who claimed to have found the headwaters while on a short solo exploration during the trip. For the remainder of their lives, the two men would argue about whether Speke was correct. While Speke found favor with the Royal Geographical Society and the public, Burton sank into bitter recriminations. He continued exploring and writing, with stops in South America, the American West, and several spots in Africa, but his abrasive personality and negative publicity about his morality and judgment left him shut out of the major expeditions he so longed for.

Today, he might even be better remembered for making the first translations of *Arabian Nights* and the *Kama Sutra*, both scandalous books during Burton's day. The following story of his trip to the secret city of Harar in Somalia, is taken from *First Footsteps in East Africa*, first published in 1856.

★ ★ ★ ★ ★

arly on the 23rd December assembled the caravan, which we were destined to escort across the Marar Prairie. Upon this neutral ground the
Eesa, Berteri, and Habr Awal meet to rob and plunder unhappy travelers. The Somal shuddered at the sight of a wayfarer, who rushed into
our encampment *in cuerpo* [naked], having barely run away with his life. Not that
our caravan carried much to lose—a few hides and pots of clarified butter, to be
exchanged for the Holcus grain of the Girhi cultivators—still the smallest contributions are thankfully received by these plunderers. Our material consisted of
four or five half-starved camels, about fifty donkeys with ears cropped as a mark,
and their eternal accompaniments in Somaliland, old women. The latter seemed
to be selected for age, hideousness, and strength; all day they bore their babes
smothered in hides upon their backs, and they carried heavy burdens apparently
without fatigue. Amongst them was a Bedouin widow, known by her "Wer," a
strip of the inner bark of a tree tied round the greasy fillet. [It is worn for a year,
during which modest women will not marry. Some tribes confine the symbol to
widowhood, others extend it to all male relations; a strip of white cotton, or even
a white fillet, instead of the usual blue cloth, is used by the more civilized]. We
were accompanied by three Widads, provided with all the instruments of their
craft, and uncommonly tiresome companions. The recited Koran *à tort et à travers*;
at every moment they proposed Fatihahs, the name of Allah was perpetually
upon their lips, and they discussed questions of divinity, like Gil Blas and his
friends, with a violence bordering upon frenzy. One of them was celebrated for
his skill in the "Fal," or Omens; he was constantly consulted by my companions,
and informed them that we had nought to fear except from wild beasts. The pre-
diction was a good hit; I must own, however, that it was not communicated to
me before fulfilment.

At half past 6 A.M., we began our march over rough and rising ground,
a network of thorns and water-courses, and presently entered a stony gap between two ranges of hills. On our right was a conical peak, bearing the remains
of a building upon its summit. Here, said Abtidon, a wild Gudabirsi hired to
look after our mules, rests the venerable Shaykh Samawai. Of old, a number of
wells existed in the gaps between the hills; these have disappeared with those
who drank of them.

Presently we entered the Barr or Prairie of Marar, one of the long
strips of plain which diversify the Somali country. Its breadth, bounded on the
east by the rolling ground over which we had passed, on the west by Gurays, a
range of cones offshooting from the highlands of Harar; is about twenty-seven
miles, the general course is north and south; in the former direction, it belongs

to the Eesa; in the latter may be seen peaks of Kadau and Madir, the property of the Habr Awal tribes; and along these ranges it extends, I was told, towards Ogadayn. The surface of the plain is gently rolling ground; the black earth, filled with the holes of small beasts, would be most productive, and the outer coat is an expanse of tall, waving, sunburnt grass, so unbroken, that from a distance it resembles the nap of yellow velvet. In the frequent Wadys, which carry off the surplus rain of the hills, scrub and thorn trees grow in dense thickets, and the grass is temptingly green. Yet the land lies fallow; water and fuel are scarce at a distance from the hills, and the wildest Bedouin dare not front the danger of foraging parties, the fatal heats of day, and the killing colds of night. On the edges of the plain, however, are frequent vestiges of deserted kraals.

About midday, we crossed a depression in the centre, where Acacias supplied us with gum for luncheon, and sheltered flocks of antelope. I endeavoured to shoot the white-tailed Sig, and the large dun Oryx; but the *brouhaha* of the caravan prevented execution. Shortly afterwards we came upon patches of holcus, which had grown wild, from seeds scattered by travellers. This was the first sight of grain that gladdened my eyes since I left Bombay; the grave of the First Murderer never knew a Triptolemus [Cain is said to repose under Jabal Shamsan at Aden—an appropriate sepulchre], and Zayla is a barren flat of sand. My companions eagerly devoured the pith of this African "sweet cane," despite its ill reputation for causing fever. I followed their example, and found it almost as good as bad sugar. The Bedouin loaded their spare asses with the bitter gourd, called Ubbah; externally it resembles the watermelon, and becomes, when shaped, dried, and smoked, the wickerwork of the Somal, and the pottery of more civilized people.

Towards evening, as the setting sun sank slowly behind the distant western hills, the colour of the Prairie changed from glaring yellow to a golden hue, mantled with a purple flush inexpressibly lovely. The animals of the waste began to appear. Shy lynxes and jackals fattened by many sheeps' tails [in the Somali country, as in Kafirland, the Duwao or jackal is peculiarly bold and fierce. Disdaining garbage, he carries off limbs and kids, and fastens upon a favourite *friandise*, the sheep's tail; the victim runs away in terror, and unless the jackal be driven off by dogs, leaves a delicate piece of fat behind it], warned my companions that fierce beasts were nigh, ominous anecdotes were whispered, and I was told that a caravan had lately lost nine asses by lions. As night came on, the Bedouin Kafilah, being lightly loaded, preceded us, and our tired camels lagged far behind. We were riding in rear to prevent straggling, when suddenly my mule, the hindermost, pricked his ears uneasily, and attempted to turn his head. Looking backwards, I distinguished the form of a large animal following us with quick and stealthy strides. My companions would not fire, thinking it was a man; at last a rifle ball, pinging through the air—the moon was too young for correct shooting—put to flight a huge lion. The terror excited by this sort of an adventure was comical to look upon; the valiant Beuh, who, according to himself, had made his *preuves* in a score of foughten fields, threw his arms in the air, wildly shouting Libah! Libah!!—the lion! The lion!!—and nothing else was talked of that evening.

The ghostly western hills seemed to recede as we advanced over the endless rolling plain. Presently the ground became broken and stony, the mules stumbled in deep holes, and the camels could scarcely crawl along. As we advanced, our Widads, who poor devils! had been "roasted" by the women all day on account of their poverty, began to recite the Koran with might, in gratitude for having escaped many perils. Night deepening, our attention was riveted by a strange spectacle; a broad sheet of bright blaze, reminding me of Hanno's fiery river [the well-known Carthaginian navigator who sailed along the west coast of Africa in the fifth century B.C., the phenomenon of the "fiery river" was later discovered to be due to a series of bush fires along the Gambia river], swept apparently down a hill, and, according to my companions, threatened the whole prairie. These accidents are common; a huntsman burns a tree for honey or cooks his food in the dry grass, the wind rises and the flames spread far and wide. On this occasion no accident occurred; the hills, however, smoked like a Solfatara for two days.

About 9 P.M. we heard voices, and I was told to discharge my rifle lest the kraal be closed to us; in due time we reached a long, low, dark line of sixty or seventy huts, disposed in a circle, so as to form a fence, with a few bushes—thorns being hereabouts rare—in the gaps between the abodes. The people, a mixture of Girhi and Gudabirsi Bedouin, swarmed out to gratify their curiosity, but we were in no humour for long conversations. Our luggage was speedily disposed in a heap near the kraal, the mules and camels were tethered for the night, then, supperless and shivering with cold, we crept under our mats and fell asleep. That day we had ridden nearly fifteen hours; our halting place lay about thirty miles from, and 240° south-west, of Koralay.

After another delay, and a second vain message to the Gerad Adan, about noon appeared that dignitary's sixth wife, sister to the valiant Beuh. Her arrival disconcerted my companions, who were too proud to be protected by a woman. "Dahabo," however, relieved their anxiety by informing us that the Gerad had sent his eldest son Shirwa, as escort. This princess was a gipsy-looking dame, coarsely dressed, about thirty years old, with a gay leer, a jaunty demeanour, and the reputation of being "fast;" she showed little shamefacedness when I saluted her, and received with noisy joy the appropriate present of a new and handsome Tobe. About 4 P.M. returned our second messenger, bearing with him a reproving message from the Gerad, for not visiting him without delay; in a token of sincerity, he forwarded his baton, a knobstick about two feet long, painted in rings of Cutch colours, red, black, and yellow alternately, and garnished on the summit with a ball of similar material.

At dawn on the 26ᵗʰ December, mounted upon a little pony, came Shirwa, heir presumptive to the Gerad Adan's knobstick. His father had sent him to us three days before, but he feared the Gudabirsi as much as the Gudabirsi feared him, and he probably hung about our camp till certain it was safe to enter. We received him politely, and he in acknowledgement positively declared that Beuh should not return before eating honey in his cottage. Our Abban's heroism now became infectious. Even the End of Time, whose hot valour had long since fallen below zero, was inspired by the occasion, and recited, as usual with him in places and times of extreme safety, the Arabs' warrior lines—

> I have crossed the steed since my eyes saw light,
> I have fronted death till he feared my sight,
> And the cleaving of helm and the riving of mail
> Were the dreams of my youth—are my manhood's delight.

As we had finished loading, a mule's bridle was missed. Shirwa ordered instant restitution to his father's stranger, on the ground that all the property now belonged to the Gerad; and we, by no means idle, fiercely threatened to bewitch the kraal. The article was presently found hard by, on a hedge. This was the first and last case of theft which occurred to us in the Somali country,—I have traveled through most civilized lands, and have lost more.

At 8 A.M. we marched towards the northwest, along the southern base of the Gurays hills, and soon arrived at the skirt of the prairie, where a well-trodden path warned us that we were about to quit the desert. After advancing six miles in line we turned to the right, and recited a Fatihah over a heap of rough stones, where, shadowed by venerable trees, lie the remains of the great Shaykh Abd al-Malik. A little beyond this spot, rises suddenly from the plain a mass of castellated rock, the subject of many a wild superstition. Caravans always encamp beneath it, as whoso sleeps upon the summit loses his senses to evil spirits. At some future day Harar will be destroyed, and "Jannah Siri" will become a flourishing town. We ascended it, and found no life but hawks, coneys, an owl, and a graceful species of black eagle; there were many traces of buildings, walls, ruined houses, and wells, whilst the sides and summit were tufted with venerable sycamores. This act was an imprudence; the Bedouin at once declared that we were "prospecting" for a fort, and the evil report preceded us to Harar.

After a mile's march from Jannah Siri, we crossed a ridge of rising ground, and suddenly, as though by magic, the scene shifted.

Before us lay a little Alp; the second step of the Æthiopian Highland. Around were high and jagged hills, their sides black with the Saj [the Arabs apply this term to teak] and Somali pine [the Dayyib of the Somal, and the Sinaubar of the Arabs; its line of growth is hereabouts an altitude of 5,000 feet], and their upper brows veiled with a thin growth of cactus. Beneath was a deep valley, in the midst of which ran a serpentine of shining waters, the gladdest spectacle we had yet witnessed; further in front, masses of hill rose abruptly from shady valleys, encircled on the far horizon by a straight blue line of ground, resembling a distant sea. Behind us glared the desert; we had now reached the outskirts of civilization, where man, abandoning his flocks and herds, settles, cultivates, and attends to the comforts of life.

The fields are either terraces upon the hill slopes or the sides of valleys, divided by flowery hedges with lanes between, not unlike those of rustic England; and on a nearer approach the daisy, the thistle, and the sweet briar pleasantly affected my European eyes. The villages are no longer movable; the kraal and wigwam are replaced by the Gambisa or bell-shaped hut of Middle Africa, circular cottages of holcus wattle, covered with coarse dab and surmounted by a stiff, conical, thatch roof, above which appears the central supporting post, crowned with a gourd or ostrich egg. A strong abattis of thorns protects these settlements, which stud the hills in all directions; near most of them are clumps of tall trees, to the southern sides of which are hung, like birdcages, long cylinders of matting, the hives of these regions. Yellow crops of holcus rewarded the peasant's toil; in some places the long stems tied in bunches below the ears as piled muskets, stood ready for the reaper; in others, the barer ground showed that the task was done. The boys sat perched upon reed platforms in the trees, and with loud shouts drove away thieving birds, whilst their fathers cut the crop with diminutive sickles, or thrashed heaps of straw with rude flails, or winnowed grain by tossing it with a flat wooden shovel against the wind. The women husked the pineapple-formed heads in mortars composed of a hollowed trunk [equally simple are the other implements. The plough, which in Eastern Africa has passed the limits of Egypt, is still the crooked tree of all primitive people, drawn by oxen; and the hoe is a wooden blade inserted into a knobbed handle], smeared the threshing floor with cow dung and water to defend it from insects, piled the holcus heads into neat yellow heaps, spanned and crossed by streaks of various colours, brick-red and brownish-purple [It is afterwards stored in deep dry holes, which are carefully covered to keep out rats and insects, thus the grain is preserved undamaged for three or four years. Like the Matamores, or underground caves of Berbers, and the grain stores of Leghorn, cachettes or silos of Algerines. When opened the grain must be eaten quickly], and stacked the Karbi or straw, which was surrounded like the grain with thorn, as a defence against the wild hog. All seemed to consider it a labour of love; the harvest-home song sounded pleasantly to our ears, and, contrasting with the silent desert, the hum of man's habitation was music.

Descending the steep slope, we reposed, after a seven miles' march, on the banks of a bright rivulet, which bisects the Kobbo or valley; it runs according to my guides, from the north towards Ogadayn, and the direction is significant—about Harar I found neither hill nor stream trending from east to west. The people of the Kutti [this word is applied to the cultivated districts, the granaries of Somaliland] flocked out to gaze upon us; they were unarmed, and did not, like the Bedouin, receive us with cries of "Bori." During the halt, we bathed in the waters, upon whose banks were a multitude of huge Mantidae, pink and tender green. Returning to the camels, I shot a kind of crow, afterwards frequently seen. It is about three times the size of our English bird, of a bluish-black with a snow-white poll, and a beak of unnatural proportion; the quantity of lead which it carried off surprised me. A number of Widads assembled to greet us, and some Habr Awal, who were returning with a caravan, gave us the salaam, and called my people cousins. "Verily," remarked the Hammal, "amongst friends we cut one another's throats; amongst enemies we become sons of uncles!"

At 3 P.M. we pursued our way over rising ground, dotted with granite blocks fantastically piled, and everywhere in sight of fields and villages and flowing water. A furious wind was blowing, and the End of Time quoted the Somali proverb, "heat hurts, but cold kills;" the camels were so fatigued, and the air became so raw, that after an hour and a half's march we planted our wigwams near a village distant about seven miles from the Gurays Hills. Till late at night we were kept awake by the crazy Widads; Ao Samattar had proposed the casuistical question, "Is it lawful to pray upon a mountain when a plain is at hand?" Some took the *pro*, others the *contra*, and the wordy battle raged with uncommon fury.

On Wednesday morning at half past seven we started downhill towards "Wilensi," a small table-mountain, at the foot of which we expected to find the Gerad Adan awaiting us in one of his many houses, crossed a fertile valley, and ascended another steep slope by a bad and stony road. Passing the home of Shirwa, who vainly offered hospitality, we toiled onwards, and after a mile and a half's march, which occupied at least two hours, our wayworn beasts arrived at the Gerad's village. On inquiry, it proved that the chief, who was engaged in selecting two horses and two hundred cows, the price of blood claimed by the Amir of Harar, for the murder of a citizen, had that day removed to Sagharrah, another settlement.

As we entered the long straggling village of Wilensi, our party was divided by the Gerad's two wives. The Hammal, the Kalendar, Shehrazade and Deenarzade remained with Bueh and his sister in her Gurgi, whilst Long Gulad, the End of Time, and I were conducted to the cottage of the Gerad's prettiest wife, Sudiyah. She was a tall woman, with a light complexion, handsomely dressed in a large Harar Tobe, with silver earrings, and the kind of necklace called Jilbah or Kardas. [It is a string of little silver bells and other ornaments made by the Arabs at Berbera.] The Geradah (princess) at once ordered our hides to be spread in a comfortable part of the hut, and then supplied us with food—boiled beef, pumpkin, and Jowari cakes. During the short time spent in that Gambisa, I had an opportunity, dear L., of seeing the manners and customs of the settled Somal.

The interior of the cottage is simple. Entering the door, a single plank with pins for hinges fitted into sockets above and below the lintel—in fact, as artless a contrivance as ever seen in Spain or Corsica—you find a space, divided by dwarf walls of wattle and dab into three compartments, for the men, women, and cattle. The horses and cows, tethered at night on the left of the door, fill the cottage with the wherewithal to pass many a *nuit blanche*; the wives lie on the right, near a large fireplace of stones and raised clay, and the males occupy the most comfortable part, opposite to and farthest from the entrance. The thatched ceiling shines jetty with smoke, which when intolerable is allowed to escape by a diminutive window; this seldom happens, for smoke, like grease and dirt, keeping man warm, is enjoyed by savages. Equally simple is the furniture; the stem of a tree, with branches hacked into pegs, supports the shields, the assegais are planted against the wall, and divers bits of wood, projecting from the sides and the central roof-tree of the cottage, are hung with clothes and other articles that attract white ants. Gourds smoked inside, and coffee cups of coarse black Harar pottery, with deep wooden platters, and prettily carved spoons of the same material, compose the household supellex. The inmates are the Geradah and her baby, Siddik, a Galla serf, the slave girls and sundry Somal; thus we hear at times three languages [Harari, Somali, and Galla, besides Arabic, and other more civilized dialects] spoken within the walls.

Long before dawn the good wife rises, wakens her handmaidens, lights the fire, and prepares for the Afur or morning meal. The quern is here unknown. A flat, smooth, oval slab, weighing about fifteen pounds, and a stone roller six inches in diameter, worked with both hands, and the weight of the body kneeling ungracefully upon it on "all fours," are used to triturate the holcus grain. At times water must be sprinkled over the meal, until a finely powered paste is ready for the oven; thus several hours' labour is required to prepare a few pounds of bread. At about 6 A.M. there appears a substantial breakfast of roast beef and mutton, with scones of Jowari grain, the whole drenched in broth. Of the men few perform any ablutions, but all use the tooth stick before sitting down to eat. After the meal some squat in the sun, others transact business, and drive their cattle to the bush till 11 A.M., the dinner hour. There is no variety in the repasts, which are always flesh and holcus; these people despise fowls, and consider vegetables food for cattle. During the day there is no privacy; men, women, and children enter in crowds, and will not be driven away by the Geradah, who inquires screamingly if they come to stare at a baboon. My kettle especially excites their surprise; some opine that it is an ostrich, others, a serpent; Sudiyah, however, soon discovered its use, and begged irresistibly for the unique article. Throughout the day her slave girls are busied with grinding, cooking, and quarrelling with dissonant voices; the men have little occupation beyond chewing tobacco, chatting, and having their wigs frizzled by a professional coiffeur. In the evening the horses and cattle return home to be milked and stabled; this operation concluded, all apply themselves to supper with a will. They sleep but little, and sit deep into the night trimming the fire, and conversing merrily over their cups of Farshu or millet beer. [In the Eastern world this well-known fermentation is generally called "Buzah," whence the old German word "busen" and our "booze." The addition of a dose of garlic converts it into an emetic.] I tried this mixture several times, and found it detestable; the taste is sour, and it flies directly to the head, in consequence of being mixed with some poisonous bark. It is served up in gourd bottles upon a basket of holcus heads, and strained through a pledget of cotton fixed across the narrow mouth, into cups of the same primitive material; the drinkers sit around their liquor, and their hilarity argues its intoxicating properties. In the morning they arise with headaches and heavy eyes; but these symptoms, which we, an industrious race, deprecate, are not disliked by the Somal—they promote sleep and give something to occupy the vacant mind.

Immediately after our arrival at Wilensi we sent Yusuf Dera, the Gerad's second son, to summon his father. I had to compose many disputes between the Hammal and the End of Time; the latter was swelling with importance; he was now accredited ambassador from the Hajj to the Girhi chief, consequently he aimed at commanding the Caravan. We then made preparations for deprarture, in case of the Gerad being unable to escort us. Shehrazade and Deenarzade, hearing that the smallpox raged at Harar, and fearing for their charms, begged hard to be left behind; the Kalendar was directed, despite his manly objections, to remain in charge of these dainty dames. The valiant Beuh was dressed in the grand Tobe promised to him; as no consideration would induce him towards the city, he was dismissed with small presents, and an old Girhi Bedouin, generally known as Sa'id Wal, or Mad Sa'id, was chosen as our escort. Camels being unable to travel over these rough mountain paths, our weary brutes were placed for rest and pasture under the surveillance of Shirwa; and not wishing the trouble and delay of hiring asses, the only transport in this country, certain moreover that our goods were safer here than nearer Harar, we selected the most necessary objects, and packed them in a pair of small leathern saddlebags which could be carried by a single mule.

All these dispositions duly made, at 10 A.M. on the 29th December we mounted our animals, and guided by Mad Sa'id, trotted round the northern side of the Wilensi table mountain down a lane fenced with fragrant dog roses. Then began the descent of a steep rocky hill, the wall of a woody chasm, through whose gloomy depths the shrunken stream of a large Fiumara wound like a thread of silver. The path would be safe to nought less surefooted than a mule; we rode slowly over rolling steps, steps of micaceous grit, and through thorny bush for about half an hour. In the plain below appeared a village of the Gerad's Migdans, who came out to see us pass, and followed the strangers to some distance. One happening to say, "Of what use is his gun?—before he could fetch fire, I should put this arrow through him!" I discharged a barrel over their heads, and derided the convulsions of terror caused by the unexpected sound.

Passing onwards we entered a continuation of the Wady Harirah. It is a long valley choked with dense vegetation, through which meandered a line of water brightly gilt by the sun's rays; my Somal remarked that were the elephants now infesting it destroyed, rice, the favourite luxury, might be grown upon its banks in abundance. Our road lay under clumps of shady trees, over rocky water-courses, through avenues of tall cactus, and down *tranchées* worn by man eight and ten feet below stiff banks of rich red clay. On every side appeared deep clefts, ravines, and earth cracks, all, at this season, dry. The unarmed cultivators thronged from the frequent settlements to stare, and my Somal, being no longer in their own country, laid aside for guns their ridiculous spears. On the way passing Ao Samattar's village, the worthy fellow made us halt whilst he went to fetch a large bowl of sour milk. About noon the fresh western breeze obscured the fierce sun with clouds, and we watered our mules in a mountain stream which crossed our path thrice within as many hundred yards. After six miles' ride reaching the valley's head, we began the descent of a rugged pass by a rough and rocky path. The scenery around us was remarkable. The hillsides were well wooded, and black with pine; their summits were bared of earth by the heavy monsun which spreads the valleys with rich soil; in many places the beds of waterfalls shone like sheets of metal upon the black rock; villages surrounded by fields and fences studded the country, and the distance was a mass of purple peak and blue table in long vanishing succession. Ascending the valley's opposite wall, we found the remains of primaeval forests—little glades which had escaped the axe—they resounded with the cries of pintados [guinea-fowl] and cynocephali. [The Somal will not kill these plundering brutes, like the West Africans believing them to be enchanted men.] Had the yellow crops of Holcus been wheat, I might have fancied myself once more riding in the pleasant neighbourhood of Tuscan Sienna.

At 4 P.M., after accomplishing fifteen miles on rough ground, we sighted Sagharrah, a snug high-fenced village of eight or nine huts nestling against a hillside with trees above, and below a fertile grain-valley. Presently Mad Sa'id pointed out to us the Gerad Ahan, who, attended by a little party, was returning homewards: we fired our guns as a salute, he however hurried on to receive us with due ceremony in his cottage. Dismounting at the door we shook hands with him, were led through the idle mob into a smoky closet contrived against the inside wall, and were regaled with wheaten bread steeped in honey and rancid butter. The host left us to eat, and soon afterwards returned: I looked with attention at a man upon whom so much then depended.

Adan bin Kaushan was in appearance a strong wiry Beduouin—before obtaining from me a turban he wore his bushy hair dyed dun—about forty-five years old, at least six feet high, with decided features, a tricky smile, and an uncertain eye. In character he proved to be one of those cunning idiots so peculiarly difficult to deal with. Ambitious and wild with greed of gain, he was withal so fickle that his head appeared ever changing its contents; he could not sit quiet for half an hour, and this physical restlessness was an outward sign of the uneasy inner man. Though reputed brave, his treachery had won him a permanent ill fame. Some years ago he betrothed a daughter to the eldest son of Gerad Hirsi of the Berteri tribe, and then, contrary to the Somali laws of honour, married her to Mohammed Wa'iz of the Jibril Abokr. This led to a feud, in which the disappointed suitor was slain. Adan was celebrated for polygamy even in Eastern Africa: by means of his five sons and dozen daughters, he has succeeded in making extensive connections [Some years ago Adan plundered one of Sharmakay's caravans; repenting the action, he offered in marriage a daughter, who, however died before nuptials], and his sister, the Gisti (Gisti is "a princess" in Harari, equivalent to the Somali Geradah) Fâtimah, was married to Abubakr, father of the present Amir. Yet the Gerad would walk into a crocodile's mouth as willingly as within the walls of Harar. His main reason for receiving us politely was an ephemeral fancy for building a fort, to control the city's trade, and rival or overawe the city. Still he did not neglect the main chance: whatever he saw he asked for; and after receiving a sword, a Koran, a turban, an Arab waistcoat of gaudy satin, about seventy Tobes, and a similar proportion of indigo-dyed stuff, he privily complained to me that the Hammal had given him but twelve cloths. A list of his wants will best explain the man. He begged me to bring him from Berbera a silver-hilted sword and some soap, 1,000 dollars, two sets of silver bracelets, twenty guns with powder and shot, snuff, a scarlet cloth coat embroidered with gold, some poison that would not fail, and any other little article of luxury which might be supposed to suit him. In return he was to present us with horses, mules, slaves, ivory, and other valuables; he forgot, however, to do so before we departed.

The Gerad Adan was powerful, being the head of a tribe of cultivators, not split up, like the Bedouin, into independent clans, and he thus exercises a direct influence upon the conterminous races. The Girhi or "Giraffes" inhabiting these hills are, like most of the other settled Somal, a derivation from Darud, and descended from Kombo. Despite the unmerciful persecutions of the Gallas, they gradually migrated westwards from Makhar, their original nest, now number 5,000 shields, possess about 180 villages, and are accounted the power paramount. Though friendly with the Hbar Awal, the Girhi seldom descend, unless compelled by want of pasture, into the plains.

The other inhabitants of these hills are the Gallas and the Somali clans of Berteri, Bursuk, Shaykhash, Hawiyah, Usbayhan, Marayhan, and Abaskul.

The Gallas about Harar are divided into four several clans, separating as usual into a multitude of septs. The Alo extend westwards from the city; the Nole inhabit the land to the east and north-east, about two days' journey between the Eesa Somal, and Harar; on the south, are situated the Babuli and the Jarsa at Wilensi, Sagharrah, and Kondura—places described in these pages.

The Berteri, who occupy the Gurays Range, south of, and limitrophe to the Gallas, and thence extend eastward to the Jigjiga hills, are estimated at 3,000 shields. Of Darud origin, they own allegience to the Gerad Hirshi, and were, when I visited the country, on bad terms with the Girhi. The chief's family has, for several generations, been connected with the Amirs of Harar, and the caravan's route to and from Berbera lying through his country, makes him a useful friend and a dangerous foe. About the Gerad Hirsi different reports were rife: some described him as cruel, violent, and avaricious; others spoke of him as a godly and prayerful person; all, however, agreed that he *had* sowed wild oats. In token of repentance, he was fond of feeding Widads, and the Shaykh Jami of Harar was a frequent guest at his kraal.

The Bursuk number about 5,000 shields, own no chief, and in 1854 were at war with the Girhi, the Berteri, and especially the Gallas. In this country, the feuds differ from those of the plains; the hill men fight for three days, as the End of Time phrased it, and make peace for three days. The maritime clans are not so abrupt in their changes; moreover they claim blood-money, a thing here unknown. The Shaykhash, or "Reverend" as the term means, are the only Somal of the mountains not derived from Dir and Darud. Claiming descent from the Caliph Abu Bakr, they assert that ten generations ago, one Ao Khutab bin Fakih Umar crossed over from al-Hijaz, and settled in Eastern Africa with his six sons, Umar the greater, Umar the less, two Abdillahs, Ahmad, and lastly Siddik. This priestly tribe is dispersed, like that of Levi, amongst its brethren, and has spread from Efat to Ogadayn. Its principal sub-families are, Ao Umar, the elder, and Bah Dumma, the junior, branch.

The Hawiyah has been noticed in a previous chapter. Of the Usbayhan I saw but few individuals; they informed me that their tribe numbered forty villages, and about 1,000 shields; that they had no chief of their own race, but owned the rule of the Girhi and Berteri Gerads. Their principal clans are the Rer Yusuf, Rer Sa'id, Rer Abokr, and Yusuf Liyo.

In the Eastern Horn of Africa, and at Ogadayn, the Marahayn is a powerful tribe, here it is inconsequential, and affiliated to the Girhi. The Abaskul also lies scattered over the Harar hills, and owns the Gerad Adan as its chief. This tribe numbers fourteen villages, and between 400 and 500 shields, and is divided into the Rer Yusuf, the Jibrailah, and the Warra Dig: the latter clan is said to be of Galla extraction.

On the morning after my arrival at Sagharrah, I felt too ill to rise, and was treated with unaffected kindness by all the establishment. The Gerad sent to Harar for millet beer, Ao Samattar went to the gardens in search of Kat, the sons Yusuf Dera and a Dwarf [the only specimen of stunted humanity seen by me in the Somali country. He was about eighteen years old and looked ten] insisted upon firing me with such ardour, that no refusal could avail: and Khayrah the wife, with her daughters, two tall dark smiling, and well-favoured girls of thirteen and fifteen, sacrificed a sheep as my Fida, or Expiatory offering. Even the Galla Christians, who flocked to see the stranger, wept for the evil fate which had brought him so far from his fatherland, to die under a tree. Nothing indeed, would have been easier than such operation: all required was the turning face to the wall, for four or five days. But to expire of a ignoble colic!—the thing was not to be thought of, and a firm resolution to live on sometimes, methinks, effects its object.

On the 1st January 1855, feeling stronger, I clothed myself in my Arab best, and asked a palaver with the Gerad. We retired to a safe place behind the village, where I read with pomposity the Hajj Sharmakay's letter. The chief appeared much pleased by our having preferred his country to that of the Eesa; he at once opened the subject of the new fort, and informed me that I was the builder, as his eldest daughter had just dreamed that the stranger would settle in the land. Having discussed the project to the Gerad's satisfaction, we brought out the guns and shot a few birds for the benefit of the vulgar. Whilst engaged in the occupation, appeared a party of five strangers, and three mules with ornamented Morocco saddles, bridles, bells, and brass neck ornaments, after the fashion of Harar. Two of these men, Haji Umar and Nur Ambar, were citizens; the others, Ali Hasan, Husayn Araleh, and HajI Mohammed, were Somal of the Habr Awal tribe, high in the Amir's confidence. They had been sent to settle with Adan the weighty matter of blood-money. After sitting with us almost half an hour, during which they exchanged grave salutations with my attendants, inspected our asses with portentous countenances, and asked me a few questions concerning my business in those parts, they went privily to the Gerad, told him that the Arab was not one who bought and sold, that he had no design but to spy our the wealth of the land, and that the whole party should be sent prisoners in their hands to Harar. The chief curtly replied that we were his friends, and bade them, "throw far those words." Disappointed in their designs, they started late in the afternoon, driving off their 200 cows, and falsely promising to present our salaams to the Amir.

It became evident that some decided step must be taken. The Gerad confessed fear of his Harari kinsman, and owned that he had lost all his villages in the immediate neighbourhood of the city. I asked him point-blank to escort us; he as frankly replied that it was impossible. The request was lowered—we begged him to accompany us as far as the frontier; he professed inability to do so, but promised to send his eldest son, Shirwa. [In his account to the Royal Geographical Society Burton said: "We remained six days under the roof of the Gerad Adan, one of the most treacherous and dangerous Chiefs in this land of treachery and danger. My Somali attendants saw with horror that preparations were being made to enter the city of evil fame. They attempted by all means in their power to deter me from the attempt, but the unfortunates little knew the persistency of a Haji" (*Journal of the Royal Geographical Society*, Vol. 25, 1855, read June 11, 1855).]

Nothing then remained, dear L., but *payer d'audace*, and throwing all forethought to the dogs, to rely upon what has made many a small man great, the good star. I addressed my companions in a set speech, advising a mount without delay. They suggested a letter to the Amir, requesting permission to enter his city; this device was rejected for two reasons. In the first place, had a refusal been returned, our journey was cut short, and our labours stultified. Secondly, the End of Time had whispered that my two companions were plotting to prevent the letter reaching its destination. He had charged his own sin upon their shoulders; the Hammal and Long Gulad were incapable of such treachery. But our hedge-priest was thoroughly terrified; "a coward body after a," his face brightened when ordered to remain with the Gerad at Sagharrah, and though openly taunted with poltroonery, he had not the decency to object. My companions were then informed that hitherto their acts had been those of old women, not soldiers, and that something savouring of manliness must be done before we could return. They saw my determination to start alone, if necessary, and to do them justice, they at once arose. This was the more courageous in them, as alarmists had done their worst; but a day before, some travelling Somali had advised them, as they valued dear life, not to accompany that Turk to Harar. Once in the saddle, they shook off sad thoughts, declaring that if they were slain, I should pay their blood-money, and if they escaped, that their reward was in my hands. When in some danger, the Hammal especially behaved with a sturdiness which produced the most beneficial results. Yet they were true Easterns. Wearied by delay at Harar, I employed myself in meditating flight; they dryly declared that after-wit serves no good purpose; whilst I considered the possibility of escape, they looked only at the prospect of being dragged back with pinioned arms by the Amir's guard. Such is generally the effect of the vulgar Moslem's blinding fatalism.

I then wrote an English letter [At first I thought of writing it in Arabic; but having no seal, a *sine qua non* in an Eastern letter, and reflecting upon the consequences of detection or even suspicion, it appeared more politic to come boldly as a European. (Burton in the report he read to the R.G.S. stated, "As I approached the city [Harar] men turned out of their villages to ask if that was the Turk who was going to his death? The question made me resolve to appear before the Amir in my own character, an Englishman." [*Journal of the Royal Geographical Society*, Vol. 25, 1855] from the Political Agent at Aden to the Amir of Harar, proposing to deliver it in person, and throw off my disguise. Two reasons influenced me in adopting this "neck or nothing" plan. All the races amongst whom my travels lay, hold him nidering who hides his origin in places of danger; and secondly, my white face had converted me into a Turk, a nation more hated and suspected than any Europeans, without our *prestige*. Before leaving

Sagharrah, I entrusted to the End of Time a few lines addressed to Lieutenant Herne at Berbera, directing him how to act in case of necessity. Our baggage was again decimated; the greater part of left with Adan, and an ass carried only what was absolutely necessary—a change of clothes, a book or two, a few biscuits, ammunition, and a little tobacco. My Girhi escort consisted of Shirwa, the Bedouin Abtidon, and Mad Sa'id mounted on the End of Time's mule.

At 10 A.M. on the 2nd January, all the villagers assembled, and recited the Fatihah, consoling us with the information that we were dead men. By the worst of footpaths, we ascended the tough and stony hill behind Sagharrah, through bush and burn and over ridges of rock. At the summit was a village, where Shirwa halted, declaring that he dared not advance; a swordsman, however, was sent on to guard us through the Galla Pass. After an hour's ride, we reached the foot of a tall table-mountain called Kondura, where our road, a goat-path rough with rocks or fallen trees, and here and there arched over with giant creepers, was reduced to a narrow ledge, with a forest above and a forest below. I could not but admire the beauty of this Valombrosa, which reminded me of scenes whilome enjoyed in fair Touraine. High up on our left rose the perpendicular walls of the misty hill, fringed with tufted pine, and on the right the shrub-clad folds fell into a deep valley. The cool wind whistled and sunbeams like golden shafts darted through tall shady trees—"bearded with moss, and in garments green"—the ground was clothed with dank grass, and around the trunks grew thistles, daisies, and blue flowers which, at a distance, might well pass for violets.

Presently we were summarily stopped by half a dozen Gallas attending upon one Rabah, the Chief who owns the Pass. [It belongs, I was informed, to two clans of Gallas, who year by year in turn monopolize the profits.] This was the African style of toll-raking; the "pike" appears in the form of a plump spearman, and the gate is a pain of lances thrown across the road. Not without trouble, for they feared to depart from the *mos majorum*, we persuaded them that the ass carried no merchandise. Then rounding Kondura's northern flank, we entered the Amir's territory; about thirty miles distant, and separated by a series of blue valleys, lay a dark speck upon a tawny sheet of stubble—Harar.

Having paused for a moment to savour success, we began the descent. The ground was a slippery black soil—mist ever settles upon Kondura—and frequent springs oozing from the rock formed beds of black mire. A few huge Birbisa trees, the remnant of a forest still thick around the mountain's neck, marked out the road; they were branchy from stem to stern, and many had a girth of from twenty to twenty-five feet. [Of this tree are made the substantial doors, the basins and the porringers of Harar.]

After an hour's ride amongst thistles, whose flowers of a bright red-like worsted were not less than a child's head, we watered our mules at a rill below the slope. Then remounting, we urged over hill and dale, where Galla peasants were threshing and storing their grain with loud songs of joy; they were easily distinguished by their African features, mere caricatures of the Somal, whose type has been Arabized by repeated immigrations from al Yemen and Hadramaut. Late in the afternoon, having gained ten miles in a straight direction, we passed through a hedge of plantains, defending the windward side of Gafra, a village of Midgans who collect the Gerad Adan's grain. They shouted delight on recognizing their old friend, Mad Sa'id, led us to an empty Gambisa, swept and cleaned it, lighted a fire, turned our mules into a field to graze, and went forth to seek food. Their hospitable thoughts, however, were marred by the two citizens of Harar, who privately threatened them with the Amir's wrath, if they dared to feed that Turk.

As evening drew on, came a message from our enemies, the Habr Awal, who offered, if we would wait till sunrise, to enter the city in our train. The Gerad Adan had counselled me not to provoke these men; so, contrary to the advice of my two companions, I returned a polite answer, purporting that we would expect them till eight o'clock the next morning.

At 7 A.M., on the 3rd January, we heard that the treacherous Habr Awal had driven away their cows shortly after midnight. Seeing their hostile intentions, I left my journal, sketches, and other books in charge of an old Midgan, with directions that they should be forwarded to the Gerad Adan, and determined to carry nothing but our arms and a few presents for the Amir. We saddled our mules, mounted, and rode hurriedly along the edge of a picturesque chasm of tender pink granite, here and there obscured by luxuriant vegetation. In the centre, fringed with bright banks a shallow rill, called Doghlah, now brawls in tiny cascades, then whirls through huge boulders towards the Erar river. Presently, descending by a ladder of rock scarcely safe even for mules, we followed the course of the burn, and emerging into the valley beneath, we pricked forward rapidly, for day was wearing on, and we did not wish the Habr Awal to precede us.

About noon we crossed the Erar river. The bed is about one hundred yards broad, and a thin sheet of clear, cool, and sweet water covered with crystal the great part of the sand. According to my guides, its course, like that of the hills, is southerly towards the Webbe of Ogadayn [The Shebelli or Shebayli river]; none, however, could satisfy my curiosity concerning the course of the only perennial stream which exists between Harar and the coast.

In the lower valley, a mass of waving holcus, we met a multitude of Galla peasants coming from the city market with new potlids and the empty gourds which had contained their butter, ghi, and milk; all wondered aloud at the Turk, concerning whom they had heard many horrors. As we commenced another ascent, appeared a Harar Grandee mounted upon a handsomely caparisoned mule and attended by seven servants who carried gourds and skins of grain. He was a pale-faced senior with a white beard, dressed in a fine Tobe and a snowy turban, with scarlet edges: he carried no shield, but an Abyssinian broadsword was slung over his left shoulder. We exchanged courteous salutations, and as I was thirsty he ordered a footman to fill a cup with water. Half way up the hill appeared the 200 Girhi cows, but those traitors, the Habr Awal, had hurried onwards. Upon the summit was pointed out to me the village of Elaoda: in former times it was a wealthy place belonging to the Gerad Adan.

At 2 P.M. we fell into a narrow, fenced land, and halted for a few minutes near a spreading tree, under which sat women selling ghi and unspun cotton. About two mils distant on the crest of a hill, stood the city—the end of my present travel—a long somber line strikingly contrasting with the whitewashed towns of the East. The spectacle, materially speaking, was a disappointment; nothing conspicuous appeared but two grey minarets of rude shape; many would have grudged exposing three lives to win so paltry a prize. But of all that have attempted, none ever succeeded in entering that pile of stones; the thorough-bred traveller, dear L., will understand my exultation, although my two companions exchanged glances of wonder.

Spurring our mules, we advanced at a long trot, when Mad Sa'id stopped us to recite a Fatihah in honor of Ao Umar Siyad and Ao Rahmah, two great saints who repose under a clump of trees near the road. The soil on both sides of the path is rich and red; masses of plantains, limes, and pomegranates denote the gardens, which are defended by a bleached cow's skull, stuck upon a short stick and between them are plantations of coffee, bastard saffron, and the graceful Kat. About half a mile eastward of the town appears a burn called Jalah or the Coffee Water; the crowd crossing it did not prevent my companions bathing, and whilst they donned clean Tobes I retired to the wayside and sketched the town.

These operations over, we resumed our way up a rough *tranchée* ridged with stone and hedged with tall cactus. This ascends to an open plain. On the right lie the holcus fields, which reach to the town wall; on the left is a heap of rude cemetery, and in front are the dark defences of Harar, with groups of citizens loitering about the large gateway, and sitting in chat near the ruined tomb of Ao Abdal. We arrived at 3 P.M., after riding about five hours, which were required to accomplish twenty direct miles.

Advancing to the gate, Mad Sa'id accosted a warder, known by his long wand of office, and sent our salaams to the Amir, saying that we came from Aden, and requested the honour of an audience. Whilst he sped upon his errand, we sat at the foot of a round bastion, and were scrutinized, derided, and catechized by the curious of both sexes, especially by that conventionally termed the fair. The three Habr Awal presently approached and scowlingly inquired why we had not apprised them of our intention to enter the city. It was now "war to the knife"—we did not deign a reply.

After waiting half an hour at the gate, we were told by the returned warder to pass the threshold, and remounting guided our mules along the main street, a narrow uphill lane, with rocks cropping out from a surface more irregular than a Perote pavement. Long Gulad had given his animals into the hands of our two Bedouin: they did not appear till after our audience, when they informed us that the people at the entrance had advised them to escape with the beasts, an evil fate having been prepared for the proprietors.

Arrived within a hundred yards of the gate of holcus stalks, which opens into the courtyard of this African St. James's, our guide, a blear-eyed, surly-faced, angry-voiced fellow, made signs—none of us understanding his Harari—to dismount. We did so. He then began to trot, and roared our apparently that we must do the same. We looked at one another, the Hammal swore that he would perish foully rather than obey, and—conceive, dear L., the idea of petticoated pilgrim venerable as to beard and turban breaking into a long "double!"—I expressed much the same sentiment. Leading our mules leisurely, in spite of the guide's wrath, we entered the gate, strode down the yard, and were placed under a tree in its left corner, close to a low building of rough stone, which the clanking of frequent fetters argued to be a state prison.

This part of the court was crowded with Gallas, some lounging about, others squatting in the shade under the palace walls. The chiefs were known by their zinc armlets, composed of thin spiral circlets, closely joined, and extending in mass from the wrist almost to the elbow; all appeared to enjoy peculiar privileges—they carried their long spears, wore their sandals, and walked leisurely about the royal precincts. A delay of half an hour, during which state of affairs were being transacted within, gave me time to inspect a place of which so many and such different accounts are current. The palace itself, as Clapperton [Hugh Clapperton, 1788–1827 "From Kano to Sackatoo (Sokato), in *Narrative Travels and Discoveries in Northern and Central Africa 1822–4*, by D. Denham, H. Clapperton, and W. Oudney, 1826] describes the Fellatah Sultan's state hall, a mere shed, a long single-storied, windowless barn of rough stone and reddish clay, with no other insignia but a thin coat of whitewash over the door. This is the royal and wazirial distinction at Harar, where no lesser man may stucco the walls of his house. The courtyard was about eighty yards long by thirty in breadth, irregularly shaped, and surrounded by low buildings: in the centre, opposite the outer entrance, was a circle of masonry against which were propped divers doors. [I afterwards learned that when a man neglects a summons his door is removed to the royal court-yard on the first day; on the second, it is confiscated. The door is a valuable and venerable article in this part of Africa. According to Brude, Ptolemy Euergetes engraved it upon the Axum Obelisk for the benefit of his newly conquered Æthiopian subjects, to whom it had been unknown.]

Presently the blear-eyed guide with the angry voice returned from within, released us from the importunities of certain forward and inquisitive youths, and motioned us to doff our slippers at a stone step, or rather line, about twelve feet distant from the palace wall. We grumbled that we were not entering a mosque, but in vain. Then ensued a long dispute, in tongues mutually unintelligible, about giving up our weapons; by dint of obstinacy we retained our daggers and my revolver. The guide raised a door curtain, suggested a bow, and I stood in the presence of the dreaded chief. [In the *Life* (p. 207, vol. 1) there is an additional paragraph: "I walked into a vast hall, a hundred feet long, between two rows of Galla spearmen, between whose lines I had to pass. They were large half-naked savages, standing like statues, with fierce movable eyes, each one holding . . . a huge spear, with a head the size of a shovel. I purposely sauntered down them coolly with a swagger, with my eyes fixed upon their dangerous-looking faces. I had a six-shooter concealed in my waist-belt, and determined, at the first show of excitement, to run up to the Amir, and put it to his head, if it were necessary, to save my own life."]

The Amir, or, as he styles himself, the Sultan Ahmad bin Sultan Abibakr, sat in a dark room with whitewashed walls, to which hung—significant decorations—rusty matchlocks and polished fetters. His appearance was that of a little Indian Rajah, an etiolated youth twenty-four or twenty-five years old, plain and thin-bearded, with a yellow complexion, wrinkled brows, and protruding eyes. His dress was a flowing robe of crimson cloth, edged with snowy fur, and a narrow white turban tightly twisted round a tall conical cap of red velvet, like the old Turkish headgear of our painters. His throne was a common Indian Kursi, or raised cot, about five feet long, with back and sides supported by a dwarf railing: being an invalid he rested his elbow upon a pillow, under which appeared the hilt of a Cutch sabre. Ranged in double line, perpendicular to the Amir, stood the "court," his cousins and nearest relations with right arms bared after fashion of Abyssinia.

I entered the room with a loud "Peace be upon ye!" to which H.H. replying graciously, and extending a hand, bony and yellow as a kite's claw, snapped his thumb and middle finger. Two chamberlains stepping forward, held my forearms, and assisted me to bend low over the fingers, which however I did not kiss, being naturally averse to performing that operation upon any but a woman's hand. My two servants then took their turn: in this case, after the back was saluted, the palm was presented for a repetition. These preliminaries concluded, we were led to and seated upon a mat in front of the Amir, who directed towards us a frowning brow and inquisitive eye.

Some inquiries were made about the chief's health; he shook his head captiously, and inquired our errand. I drew from my pocket my own letter; it was carried by a chamberlain, with hands veiled in his Tobe, to the Amir, who after a brief glance laid it upon the couch, and demanded further explanation. I then represented in Arabic that we had come from Aden, bearing the compliments of our Daulah or governor, and that we had entered Harar to see the light of H.H.'s countenance; this information concluded with a little speech, describing the changes of Political Agents in Arabia, and alluding to the friendship formerly existing between the English and the deceased chief Abibakr.

The Amir smiled graciously.

This smile I must own, dear L., was a relief. We had been prepared for the worst, and the aspect of affairs in the palace was by no means reassuring.

Whispering to his Treasurer, a little ugly man with a badly shaven head, coarse features, pug nose, angry eyes, and a stubby beard, the Amir made a sign for us to retire. The *baise main* was repeated, and we backed out of the audience-shed in high favour. According to grandiloquent Bruce, "the Court of London and that of Abyssinia are, in their principles, one:" the loiterers in the Harar palace yards who had before regarded us with cut-throat looks, now smiled as though they loved us. Marshalled by the guard, we issued from the precincts, and after walking a hundred yards entered the Amir's second palace, which we were told to consider our home. There we found the Bedouin, who, scarcely believing that we had escaped alive, grinned in the joy of their hearts, and we were at once provided from the chief's kitchen with a dish of Shabta, holcus cakes soaked in sour milk, and thickly powdered with red pepper, the salt of this inland region.

When we had eaten, The treasurer reappeared, bearing the Amir's command that we should call upon his Wazir, the Gerad Mohammed. Resuming our peregrinations, we entered an abode distinguished by its eternal streak of chunam [plaster made of shell-lime and sand], and in a small room on the ground floor, cleanly whitewashed and adorned, like an old English kitchen, with varnished wooden porringers of various sizes, we found a venerable old man whose benevolent countenance belied the reports current about him in Somaliland. [About seven years ago the Hajj Sharmakey of Zayla chose as his agent at Harar, one of the Amir's officers, a certain Hajj Janitay. When this man died Sharmakey demanded an account from his sons; at Berbera they promised to give it, but returning to Harar they were persuaded, it is believed, by the Gerad Mohammed, to forget their word. Upon this Sharmakay's friends and relations, incited by one Husayn, a Somali who had lived many years at Harar in the Amir's favour, wrote an insulting letter to the Gerad, beginning with "No peace be upon thee, and no blessings of Allah, thou butcher! son of a butcher, etc., etc!" and concluding with a threat to pinion him in the market-place as a warning to men. Husayn carried the letter, which at first excited general terror; when, however, the attack did not take place, the Amir Abibakr imprisoned the imprudent Somali till he died. Sharmakay by way of reprisals, persuaded Alu, son of Sahlah Saleseh, king of Shoa, to seizure about three hundred Harari citizens living in his dominions and to keep them two years in durance.

The Amir Abibakr is said on his deathbed to have warned his son against the Gerad. When Ahmed reported his father's decease to Zayla, the Hajj Sharmakay ordered a grand Maulid or Mass in honour of the departed. Since that time, however, there has been little intercourse and no cordiality between them]. Half rising, although his wrinkled brow showed suffering, he seated me by his side upon the carpeted masonry bench, where lay the implements of his craft, reeds, inkstands and whitewashed boards for paper, politely welcomed me, and gravely stroking his cotton-coloured beard, in good Arabic desired my object.

I replied almost in the words used to the Amir, adding however some details how in the old days one Madar Farih had been charged by the late Sultan Abibakr with a present to the governor of Aden, and that it was the wish of our people to re-establish friendly relations and commercial intercourse with Harar.

"Khayr Inshallah!—it is well if Allah please!" ejaculated the Gerad; I then bent over his hand, and took leave.

Returning, we inquired anxiously of the Treasurer about my servants' arms which had not been returned, and were assured that they had been placed in the safest of store-houses, the palace. I then sent a common six-barrelled revolver as a present to the Amir, explaining its use to the bearer, and we prepared to make ourselves as comfortable as possible. The interior of our new house was a clean room, with plain walls, and a floor of tamped earth; opposite the entrance were two broad steps of masonry, raised about two feet, and a yard above the ground, and covered with hard matting. I contrived to make upon the higher ledge a bed with the cushions which my companions used as shabracques, and after seeing the mules fed and tethered, lay down to rest worn out by fatigue and profoundly impressed with the *poésie* of our position. I was under the roof of a bigoted prince whose least word was death; amongst a people who detested foreigners; the only European that had ever passed over their inhospitable threshold, and the fated instrument of their future downfall.

Down the Amazon

BY WILLIAM HERNDON

There have been many explorations of the mighty Amazon through the years, from Spanish conquistadors to naturalist Alfred Russell Wallace to Teddy Roosevelt. William Herndon's trip was more low-key. He traveled a fairly well-known route down the river, although there were still many dangers along the way. And while his narrative lacks the tension of many of the best tales of exploration, his easy-going style and interesting observations make it one of the best reads in early travel literature.

The story of Herndon's trip had such an effect on one young man, who eventually took the name Mark Twain, that he quit his job and started down the Mississippi to New Orleans, with every intention of heading off into the Brazilian jungles. Fortunately for the world of literature, he got sidetracked along the way.

This pleasant excerpt from Herndon's *Exploration of the Valley of the Amazon* describes the start of the more serious portion of his canoe journey.

★   ★   ★   ★   ★

ugust 2. Tingo Maria is a prettily situated village, of forty eight able-bodied men, and an entire population of one hundred and eighty-eight. This includes those who are settled at Juana del Rio and the houses within a mile or two.

The pueblo is situated in a plain on the left bank of the river, which is about six miles in length and three miles in its broadest part, where the mountains back of it recede in a semi-circle from the river. The height above the level of the sea is two thousand two hundred and sixty feet. The productions of the plain are sugar-cane, rice, cotton, tobacco, indigo, maize, sweet potatoes, yuccas, and *sachapapa* (potato of the woods), the large, mealy, purple-streaked tuberous root of a vine, in taste like a yam, and very good food. The woods are stocked with wild game such as *pumas*, or American tigers; deer; peccary, or wild hog; *ronsoco*, or river hog; monkeys, &c. For birds there are several varieties of *curassow*, a large bird, something like a turkey, but with, generally, a red bill, a crest, and shining blue-black plumage; a delicate *pava del monte*, or wild turkey; a great variety of parrots; large, black, wild ducks; and cormorants. There are also rattlesnakes and vipers. But even with all these, I would advise no traveller to trust to his gun for support. The woods are so thick and tangled with undergrowth that no one but an Indian can penetrate them, and no eyes but those of an Indian could see the game. Even he only hunts from necessity and will rarely venture into the thick forest alone, for fear of the tiger and the viper. There are also good and delicate fish in the river, but in no great abundance.

Ijurra shot a large bat, of the vampire species, measuring about two feet across the extended wings. This is a very disgusting-looking animal, though its fur is very delicate and of a glossy, rich maroon color. Its mouth is amply provided with teeth, looking like that of a miniature tiger. I never heard it doubted, until my return home, that these animals were blood-suckers; but the distinguished naturalist Mr. T.R. Peale tells me that no one has ever seen them engaged in that operation and that he has made repeated attempts for that purpose, but without success. Never having heard this doubt, it did not occur to me to ask the Indians if they had ever seen the bat sucking, or to examine the wounds of the horses that I had seen bleeding from this supposed cause.

I saw here, for the first time, the blow-gun of the Indians, called by the Spaniards *cerbatana*; by the Portuguese of the river, *gravatana* (a corruption, I imagine, of the former, as I find no such Portuguese word); and by the Indians, *pucuna*. It is made of any long, straight piece of wood, generally of a species of palm called chonta—a heavy, elastic wood, of which bows, clubs, and spears are also made. The pole or staff, about eight feet in length and two inches diameter near the mouth end, and, tapering down to half an inch at the extremity, is divided longitudinally; a canal is hollowed out along the centre of each part, which is well smoothed and polished by rubbing with find sand and wood. The two parts are then brought together, nicely wound with twine, and the whole covered with wax, mixed with some resin of the forest to make it hard. A couple of boar's teeth are fitted on each side of the mouth end, and one of the curved front teeth of a small animal resembling a cross between a squirrel and a hare is placed on top for a sight. The arrow is made of any light wood, generally the wild cane, or the middle fibre of a species of palm-leaf, which is about a foot in length and of the thickness of an ordinary match. The end of the arrow, which is placed next to the mouth, is wrapped with a light, delicate sort of wild cotton which grows in a pod upon a large tree and is called *huimba.* The other end, very sharply pointed, is dipped in a vegetable poison prepared from the juice of the creeper, called *bejuco de ambihuasca,* mixed with *aji,* or strong red pepper, *barbasco, sarnango,* and whatever sustance the Indians know to be deleterious.

The marksman, when using his pucuna, instead of stretching out the left hand along the body of the tube, places it to his mouth by grasping it, with both hands together, close to the mouthpiece, in such a manner that it requires considerable strength in the arms to hold it out at all, much less steadily. If a practised marksman, he will kill a small bird at thirty or forty paces. In an experiment that I saw, the Indian held the pucuna horizontally and the arrow blown from it struck the ground at thirty-eight paces. Commonly the Indian has quite an affection for his gun and many superstitious notions about it. I could not persuade one to shoot a very pretty black-and-yellow bird for me because it was a carrion bird; the Indian said that it would deteriorate and make useless all the poison in his gourd. Neither will he discharge his pucuna at a snake, for fear of the gun being made crooked like the reptile, and a fowling-piece or rifle that has once been discharged at an alligator is considered entirely worthless. A round gourd, with a hole in it for the huimba, and a joint of the *caña brava* as a quiver, completes the hunting apparatus.

August 3. Went to church. The congregation—men, women, and children—numbered about fifty. The service was conducted by the governor, assisted by the alcalde. A little naked, bow-legged Indian child, of two or three years, and Ijurra's pointer puppy, which he had brought all the way from Lima on his saddlebow, worried the congregation with their tricks and gambols; but altogether they were attentive to their prayers, and devout. I enjoyed exceedingly the public worship of God with these simple people of the forest; and although they probably understood little of what they were about, I thought I could see its humanizing and fraternizing effect upon all.

At night we had a ball at the governor's house. The alcalde, who was a trump, produced his fiddle. Another had a rude sort of guitar, or banjo. Under the excitement of the music we danced till eleven o'clock. The *Señor Commandante* was in considerable request, and a fat old lady, who would not dance with anybody else, nearly killed me. The governor discharged our guns several times and let off some rockets that we had brought from Huanuco. I doubt if Tingo Maria had ever witnessed such a brilliant affair before.

August 4. I waked up with pain in the legs and headache from dancing, and found our men and canoes ready for embarkation. After breakfast the governor and his wife (though I grievously fear that there had been no intervention of the priest in the matter of the union), together with several of our partners of the previous night, accompanied us to the port. After loading the canoes, the governor made a short address to the canoe-men, telling them that they were to take good care of us; whereupon, after a glass all round, from a bottle brought down specially by our hostess, and a hearty embrace from the governor, his lady, and my fat friend of the night before, we embarked and shoved off, the boatmen blowing their horns as we drifted rapidly down with the current of the river, and the party on shore waving their hats and shouting their adieus.

We had two canoes, the larger about forty feet long by two and a half feet broad. Each was hollowed out from a single log, and manned by five men and a boy. They are conducted by a *puntero*, or bowman, who looks out for rocks or sunken trees ahead; a *popero*, or steersman, who stands on a little platform at the stern of the boat and guides her motions; and the *bogas*, or rowers, who stand up to paddle, having one foot in the bottom of the boat and the other on the gunwale. When the river was smooth and free from obstructions, we drifted with the current, the men sitting on trunks and boxes, chatting and laughing with each other; but as we approached a *mal-paso*, their serious looks and the firm position in which each had planted himself at his post showed that work was to be done. I felt a little nervous at first, but when we had fairly entered the pass, the rapid gesture of the puntero, indicating the channel; the elegant and graceful position of the popero; giving the boat a broad sheer with the sweep of his long paddle; the desperate exertions of the bogas; the railroad rush of the canoe; and the wild, triumphant screaming laugh of the Indians, as we shot past the danger, made a scene that was much too exciting to admit of any other emotion than that of admiration.

At half-past five we camped on the beach. The first business of the boatmen when the canoe is secured is to go off to the woods and cut stakes and palm branches to make a house for the *patron*. By sticking long poles in the sand, chopping them half in two, about five feet above the ground, and bending the upper parts together, they make, in a few minutes, the frame of a little shanty, which, thickly thatched with palm leaves, will keep off the dew or an ordinary rain. Some bring the drift-wood that is lying about the beach and make a fire; the provisions are cooked and eaten; the bedding laid down upon the leaves that cover the floor of the shanty; the mosquito nettings spread; and, after a cup of coffee, a glass of grog, and a cigar (if they are to be had), everybody retires for the night by eight o'clock. The Indians sleep around the hut, each under his narrow cotton mosquito curtain, and the curtains glisten in the moon-light like so many tombstones.

August 5. Started at eight. River seventy yards broad, nine feet deep, pebbly bottom; current three miles per hour. We find in some places, where hills come down to the river, as much as thirty feet of depth. I was surprised that we saw no animals all day, but only river birds, such as ducks, cormorants, and king-fishers. We also saw many parrots of various kinds and brilliant plumage, but they always kept out of shot. We camped at half-past five, tired and low-spirited, having had nothing to eat all day but a little rice boiled with cheese early in the morning. My wrists were sore and painful from sunburn, and the sand-flies were very troublesome.

August 6. Soon after starting we saw a fine doe coming down towards the river. We steered in and got within about eighty yards of her, when Ijurra and I fired together, the guns loaded with a couple of rifle-balls each. The animal stood quite still for a few minutes, and then walked slowly off towards the bushes. I gave my gun, loaded with three rifle-balls, to the puntero, who got a close shot, but without effect. One of the balls, a little flattened, was picked up close to where the deer stood. These circumstances made the Indians doubt if she were a deer; and I judged from their gestures and exclamations, that they thought it was some evil spirit that was ball-proof.

These Indians have very keen senses and see and hear things that are inaudible and invisible to us. Our canoe-men this morning commenced paddling with great vigor. When I asked the cause, they said that they heard monkeys ahead. I think we must have paddled a mile before I heard the sound they spoke of. When we came up to them, we found a gang of large red monkeys in some tall trees on the river-side, making a noise like the grunting of a herd of enraged hogs. We landed, and in a few minutes I found myself beating my way through the thick undergrowth and hunting monkeys with as much excitement as ever I had hunted squirrels when I was a boy. I had no balls with me, and my No.3 shot only served to sting them from their elevated positions in the tops of the trees, and bring them within reach of the pucunas of the Indians. They got two and I one, after firing about a dozen shots into him. I never saw animals so tenacious of life; this one was, as the Indians expressed it, *bathed in shot* (*banado en municion*). These monkeys, about the size of a common terrier, were clad with a long, soft, maroon-colored hair. I believe they are of the species commonly called "howling monkeys."

·When I arrived at the beach with my game, I found that the Indians had made a fire and were roasting theirs. They did not take the trouble to skin and clean the animal, but simply put him in the fire, and, when well scorched, took him off and cut pieces from the fleshy parts with a knife. If these were not sufficiently well done, they roasted them further on little stakes stuck up before the fire. I tried to eat a piece, but it was so tough that my teeth would make no impression upon it.

We also saw today several river hogs and had an animated chase after one, which we encountered on the river-side, immediately opposite a nearly precipitous bank of loose earth, which crumbled under his feet so that he could not climb it. He hesitated to take the water in face of the canoes, so that we thought we had him; but after a little play, up and down the river-side, he broke his way through the line of his adversaries, capsizing two Indians as he went, and took to the water. This animal is amphibious, about the size of a half-grown hog. It reminded me, in its appearance and movements, of the rhinoceros. It is also red, and I thought it remarkable that the only animals we had seen—the deer, the monkeys, and the hog—should all be of this color.

We found the river today much choked with islands, shoals, and grounded drift-wood; camped at half-past five, and supped upon monkey soup. The monkey, as it regards toughness, was monkey still; but the liver, of which I ate nearly the whole, was tender and good. Jocko, however, had his revenge, for I nearly perished of nightmare. Some devil, with arms as nervous as the monkey's, had me by the throat, and staring on me with his cold, cruel eye, expressed his determination to hold on to the death. I thought it hard to die by the grasp of this fiend on the banks of the strange river, and so early in my course. Upon making a desperate effort and shaking him off, I found that I had forgotten to take off my cravat, which was choking me within an inch of my life.

August 7. Today presented a remarkable contrast to yesterday for sportsmen. We saw not a single animal, and very few birds; even parrots, generally so plentiful, were scarce today. It was a day of work. The men paddled well and we must have made seventy miles. On approaching Tocache, which was their last stage with us, the Indians almost deafened me with the noise of their horns. These horns are generally made of pieces of wood hollowed out thin, joined together, wrapped with twine, and coated with wax. They are shaped like a blunderbuss and are about four feet long; the mouthpiece is of reed, and the sound deep and mellow. The Indians always make a great noise on approaching any place to indicate that they come as friends. They fancy that they might otherwise be attacked, as hostile parties always move silently.

We arrived at five. Wearied with the monotonous day's journey and the heat of the sun, I anticipated the arrival with pleasure, thinking that we were going to stop at a large village and get something good to eat, but I was grievously disappointed. We arrived only at the port, which was, as usual, a shed on a hill. The village itself was nine miles off. There was nothing to eat where we were, so we determined to start inland and see what we could pick up. A rapid walk of an hour and a quarter brought us to Lamasillo, which I had been told was a pueblo of whites, but which we found to be but a single house.

I had been under the impression that "pueblo" meant a village, but I think now it signifies any settled country, though the houses may be miles apart. With much persuasion we induced the people of the house to sell us a couple of bottles of aguadiente and a pair of chickens. We were given to understand that Tocache was two *coceadas* further on, or about the same distance that we had come over from the port to this place. Distance is frequently estimated by the time that a man will occupy in taking a chew of coca. From the distance between the port and Lamasillo, it appears that a chew of coca is about three-fourths of a league, or thirty-seven and a half minutes.

We walked back by moonlight and had a fowl cooked forthwith. As we had had nothing but a little monkey soup early in the morning, we devoured it more like tigers than Christian men. We made our beds in the canoes under the shed, and, tired as we were, slept comfortably enough. It seems a merciful dispensation of Providence that the sand-flies go to bed at the same time with the people; otherwise I think one could not live in this country.

August 8. I sent Ijurra to Tocache to communicate with the governor, while I spent the day in writing up my journal and drying the equipage that had been wetted in the journey. In the afternoon I walked into the woods with an Indian, for the purpose of seeing him kill a bird or animal with his blow-gun. I admired the stealthy and noiseless manner with which he moved through the woods, occasionally casting a wondering and reproachful glance at me as I would catch my foot in a creeper and pitch into the bushes with sufficient noise to alarm all the game within a mile round. At last he pointed out to me a toucan, called the Spaniards *predicador*, or preacher, sitting on a branch of a tree out of the reach of his gun. I fired and brought him down with a broken wing. The Indian started into the bushes after him, but, finding him running, he came back to me for his blow-gun, which he had left behind. In a few minutes he brought the bird to me with an arrow sticking in its throat. The bird was dead in two minutes after I saw it, and probably in two and a half minutes from the time it was struck. The Indian said that his poison was good, but that it was in a manner ejected by the flow of blood, which covered the bird's breast, and which showed that a large blood-vessel of the neck had been pierced. I do not know if his reasoning was good or not.

Ijurra returned at eight, tired and in a bad humor. He reported that he had hunted the governor from place to place all day; had come up with him at last and obtained the promise that we should have canoes and men to prosecute our journey. My companion, who has been sub-prefect or governor of the whole province which we are now in (Mainas) and who has appointed and removed these governors of districts at pleasure, finds it difficult to sue where he has formerly commanded. He consequently generally quarrels with those in authority, and I have put myself to some trouble to reconcile the difference and cool down the heats which his impatience and irritability often occasion. He, however, did good service to the cause, by purchasing a hog and some chickens.

August 9. We had people to work killing and salting our hog. We had difficulty in getting someone to undertake this office, but the man from whom we purchased the hog brought down his family from Lamasillo to do the needful. We had very little benefit from our experiment in this way. We paid eight dollars for the hog, twenty-five cents for salt, twenty-five cents to Don Isidro, who brought him down to the port, and fifty cents to the same gentleman for butchering him.

Everybody is a Don in this country. Our Indian boatmen, at least the poperos, are Dons. Much ceremonious courtesy is necessary in intercourse with them. I have to treat the governors of the districts with all manner of ceremony. At the same time, while they exact this, and will get sulky and afford me no facilities without it, every last one of them will entertain the proposition to go along with me as my servant.

August 10. Whilst bathing in the river, I saw an animal swimming down the stream towards me, which I took to be a fox or cat. I threw stones at it and it swam to the other side of the river and took to the forest. Very soon after, a dog, who was evidently in chase, came swimming down, and missing the chase from the river, swam round in circles for some minutes before giving up. This animal, from my description, was pronounced to be an *ounce*, or tiger-cat. It is called *tigre* throughout all this country, but is never so large or ferocious as the Indian tiger. They are rather spotted like the leopard, than striped like the tiger. They are said, when hungry, to be sufficiently dangerous, and no one cares to bring them to bay without good dogs and a good gun. We talked so much about tigers and their carrying people off while asleep, that I, after going to bed, became nervous, and every sound near the shed made me grasp the handles of my pistols.

August 12. Had a visit from the governor last night. He is a little, barefooted Mestizo, dressed in the short frock and trousers of the Indians. He seemed disposed to do all in his power to facilitate us and forward us on our journey. I asked him about the tigers. He said he had known three instances of their having attacked men in the night; two of them were much injured, and one died.

Our boatmen made their appearance at 10 A.M. accompanied by their wives. The women carry their children (lashed flat on the back to a frame of reeds) by a strap around the brow as they do any other burden. The Indians of this district are Ibitos. They are less civilized than the Cholones of the Tingo Maria, and are the first whose faces I have seen regularly painted. They seem to have no fixed pattern, but each man paints according to his fancy; using, however, only two colors, blue and red.

We started at twelve with two canoes and twelve men. River fifty yards broad, eighteen feet deep, and with three miles an hour current; a stream called the Tocache empties into it about half a mile below the port. It forces its way through five channels, over a bank of stones and sand. The river is now entirely broken up by islands and rapids. In passing one of these, we came very near being capsized. Rounding suddenly the lower end of an island, we met the full force of the current from the other side, which, striking us on the beam, nearly rolled the canoe over. The men, in their fright, threw themselves on the upper gunwale of the boat which gave us a *heel* the other way, and we very nearly filled. Had the popero fallen from his post (and he tottered fearfully), we should probably have been lost; but by great exertions he got the boat's head downstream, and we shot safely by the rocks that threatened destruction.

At six we arrived at the port of Bolsayacu. The pueblo, which I found, as usual, to consist of one house, was a pleasant walk of half a mile from the port. We slept there instead of at the beach, and it was well that we did, for it rained heavily all night. The only inhabitants of the rancho seemed to be two little girls, but I found in the morning that one of them had an infant, though she did not appear to be more than twelve or thirteen years of age. I suppose there are more houses in the neighborhood; but, as I have before said, a pueblo is merely a settlement and may extend over leagues. We travelled today about twenty-five miles.

August 13. Last night Ijurra struck with a fire-brand one of the boatmen, who was drunk and disposed to be insolent, and blackened and burned his face. The man—a powerful Indian, of full six feet in height—bore it like a corrected child in a blubbering and sulky sort of manner.

Between ten and eleven we passed the mal-paso of Matagalla, just below the mouth of the river of the same name, which comes in on the left, clear and cool into the Huallaga. This mal-paso is the worst that I have yet encountered. We dared not attempt it under oar. The canoe was let down along the shore, stern foremost, by a rope from its bows, and guided between the rocks by the popero—sometimes with his paddle, and sometimes overboard, up to his middle in water.

Livingstone in Africa

BY DAVID LIVINGSTONE

Livingstone traveled extensively through southern and central Africa, starting as a missionary doctor in South Africa and working his way north. While he is most famous for being "found" by Stanley, his rambling did much to fill in the blank spots on the map of the African interior. He died while continuing to search for the source of the Nile, mistakenly believing that its headwaters were in the area of the Upper Congo.

This account is taken from *Travels and Researches in South Africa*. Like most African explorers, his attempts to pass from the lands of one tribe to another were more of a struggle than dealing with fever, rough terrain, or dangerous animals. A mix of threats, friendship, diplomacy, gifts, and violence were necessary at almost every turn.

★   ★   ★   ★   ★

It happened that the head-man of the village where I had lain twenty-two days, while bargaining and quarrelling in my camp for a piece of meat, had been struck on the mouth by one of my men. My principal men paid five pieces of cloth and a gun as an atonement; but the more they yielded the more exorbitant he became, and he sent word to all the surrounding villages to aid him in avenging the affront of a blow on the beard. As their courage usually rises with success, I resolved to yield no more, and departed. In passing through the forest in the country beyond, we were startled by a body of men rushing after us. They began by knocking down the burdens of the hindermost of my men, and several shots were fired, each party spreading out on both sides of the path. I fortunately had a six-barreled revolver, which my friend Captain Henry Need, of her majesty's brig "Linnet," had considerably sent to Golungo Alto after my departure from Loanda. Taking this in my hand,

182

and forgetting fever, I staggered quickly along the path with two or three of my men, and fortunately encountered the chief. The sight of the six barrels gaping into his stomach, with my own ghastly visage looking daggers at his face, seemed to produce an instant revolution in his martial feelings; for he cried out, "Oh, I have only come to speak to you, and wish peace only." Mashauana had hold of him by the hand, and found him shaking. We examined his gun, and found that it had been discharged. Both parties crowded up to their chiefs. One of the opposite party coming too near, one of mine drove him back with a battle-axe. The enemy protested their amicable intentions, and my men asserted the fact of having the goods knocked down as evidence of the contrary. Without waiting long, I requested all to sit down; and Pitsane, placing his hand upon the revolver, somewhat allayed their fears. I then said to the chief, "If you have come with peaceable intentions, we have no other; go away home to your village." He replied, "I am afraid lest you shoot me in the back." I rejoined, "If I wanted to kill you, I could shoot you in the face as well." Mosantu called out to me, "That's only a Makalaka trick; don't give him your back." But I said, "Tell him to observe that I am not afraid of him," and, turning, mounted my ox. There was not much danger in the fire that was opened at first, there being so many trees. The enemy probably expected that the sudden attack would make us forsake our goods and allow them to plunder with ease. The villagers were no doubt pleased with being allowed to retire unscathed, and we were also glad to get away without having shed a drop of blood or having compromised ourselves for any future visit. My men were delighted with their own bravery, and made the woods rings with telling each other how "brilliant their conduct before the enemy" would have been, had hostilities not been brought to a sudden close.

I do not mention this little skirmish as a very frightful affair. The negro character in these parts, and in Angola, is essentially cowardly, except when influenced by success. A partial triumph over any body of men would induce the whole country to rise in arms; and this is the chief danger to be feared. These petty chiefs have individually but little power, and with my men, now armed with guns, I could have easily beaten them off singly; but, being of the same family, they would readily unite in vast numbers if incited by the prospect of successful plunder. They are by no means equal to the Cape Caffres in any respect whatever.

In the evening we came to Moena Kikanje, and found him a sensible man. He is the last of the Chiboque chiefs in this direction, and is in alliance with Matiamvo, whose territory commences a short distance beyond. His village is placed on the east bank of the Quilo, which is here twenty yards wide and breast deep.

The country was generally covered with forest, and we had slept every night at some village. I was so weak, and had become so deaf from the effects of the fever, that I was glad to avail myself of the company of Senhor Pascoal and the other native traders. Our rate of travelling was only two geographical miles per hour, and the average number of hours three and a half per day, or seven miles. Two-thirds of the month was spent in stoppages, there being only ten travelling days in each month. The stoppages were caused by sickness, and the necessity of remaining in different parts to purchase food; and also because when one carrier was sick the rest refused to carry his load.

We crossed the Loange, a deep but narrow stream, by a bridge. It becomes much larger, and contains hippopotami, lower down. It is the boundary of Londa on the west. We also slept on the banks of the Pezo, now flooded, and could not but admire their capabilities for easy irrigation. On reaching the river Chikapa (lat. 10° 10'S., long. 19° 42'E.), the 25th of March, we found it fifty or sixty yards wide, and flowing E.N.E. into the Kasai. The adjacent country is of the same level nature as that part of Londa formerly described; but, having come farther to the eastward than our previous course, we found that all the rivers had worn for themselves much deeper valleys than at the points we had formerly crossed them.

Surrounded on all sides by large gloomy forests, the people of these parts have a much more indistinct idea of the geography of their country than those who live in hilly regions. It was only after long and patient inquiry that I became fully persuaded that the Quilo runs into the Chikapa. As we now crossed them both considerably farther down, and were greatly to the eastward of our first route, there can be no doubt that these rivers take the same course as the others, into the Kasai, and that I had been led into a mistake in saying that any of them flowed to the westward. Indeed, it was only at this time that I began to perceive that all the western feeders of the Kasai, except the Quango, flow first from the western side toward the centre of the country, then gradually turn, with the Kasai itself, to the north, and after the confluence of the Kasai with the Quango, an immense body of water, collected from all these branches, finds its way out of the country by means of the river Congo or Zaire, on the west coast.

The people living along the paths we are now following were quite accustomed to the visits of native traders, and did not feel in any way bound to make presents of food except for the purpose of cheating; thus, a man gave me a fowl and some meal, and after a short time returned. I offered him a handsome present of beads; but these he declined, and demanded a cloth instead, which was far more than the value of his gift. They did the same with my men, until we had to refuse presents altogether. Others made high demands because I slept in a "house of cloth" and must be rich. They seemed to think that they had a perfect right to payment for simply passing through the country.

Beyond the Chikapa we crossed the Kamáue, a small, deep stream proceeding from S.S.W. and flowing into the Chikapa.

On the 30ᵗʰ of April we reached the Loajima, where we had to form a bridge to effect our passge. This was not so difficult an operation as one might imagine; for a tree was growing in a horizontal position across part of the stream, and there being no want of the tough climbing plants which admit of being knitted like ropes, Senhor P. soon constructed a bridge. The Loajima was here about twenty-five yards wide, but very much deeper than where I had crossed before on the shoulders of Mashauana. The last rain of this season had fallen on the 28ᵗʰ, and had suddenly been followed by a great decrease of the temperature. The people in these parts seemed more slender in form, and their color a lighter olive, than any we had hitherto met. The mode of dressing the great masses of woolly hair which lay upon their shoulders, together with their general features, again reminded me of the ancient Egyptians. Several were seen with the upward inclination of the outer angles of the eye; but this was not general. A few of the ladies adopt a curious custom of attaching the hair to a hoop which encircles the head, giving it somewhat the appearance of the glory round the head of the Virgin. Some have a small hoop behind that represented in the wood-cut. Others wear an ornament of woven hair and hide adorned with beads. The hair of the tails of buffalos, which are to be found farther east, is sometimes added; while others weave their own hair on pieces of hide in the form of buffalo horns, or make a single horn in front. Many tattoo their bodies by inserting some black substance beneath the skin; which leaves an elevated cicatrix about half an inch long: these are made in the form of stars and other figures of no particular beauty.

We made a little détour to the southward, in order to get provisions in a cheaper market. This led us along the rivulet called Tamba, where we found the people, who had not been visited so frequently by the slave traders as the rest, rather timid and very civil.

We reached the river Moamba (lat. 9° 38' S., long. 20° 13' 34" E.) on the 7ᵗʰ of May. This is a stream of thirty yards wide, and, like the Quilo, Loange, Chikapa, and Loajima, it contains both alligators and hippopotami. We crossed it by means of canoes.

We crossed two small streams, the Kanesi and Fombeji, before reaching Cobango, a village situated on the banks of the Chihombo. The country was becoming more densely peopled as we proceeded, but it bears no population compared to what it might easily sustain.

Cabango (lat. 9° 31' S., long. 20° 31' or 32' E.) is the dwelling-place of Muanzánza, one of Matiamvo's subordinate chiefs. His village consists of about two hundred huts and ten or twelve square houses, constructed of poles with grass interwoven. The latter are occupied by half-caste Portuguese from Ambaca, agents for the Cassange traders. The cold in the mornings was now severe to the feelings, the thermometer ranging from 58° to 60°, though, when protected, sometime standing as high as 64° at 6 A.M. When the sun is well up, the thermometer in the shade rises to 80°, and in the evenings it is about 78°.

Having met with an accident to one of my eyes by a blow from a branch in passing through a forest, I remained some days here, endeavoring, though with much pain, to draw a sketch of the country thus far, to be sent back to Mr. Gabriel at Loanda. I was always anxious to transmit an account of my discoveries on every possible occasion, lest, any thing happening in the country to which I was going, they should be entirely lost. I also fondly expected a package of letters and papers which my good angel at Loanda would be sure to send if they came to hand; but I afterward found that, though he had offered a large sum to anyone who would return with an assurance of having delivered the last packet he sent, no one followed me with it to Cabango. The unwearied attentions of this good Englishman, from his first welcome to me, when, a weary, dejected, and worn-out stranger, I arrived at his residence, and his whole subsequent conduct, will be held in lively remembrance by me to my dying day.

As we thought it best to strike away to the S.E. from Cabango to our old friend Katema, I asked a guide from Muanzánza. He agreed to furnish one, and also accepted a smaller present from me than usual, when it was represented to him by Pascoal and Faria that I was not a trader.

We were forced to prepay our guide and his father too; and he went but one day, though he promised to go with us to Katema.

The reason why we needed a guide at all was to secure the convenience of a path, which, though generally no better than a sheep-walk, is much easier than going straight in one direction through entangled forests and tropical vegetation. We knew the general direction we ought to follow, and also if any deviation occurred from our proper route; but, to avoid impassable forests

and untreadable bogs, and to get to the proper fords of the rivers, we always
tried to procure a guide, and he always followed the common path from one
village to another when that lay in the direction we were going.

After leaving Cabango, on the 21st, we crossed several little streams
running into the Chihombo on our left.

On the 28th we reached the village of the chief Bango (lat. 12° 22' 53"
S., long. 20° 58' E.), who brought us a handsome present of some meal and the
mean of an entire pallah. We here slaughtered the last of the cows presented to
us by Mr. Schut, which I had kept milked until it gave only a teaspoonful at a
time. My men enjoyed a hearty laugh when they found that I had given up all
hope of more, for they have been talking among themselves about my perseverance.

May 30—We left Bango, and proceeded to the river Loembwe, which
flows to the N.N.E. and abounds in hippopotami. It is about sixty yards wide
and four feet deep, but usually contains much less water than this, for there are
fishing-weirs placed right across it. Like all the African rivers in this quarter, it
has morasses on each bank; yet the valley in which it winds, when seen from
the high lands above, is extremely beautiful.

Having passed the Loembwe, we were in a more open country, with
every few hours a small valley, through which ran a little rill in the middle of a
bog. These were always difficult to pass, and being numerous, kept the lower
part of the person constantly wet.

On the evening of the 2nd of June we reached the village of Kawawa,—
rather an important personage in these parts. This village consists of forty or
fifty huts, and is surrounded by forest. Drums were beating over the body of a
man who had died the preceding day, and some women were making a clam-
orous wail at the door of his hut, and addressing the deceased as if alive.

In the morning we had agreeable intercourse with Kawawa; he visited
us, and we sat and talked nearly the whole day with him and his people. When
we visited him in return, we found him in his large court-house which, though
of a beehive shape, was remarkably well built. As I had shown him a number of
curiosities, he now produced a jug, of English ware, shaped like an old man
holding a can of beer in his hand, as the greatest curiosity he had to exhibit.

We exhibited the pictures of the magic lantern in the evening, and all
were delighted except Kawawa himself. He showed symptoms of dread, and
several times started up as if to run away, but was prevented by the crowd behind. Some of the more intelligent understood the explanations well, and ex-
patiated eloquently on them to the more obtuse. Nothing could exceed the

civilities which had passed between us during this day; but Kawawa had heard that the Ciboque had forced us to pay an ox, and now thought he might do the same. When, therefore, I sent next morning to let him know that we were ready to start, he replied, in his figurative way, "If an ox come in the way of a man, ought he not to eat it? I had given one to the Chiboque, and must give him the same, together with a gun, gunpowder, and a black robe, like that he had seen spread out to dry the day before; that, if I refused an ox, I must give one of my men, and a book by which he might see the state of Matiamvo's heart toward him, and which would forewarn him should Matiamvo ever resolve to cut off his head." Kawawa came in the coolest manner possible to our encampment after sending this message, and told me he had seen all our goods and must have all he asked, as he had command of the Kasai in our front, and would prevent us from passing it unless we paid this tribute. I replied that the goods were my property and not his; that I would never have it said that a white man had paid tribute to a black, and that I should cross the Kasai in spite of him. He ordered his people to arm themselves, and when some of my men saw them rushing for their bows, arrows, and spears, they became somewhat panic-stricken. I ordered them to move away, and not to fire unless Kawawa's people struck the first blow. I took the lead, and expected them all to follow, as they usually had done; but many of my men remained behind. When I knew this, I jumped off the ox and made a rush to them with the revolver in my hand. Kawawa ran away among his people, and they turned their backs too. I shouted to my men to take up their luggage and march; some did so with alacrity, feeling that they had disobeyed orders by remaining; but one of them refused, and was preparing to fire at Kawawa, until I gave him a punch on the head with the pistol and made him go too. I felt here, as elsewhere, that subordination must be maintained at all risks. We all moved into the forest, the people of Kawawa standing about a hundred yards off, gazing, but not firing a shot or an arrow. It is extremely unpleasant to part with these chieftains thus, after spending a day or two in the most amicable intercourse, and in a part where the people are generally civil. This Kawawa, however, is not a good specimen of the Balonda chiefs, and is rather notorious in the neighborhood for his folly. We were told that he has good reason to believe that Matiamvo will some day cut off his head for his disregard for the rights of strangers.

Kawawa was not to be balked of his supposed rights by the unceremonious way in which we had left him; for, when we reached the ford of the Kasai, about ten miles distant, we found that he had sent four of his men with orders to the ferryman to refuse us passage. We were here duly informed that we must deliver up all the articles mentioned, and one of our men besides. This demand for one of our number always nettled every heart. The canoes were taken away before our eyes, and we were supposed to be quite helpless without them, at a river a good hundred yards broad, and very deep. Pitsane stood on the bank, gazing with apparent indifference on the stream, and made an accurate observation of where the canoes were hidden among the reeds. The ferrymen casually asked one of my Batoka if they had rivers in his country, and he answered, with truth, "No; we have none." Kawawa's people then felt sure we could not cross. I thought of swimming when they were gone; but, after it was dark, by the unasked loan of one of the hidden canoes, we soon were snug in our bivouac on the southern bank of the Kasai. I left some beads as payment for some meal which had been presented by the ferrymen; and, the canoe having been left on their own side of the river, Pitsane and his companions laughed uproariously at the disgust our enemies would feel, and their perplexity as to who had been our paddler across. They were quite sure that Kawawa would imagine that we had been ferried over by his own people and would be divining to find out who had done the deed. When ready to depart in the morning, Kawawa's people appeared on the opposite heights, and could scarcely believe their eyes when they saw us prepared to start away to the south. At last one of them called out, "Ah! Ye are bad;" to which Pitsane and his companions retorted, "Ah! Ye are good, and we thank you for the loan of your canoe." We were careful to explain the whole of the circumstance to Katema and the other chiefs, and they all agreed that we were perfectly justifiable under the circumstances, and that Matiamvo would approve our conduct. When any thing that might bear an unfavorable construction happens among themselves, they send explanations to each other. The mere fact of doing so prevents them from losing their character, for there is public opinion even among them.

Witchcraft in West Africa

BY PAUL DU CHAILLU

In the annals of African exploration, Paul Du Chaillu's name is rarely mentioned with men like Speke, Baker, Livingstone, or Stanley. But his travels in West Africa in the 1850s made him one of the first white explorers to learn about the mysterious gorilla, pygmies, and cannibals. His first book, *Explorations and Adventures in Equatorial Africa*, was widely discredited as fiction. Stung by the criticism, Du Chaillu returned to Africa to bring back more scientific evidence of his claims. His second book, *A Journey to Ashango Land*, restored his reputation, and later West African explorers like Mary Kingsley and Richard Burton confirmed his claims.

Du Chaillu's method of travel also distinguished him. He usually went without white companions, spoke enough native languages to communicate with the tribes he encountered, and survived the fevers that took the lives of so many Europeans in Africa. Part of his youth was spent at a trading post on the African coast, giving him a better understanding of the physical rigors of travel in Africa and its system of trade—both in slaves and goods—which allowed him access to interior tribes that no white man had ever visited.

He was also a surprisingly good observer and writer. This account of native customs and witchcraft, followed by a description of an ant species that caused even the largest beasts in the jungle to flee for their lives, is from his first book.

★　★　★　★　★

At last I was ready to make another start; my health restored, my spirits in some measure recovered, and eager for the new region.

On the 10th of October, 1859, Quengueza was still too weak to travel, so I determined to start without him.

Ranpano and his people had been urging me for some time not to go; and now, when I was all ready, the old king called a grand palaver, which I attended, and of which the chief purpose was to persuade me not to venture into the interior.

My good old friend Ranpano was really solicitous about me. He made me an address, in which he informed me that he had heard the interior people wanted to get me in their power. They wanted to kill me, in order to make a fetich of my hair. They had very many fetiches already, and were very anxious to make their collection complete—so it appeared.

I replied that I had no fear of them; that, so far, I had been brought back safely to them, and I was willing to trust my God again.

Then he said, "We love you. You are our white man (ntangani). What you tell us we do. When you say it is wrong, we do not do it. We take care of your house, your goats, your fowl, your parrots, your monkeys. You are the first white man that settled among us, and we love you."

To which all the people answered, "Yes, we love him! He is our white man, and we have no other white man."

Then the king said, "We know that writing talks. Write us, therefore, a letter to prove to your friends, if you do not come back, that it was not we who hurt you."

To this followed various objections to my going, to all of which I was obliged to make grave answers.

Finally, when they gave me up, all exclaimed in accents of wonder, "Ottangani angani (man of the white men)! What is the matter with you that you have no fear? God gave you the heart of a leopard! You were born without fear!"

More than a year ago the Camma gave me the title of "*makaga*," an honourable name, which only one man, and he the bravest and best hunter in the tribe, may bear. The office of the makaga is to lead in all desperate affairs. For instance, if anyone has murdered one of his fellow-villagers, and the murderer's town refuses to give him up (which is almost always the case, they thinking it a shame to surrender anyone who has taken refuge with them), then it is the business of the makaga to take the best men of the villages, lead them to the assault of that which protects the murderer, and destroy that, with its inhabitants. It is remarkable that, in all of the Camma country, the murder of a free man is punished with the death of the murderer. My title was rather an honorary one, as I was never called on the execute justice among them.

At last Ranpano gave me sixteen men to take me to Goumbi, from where Quengueza's people were to set me on. Makondai, the little fellow who had so bravely accompanied me on my last tour, asked to be taken again, and I took him gladly. He is a brave, intelligent lad, and by his care for my coffee and many other matters, added much to my comfort.

Quengueza could not come with us; but he sent orders to his brother, who reigned in his stead at Goumbi, to give me as many people as I wanted, and to afford me protection as far as I needed it; and specially named Adouma to be the chief of the party who were to accompany me to the Ashira country.

When all this was done, there was, according to African custom, a formal leave-taking. Quengueza's men, Ranpano's, and mine gathered before the old king, who solemnly bade us God-speed, taking my two hands in his and blowing upon them, as their custom is; saying, "Go thou safely, and return safely."

It is now (October) the full rainy season, and not the most comfortable for travelling. But it is probably the healthiest, and, as for the rest, there is little choice. Besides provisions, I took with me some wine and brandy to help me in rainy nights, and a goodly quantity of quinine—the one indispensable requisite, without which let no man travel in Western Africa. I know the prejudice which exists against this remedy; but I have within this last four years taken fourteen ounces, and live as a proof that it is a useful medicine and a very slow poison.

We arrived at Goumbi on the 13th, after meeting with two very heavy storms of wind and rain on the way. The people asked after their king, who had gone away well, and whom, they thought, I ought to have brought back in the same condition.

I was asked to go and see an old friend of mine, Mpomo, who was now sick. They had spent the night before drumming about his bedside to drive out the devil. But I soon saw that neither drumming nor medicine would help the poor fellow. The film of death was already in his eyes, and I knew he could scarce live through the approaching night. He held out his hand to me in welcome, and feebly said, "Chally, save me, for I am dying."

He was then surrounded by hundreds of people, most of them moved to tears at their friend's pitiable condition.

I explained to him that I had no power to save him; that my life and his were alike in the hands of God; and that he should commend both body and soul to that one God. But he and all around had the conviction that, if only I wished, I could cure him. They followed me to my house, asking for medicine; and at last, not to seem heartless, I sent him a restorative—something, at least, to make his remaining moments easy. At the same time I warned them that he would die, and they must not blame me for his death. This was necessary, for their ignorance makes them very suspicious.

When I awoke the next morning I heard the mournful wail which proclaimed that poor Mpomo was gone to his long rest. This cry of the African mourners is the saddest I ever heard. Its burden is really and plainly, "All is done. There is no hope. We loved him. We shall *never* see him again." They mourn literally as those who have no hope.

In the last moments of a Camma man who lies at the point of death, his head-wife comes and throws herself by him on his bed. Then, encircling his form with her arms, she sings to him songs of love, and pours out a torrent of endearing phrases, all the village standing by uttering wailings and shedding tears. Such a scene was always very touching to me.

When I went to Mpomo's house I saw his poor wives sitting in tears upon the ground, throwing moistened ashes and dust over their bodies, shaving their heads, and rending their clothes.

In the afternoon I heard talk of witchcraft.

The mourning lasted for two days. On the 17th the body, already in a state of decomposition, was put in a canoe and taken to the cemetery of the Goumbi people down the river some fifty miles. It was pitiable to see the grief of his poor wives. They seemed to have really loved him, and sorrowed for him now that he was dead, as they had carefully and lovingly attended upon him till he died. I saw them, on the night of his death, weeping over him, one after the other taking him in her arms. It was a strange sight. In these sorrowful moments there was no sign of jealousy between the poor women, that I could see. All were united by their love for the same object.

Those who have studied the African character, and know how much they are given to dissimulation, cannot be certain whether the display of love come from real sorrow or not. Of course, every wife ought to appear much distressed, for should they not show a profound sorrow they would certainly be accused of bewitching their husbands. I have even known cases where the mother was killed as the cause of death of her own child.

On the day Mpomo was buried proceedings were begun to discover the persons who had bewitched the poor fellow. They could not be persuaded that a young man, hale and hearty but a few weeks ago, could die by natural causes. A great doctor was brought from up the river, and for two nights and days the rude scenes which I have already once given an account of were repeated.

At last, on the third morning, when the excitement of the people was at its height—when old and young, male and female, were frantic with the desire for revenge on the sorcerers, the doctor assembled them about him in the centre of the town, and began his final incantation, which should disclose the names of the murderous sorcerers.

Every man and boy was armed, some with spears, some with swords, some with guns and axes, and on every face was shown a determination to wreak bloody revenge on those who should be pointed out as the criminals. The whole town was rapt in an indescribable fury and horrid thirst for human blood. For the first time I found my voice without authority in Goumbi. I did not even get a hearing. What I said was passed by as though no one had spoken. As a last threat, when I saw proceedings begun, I said I would make Quenguez punish them for the murders done in his absence. But alas! Here they had out-witted me. On the day of Mpomo's death they had sent secretly to Quengueza to ask if they could kill the witches. He, poor man! Sick himself, and always afraid of the power of sorcerers, and without me to advise him, at once sent back word to kill them all without mercy. So they almost laughed in my face.

Finding all my endeavours in vain, and that the work of bloodshed was to be carried through to its dreadful end, I determined, at least, to see how all was conducted.

At a motion from the doctor, the people became at once quite still. This sudden silence lasted about a minute, when the loud, harsh voice of the doctor was heard:

"There is a very black woman, who lives in a house"—describing it fully, with its location—"she bewitched Mpomo."

Scarce had he ended when the crowd, roaring and screaming like so many hideous beasts, rushed frantically for the place indicated. They seized upon a poor girl named Okandaga, the sister of my good friend and guide Adouma. Waving their weapons over her head, they tore her away towards the water-side. Here she was quickly bound with cords, and then all rushed away to the doctor again.

As poor Okandaga passed in the hands of her murderers, she saw me, though I thought I had concealed myself from view. I turned my head away and prayed she might not see me. I could not help her. But presently I heard her cry out, "Chally, Chally, do not let me die!"

It was a moment of terrible agony to me. For a minute I was minded to rush into the crowd and attempt the rescue of the poor victim. But it would have been of not the slightest use. The people were too frantic and crazed to even notice my presence. I should only have sacrificed my own life without helping her. So I turned away into a corner behind a tree, and—I may confess, I trust—shed bitter tears at my utter powerlessness.

Presently silence again fell upon the crowd. Then the harsh voice of the devilish doctor again rang over the town. It seemed to me like the hoarse croak of some death-foretelling raven:

"There is an old woman in a house"—describing it—"she also bewitched Mpomo."

Again the crowd rushed off. This time they seized a niece of King Quengueza, a noble-hearted and rather majestic old woman. As they crowded around her with flaming eyes and threats of death, she rose proudly from the ground, looked them in the face unflinchingly, and motioning them to keep their hands off, said, "I will drink the mboundou; but woe to my accusers if I do not die!"

Then she, too, was escorted to the river, but without being bound. She submitted to all without a tear or a murmur for mercy.

Again, a third time the dreadful silence fell upon the town, and the doctor's voice was heard:

"There is a woman with six children. She lives on a plantation towards the rising sun. She, too, bewitched Mpomo."

Again there was a furious shout, and in a few minutes they brought to the river one of Quengueza's slave-women, a good and much-respected woman, whom also I knew.

The doctor now approached with the crowd. In a loud voice he recited the crime of which these women were accused. The first taken, Okandaga, had—so he said—some weeks before asked Mpomo for some salt, he being her relative. Salt was scarce, and he had refused her. She had said unpleasant words to him them, and had by sorcery taken his life.

Then Quengueza's niece was accused. She was barren, and Mpomo had children. She envied him. Therefore she had bewitched him.

Quengueza's slave had asked Mpomo for a looking-glass. He had refused her. Therefore she had killed him with sorcery.

As each accusation was recited the people broke out into curses. Even the relatives of the poor victims were obliged to join in this. Everyone rivalled his neighbour in cursing, each fearful lest lukewarmness in the ceremony should expose him to a like fate.

Next the victims were put into a large canoe with the executioners, the doctor, and a number of other people, all armed.

Then the tam-tams were beaten, and the proper persons prepared the mboundou. Quabi, Mpomo's eldest brother, held the poisoned cup. At sight of it poor Okandaga began again to cry, and even Quenguez's niece turned pale in the face—for even the negro face has at such times a pallor which is quite perceptible. Three other canoes now surrounded that in which the victims were. All were crowded with armed men.

Then the mug of mboundou was handed to the old slave-woman, next to the royal niece, and last to Okandaga. As they drank, the multitude shouted, "If they are witches, let the mboundou kill them; if they are innocent, let the mboundou go out."

It was the most exciting scene of my life. Though horror almost froze my blood, my eyes were riveted upon the spectacle. A dead silence now occurred. Suddenly the slave fell down. She had not touched the boat's bottom ere her head was hacked off by a dozen rude swords.

Next came Quengueza's niece. In an instant her head was off, and the blood was dyeing the waters of the river.

Meantime poor Okandaga staggered, and struggled, and cried, vainly resisting the working of the poison in her system. Last of all she fell too, and in an instant her head was hewed off.

Then all became confused. An almost random hacking ensued, and in an incredibly short space of time the bodies were cut in small pieces, which were cast into the river.

When this was done the crowd dispersed to their houses, and for the rest of the day the town was very silent. Some of these rude people felt that their number, in their already almost extinguished tribe, was becoming less, and the dread of death filled their hearts. In the evening poor Adouma came secretly to my house to unburden his sorrowing heart to me. He, too, had been compelled to take part in the dreadful scene. He dared not even refrain from joining in the curses heaped upon his poor sister. He dared not mourn publicly for her who was considered so great a criminal.

I comforted him as well as I could, and spoke to him of the true God, and of the wickedness of the conduct we had witnessed that day. He said at last, "Oh Chally! When you go back to your far country, let them send men to us poor people to teach us from that which you call God's mouth," meaning the Bible. I promised Adouma to give the message, and I now do so.

I have often endeavoured to get at the secret thoughts of the doctors or wonder-workers among these people. They lead the popular superstition in such manner that it is almost impossible to suppose that they are themselves deceived, and yet it is certain that most them have a kind of faith in it. Nevertheless, it is not likely that they are imposed upon to the same extent as the common people, and this because they are most barefaced imposters themselves. They go about covered with charms, which they themselves give importance to. They relate most wonderful dreams and visions, which are almost certainly spun out of their own brains. They practise all manner of cheats; and when they fasten a charge of sorcery on any person, it is scarce possible to conceive that in such a case they are the victims of delusions which they themselves create. Indeed I must say, that generally for months before popular feeling points to those who are believed to be wizards. I have never found them very friendly to myself, and never disposed to assert or deny anything. One thing only I *can* assert about them; they can drink great quantities of mboundou without taking harm from it. And this is one great source of their power over the people.

Before leaving Goumi, a grand effort was made by the people to ascertain the cause of the king's sufferings. Quengueza had sent word by my men to his people to consult *Ilogo*, a spirit said to live in the moon. The rites were very curious. To consult Ilogo, the time must be near full moon. Early in the evening the women of the town assembled in front of Quengueza's house, and sang songs to and in praise of Ilogo, the spirit of Ogouayli (the moon), the latter name being often repeated. Meantime a woman was seated in the centre of the circle of singers, who sang with them, and looked constantly towards the moon. She was to be inspired by the spirit, and to utter prophecies.

Two women made trial of this post without success. At last came a third, a little woman, wiry and nervous. When she seated herself the singing was redoubled in fury; the excitement of the people had had time to become intense; the drums beat; the outsiders shouted madly. Presently the woman, who, singing violently, had looked constantly towards the moon, began to tremble. Her nerves twitched; her face was contorted; her muscles swelled; and at last her limbs straightened out, and she lay extended on the ground, insensible.

The excitement was not intense and the noise horrible. The songs to Ilogo were not for a moment discontinued. The words were little varied, and were to this purport—

> Ilogo, we ask thee!
> Tell who has bewitched the king!
> Ilogo we ask thee,
> What shall we do to cure the king?
> The forests are thine, Ilogo!
> The rivers are thine, Ilogo!
> The moon is thine!
> O moon! O moon! O moon!
> Thou art the house of Ilogo!

Shall the king die? O Ilogo!
O Ilogo! O moon! O moon!

These words were repeated again and again, with little variation. The woman, who lay for some time insensible, was then supposed to be able to see things in the world of Ilogo, and was expected to bring back a report thereof. When she at last came to her senses, after half an hour's insensibility, she looked very much prostrated. She averred that she had seen Ilogo; that he had told her Quengueza was not bewitched; that a remedy prepared from a certain plant would cure him; and so on. I am convinced the woman believed what she said, as did all the people. It was a very curious instance of the force of the imagination and extreme excitement combined.

I should have mentioned before that, as we were sailing up the river a little above Biagano, we had a fight. The crew of one of my canoes got into a quarrel with a canoe from one of the villages, and presently we came to hard blows. The noise was deafening, and the blows which were given on both sides were tremendous, and showed to great advantage the superior thickness of the African skull. The weapons used were a kind of pole, of very heavy and hard wood, called the *tongo*. It is an unwieldy weapon, being seven feet long, and about an inch in diameter. The outer end is heavier, and is notched so as to inflict severer wounds, and when the battle was over I noticed that every tongo was covered with blood and wool. I am sure that one blow from a tongo would have fractured the skull of a white man. The length of the tongo makes it an awkward and ineffective weapon; but the African does not like to come to close quarters with his enemy.

When we had beaten off the assailants, they retired, followed by the abusive songs of our side, who were very proud of their victory. Abuse is the negro's *forte* and his delight, and my fellows bubbled over with the most ridiculous reproaches, already set to a sort of impromptu tune.

"Your chief has the leg of an elephant!" sang one; and another,

"Ho! His eldest brother has the neck of a wild ox!"

"Your women are dirty and ugly!"

"You have no food in your village, poor fellows. Ho! Ho!"

And so they went on, pouring out ridicule upon the discomfited foe. Nothing touches a negro so quickly as ridicule, and I fancy my men will have to pay for theirs when they return. Their words were felt to be harder than their blows.

On the 21st I sent my Biagano people back. On the next day I left for Obindji's town and the far interior, with thirty-five Goumbi men and Adouma for my head-man. The men I had to pay each about six dollars' worth of cloth. To Adouma I only promised that I would "make his heart glad," which means that he should be well paid.

I was glad to take poor Adouma along, not only to cheer him up, but because thus I was likely to save him, for a while, at least, from his sister's fate. These tribes have a belief that the powers of sorcery are inherited, and go from generation to generation in certain families. Now several of Adouma's ancestors had been killed for witchcraft at different times; his sister had but just met the same fate, and the poor fellow himself was quite likely to be a victim when the next sorcery row took place.

While I remained in the town I refused to speak to the men who had been most active in the killing of the women. They felt ashamed when they saw that I was not inclined to notice them, and tried to express their sorrow; but I would hear nothing from them. I was determined to show my horror at their conduct, and to hold out to them the threat that if they would do so they need expect nothing from me.

While I staid at Goumbi this time I noticed again that the people do not like to drink of the water of the river. This dislike is found in all tribes that live on the larger streams. Their women have to bring water for drinking from the springs and streamlets, often at considerable distances. This is because they have a horror of drinking from water into which slaves who die, and persons executed for witchcraft, are thrown.

On the 22nd we at last got off. My goods were so heavy that I required several canoes. I carried, besides plenty of ammunition, a large supply of beads, tobacco, calico, looking-glasses, files, fire-steels, etc. Some of the men who are with me this time have most curious names, such as Gooloo-Gani, Biembia, Agambic-Mo, Jombai, Manda, Akongogo.

We left the shores of Goumbi without the customary singing. Scarce a word was said. We were going to explore an unknown, and, to the negroes, fearful region; and moreover, Mpomo's death made singing out of order.

The day was very hot, and towards evening we were overtaken by a terrible storm of rain and wind. I was glad when, towards sunset, we reached the village of Acaca, where my friend Acoundie soon made me comfortable and dry. I was prevailed upon to spend a day here to hunt the *manga*, a species of manatee, of whose meat the people are very fond.

During the day we passed the celebrated oloumi-tree; and here the men fortified their courage by a curious superstitious rite. They went ashore, and presently stripped bark from the tree, which they boiled in water. With this water they then washed themselves thoroughly, thus securing to themselves good fortune for the trip, and success in certain speculations which they hoped to be able to make in the Ashira country, where they expect to get "trusted" with slaves, and ivory, and cloth to sell on the coast.

The morning after our arrival at Acaca we set off in small, very flat canoes, made on purpose for this sport. A manga doctor accompanied us. We went into the Niembai, on whose grassy bottom the manga dwells, and here stationed the boat among the high reeds which lined the shore. The doctor spread a powder he had in a pouch thickly on the water, and returned then towards the reeds. Presently, while we kept silence, a great beast came to the surface, and began greedily sucking in the powder. Immediately they stole upon it with the canoe, and, when they got near enough, fastened a harpoon to it. To this was attached a long strip of native rope. The animal immediately made for the bottom, but in a few minutes came to the top, and presently, after some struggles, died. They they brought an empty canoe, which was upset, and the body of the animal put into it, whereupon we returned to the village.

Before it was cut up the manga doctor went through some ceremonies which I did not see, and nobody was permitted to see the animal while he was cutting it up.

This manga is a new species of manatee. Its body is of a dark lead colour; the skin is smooth, very thick, and covered in all parts with single bristly hairs from half an inch to an inch in length. The eyes are small; the paddles are without nails. The specimen we killed was ten feet long. Its circumference was very considerable, but I could not get at it to measure it. This animals feeds on the leaves and grass growing on the river-banks.

The people were greatly rejoiced. The beast weighed about 1,500 pounds, as I calculate from its requiring eighteen men to drag it, and the meat is delicious—something like pork, but finer grained and of a sweeter flavour. Tonight all hands were smoking it. The doctor was greatly rejoiced at his success, and praised himself to me at a great rate. But I could not discover the composition of his powder, which was certainly quite efficacious.

On the 24th we started for the interior. When we got to Mpopo I found my men would not be able to carry all my luggage. I had to hire more. The chief asked his wives to furnish some slaves for me, but they asked such a price for their services that I would not give it. It is curious how seldom a husband in this country interferes with that property which he has given to his wives. The women jealously guard their rights in this respect; and so long as they feed their husbands and make them comfortable, they are not, in many things, subject to any rule at all.

On the 26th we got to Obindji's town. The old fellow was rejoiced to see me, and here I got several Ashira men and two Bakalai, which makes my troop up to thirty-two men all told, and sets me on my way rejoicing.

One of the Ashira fellows was here last spring when I was here. He had brought a slave to Obindji to sell for him, and had been waiting for the proceeds ever since. He might have waited a year or two longer if I had not come, and he would have done so quite willingly. The creditor in such case lives with the debtor. Okendjo was fed by Obindji's wife; and, to comfort and cheer him while he was waiting, Obindji gave him one of his own wives—a hospitable custom in this part of Africa, which a man is always expected to observe towards his visitors. Whenever I entered a strange village, the chief always made haste to place a part, and often his whole harem at my service. Time was literally of no account to Okendjo. Obindji's town was as jolly a place as any village in his own country. And perhaps, in a few months, his goods would come. So the days went on pleasantly with him.

When he heard my destination mentioned, he at once conceived the brilliant idea of having the honour of guiding the first white man to his king, and thus gaining imperishable renown to himself. I was very glad to have him, as he was a very intelligent negro.

Yesterday, as we approached Obindji's town, we came to the plantation of my old friend Querlaouen. I got out of the canoe, and went ashore to greet the good old African and his wife and children, for whom I had brought presents such as they wished. But alas! I found no house or plantation. The place was deserted; the jungle was thickest where his little clearing had been, and I walked back with disappointed and foreboding heart. On the river-bank I met a Bakalai, who told me poor Querlaouen's story. Some months before the old hunter had gone out after an elephant. His slave who was with him heard the report of the gun, and finding that his master did not return, set out to seek him. He found him in the forest, dead, and trampled into a shapeless mass by the beast, which he had wounded mortally, but which had strength enough left to rush at and kill its enemy. The poor body was brought in and buried. But now came in the devilish superstitions of the Africans. This family really loved each other. They lived together in peace and unity. But the people declared that Querlaouen's brother had bewitched him and caused his death. The brother was killed by the mboundou ordeal, and the women and children had gone to live with those to whom they belonged by the laws of inheritance, and were thus scattered in several villages. I was consequently prevented repaying this family for their kind deeds to me.

Early on the 27th we were awakened by the voice of Obindji, who was recommending Okendjo to take great care of "his white man," and see that nothing hurt him. We were soon underway. Our road led up the Ofoubou for some three miles and a half. Then we struck off due east, and after half an hour's arduous travel we got through the marshy bottom land which bounds the river, and stood at the foot of a mountain ridge, along which lay the route to Ashira-land. Here we gave three cheers, and with great hopes I led the way into a new terra incognita.

By five that night, when we encamped, we had advanced in a straight line about twenty miles from the Ofoubou. The country was mountainous, very rugged, and very thickly wooded with great trees. The ground was in many place thickly strewn with the immense boulders which I had noticed in my journey to the Fans, only here quartz rock was more abundant. Numerous streams of the purest and most crystalline water rolled in every direction, tumbling over the rocks in foaming cascades, or purling along in a bed of white pebbles, which was delightfully reminiscent of the hill-streams and trout-brooks of home.

This night we had no rainstorm, which was very lucky, as, when camping time came, we were too tired to build ourselves shelters. Before this not a night had passed since I started from Biagano without our having one of the powerful storms of mixed wind and rain for which this is the proper season. Several times they even overtook us by day.

Our camp was full of life this evening. The men were rejoicing in anticipation of great trade in slaves and ivory, and gave their imagination full swing. When trade was exhausted, they rejoiced over the wives they would get among the Ashira, where they expect, as strangers from a far land, to be sumptuously entertained. And at last Okendjo capped their pleasure by promising them great feasts of goats and plantains, the Goumbi and Bakalai regarding Ashira-land as the country of goats and plantains.

We were kept awake between one and three o'clock by the roarings of a leopard, which, however, could not face the fire, which we had kept bright so he could not make his breakfast upon one of us as he desired. But neither did I think it quite safe to venture into the gloom after him. The leopard is a beast that cannot be trifled with even by white men. As for the negroes, they are very much afraid of him; and I have known cases where so many persons were carried away out of a village by a persistent leopard, who had got a taste of black meat and liked it, that the survivors had to move away.

Next morning (29th) I found that the fellows had slyly thrown away a quantity of my plantains, to be relieved of the burden. I warned them that if we were short of food, they would have to starve first.

This day the country was much as yesterday. Ebony grows in great abundance on all hands. The poorer the soil, the taller the trees, and the more numerous. In many places the rains had washed away the soil from the immense and wide-spreading roots, which ran along the ground looking like huge serpents. Today we saw for the first time a tree new to me, and which my men called the *indoonoo*. It has an immense girth, and is a much taller and better shaped tree than the baobab, which is not found in this part of Africa. I measured one, of only moderate size, which had fallen down, and found it, at some feet from the base, eight feet in diameter. This tree is not known on the Rembo, and was as new to my Bakalai as to me. The Ashira fellows, however, knew it very well.

I think the blocks of quartz grow more and more immense as we proceed. Today there were some which were really stupendous masses, and it was a most curious sight to see our caravan filing between two such ponderous blocks, looking like pigmies alongside of these huge boulders.

Towards evening, at last, we began to see signs of a change in the face of the country. Plantations could be seen from time to time; the soil became more clayey; and at last we emerged from the immense forest. I saw spread out before me the great Ashira prairie-land, dotted plentifully with villages, which looked in the distance like ant-heaps. I stood for a long time on the edge of a bluff, taking in this, one of the finest landscapes I ever saw in my life. Far as the eye could reach was a high rolling prairie. As I afterwards discovered, the plain is about fifty-five miles long by ten wide. All over this vast plain were scattered collections of little Ashira huts. The hills and valleys were streaked with ribbon-like paths, and here and there the eye caught the silver sheen of a brook winding along through the undulating land. In the far distance loomed up mountains higher than any I had yet seen, and whose peaks were lost in the clouds. It was a grand sight.

In the forests of this part of Africa are found vast numbers of ants, some of whose tribes are so terrible to man, and even to the beasts of the wood, from their venomous bites, their fierce temper and voracity, that their patch is freely abandoned to them, and they may well be called lords of the forest.

I know of ten different species of ants found in these regions, all differing widely in their choice of food, the quality of their venom, the manner of their attack, or the time of their operation. The most remarkable and most dreaded of all is the *bashikouay*.

This ant, also called *nchounou* by the Mpongwe, is very abundant in the whole region I have travelled over in Africa, and is the most voracious creature I ever met. It is the dread of all living animals, from the leopard to the smallest insect.

I do not think that they build a nest or home of any kind. At any rate they carry nothing away, but eat all their prey on the spot. It is their habit to march through the forests in a long regular line—a line about two inches broad and often several miles in length. All along this line are the larger ants, which act as officers, stand outside the ranks, and keep this singular army in order. If they come to a place where there are no trees to shelter them from the sun, whose heat they cannot bear, they immediately build underground tunnels, through which the whole army passes in columns to the forest beyond. These tunnels are four or five feet underground, and are used only in the heat of the day or during a storm.

When they grow hungry the long file spreads itself through the forest in a front line, and attacks and devours all it overtakes with a fury which is quite irresistible. The elephant and gorilla fly before this attack. The black men run for their lives. Every animal that lives in their line of march is chased. They seem to understand and act upon the tactics of Napoleon, and concentrate, with great speed, their heaviest forces upon the point of attack. In an incredibly short space of time the mouse, or dog, or leopard, or deer is overwhelmed, killed, eaten, and the bare skeleton only remains.

They seem to travel night and day. Many a time have I been awakened out of a sleep, and obliged to rush from the hut and into the water to save my life, and after all suffered intolerable agony from the bites of the advance-guard, who had got into my clothes. When they enter a house they clear it of all living things. Cockroaches are devoured in an instant. Rats and mice spring round the room in vain. An overwhelming force of ants kills a strong rat in less than a minute, in spite of the most frantic struggles, and in less than another minute its bones are stripped. Every living thing in the house is devoured. They will not touch vegetable matter. Thus they are in reality very useful (as well as dangerous) to the negroes, who have their huts cleaned of all the abounding vermin, such as immense cockroaches and centipedes, at least several times a year.

When on their march the insect-world flies before them, and I have often had the approach of a bashikouay army heralded to me by this means.

Wherever they go they make a clean sweep, even ascending to the tops of the highest trees in pursuit of their prey. Their manner of attack is an impetuous *leap*. Instantly the strong pincers are fastened, and they only let go when the piece gives way. At such times this little animal seems animated by a kind of fury which causes it to disregard entirely its own safety, and to seek only the conquest of its prey. The bite is very painful.

The negroes relate that criminals were in former times exposed in the path of the bashikouay ants, as the most cruel manner of putting them to death.

Two very remarkable practices of theirs remain to be related. When on their line of march they require to cross a narrow stream, they throw themselves across and form a tunnel—a living tunnel—connecting two trees or high bushes on opposite sides of the little stream, whenever they can find such to facilitate the operation. This is done with great speed, and is effected by a great number of ants, each of which clings with its fore claws to its next neighbour's body or hind claws. Thus they form a high, safe tubular bridge, *through* which the whole vast regiment marches in regular order. If disturbed, or if the arch is broken by the violence of some animal, they instantly attack the offender with the greatest animosity.

The bashikouay have the sense of smell finely developed, as indeed have all the ants I know, and they are guided very much by it. They are larger than any ant we have in America, being at least half an inch long, and are armed with very powerful fore legs and sharp jaws, with which they bite. They are red or dark-brown in colour. Their numbers are so great that one does not like to enter into calculations; but I have seen one continuous line passing at good speed a particular place for *twelve hours*. The reader may imagine for himself how many millions on millions there may have been contained here.

There is another species of bashikouay which is found in the mountains to the south of the equator. It is of great size. The body is grayish-white in color; the head of a reddish-black. Its fangs are very powerful, and it is able to make a clean bite out of a piece of flesh. It is thus a very formidable animal; but fortunately its motions are not so quick as those of its fierce brother; it does not march in such vast armies nor does it precipitate itself upon its prey with such irresistible fury. In its motions it is almost sluggish. They do not invade villages, nor climb trees in pursuit of prey; and I do not think them nearly so voracious as their fellows before mentioned. If they were, they could doubtless clear the country of every living thing, for they are much more powerful. They are, in fact, to ants what whales are to fish.

Next to the bashikouay come the *nchellelay*, or white ants. These troublesome animals do not bite or attack living things at all. They live on vegetable substances, and are particularly fond of cotton-cloth, paper, and old wood. They have a great aversion to daylight, and use all means possible to avoid it. To reach an object which is situated in the light they build a clay tunnel, through which they pass in safety. The clay seems to be moistened with some juices of their own, and becomes quite firm on exposure to the air. Their nests, which are curiously shaped, with overhanging flat roofs (exactly like a toadstool or gigantic mushroom), are constructed in the same manner, and are built up from within, the underground excavations doubtless furnishing clay for this purpose.

It is almost impossible to keep anything safe from these destroyers. They work in silence, unseen, and with wonderful rapidity. One night's negligence suffices to spoil a box of clothing or books. They seem to be attracted by smell rather than sight to their prey. They are always near; and they cut through any—the hardest—wood, in order to reach the object of their desires. I have noticed that they always cut through the middle of a piece of cloth first, as though they were trying to do as much mischief as possible. Such is their perseverance and destructiveness, that I think one of the greatest boons to this part of Africa would be to rid it of this pest.

The earth of which they build their houses becomes so hard, after it has been mixed with their saliva, that it stands the heaviest and longest rainstorms without melting or breaking away, and they last many rainy reasons. They leave no opening in their house for air or light, for both which they seem to have a particular aversion. And thus, too, they are protected from other ants which are their enemies, and against whom, being unarmed, they would find it difficult to protect themselves.

Among these enemies the chief is the bashikouay ant, which pursues the white ant with great fury. I have sometimes, when I noticed some of these white-ant-hills in the track of an army of bashikouay, knocked away the top. No sooner was this done than the bashikouay rushed to their work, and in a short time not a white ant was left. When the house is only slightly injured, the working ants are called, and immediately set to work to mend the hole, using clay brought from the interior. The outside work is only carried on during the night.

These ants, though called white, are really of a straw colour. They emit a strong smell, especially if crushed.

The Source of the Nile

BY JOHN HANNING SPEKE

Although it wasn't generally agreed upon before his death, John Hanning Speke correctly surmised the source of the Nile during his third trip to Africa in the early 1860s. He had accompanied the explorer Richard Burton on two earlier trips, one to Somalia and one to search for the Nile's headwaters. Those trips sowed the seeds of bitterness between the two men that spilled over among all of England's leading geographers. While Speke was much less articulate than Burton, he was by far the more popular. Just before the two men were to meet for a public debate on the Nile's source, Speke died in a hunting accident. As he was one of England's greatest sportsmen and unlikely to be careless around firearms, many historians believe he committed suicide.

Despite Speke's findings on that third trip, presented here from his *Journal of the Discovery of the Source of the Nile*, the fascinating, convoluted, centuries-old Nile debate raged on until Henry Stanley finally laid it to rest some years later by circumnavigating Lakes Victoria and Tanganyika. The experiences Speke has with local kings is similar to that of most African explorers, with petty politics, endless delays, and patient diplomacy all playing a role in successful travel.

In this portion of his journey, Speke is finally closing in on the massive falls on the upper Nile just below Lake Victoria.

★ ★ ★ ★ ★

7*th* to 11*th*—With Budja appointed as the general director, a lieutenant of the Sakibobo's to furnish us with sixty cows in his division at the first halting-place, and Kasoro (Mr Cat), a lieutenant of Jumba's, to provide the boats at Urondogani, we started at 1 P.M. on the journey northwards. The Wanguana still grumbled, swearing they would carry no loads, as they got no rations and threatening to shoot us if we pressed them, forgetting that their food had been paid for to the king in rifles, chronometers, and other articles, costing about 2,000 dollars, and what was more to the point, that all the ammunition was in our hands. A judicious threat of the stick, however, put things right, and on we marched five successive days to Kari—as the place was afterwards named, in consequence of the tragedy mentioned below—the whole distance accomplished being thirty miles from the capital, through a fine hilly country, with jungles and rich cultivation alternating. The second march, after crossing the Katawana river with its many branches flowing north-east into the huge rush-drain of Luajerri, carried us beyond the influence of the higher hills, and away from the huge grasses which characterise the southern boundary of Uganda bordering on the lake.

Each day's march to Kari was directed much in the same manner. After a certain number of hours' travelling, Budja appointed some village of residence for the night, avoiding those which belonged to the queen, lest any rows should take place in them, which would create disagreeable consequences with the king, and preferring those the heads of which had been lately seized by the orders of the king. Nevertheless, wherever we went, all the villagers forsook their homes, and left their houses, property, and gardens an easy prey to the thieving propensities of the escort. To put a stop to this vile practice was now beyond my power; the king allowed it, and his men were the first in every house, taking goats, fowls, skins, mbugus, cowries, beads, drums, spears, tobacco, pombé—in short, everything they could lay their hands on—in the most ruthless manner. It was a perfect marauding campaign for them all, and all alike were soon laden with as much as they could carry.

A halt of some days had become necessary at Kari to collect the cows given by the king; and, as it is one of his most extensive pasture-grounds, I strolled with my rifle (11th) to see what new animals could be found; but no sooner did I wound a zebra than messengers came running after me to say Kari, one of my men, had been murdered by the villagers three miles off; and such was the fact. He, with others of my men, had been induced to go plundering, with a few boys of the Waganda escort, to a certain village of potters, as pots were required by Budja for making plantain wine, the first thing ever thought of when a camp is formed. On nearing the place, however, the women of the village, who were the only people visible, instead of running away, as our braves expected, commenced hullalooing and brought out their husbands. Flight was now the only thought of our men, and all would have escaped had Kari not been slow and his musket empty. The potters overtook him, and, as he pointed his gun, which they considered a magic-horn, they speared him to death, and then fled at once. Our survivors were not long in bringing the news into camp, when a party went out, and in the evening brought in the young man's corpse and everything belonging to him, for nothing had been taken.

12*th*—To enable me at my leisure to trace up the Nile to its exit from the lake, and then go on with the journey as quickly as possible, I wished the cattle to be collected and taken by Budja and some of my men with the heavy baggage overland to Kamrasi's. Another reason for doing so was, that I thought it advisable Kamrasi should be forewarned that we were coming by the water route, lest we should be suspected and stopped as spies by his officers on the river, or regarded as enemies, which would provoke a fight. Budja, however, objected to move until a report of Kari's murder had been forwarded to the king, lest the people, getting bumptious, should try the same trick again; and Kasoro said he would not go up the river, as he had received no orders to do so.

In this fix I ordered a march back to the palace, mentioning the king's last words, and should have gone, had not Budja ordered Kasoro to go with me. A page then arrived from the king to ask after Bana's health, carrying the Whitworth rifle as his master's card, and begging for a heavy double-barrelled gun to be sent him from Gani. I called this lad to witness the agreement I had made with Budja, and told him, if Kasoro satisfied me, I would return by him, in addition to the heavy gun, a Massey's patent log. I had taken it for the navigation of the lake, and it was now of no further use to me, but, being an instrument of complicated structure, it would be a valuable addition to the king's museum of magic charms. I added I should like the king to send me the robes of honour and spears he had once promised me, in order that I might, on reaching England, be able to show my countrymen a specimen of the manufactures of his country. The men who were with Kari were now sent to the palace, under accusation of having led him into ambush, and a complaint was made against the villagers, which we waited the reply to. As Budja forbade it, no men would follow me out shooting, saying the villagers were out surrounding our camp, and threatening destruction on anyone who dared show his face; for this was not the highroad to Uganda, and therefore no one had a right to turn them out of their houses and pillage their gardens.

13*th*—Budja lost two cows given to his party last night, and seeing ours securely tied by their legs to trees, asked by what spells we had secured them; and would not believe our assurance that the ropes that bound them were all the medicines we knew of. One of the queen's sisters, hearing of Kari's murder, came on a visit to condole with us, bringing a pot of pombé, for which she received some beads. On being asked how many sisters the queen had, for we could not help suspecting some imposition, she replied she was the only one, till assured ten other ladies had presented themselves as the queen's sisters before, when she changed her tone, and said, "That is true, I am not the only one; but if I had told you the truth I might have lost my head." This was a significant expression of the danger of telling court secrets.

I suspected that there must be a considerable quantity of game in this district, as stake-nets and other traps were found in all the huts, as well as numbers of small antelope hoofs spitted on pipe-sticks—an ornament which is counted the special badge of the sportsman in this part of Africa. Despite, therefore, of the warnings of Budja, I strolled again with my rifle, and saw pallah, small plovers, and green antelopes with straight horns, called mpéo, the skin of which makes a favourite apron for the Mabandwa.

14th—I met today a Mhuma cowherd in my strolls with the rifle, and asked him if he knew where the game lay. The unmannerly creature, standing among a thousand of the sleekest cattle, gruffishly replied, "What can I know of any other animals than cows?" and went on with his work, as if nothing in the world could interest him but his cattle-tending. I shot a doe, leucotis, called here nsunnu, the first one seen upon the journey.

15th—In the morning, when our men went for water to the springs, some Waganda in ambush threw a spear at them, and this time caught a Tartar, for the "horns" as they called their guns, were loaded, and two of them received shot wounds. In the evening, whilst we were returning from shooting, a party of Waganda, also lying in the bush, called out to know what we were about; saying, "Is it not enough that you have turned us out of our homes and plantations, leaving us to live like animals in the wilderness?" and when told we were only searching for sport, would not believe that our motive was any other than hostility to themselves.

At night one of Budja's men returned from the palace, to say the king was highly pleased with the measures adopted by his Wakungu, in prosecution of Kari's affair. He hoped now as we had cows to eat, there would be no necessity for wandering for food, but all would keep together "in one garden." At present no notice would be taken of the murderers, as all the culprits would have fled far away in their fright to escape chastisement. But when a little time had elapsed, and all would appear to have been forgotten, officers

would be sent and the miscreants apprehended, for it was impossible to suppose anybody could be ignorant of the white men being the guests of the
king, considering they had lived at the palace so long. The king took this opportunity again to remind me that he wanted a heavy solid double gun, such
as would last him all his life; and intimated that in a few days the arms and
robes of honour were to be sent.

16*th*—Most of the cows for ourselves and the guides—for the king
gave them also a present, ten each—were driven into camp. We also got 50
pounds of butter, the remainder to be picked up on the way. I strolled with
the gun, and shot two zebras, to be sent to the king, as, by the constitution of
Uganda, he alone can keep their royal skins.

17*th*—We had to halt again, as the guides had lost most of their cows,
so I strolled with my rifle and shot a ndjezza doe, the first I had ever seen. It is
a brown animal, a little smaller than leucotis, and frequents much the same
kind of ground.

18*th*—We had still to wait another day for Budja's cows, when, as it
appeared all important to communicate quickly with Petherick, and as Grant's
leg was considered too weak for traveling fast, we took counsel together, and
altered our plans. I arranged that Grant should go to Kamrasi's direct with the
property, cattle, and women, taking my letters and a map for immediate dis-
patch to Petherick at Gani, whilst I should go up the river to its source or exit
from the lake, and come down again navigating as far as practicable.

At night the Waganda startled us by setting fire to the huts our men
were sleeping in, but providentially did more damage to themselves than to
us, for one sword only was buried in the fire, whilst their own huts, intended to be vacated in the morning, were burnt to the ground. To fortify
ourselves against another invasion, we cut down all their plantains to make a
boma or fence.

We started all together on our respective journeys; but, after the third
mile, Grant turned west, to join the highroad at Kamrasi's, whilst I went east
for Urondogani, crossing the Luajerri, a huge rush-drain three miles broad,
fordable nearly to the right bank, where we had to ferry in boats, and the
cows to be swum over with men holding onto their tails. It was larger than
the Katonga, and more tedious to cross, for it took no fewer than four hours
mosquitoes in myriads biting our bare backs and legs all the while. The Luajerri is said to rise in the lake and fall into the Nile, due south of our crossing-
point. On the right bank wild buffalo are described to be as numerous as
cows, but we did not see any, though the country is covered with a most

inviting jungle for sport, with intermediate lays of fine grazing grass. Such is the nature of the country, all the way to Urondogani, except in some favoured spots, kept as tidily as in any part of Uganda, where plantains grow in the utmost luxuriance. From want of guides, and misguided by the exclusive ill-natured Wahuma who were here in great numbers tending their king's cattle, we lost our way continually, so that we did not reach the boat station until the morning of the 21st.

Here at last I stood on the brink of the Nile: most beautiful was the scene, nothing could surpass it! It was the very perfection of the kind of effect aimed at in a highly kept park; with a magnificent stream from 600 to 700 yards wide, dotted with islets and rocks, the former occupied by fishermen's huts, the latter by sterns and crocodiles basking in the sun—flowing between high grassy banks, with rich trees and plantains in the background, where herds of the nsunnu and hartebeest could be seen grazing, while the hippopotami were snorting in the water, and florikan and guinea-fowl rising at our feet. Unfortunately, the chief district officer, Mlondo, was from home, but we took possession of his huts—clean, extensive, and tidily kept—facing the river, and felt as if a residence here would do one good. Delays and subterfuges, however, soon came to damp our spirits. The acting officer was sent for, and asked for the boats; they were all scattered, and could not be collected for a day or two; but, even if they were at hand, no boat ever went up or down the river. The chief was away and would be sent for, as the king often changed his orders, and, after all, might not mean what had been said. The district belonged to the Sakibobo, and no representative of his had come here. These excuses, of course, would not satisfy us. The boats must be collected, seven, if there are not ten, for we must try them, and come to some understanding about them, before we march upstream, when, if the officer values his life, he will let us have them, and acknowledge Karoso as the king's representative, otherwise a complaint will be sent to the palace, for we won't stand trifling.

We were now confronting Usoga, a country which may be said to be the very counterpart of Uganda in its richness and beauty. Here the people use such huge iron-headed spears with short handles, that, on seeing one today, my people remarked that they were better fitted for digging potatoes than piercing men. Elephants, as we had seen by their devastations during the last two marches, were very numerous in this neighbourhood. Till lately, a party from Unyoro, ivory-hunting, had driven them away. Lions were also described as very numerous and destructive to human life. Antelopes were common in the jungle, and the hippopotami, though frequenters of the plantain-garden and constantly heard, were seldom seen on land in consequence of their unsteady habits.

The king's page again came, begging I would not forget the gun and stimulants, and bringing with him the things I asked for—two spears, one shield, one dirk, two leopard-cat skins, and two sheets of small antelope skins. I told my men they ought to shave their heads and bathe in the holy river, the cradle of Moses—the waters of which, sweetened with sugar, men carry all the way from Egypt to Mecca, and sell to the pilgrims. But Bombay, who is a philosopher of the Epicurean school, said, "We don't look on those things in the same fanciful manner that you do; we are contented with all the common-places of life, and look for nothing beyond the present. If things don't go well, it is God's will; and if they do go well, that is His will also."

22*nd*—The acting chief brought a present of one cow, one goat, and pombé, with a mob of his courtiers to pay his respects. He promised that the seven boats, which are all the station could muster, would be ready next day, and in the meanwhile a number of men would conduct me to the shooting-ground. He asked to be shown the books of birds and animals, and no sooner saw some specimens of Wolf's handiwork, than, in utter surprise, he exclaimed, "I know how these are done; a bird was caught and stamped upon the paper," using action to his words, and showing what he meant, while all his followers n'yanzigged for the favour of the exhibition.

In the evening I strolled in the antelope parks, enjoying the scenery and sport excessively. A noble buck nsunnu, standing by himself, was the first thing seen on this side, though a herd of hartebeests were grazing on the Usoga banks. One bullet rolled my fine friend over, but the rabble looking on no sooner saw the hit than they rushed upon him and drove him off, for he was only wounded. A chase ensued, and he was tracked by his blood when a pongo (bush boc) was started and divided the party. It also brought me to another single buck nsunnu, which was floored at once, and left to be carried home by some of my men in company with Waganda, whilst I went on, shot a third nsunnu buck, and tracked him by his blood till dark, for the bullet had pierced his lungs and passed out on the other side. Failing to find him on the way home, I shot, besides florikan and guinea-chicks, a wonderful goatsucker, remarkable for the exceeding length of some of its feathers floating out far beyond the rest in both wings. [Named by Dr. P.L. Sclater, *Cosmetornis Spekii*. The seventh pen feathers are double the length of the ordinaries, the eighth double that of the seventh, and the ninth 20 inches long. Bombay says the same bird is found in Uhiyow.] Returning home, I found the men who had charge of the dead buck all in a state of excitement; they no sooner removed his carcass, than two lions came out of the jungle and lapped his blood. All the Waganda ran away at once; but my braves feared my anger more than the lions, and came off safely with the buck on their shoulders.

23rd—Three boats arrived, like those used on the Murchison Creek, and when I demanded the rest, as well as a decisive answer about going to Kamrasi's, the acting Mkungu said he was afraid accidents might happen, and he would not take me. Nothing would frighten this pig-headed creature into compliance, though I told him I had arranged with the king to make the Nile the channel of communication with England. I therefore applied to him for guides to conduct me up the river, and ordered Bombay and Kasoro to obtain fresh orders from the king, as all future Wazungu, coming to Uganda to visit or trade, would prefer the passage by the river. I shot another buck in the evening, as the Waganda love their skins, and also a load of guinea-fowl—three, four, and five at a shot—as Kasoro and his boys prefer them to anything.

24th—The acting officer absconded, but another man came in his place, and offered to take us on the way up the river tomorrow, humbugging Kasoro into the belief that his road to the palace would branch off from the first stage, though in reality it was here. The Mkungu's women brought pombé, and spent the day gazing at us, till, in the evening, when I took up my rifle, one ran after Bana to see him shoot, and followed like a man; but the only sport she got was on an ant-hill, where she fixed herself some time, popping into her mouth and devouring the white ants as fast as they emanated from their cells—for, disdaining does, I missed the only pongo buck I got a shot at in my anxiety to show the fair one what she came for.

Reports came today of new cruelties at the palace. Kasoro improved on their off-hand manslaughter by saying that two Kamravionas and two Sakibobos, as well as all the old Wakungu of Sunna's time, had been executed by the order of king Mtésa. He told us, moreover, that if Mtésa ever has a dream that his father directs him to kill anybody as being dangerous to his person, the order is religiously kept. I wished to send a message to Mtésa by an officer who is starting at once to pay his respects to the court; but although he received it and promised to deliver it, Kasoro laughed at me for expecting that one word of it would ever reach the king; for, however appropriate or important the matter might be, it was more than anybody dare do to tell the king, as it would be an infringement of the rule that no one is to speak to him unless in answer to a question. My second buck of the first day was brought in by the natives, but they would not allow it to approach the hut until it had been skinned; and I found their reason to be a supersitition that otherwise no others would ever be killed by the inmates of that establishment.

I marched up the left bank of the Nile at a considerable distance from the water, to the Isamba Rapids, passing through rich jungle and plantain-gardens. Nango, an old friend, and district officer of the place, first refreshed us with a dish of plantain-squash and dried fish, with pombé. He told us he is often threatened by elephants, but he sedulously keeps them off with charms; for if they ever tasted a plantain they would never leave the garden until they had cleared it out. He then took us to see the nearest falls of the Nile—extremely beautiful, but very confined. The water ran deep between its banks, which were covered with fine grass, soft cloudy acacias, and festoons of lilac convolvuli; whilst here and there, where the land had slipped above the rapids, bared places of red earth could be seen, like that of Devonshire; there, too, the waters, impeded by a natural dam, looked like a huge mill pond, sullen and dark, in which two crocodiles laving about, were looking for prey. From the high banks we looked down upon a line of sloping wooded islets lying across the stream, which divide its waters, and by interrupting them, cause at once both dams and rapids. The whole was more fairy-like, wild, and romantic than—I must confess that my thoughts took that shape—anything I ever saw outside of a theatre. It was exactly the sort of place, in fact, where, bridged across from one side-slip to the other, on a moonlight night, brigands would assemble to enact some dreadful tragedy. Even the Wanguana seemed spellbound at the novel beauty of the sight, and no one thought of moving till hunger warned us night was setting in, and we had better look out for lodgings.

Start again, and after drinking pombé with Nango, when we heard that three Wakungu had been seized at Kari in consequence of the murder, the march was commenced, but soon after stopped by the mischievous machinations of our guide, who pretended it was too late in the day to cross the jungles on ahead, either by the road to the source or the palace, and therefore would not move till the morning; then, leaving us on the pretext of business, he vanished, and was never seen again. A small black fly, with thick shoulders and bullet-head, infests the palace, and torments the naked arms and legs of the people with its sharp stings to an extent that must render life miserable to them.

After a long struggling march, plodding through huge grasses and jungle, we reached a district which I cannot otherwise describe than by calling it a "Church Estate." It is dedicated in some mysterious manner to Lubari (Almighty), and although the king appeared to have authority over some of the inhabitants of it, yet others had apparently a sacred character, exempting them from the civil power, and he had no right to dispose of the land itself. In this territory, there are small villages only at every fifth mile, for there is no road, and the lands run high again, whilst, from want of a guide, we often lost the track. It now transpired that Budja when he told at the palace that there was no road down the banks of the Nile, did so in consequence of his fear that if he sent my whole party there they would rob from these church lands, and so bring him into a scrape with the wizards or ecclesiastical authorities. Had my party not been under control, we could not have put up here; but on my being answerable that no thefts should take place, the people kindly consented to provide us with board and lodgings, and we found them very obliging. One elderly man, half-witted—they said the king had driven his senses from him by seizing his house and family—came at once on hearing of our arrival, laughing and singing in a loose jaunty maniacal manner, carrying odd sticks, shells, and a bundle of mbugu rags, which he deposited before me, dancing and singing again, then retreating and bringing some more, with a few plantains from a garden, when I was to eat, as kings lived upon flesh, and "poor Tom" wanted some, for he lived with lions and elephants in a hovel beyond the gardens, and his belly was empty. He was precisely a black specimen of the English parish idiot.

At last, with a good push for it, crossing hills and threading huge grasses, as well as extensive village plantations lately devastated by elephants— they had eaten all that was eatable, and what would not serve for food they had destroyed with their trunks, not one plantain or one hut being left entire—we arrived at the extreme end of the journey, the farthest point ever visited by the expedition on the same parallel of latitude as king Mtésa's palace and just forty miles east of it.

We were well rewarded; for the "stones," as the Waganda call the falls, was by far the most interesting sight I had seen in Africa. Everybody ran to see them at once, though the march had been long and fatiguing, and even my sketch-block was called into play. Though beautiful, the scene was not exactly what I expected; for the broad surface of the lake was shut out from view by a spur of hill, and the falls, about 12 feet deep, and 400 to 500 feet broad, were broken by rocks. Still it was a sight that attracted one to it for hours—the roar of the waters, the thousands of passenger fish, leaping at the falls with all their might; the Wasoga and Waganda fishermen coming out in boats and taking post on all the rocks with rod and hook, hippopotami and crocodiles lying sleepily on the water, the ferry at work above the falls, and cattle driven down to drink at the margin of the lake—made, in all, with the pretty nature of the country—small hills, grassy-topped, with trees in the folds, and gardens on the lower slopes—as interesting a picture as one could wish to see.

The expedition had now performed its functions. I saw that old father Nile without any doubt rises in the Victoria N'yanza, and, as I had foretold, that lake is the great source of the holy river which cradled the first expounder of our religious belief. I mourned, however, when I thought how much I had lost by the delays in the journey having deprived me of the pleasure of going to look at the north-east corner of the N'yanza to see what connection there was, by the strait so often spoken of, with it and the other lake where the Waganda went to get their salt, and from which another river flowed to the north, making "Usoga an island." But I felt I ought to be content with what I had been spared to accomplish; for I had seen full half of the lake, and had information given me of the other half, by means of which I knew all about the lake, as far, at least, as the chief objects of geographical importance were concerned.

Let us now sum up the whole and see what it is worth. Comparative information assured me that there was as much water on the eastern side of the lake as there is on the western—if anything, rather more. The most remote waters, *or top head of the Nile*, is the southern end of the lake, situated close on the third degree of south latitude, which gives to the Nile the surprising length, in direct measurement, rolling over thirty-four degrees of latitude, of above 2,300 miles, or more than one-eleventh of the circumference of our globe. Now from this southern point, round by the west, to where the *great* Nile stream issues, there is only one feeder of any importance, and that is the Kitangulé river; whilst from the southernmost point, round by the east, to the strait, there are no rivers at all of any importance; for the travelled Arabs one and all aver, that from the west of the snow-clad Kilimandjaro to the lake where it is cut by the second degree, and also the first degree of south latitude, there are salt lakes and salt plains, and the country is hilly, not unlike Unyamuézi; but they said there were not great rivers, and the country was so scantily watered, having only occasional runnels and rivulets, that they always had to make long marches in order to find water when they went on their trading journeys; and further, those Arabs who crossed the strait when they reached Usoga, as mentioned before, during the late interregnum, crossed no river either.

There remains to be disposed of the "salt lake," which I believe is not a salt, but a fresh-water lake; and my reasons are, as before stated, that the natives call all lakes salt, if they find salt beds or salt islands in such places. Dr. Krapf, when he obtained a sight of the Kenia mountain, heard from the natives there that there was a salt lake to its northward, and he also heard that a river ran from Kenia towards the Nile. If his information was true on this latter point, then, without doubt, there must exist some connection between his river and the salt lake I have heard of, and this in all probability would also establish a connection between my salt lake and his salt lake which he heard was called Baringo. [It is questionable whether or not this word is a corruption of Bahr (sea of) Ingo]. In no view that can be taken of it, however, does this unsettled matter touch the established fact that the head of the Nile is in 3° south latitude, where, in the year 1858, I discovered the head of the Victoria N'yanza to be.

I now christened the "stones" Ripon Falls, after the nobleman who presided over the Royal Geographical Society when my expedition was got up; and the arm of water from which the Nile issued, Napoleon Channel, in token of respect to the French Geographical Society, for the honour they had done me, just before leaving England, in presenting me with their gold medal for the discovery of the Victoria N'yanza. One thing seemed at first perplexing—the volume of water in the Kitangulé looked as large as that of the Nile; but then the other one was a slow river and the other swift, and on this account I could form no adequate judgment of their relative values.

Not satisfied with my first sketch of the falls, I could not resist sketching them again; and then, as the cloudy state of the weather prevented my observing for latitude, and the officer of the place said a magnificent view of the lake could be obtained from the hill alluded to as intercepting the view from the falls, we proposed going there; but Kasoro, who had been indulged with nsunnu antelope skins, and with guinea-fowl for dinner, resisted this, on the plea that I never should be satisfied. There were orders given only to see the "stones," and if he took me to one hill I should wish to see another and another, and so on. It made me laugh, for that had been my nature all my life; but, vexed at heart, and wishing to trick the young tyrant, I asked for boats to shoot hippopotami, in the hope of reaching the hills to picnic; but boating had never been ordered, and he would not listen to it. "Then bring fish," I said, that I might draw them; no, that was not ordered. "Then go you to the palace, and leave me to go to Urondogani tomorrow, after I have taken a latitude;" but the willful creature would not go until he saw me underway. And as nobody would do anything for me without Kasoro's orders, I amused the people by firing at the ferry-boat upon the Usoga side, which they defied me to hit, the distance being 500 yards; but nevertheless a bullet went through her, and was afterwards brought by the Wasoga nicely folded up in a piece of mbugu. Bombay then shot a sleeping crocodile with his carbine, whilst I spent the day out watching the falls.

A Canyon Voyage

BY FREDERICK DELLENBAUGH

Frederick Dellenbaugh was just eighteen when he accompanied Major Powell on his pioneering river voyage through the Grand Canyon in 1871. The trip, made by starving men in leaky boats and led by the one-armed Powell, was a seminal event in the exploration of the American West.

The following year Powell again decided to tackle the mighty Colorado, and Dellenbaugh's account, *A Canyon Voyage*, was the only one ever written about that expedition. In the summer of 1872, the river was phenomenally high. It was like facing entirely new water, with previously used portages wiped out, forcing them to run rapids they had intended to avoid.

Here, they are just entering the worst stretch of the Colorado.

★　　★　　★　　★　　★

E verything now developed on a still larger and grander scale; we saw before us an enormous gorge, very wide at the top, which could engulf an ordinary mountain range and lose it within its vast depths and ramifications. Multitudinous lofty mesas, buttes, and pinnacles began to appear, each a mighty mountain in itself, but more or less overwhelmed by the greater grandeur of the Cyclopean environment.

Tuesday, August 27, after Prof. had put a new tube in the second barometer which had somehow been broken, we pushed off once more to see what the day would develop. The rapid just below camp we ran through easily and then made swift progress for seven miles, running nine more rapids, two rather bad ones. The *Cañonita* grounded once on a shoal but got off without damage. Where we stopped for dinner we caught sight of two mountain sheep drinking, and Andy and I got our guns out of the cabins as quickly as possible and started after them, but they flew away like birds of the air. Near this point there was a small abandoned hut of mesquite logs. We went into camp farther down on the left for investigations, the Major and I going up the river and finding a small salty creek which we followed for a time on an old trail, the Major studying the geology and collecting specimens of the rocks, which we carried back to camp, arriving after dark. The geology and topography here were complicated and particularly interesting, and we ought to have been able to spend more days, but the food questions, as well as time, was a determining factor in our movements, and with only two boats our rations would carry us with necessary stops only to the mouth of the Kanab Canyon where our pack-train would meet us on September 4. There was no other place above Diamond Creek known at that time, except perhaps the spot near Mount Trumbull, where supplies could be brought in. On Wednesday we ran two or three miles and stopped for our photographers to get some views opposite a rust-coloured sandstone. We also had dinner at this place and then continued the descent. After running four rapids successfully making a let-down at another, and a portage over the upper end of a sixth we were ready, having made in all six miles, to go into camp part way down the last, one of the heaviest falls we had so far encountered. It was perhaps half a mile long, with a declivity of at least forty feet, studded by numerous enormous boulders. A heavy rain began during our work of getting below, and our clothes being already wet the air became very chilly. We had to carry the cargoes only a short distance, with no climbing, and there was ample room so the portage was not difficult in that respect. But though we could manoeuvre the empty boats down along the shore amidst the big rocks, they were exceedingly heavy for our small band, and in sliding them down between the huge masses, with the water pouring around and often into them, we sometimes had as much as we could do to manage them, each man being obliged to strain his muscle to the limit. Jack from this cause hurt his back so badly that he could not lift at all, and overcome by the sudden weakness and pain he came near sinking into the swift river at the stern of the *Dean* where he happened at the moment to be working. I heard his cry and clambered over to seize him as quickly as I could, helping him to shore, where we did all that was possible for his comfort. As we were going no farther that day he was able to rest, and in the morning felt much better, though his back was still weak. Andy took his place in our boat to run the lower end of the rapid, which was easily done. We landed below on the same side, enabling Andy to go back to help bring down the *Cañonita*, while Jack walked along the rocks to where we were. Here we remained for a couple of hours while I climbed up for the Mayor and measured the "Red

Beds," and Jack rested again, improving very fast. When we were ready to go on his trouble had almost disappeared.

A dark granite formation had run up at the foot of the last fall and it rose rapidly higher, hemming the water in with steep, forbidding cliffs close together. The river became much narrower and swirled with an oily-looking current around the buttresses of granite that thrust themselves from one side or the other into it. The declivity was not great and the torrent was otherwise placid. After two miles of this ominous docility, just as the dinner hour was near and the threatening black granite had risen to one thousand feet above the water, we heard a deep, sullen roar ahead and from the boats the whole river seemed to vanish instantly from earth. At once we ran in on the right to a small area of great broken rocks that protruded above the water at the foot of the wall, and stepping out on these we could look down on one of the most fearful places I ever saw or ever hope to see under like circumstances—a place that might have been the Gate to Hell that Steward had mentioned. We were near the beginning of a tremendous fall. The narrow river dropped suddenly and smoothly away, and then, beaten to foam, plunged and boomed for a third of a mile making an exceedingly angry looking place. We were deeply impressed by its violence at this high stage of the river and wondered how the boats would fare. [This was the now famous "Sockdologer." The amount of fall has been variously estimated; from 30 to 130 feet. It looks the latter, but measured in 1923 turns out to be 19 feet, most of this in the first one hundred yards. I called it 40 feet in Sept. 1872—in a letter. Powell called it 30 in 1869. Stone in 1909 made it 34 feet 9 inches by leveling, if it was the same rapid.] On each side were the steep, ragged granitic walls, with the tumultuous waters lashing and pounding against them in a way that precluded all idea of portage or let-down. It needed no second glance to tell us that there was only one way of getting below. If the rocks did not stop us we could "cross to Killiloo," and when a driving rain had ceased Andy gathered the few sticks of driftwood available for a fire, by which he prepared some dinner in advance of the experiment. Jack and Clem took three negatives, and when the dinner was disposed of we stowed all loose articles snugly away in the cabins, except a camp-kettle in each standing-room to bail with, and then battening down the hatches with extra care, and making everything shipshape, we pulled the *Dean* upstream, leaving the *Canoñita* and her crew to watch our success or failure and profit by it. The Major had on his life preserver and so had Jones, but Jack and I put ours behind our seats, where we could catch them up quickly, for they were so large we thought they impeded the handling of the oars. Jack's back fortunately had now recovered, so that he was able to row almost his usual stroke. We pulled up-stream about a quarter of a mile close to the right-hand wall, in order that we might get well into the middle of the river before making the great plunge, and then we turned our bow out and secured the desired position as speedily as possible, heading down upon the roaring enemy—roaring as if it would surely swallow us at one gulp.

My back being towards the fall I could not see it, for I could not turn round while waiting every instant for orders. Nearer and nearer came the angry tumult; the Major shouted "Back water!" there was a sudden dropping away of all support; then the mighty wavers smote us. The boat rose to them well, but we were flying at twenty-five miles an hour and at every leap the breakers rolled over us. "Bail!" shouted the Major,—"Bail for your lives!" and we dropped the oars to bail, though bailing was almost useless. The oars could not get away, for they had rawhide rings nailed around near the handle to prevent them from slipping through the rowlocks. The boat rolled and pitched like a ship in a tornado, and as she flew along Jack and I, who faced backwards, could look up under the canopies of foam pouring over gigantic black boulders, first on one side, then on the other. Why we did not land on top of one of these and turn over I don't know, unless it might be that the very fury of the current causes a recoil. However that may be, we struck nothing but the waves, the boats riding finely and certainly leaping at times almost half their length out of water, to bury themselves quite as far at the next lunge. If you will take a watch and count by it ninety seconds, you will probably have about the time we were in this chaos, though it seemed much longer to me. Then we were through, and immediately took advantage of an eddy on one side to lie to and bail out, for the boat was full of water. Setting her to rights as quickly as we could, we got ready to make a dash for the crew of the *Cañonita* in case she fared worse than we did. We looked anxiously for her to appear, and presently, at the top of what seemed to us now to be a straight wall of foam, her small white bulk hung for an instant and then vanished from our sight in the mad flood. Soon appearing at the bottom uninjured, she ran in to where we were waiting. The *Cañonita*, being lighter than our boat, did not ship as much water as in some other places, and altogether we agreed that notwithstanding its great descent and furious aspect the passage was not more difficult than we had made in several previous rapids.

Continuing on down the narrow and gloomy granite gorge, we en-countered about a mile farther down a singular rapid, which turned the *Cañonita* completely around. About four o'clock we found ourselves before another tremendous fall, and a very ugly one. Landing on the left, we discovered that to be the wrong side, and crossed over to a little cove where there was a patch of gravel, surrounded by vertical walls, the crossing being easily made because the water seemed to slacken before the plunge. We did not intend to run the place if it could be avoided, and the south side gave no opportunity whatever for a portage, while the north side offered no very easy course. Prof. declared this to be one of the worst rapids we had seen, and we were now about two hundred feet above the head of it, with the vertical cliffs between. Immediately at the beginning of the drop on the same side that we were on was a pile of boulders, and our plan was to engineer the boats by lines from where we had landed down to these rocks, from which we believed we could work around over the rocks into an alcove there was there, and thence go down till we reached the lower part of the descent, through which we could navigate. Consequently several of the men entered one boat, and we lowered her from the stern of the second as far as her line would reach, and then lowered the second till the first lodged in the rocks at the desired point at the head of the fall. Then, pulling up the second boat, we who had remained got on board, and by clinging to the projections of the wall, the current close in being quite slow, we succeeded in arriving alongside the first boat. The next thing was to get around into the alcove. The sky above was heavy and rain began to come down steadily, making the dark granite blacker and intensifying the gloomy character of the locality. By hard work we finally got our boats across the rocks and down about two hundred feet farther into a cove, where they rested easily. Up to this time we had made in all, during the day, seven and one-quarter miles. As night was now dropping fast we had to make camp on a pile of broken granite, where a close search yielded an armful or two of small pieces of driftwood, all wet. Under a rock several dry sticks were discovered, and by their aid a fire soon blazed up by which the indomitable Andy proceeded to get supper. There was no use changing wet clothes for dry ones from the rubber bags as long as the rain fell, and it increased till water was dashing off the walls in streams. The thunder roared and crashed as if it were knocking the cliffs about to rearrange them all, and a deluge swept down in which Andy's struggling little fire died with hardly a sputter. The only thing remaining for us to do was to all stand with our backs against the foot of the wall, which was still warm from the day, and wait for something else to happen. The bread-pan seen through the dim and dismal light was a tempestuous lake, with an island of dough in it, while Andy the undaunted stood grimly gazing at it, the rain dribbling from his hat and shoulders till he resembled the fabled ferryman of the River Styx. The situation was so ludicrous that everyone laughed, and the Weather God finding we were not downcast slackened the downpour immediately. Then we put some oars against the wall and stretched a paulin to protect our noble chef, who finally got the wet firewood once more ignited, and succeeded in getting the bread almost baked and the coffee nearly hot and some dried peaches almost stewed. The rain ceasing, we hurriedly donned dry clothes and applied ourselves to the destruction of these viands, which tasted better than might be imagined. Each man then took his blankets, and, selecting rocks that in his judgment were the softest, he went to sleep.

There was another alcove, about three hundred yards below our camp, and in the morning, Friday, August 30th, we proceeded to work our way down to this, several men clambering along a ledge about 150 feet above the water with the line, while I remained each time in the boat below with an oar to keep the bow in against the wall, so that she could not take the current on the wrong side—that is, on the side next to the wall—and cut out into the river. In this way we got both boats down to the alcove, whence we intended to pull out into the current and run the lower portion of the rapid. It was only noon when we reached the place, but then we discovered that both boats had been so pounded that they badly needed repairs—in fact, it was imperative to halt there for this purpose—and we hauled them out on a patch of broken rocks, thirty or forty feet square, filling the curve of the alcove and bounded by vertical rocks and the river. While at work on them we happened to notice that the river was rapidly rising, and, setting a mark, the rate was found to be three feet an hour. The rocks on which we were standing and where all the cargo was lying were being submerged. We looked around for some way to get up the cliff, as it was now too late to think of leaving. About fifteen feet above the top of the rocks on which we were working there was a shelf five or six feet wide, to which some of the men climbed, and we passed up every article to them. When the repairs were done darkness was filling the great gorge. By means of lines from above and much hard lifting we succeeded in raising the boats up the side of the cliff, till they were four or five feet above the highest rocks of the patch on which we stood. This insured their safety for the time being, and if the river mounted to them we intended to haul them higher. The next thing was to find a place to sleep. By walking out on a ledge from the shelf where our goods were we could turn a jutting point above the rushing river by clinging closely to the rocks, and walk back on a shelf on the other side to a considerable area of finely broken rocks, thirty feet above the torrent, where there was room enough for a camp. Rain fell at intervals, and the situation was decidedly unpromising. While Andy and the others were getting the cook outfit and rations around the point, I climbed the cliffs hunting for wood. I found small pieces of driftwood lodged behind mesquite bushes fully one hundred feet above the prevailing stage of water. I collected quite an armful of half-dead mesquite, which has the advantage of being so compact that it makes a fire hot as coal, and little is needed to cook by. Supper was not long in being dispatched, and then, every man feeling about worn out, we put on dry clothes, the rain having ceased, and went to sleep on the rocks. Before doing so we climbed back to examine the boats, and found the river was not coming up farther, though it had almost completely covered the rocks.

Saturday, the 31st of August, 1872, was about the gloomiest morning I ever saw. Rain was falling, the clouds hung low over our heads like a lid to the box-like chasm in the black, funereal granite enclosing us, while the roar of the big rapid seemed to be intensified. We felt like rats in a trap. Eating breakfast as quickly as possible, we got everything together again on the shelf and lowered the boats. Though the river was not rising, it beat and surged into the cove in a way that made the boats jump and bounce the moment they touched the water. To prevent their being broken by pounding, one man at each steadied them while the others passed down the sacks and instrument boxes. Then it was seen that either a new leak had sprung in the *Dean* amidships or a hole had not been caulked, for a stream as wide as two fingers was spurting into the middle cabin. To repair her now meant hauling both boats back against the side of the cliff and spending another day in this trap, with the chance of the river rising much higher before night so that we might not be able to get away at all—at least not for days. For an instant the Major thought of pulling the boats out again, but as his quick judgment reviewed the conditions he exclaimed, "By God, we'll start! Load up!" It was the rarest thing for him to use an oath, and I remember only one other occasion when he did so—in Marble Gorge when he thought we were going to smash. We threw the things in as fast as we could, jammed a bag of flour against the leak in the *Dean*, battened down the hatches, threw our rifles into the bottom of the standing rooms where the water and sand washed unheeded over them, and jumped to our oars. The crew of the *Cañonita* held our stern till the bow swung out into the river, and then at the signal Jack and I laid to with all our strength—to shoot clear of an enormous rock about fifty feet below against which the fierce current was dashing. The *Dean* was so nearly water-logged that she was sluggish in responding to the oars, but we swept past the rock safely and rolled along down the river in the tail of the rapid with barely an inch of gunwale to spare—in fact, I thought the boat might sink. As soon as we saw a narrow talus on the right we ran in and landed.

When the *Cañonita* was ready to start one of Clem's oars could not be found, and Prof. had to delay to cut down one of the extras for him. Then they got their boat up as far as they could, and while Prof. and Andy kept her from pounding to pieces, Clem got in, bailed out, and took his oars. Prof. then climbed in at the stern, but the current was so strong that it pulled Andy off his feet and he was just able to get on, the boat drifting down stern first toward the big rock. Prof. concluded to let the stern strike and then try to throw the boat around into the river. By this time Andy had got hold of his oars, and the eddy seemed to carry them up-stream some twenty-five feet, so perverse and capricious is the Colorado. They swung the bow to starboard into the main current, and with a couple of strong oar-strokes the dreaded rock was cleared, and down the *Cañonita* came to us over the long waves like a hunted deer. We unloaded the *Dean* and pulled her out for repairs, but it was after four o'clock when we were able to go on again with a fairly tight boat. Then for eight miles the river was a continuous rapid broken by eight heavy falls, but luckily there were no rocks in any of·them at this stage of water, and we were able to dash through one after another at top speed, stopping only once for examination. Two of these rapids were portages on the former trip; proving the ease and advantage of high water in some places; but the disadvantages are much greater. Through a very narrow canyon on the right we caught a glimpse of a pretty creek, but we were going so fast the view was brief and imperfect. At 5:15 o'clock we ran up to a wide sandbank on which grew a solitary willow tree and there Camp 99 was made. For a space the inner canyon was much wider than above and the mouth of Bright Angel Creek was just below us; a locality now well known because a trail from the Hotel Tovar on the south rim comes down at this point. The name was applied by the Major on his first trip to offset the name Dirty Devil applied farther up.

The next day was Sunday, September 1st, and after the Major had climbed the south wall for observations we started once more on a powerful current. For the first three miles there was a continuous rapid with no opportunity to land. We dashed through waves that tossed us badly and filled the boats half full and then half full again before we had a chance to bail. In fifteen minutes we made the three miles and a half mile more, to arrive at a heavy rapid, which we ran and in two miles reached another with fearful waves, which we also ran. In one Jones was overbalanced by his oar hitting the top of a big wave behind the boat and he was knocked out. He clung by his knees and hands, his back in the water, and the boat careened till I thought she would go over. We could not move to help him without upsetting and were compelled to leave him to his own resources. In some way he succeeded in scrambling back. The waves were tremendous and sometimes seemed to come from all directions at once. There were whirlpools, too, that turned us round in spite of every effort to prevent it. The river was about one hundred and fifty feet wide. After an extremely strenuous morning we halted on the right for dinner, continuing as soon as we had disposed of it. Presently we arrived at a sharp fall of about twenty feet, where we made a portage, and waited at the foot for the photographers to take some negatives and also for repairing the *Cañonita*. Finally it was decided to camp on the spot. It was Camp 100. Our record for the day was a trifle over seven miles with nine rapids run and one portage.

Almost the first thing in the morning of September 2nd was a portage, after which we had fair water for two or three miles, and then reached a very heavy fall, where we landed on the left and had dinner after making another portage. This accomplished, we proceeded on a river still rising and ran a great many bad rapids, some of them having tremendous falls. In one the fierce current set against the cliff so strongly that we were carried within an oar's length of it, notwithstanding our severe effort to avoid so close an acquaintance with the rough wall. Even between the rapids the velocity of the water was extremely high and we flew along at terrific speed, while in the huge waves of the rapids the boats leaped and plunged with startling violence. Toward night a sudden halt was made on the left to examine a bad-looking place half a mile below. The Major and Prof. tried to climb where they could get a good view of it, but they failed. The Major said we would run it in the morning, though Prof. was dubious about the feasibility of doing so successfully and said he thought it about the worst place we had yet seen. We camped on a rocky talus where we were. A small sandbank was found nearby for our beds, and made another discovery, a small pool of clear, pure water, a rare treat after the muddy Colorado which we had been drinking for so long. Twenty rapids were placed to our credit for this one day in a trifle over fifteen miles, and we felt that we were vanquishing the Grand Canyon with considerable success.

Our life now was so strenuous every hour of the day that our songs were forgotten, and when night came every man was so used up that as soon as supper was over rest and sleep were the only things that interested us. Though our beds were as hard and rough as anything could be, we slept with the intensity of the rocks themselves, and it never seemed more than a few minutes before we were aroused by the Major's rising signal, "Oh-ho, boys!" and we rose to our feet to pack the blankets in the rubber bags, sometimes with a passing thought as to whether we would ever take them out again. For my part, never before nor since have I been so tired. One night when the Major called us to look out for the boats I did not hear him and no one waked me so I slept on, learning about it only the next morning. Our food supply was composed partly of jerked beef, and as this could not be put in rubber because of the grease it became more or less damp and there developed in it a peculiar kind of worm, the largest about an inch long, with multitudinous legs. There were a great many of them and they gave the beef a queer taste. In order to clear the sacks as far as possible of these undesirable denizens I several times emptied them on wide smooth rocks, and while the worms were scrambling about I scraped up the beef without many of them, but could not get rid of all. Andy's method of cooking this beef was to make a gravy with bacon fat and scorched flour and then for a few moments stew the beef in the gravy. Ordinarily this made a very palatable dish but the peculiar flavour of the beef now detracted from it, though we were so hungry that we could eat anything without a query, and our diminishing supply of rations forbade the abandonment of the valuable beef.

When we arose on the morning of September 3rd the dubious rapid was tossing its huge waves exactly as on the night before and humanity seemed to be out of the reckoning. By eight o'clock we were ready for it, and with everything in good trim we pushed off. The current was strong from the start, and a small rapid just below camp gave additional speed, so that we were soon baring down on the big one with wild velocity. The river dropped away abruptly, to rise again in a succession of fearful billows whose crests leaped and danced high in air as if rejoicing at the prospect of annihilating us. Just then the Major changed his mind as to running the place, for now standing on the boat's deck he could see it better than before from the region of the camp. He ordered us to pull hard to our left, intending to land at a spot that was propitious on the left or south bank, but no sooner had he given this command than he perceived that no landing above the fall was possible. He gave another order which put us straight in the middle gain and down we flew upon the descent. The Major as usual had put on his life preserver and think Jones had on his, but Jack and I, as was our custom, placed ours inflated immediately behind our seats, not wishing to be hampered by them. The plunge was exceedingly sharp and deep, and then we found ourselves tossing like a chip in a frightful chaos of breakers which almost buried us, though the boats rose to them as well as any craft possibly could. I bailed with a camp kettle rapidly and Jack did the same, but the boat remained full to the gunwales as we were swept on. We had passed the worst of it when, just as the *Dean* mounted a giant wave at an angle of perhaps forty or fifty degrees, the crest broke in a deluge against the port bow with a loud slap. In an instant we were upside-down going over to starboard. I threw up my hand instinctively to grasp something, and luckily caught hold of a spare oar which was carried slung on the side, and by this means I pulled myself above water. My hat was pasted down over my eyes. Freeing myself from this I looked about. Bottom up the boat was clear of the rapid and sweeping on down with the swift, boiling current toward a dark bend. The *Cañonita* was nowhere to be seen. No living thing was visible. The narrow black gorge rose in somber majesty to the everlasting sky. What was a mere human life or two in the span of eternity? I was about preparing to climb up on the bottom of the boat when I perceived Jones clinging to the ring in the stern, and in another second the Major and Jack shot up alongside as if from a gun. The whole party had been kept together in a kind of whirlpool, and the Major and Jack had been pulled down headfirst till, as is the nature of these suctions on the Colorado, it suddenly changed to an upward force and threw them out into the air.

There was no time to lose, for we did not wish to go far in this condition; another rapid might be waiting around the corner. Jack and I carefully got up on the bottom, leaving the Major at the bow and Jones at the stern, and leaning over we took hold of the starboard gunwale under water, and throwing ourselves back quickly together we brought the *Dean* up on her keel, though she came near rolling clear over the other way. She was even full of water, but the cabins supported her. Jack helped me in and then I balanced his effort so as not to capsize again. The bailing kettles were gone, but as our hats had strangely enough remained on our heads through it all we bailed with them as fast as possible for a few seconds till we lowered the water sufficiently to make it safe to get the others on board. The Major came aft along the gunwale and I helped him in, then Jack helped Jones. The oars, fortunately, had not come out of the locks, thanks to our excellent arrangement, and grasping them, without trying to haul in the bow line trailing a hundred feet in the water, we pulled hard for a slight eddy on the left where we perceived a footing on the rocks, and as soon as we were near enough I caught up the rope, made the leap, and threw the bight over a projection, where I held the boat while Jack and Jones bailed rapidly and set things in order so that we could go to the assistance of the *Cañonita*. The Major's Jurgenssen chronometer had stopped at 8:26:30 from the wetting.

The *Cañonita*, being more lightly laden than the *Dean*, and also not meeting the peculiar coincidence of mounting a wave at the instant it broke, came down with no more damage than the loss of three oars and the breaking of a rowlock. Probably if the Major had sat down on the deck instead of in the chair we might also have weathered the storm. About a mile and a half below we made a landing at a favourable spot on the right, where the cargoes were spread out to dry and the boats were overhauled, while the Major and I climbed up the wall to where he desired to make a geological investigation. We joked him a good deal about his zeal in going to examine the geology at the bottom of the river, but as a matter of fact he came near departing by that road to another world.

We were now in an exceedingly difficult part of the granite gorge, for, at the prevailing stage of water, landings were either highly precarious or not possible at all; so we could not examine places before running, and could not always make a portage where we deemed it necessary. There were also all manner of whirlpools and bad places. Starting on about three o'clock we descended several rapids in about six miles, when we saw one ahead that looked particularly forbidding. The granite came down almost vertically to the water, projecting in huge buttresses that formed a succession of little bays, especially on the left, where we manoeuvered in and out, keeping close against the rocks, the current there being slack. The plan was for me to be ready, on turning the last point, to jump out on some rocks we had noticed from above not far from the beginning of the rapid. As we crept around the wall I stood up with the bight of the line in one hand, while Jack pulled in till we began to drift down stern foremost alongshore. At the proper moment I made my leap exactly calculated. Unluckily at the instant the capricious Colorado threw a "boil" up between the bow and the flat rock I was aiming at, turning the bow out several feet, and instead of landing were I intended I disappeared in deep water. I clung to the line and the acceleration of the boat's descent quickly pulled me back to the surface. She was gliding rapidly past more rocks and the Major jumped for them with the purpose of catching the rope, but they were so isolated and covered with rushing water that he had all he could do to take care of himself. Jones then tried the same thing, but with the same result. Jack stuck to his post. I went hand over hand to the bow as fast as I could, and reaching the gunwale I was on board in a second. One of my oars had somehow come loose, but Jack had caught it and now handed it to me. We took our places and surveyed the chances. Apparently we were in for running the rapid stern foremost and we prepared for it, but in the middle of the stream there was a rock of most gigantic proportions sloping up the river in such a way that the surges alternately rolled upon it and then slid back. Partly up the slope we were drawn by this power, and on the down rush the boat turned and headed diagonally just right for reaching the left bank. We saw our opportunity and, pulling with every muscle, lodged the *Dean* behind a huge boulder at the very beginning of the main rapid, where I made the line fast in the twinkle of an eye. Meanwhile the Major had hastily scrambled up to where he could see down the canyon, and he heard Jack's hearty shout of "All right!" Lowering the *Dean* a couple of rods farther to a sandbank at the mouth of a gulch we went into camp feeling that we had done enough river work for one day, and the *Canonita's* crew without accident lowered down to the same place before Andy had supper ready. My hat had come off in my deep plunge and beyond this I did not have another one. Near by was a small clear spring that gave us another treat of palatable water, the Colorado now being muddier than ever, as it was still on the rise, coming up three feet more while we were here. The entire day's run was eight and one-eighth miles. The Major and Prof. succeeded in getting down three miles on foot to reconnoitre.

Continuing in the morning, September 4th, we lowered the boats past the remainder of the rapid and then shoved out into the terrific current once more. Water could hardly run faster than it now did, except in a fall or rapid. The canyon was narrow and for five miles we encountered the worst whirlpools we had anywhere seen. The descent was swift and continuous, but the river was broken only by the whirlpools and "boils" as we called them, the surface suddenly seeming to boil up and run over. These upshots, as a rule, seemed to follow whirlpools. In the latter the water for a diameter of twenty or twenty-five feet would revolve around a centre with great rapidity, the surface inclining to the vortex, the top of which was perhaps eighteen or twenty inches lower than the general level. The vortex itself was perfectly formed, like a large funnel, and about six or eight inches in diameter, where it began to be a hole in the water, taping thence down in four or five feet to a mere point. The same effect is often seen when the water is flowing out of a round wash-basin through a pipe at the bottom. These were the most perfect whirlpools I have ever seen, those above having been lacking in so distinct a vortex. There were many and we could often see them ahead, but try as we would to cleave through without a complete revolution or two of the boat we could not do it. The boats sank down into the hollow, enabling one to look over the side into the spinning opening, but the boats, being almost as long as the whirlpool's usual diameter, could not be pulled in and we were not alarmed. We found it rather interesting to see if we could get through without turning, but we never did. Any ordinary short object or one that could be tipped on end would surely go out of sight. So furious ran the river along this stretch that we found it impossible to stop, the boats being like bits of paper in a mill-race, swinging from one side to the other, and whirling round and round as we were swept along between the narrow walls till we ran the granite under about five miles from our last camp. Finally, after a run all told of fourteen miles with twenty-three rapids, we made Camp 103 with walls of friendly sandstone about us. Here again we discovered a small clear spring for drinking and cooking purposes. There was no rain this day and at night we put on our dry clothes with confidence and had a warm comfortable camp with a good sound sleep.

Down the Congo

BY HENRY MORTON STANLEY

Henry Morton Stanley was one of history's greatest explorers, mapping much of the interior of Africa over the course of several expeditions and settling the source of the Nile—Africa's last great secret. His life was one adventure after another, starting with his youth in a notorious English workhouse and continuing through his enlistment in the Confederate army during the American Civil War, his subsequent capture, switching sides to join the U.S. Navy, and his eventual desertion after the war.

Later work as a journalist led to his being offered the chance to lead an expedition to find David Livingstone, who had disappeared several years earlier while searching for the source of the Nile. Upon meeting him, Stanley uttered the famous but prosaic words: "Dr. Livingstone, I presume?"

He set out on a more ambitious expedition to Africa in 1874, proving conclusively that Speke was right about the Nile's source and showing that Livingstone's Lualaba River was really the Congo, not the Nile. While many African explorers traveled in small groups that often suffered at the hands of local warlords, Stanley set out with a veritable army and shot and hacked his way through hostile lands. When he finally made it back to civilization, his party of 356 was reduced to just 115, and his three English companions were all dead.

His book *Through the Dark Continent* gives a fascinating account of this harrowing journey. In the following episode, he is taking leave of Tippu Tip, an Arab trader who had agreed to travel with him for added protection. The trader and his men wanted nothing more to do with the incessant fighting with cannibalistic tribes. But Stanley and his last white companion, Frank Pocock, set out to float down a river no white man had ever seen. (Frank eventually drowned in the succession of rapids they encountered.) They really had no idea where the river would take them, and although they faced wholesale desertion by their men, illness, and almost constant fighting with cannibals, they embarked with an enthusiasm that only true explorers can muster.

★   ★   ★   ★   ★

I n the evening, while sleep had fallen upon all save the watchful sentries in charge of the boat and canoes, Frank and I spent a serious time. Frank was at heart as sanguine as I that we should finally emerge somewhere, but, on account of the persistent course of the great river towards the north, a little uneasiness was evident in his remarks.

"Before we finally depart, sir," said he, "do you really believe, in your innermost soul, that we shall succeed? I ask this because there are such odds against us—not that I for a moment think it would be best to return, having proceeded so far."

"Believe? Yes, I do believe that we shall all emerge into light again some time. It is true that our prospects are as dark as this night. Even the Mississippi presented no such obstacles to De Soto as this river will necessarily present to us. Possibly its islands and its forests possessed much of the same aspect, but here we are at an altitude of sixteen hundred and fifty feet above the sea. What conclusions can we arrive at? Either that this river penetrates a great distance north of the Equator, and, taking a mighty sweep round, descends into the Congo—this, by the way, would lessen the chances of there being many cataracts in the river—or that we shall shortly see it in the neighbourhood of the Equator, take a direct cut towards the Congo, and precipitate itself, like our Colorado river, through a deep cañyon, or down great cataracts; or that it is either the Niger or the Nile. I believe it will prove to be the Congo; if the Congo then, there must be many cataracts. Let us only hope that the cataracts are all in a lump, close together.

"Any way, whether the Congo, the Niger, or the Nile, I am prepared, otherwise I should not be so confident. Though I love life as much as you do, or any other man does, yet on the success of this effort I am about to stake my life, my all. To prevent its sacrifice foolishly I have devised numerous expedients with which to defy wild men, wild nature, and unknown terrors. There is an enormous risk, but you know the adage, 'Nothing risked, nothing won.'

"Now look at this, the latest chart which Europeans have drawn of this region. It is a blank, perfectly white. We will draw two curves just to illustrate what I mean. One shows the river reaching the Equator and turning westward. Supposing there are no cataracts, we ought to reach 'Tuckey's Furthest' by the 15th February; but if the river takes that wider sweep from 2° north of the Equator, we may hope to reach by the 15th March, and if we allow a month for cataracts or rapids, we have a right to think that we ought to see the ocean by either the middle or the end of April 1877.

"I assure you, Frank, this enormous void is about to be filled up. Blank as it is, it has a singular fascination for me. Never has white paper possessed such a charm for me as this has, and I have already mentally peopled it, filled it with the most wonderful pictures of towns, villages, rivers, countries, and tribes—all in the imagination—and I am burning to see whether I am correct or not. *Believe*? I see us gliding down by tower and town, and my mind will not permit a shadow of doubt. Good night, my boy! Good night! And may happy dreams of the sea, and ships, and pleasure, and comfort, and success attend you in your sleep! Tomorrow, my lad, is the day we shall cry—"Victory or death!""

The crisis drew nigh when the 28th December dawned. A grey mist hung over the river, so dense that we could not see even the palmy banks on which Vinya-Njara was situated. It would have been suicidal to begin our journey on such a gloomy morning. The people appeared as cheerless and dismal as the foggy day. We cooked our breakfasts in order to see if, by the time we had fortified the soul by satisfying the cravings of the stomach, the river and its shores might not have resumed their usual beautiful outlines, and their striking contrasts of light and shadow.

Slowly the breeze wafted the dull and heavy mists away until the sun appeared, and bit by bit the luxuriantly wooded banks rose up solemn and sad. Finally the grey river was seen, and at 9 A.M. its face gleamed with the brightness of a mirror.

"Embark, my friends! Let us at once away! And a happy voyage to us."

The drum and trumpet proclaimed to Tippu-Tib's expectant ears that we were ascending the river. In half an hour we were pulling across to the left bank, and when we reached it a mile above Vinya-Njara we rested on our oars. The strong brown current soon bore us down within hearing of a deep and melodious diapason of musical voices chanting the farewell song. How beautiful it sounded to us as we approached them! The dense jungle and forest seemed to be penetrated with the vocal notes, and the river to bear them tenderly towards us. Louder the sad notes swelled on our ears, full of a pathetic and mournful meaning. With bated breath we listened to the rich music which spoke to us unmistakably of parting, of sundered friendship, a long, perhaps an eternal, farewell. We came in view of them, as ranged along the bank in picturesque costume the sons of Unyamwezi sang their last song. We waved our hands to them. Our hearts were so full of grief that we could not speak. Steadily the brown flood bore us by, and fainter and fainter came the notes down the water, till finally they died away, leaving us all alone in our loneliness.

But, looking up, I saw the gleaming portal to the Unknown: wide open to us and away down, for miles and miles, the river lay stretched with all the fascination of its mystery. I stood up and looked at the people. How few they appeared to dare the region of fable and darkness! They were nearly all sobbing. They were leaning forward, bowed, as it seemed, with grief and heavy hearts.

"Sons of Zanzibar," I shouted, "the Arabs and the Wanyamwezi are looking at you. They are now telling one another what brave fellows you are. Lift up your heads and be men. What is there to fear? All the world is smiling with joy. Here we are all together like one family, with hearts united, all strong with the purpose to reach our homes. See this river; it is the road to Zanzibar. When saw you a road so wide? When did you journey along a path like this? Strike your paddles deep, cry out Bismillah! And let us forward."

Poor fellows! With what wan smiles they responded to my words! How feebly they paddled! But the strong flood was itself bearing us along, and the Vinya-Njara villages were fast receding into distance.

Then I urged my boat's crew, knowing that thus we should tempt the canoes to quicker pace. Three or four times Uledi, the coxswain, gallantly attempted to sing, in order to invite a cheery chorus, but his voice soon died into such piteous hoarseness that the very ludicrousness of the tones caused his young friends to smile even in the midst of their grief.

We knew that the Vinya-Njara district was populous from the numbers of natives that fought with us by land and water, but we had no conception that it was so thickly populated as the long row of villages we now saw indicated. I counted fourteen separate villages, each with its respective growth of elais palm and banana, and each separated from the other by thick bush.

Every three or four miles after passing Vinya-Njara, there were small villages visible on either bank, but we met with no disturbance, fortunately.

At 5 P.M. we made for a small village called Kali-Karero, and camped there, the natives having retired peacefully. In half an hour they returned, and the ceremony of brotherhood was entered upon, which insured a peaceful night. The inhabitants of Rukura, opposite us, also approached us with confidence, and an interchange of small gifts served us as a healthy augury for the future.

On the morning of the 29th, accompanied by a couple of natives in a small fishing-canoe, we descended the river along the left bank, and after about four miles, arrived at the confluence of the Kasuku, a dark-water stream of a hundred yards' width at the mouth. Opposite the mouth, at the southern end of Kaimba—a long wooded island on the right bank, and a little above the confluence—stands the important village of Kisanga-Sanga.

Below Kaimba Island and its neighbour, the Livingstone assumes a breadth of 1,800 yards. The banks are very populous; the villages of the left bank comprise the district of Luavala. We thought for some time we should be permitted to pass by quietly, but soon the great wooden drums, hollowed out of huge trees, thundered the signal along the river that there were strangers. In order to lessen all chances of a rupture between us, we sheered off to the middle of the river, and quietly lay on our paddles. But from both banks at once, in fierce concert, the natives, with their heads gaily feathered, and armed with broad black wooden shields and long spears, dashed out towards us.

Tippu-Tib before our departure had hired to me two young men of Ukusu—cannibals—as interpreters. These were now instructed to cry out the word "Sennenneh!" ("Peace!"), and to say that we were friends.

But they would not reply to our greeting, and in a bold peremptory manner told us to return.

"But we are doing no harm, friends. It is the river that takes us down, and the river will not stop or go back."

"This is our river."

"Good. Tell it to take us back, and we will go."

"If you do not go back, we will fight you."

"No, don't; we are friends."

"We don't want you for our friends; we will eat you."

But we persisted in talking to them, and as their curiosity was so great they persisted in listening, and the consequence was that the current conveyed us near to the right bank; and in such near neighbourhood to another district, that our discourteous escort had to think of themselves, and began to scurry hastily up river, leaving us unattacked.

The villages on the right bank also maintained a tremendous drumming and blowing of war-horns, and their wild men hurried up with menace towards us, urging their sharp-prowed canoes so swiftly that they seemed to skim over the water like flying fish. Unlike the Luavala villagers, they did not wait to be addressed, but as soon as they came within fifty or sixty yards they shot out their spears, crying out, "Meat! meat! Ah! Ha! We shall have plenty of meat! Bo-bo-bo-bo, Bo-bo-bo, bo-o-o!"

Undoubtedly these must be relatives of the terrible "Bo-bo-bos's" above, we thought, as with one mind we rose to respond to this rapid man-eating tribe. Anger we had none for them. It seemed to me so absurd to be angry with people who looked upon one only as an epicure would regard a fat capon. Sometimes also a faint suspicion came to my mind that this was all but a part of a hideous dream. Why was it that I should be haunted with the idea that there were human beings who regarded me and my friends only in the light of meat? Meat! *We*? Heavens! What an atrocious idea!

"Meat! Ah! We shall have meat today. Meat! Meat! Meat!"

There was a fat-bodied wretch in a canoe, whom I allowed to crawl within spear-throw of me; who, while he swayed the spear with a vigour far from assuring to one who stood within reach of it, leered with such a clever hideousness of feature that I felt, if only within arm's length of him, I could have bestowed upon him a hearty thump on the back, and cried out applaudingly, "Bravo, old boy! You do it capitally!"

Yet not being able to reach him, I was rapidly being fascinated by him. The rapid movements of the swaying spear, the steady wide-mouthed grin, the big square teeth, the head poised on one side with the confident pose of a practised spear-thrower, the short brow and square face, hair short and thick. Shall I ever forget him? It appeared to me as if the spear partook of the same cruel inexorable look as the grinning savage. Finally, I saw him draw his right arm back, and his body incline backwards, with still that same grin on his face, and I felt myself begin to count, one, two, three, four—and *whizz!* The spear flew over my back, and hissed as it pierced the water. The spell was broken.

It was only five minutes' work clearing the river. We picked up several shields, and I gave orders that all shields should be henceforth religiously preserved, for the idea had entered my head that they would answer capitally as bulwarks for our canoes. An hour after this we passed close to the confluence of the Urindi—a stream 400 yards in width at the mouth, and deep with water of a light colour, and tolerably clear.

We continued down river along the right bank, and at 4 P.M. camped in a dense low jungle, the haunt of the hippopotamus and elephant during the dry season. When the river is in flood a much larger tract must be under water.

The left bank was between seventy and eighty feet high; and a point bearing from camp north west was about one hundred and fifty feet high.

The traveller's first duty in lands infested by lions and leopards, is to build a safe corral, kraal, or boma, for himself, his oxen, horses, servants; and in lands infested like Usongora Meno and Kasera—wherein we now were— by human lions and leopards, the duty became still more imperative. We drew our canoes, therefore, half-way upon the banks, and our camp was in the midst of an impenetrable jungle.

On the high bluffs opposite was situated Vina-Kya. The inhabitants at once manned their drums and canoes, and advanced towards our camp. We could not help it. Here we were camped in a low jungle. How could the most captious, or the most cruel, of men find any cause or heart to blame us for resting on this utterly uninhabitable spot? Yet the savages of Vina-Kya did. Our interpreters were urged to be eloquent. And indeed they were, if I may judge by the gestures, which was the only language that was comprehensible to me. I was affected with a strange, envious admiration for those two young fellows, cannibals it is true, but endowed, nonetheless, with a talent for making even senseless limbs speak—and they appeared to have affected the savages of Vina-Kya also. At any rate, the wild natures relented for that day; but they promised to decapitate us early in the morning, for the sake of a horrid barbecue they intended to hold. We resolved not to wait for the entertainment.

At dawn we embarked, and descended about two miles, close to the right bank, when, lo! The broad mouth of the magnificent Low-wa, or Rowwa, river burst upon the view. It was over a thousand yards wide, and its course by compass was from the south-east, or east- south-east true. A sudden rain-storm compelled us to camp on the north bank, and here we found ourselves under the shadows of the primeval forest.

Judging from the height and size of these trees, I doubt whether the right bank of the Livingstone at the mouth of the Lowwa river was ever at any time inhabited. An impenetrable undergrowth consisting of a heterogeneous variety of ferns, young palms, date, doum, *Raphia viniferous*, and the

Mucuna pruriens—the dread of the naked native for the tenacity with which its stinging sharp-pointed bristles attach themselves to the skin—masses of the capsicum plant, a hundred species of clambering vines, caoutchouc creepers, llianes, and endless lengths of rattan cane intermeshed and entangled, was jealously sheltered from sunlight by high, over-arching, and interlacing branches of fine grey-stemmed Rubiaceae, camwood and bombax, teak, elais palms, ficus, with thick fleshy leaves, and tall gum-trees. Such is the home of the elephants which through this undergrowth have trodden the only paths available. In the forks of the trees were seen large lumps, a spongy excrescence, which fosters orchids and tender ferns, and from many of the branches depended the Usneae moss in graceful and delicate fringes. Along the brown clayey shores ,wherever there is the slightest indentation in the banks and still water, were to be found the Cyperaceae sedge and in deeper recesses and shallow water the papyrus.

In such cool, damp localities as the low banks near the confluence of these two important streams, entomologists might revel. The Myriapedes, with their lengthy sinuous bodies of bright shiny chocolate or deep black colour, are always one of the first species to attract one's attention. Next come the crowded lines of brown, black, or yellow ants, and the termites, which with an insatiable appetite for destruction, are ever nibbling, gnawing, and prowling. If the mantis does not arrest the eye next, it most assuredly will be an unctuous earth caterpillar, with its polished and flexible armour, suggestive of slime and nausea. The mantis among insects is like the python among serpents. Its strange figure, trance-like attitudes, and mysterious ways have in all countries appealed to the imagination of the people. Though sometimes five inches in length, its waist is only about the thickness of its leg. Gaunt, weird, and mysterious in its action, it as much a wonder among insects as a mastodon would be in a farmyard. The ladybird attracts the careless eye as it slowly wanders about by its brilliant red, spotted with black—but if I were to enter into details of the insect life I saw within the area of a square foot, an entire chapter might readily be filled. But to write upon the natural wonders of the tropics seems nowadays almost superfluous; it is so well understood that in these humid shades the earth seethes with life, that in these undrained recesses the primitive laboratory of nature is located, for disturbing which the unacclimatized will have to pay the bitter penalty of malarial fever.

One hears much about "the silence of the forest"—but the tropical forest is not silent to the keen observer. The hum and murmur of hundreds of busy insect tribes make populous the twilight shadows that reign under the primeval growth. I hear the grinding of millions of mandibles, the furious hiss of a tribe just alarmed or about to rush into battle, millions of tiny wings rustling through the nether air, the march of an insect tribe under the leaves, the startling leap of an awakened mantis, the chirp of some eager and garrulous cricket, the buzz of an ant-lion, the roar of a bull-frog. Add to these the crackle of twigs, the fall of leaves, the dropping of nut and berry, the occasional crash of a branch, or the constant creaking and swaying of the forest tops as the strong wind brushes them or the gentle breezes awaken them to whispers. Though one were blind and alone in the midst of a real tropical forest, one's sense of hearing would be painfully alive to the fact that an incredible number of minute industries whose number one could never hope to estimate, were active in the shades. Silence is impossible in a tropical forest.

About ten o'clock, as we cowered in the most miserable condition under the rude, leafy shelters we had hastily thrown up, the people of the wooded bluffs of Iryamba, opposite the Lowwa confluence, came over to see what strange beings were those who had preferred the secrecy of the uninhabited grove to their own loud roistering society. Stock still we sat cowering in our leafy coverts, but the mild reproachful voice of Katembo, our cannibal interpreter, was heard labouring in the interests of peace, brotherhood, and good will. The rain pattered so incessantly that I could from my position only faintly hear Katembo's voice pleading, earnestly yet mildly, with his unsophisticated brothers of Iryamba, but I felt convinced from the angelic tones that they would act as a sedative on any living creature except a rhinoceros or a crocodile. The long-drawn bleating sound of the word "Sen-nen-neh," which I heard frequently uttered by Katembo, I studied until I became quite as proficient in it as he himself.

Peace was finally made between Katembo on the one hand and the canoe-men of Iryamba on the other, and they drew near to gaze at their leisure at one of the sallow white men, who with great hollow eyes peered, from under the vizor of his cap, on the well-fed bronze-skinned aborigines.

After selling us ten gigantic plantains, 13 inches long and 3 inches in diameter, they informed us that we had halted on the shore of Luru, or Lulu, in the uninhabited portion of the territory of Wanpuma, a tribe which lived inland; that the Lowwa came from the east, and was formed of two rivers, called the Lulu from the north-east, and the Lowwa from the southeast; that about a day's journey up the Lowwa river was a great cataract, which was "very loud."

The Livingstone, from the base of Iryamba bluffs on the left bank to our camp on the right bank, a mile below the confluence, was about two thousand yards in width. By dead reckoning we ascertained the latitude to be south 1° 28', or 24 miles north of the Urindi affluent of the Livingstone, 95 miles north of the Lira, and 199 geographical miles north of the mountain of the Luama affluent.

The relative rank of these four great tributaries may be estimated by their width, at or near the confluence. The Luama was 400 yards wide; the Lira 300 yards, but deep; the Urindi 500 yards; the Lowwa 1,000 yards. The parallel of latitude in which the Lowwa mouth is situated is fifty miles north of the extreme north end of Lake Tanganika. From all I could gather by a comparison of names and the relative authenticity of my informants, I am inclined to believe that the sources of this last great river may be placed near the south-west corner of Lake Muta-Nzigé; also, that the Urindi's head streams must approach the sources of the Luanda, which joins the Rusizi, and flows into Lake Tanganika, and that the Lira must drain the country west of Uvira.

The length of the Urindi river which empties into the Livingstone only fifteen miles south of the Lowwra, may be estimated by a glance at the course of the Luama, which I followed from its source to its confluence with the Lualaba. In the same manner, the Lira's course and length may be judged.

The growing importance and volume of the tributaries as we proceed north also proves a northern prolongation of the mountain chain, which shuts in Tanganika on the west, and probably a slight deflection to the eastward. It will be observed also that while the Luama, the Lulindi, the Kundra, the Kariba, the Rumuna, the Kipembwé, the Lira, Urindi, and Lowwa rivers all issue from the country east, within a length of about two hundred miles of the Livingstone, we have only discovered two comparatively small rivers, the Ruiki and the Kasuku, issuing from the west side during the same course. The nature of the eastern country may be judged after a study of the chapter descriptive of our journey from Lake Tanganika to the mouth of the Luama.

At 2 P.M. we left our camp in the forest of Luru, and pulled across to the Ibyamba side of the Livingstone. But as soon as the rain had ceased, a strong breeze had risen, which, when we were in mid-river, increased to a tempest from the north, and created great heavy waves, which caused the foundering of two of our canoes, the drowning of two of our men, Farjalla Baraka and Nasib, and the loss of four muskets and one sack of beads. Half a dozen other canoes were in great danger for a time, but no more fatal accidents occurred.

I feared lest this disaster might cause the people to rebel and compel me to return, for it had shocked them greatly; but I was cheered to hear them remark that the sudden loss of their comrades had been ordained by fate, and that no precautions would have availed to save them. But though omens and auguries were delivered by the pessimists among us, not one hazarded aloud the belief that we ought to relinquish our projects; yet they were all evidently cowed by our sudden misfortune.

On the 31st, the last day of the year 1876, we resumed our voyage. The morning was beautiful, the sky blue and clear, the tall forest still and dark, the river flowed without a ripple, like a solid mass of polished silver. Everything promised fair. But from the island below, the confluence of the Lowwa and the Livingstone, the warning drum sounded loudly over the river, and other drums soon echoed the dull boom.

"Keep together, my men, " I cried, "there may be hot work for us below."

We resolved to keep in mid-stream, because both the island and the left bank appeared to be extremely populous, and to paddle slowly and steadily down river. The canoes of the natives darted from either shore, and there seemed to be every dispostion made for a furious attack; but as we drew near, we shouted out to them, "Friends, Sennenneh! Keep away from us. We shall not hurt you; but don't lift your spears, or we'll fight." ·

There was a moment's hesitation, wherein spears were clashed against shields, and some fierce words uttered, but finally the canoes drew back, and as we continued to paddle, the river with its swift current soon bore us down rapidly past the populous district and island.

Before we finally passed by the latter, we came to another island which was uninhabited, and, after descending by a narrow channel, we crossed the mouth of a stream about twenty-five yards wide, flowing from the west side, in which were several small canoes and some dozen fishermen, lifting their nets from among the sedge.

At noon of this day we came to the southern end of an uninhabited low and sandy island, where I ascertained the latitude to be south 1°, 20' 3". The altitude, above sea level, of the river at this place is 1,729 feet.

South of this position we struck across to the right bank again and discovered a small river 40 yards wide at the mouth, nearly opposite which, about mid-stream, are five low and bush-covered islets. After descending some five miles we formed our camp in the woods on the right bank.

The beginning of the new year, 1877, commenced the first three hours after sunrise, with a delicious journey past an uninhabited tract, when my mind, wearied with daily solicitude, found repose in dwelling musingly upon the deep slumber of Nature. Outwardly the forest was all beauty, solemn peace, and soft dreamy rest, tempting one to sentiment and mild melancholy. Though it was vain to endeavour to penetrate with our eyes into the dense wall of forest—black and impervious to the sunlight which almost seemed to burn up the river—what could restrain the imagination? These were my calm hours, periods when my heart, oblivious of the dark and evil days we had passed, resolutely closed itself against all dismal forebodings, and reveled in the exquisite stillness of the uninhabited wilderness.

But soon after nine o'clock we discovered we were approaching settlements, both on islands and on the banks, and again the hoarse wardrums awakened the echoes of the forest, boomed along the river, and quickened our pulses.

We descend in close order as before, and steadily pursue our way. But, heading us off, about ten long canoes dart out from the shadow of palmy banks, and the wild crews begin to chant their war-songs, and now and then, in attitudes of bravado and defiance, raise spears and shields aloft and bring them downward with sounding clash.

As we approached them, we shouted out, "Sen-nen-neh"—our Sesame and Shibboleth, our watchword and countersign. But they would not respond.

Hitherto they had called us Wasambye; we were now called Wajiwa (people of the sun?); our guns were called Katadzi, while before they were styled Kibongeh, or lightning. Katembo was implored to be eloquent, mild of voice, pacific in gesture.

They replied, "We shall eat Wajiwa meat today. Oho, we shall eat Wajiwa meat!" and then an old chief gave some word of command, and at once 100 paddles beat the water into foam, and the canoes darted at us. But the contest was short, and we were permitted to pursue our voyage.

The river, beyond these islands, expanded to a breadth of 3,000 yards; the left bank being high, and the right low. At noon we were in south latitude 1° 10'.

Five miles below, the river narrowed to almost 2,800 yards, and then we floated down past an uninhabited stretch, the interval affording us rest, until, reaching the southern end of a large island, we camped, lest we might be plunged into hostilities once more.

The 2nd January was a lively day. We first ran the gauntlet past Kirembuka, an exciting affair, and next we were challenged by Mwana-Mara's fierce sons, who were soon joined by Mwana Vibondo's people, and about 10:30 A.M. we had to repulse an attack made by the natives of Lombo a Kiriro. We had fought for three hours almost without a pause, for the Kewenjawa and Watomba tribe from the left bank had joined in the savage mêlée, and had assisted the tribes of the right bank. Then for an hour we had rest; but after that we came to islands, which we afterwards discovered were called Kibombo, and finding the tribe of Amu Nyam preparing for battle with animation, we took advantage of one of the group to see if we could not negotiate a peaceful passage before risking another fight. The latitude of this island was south 0°, 52'0".

Katembo, our interpreter, and his friend, were dispatched in a canoe manned by eight men, halfway to the shore, to speak fair and sweet words of peace to the Amu Nyam. No verbal answer was given to them, but they had to retreat in a desperate hurry before a rapidly advancing crowd of canoes. The Amu Nyams had evidently not had time to be undeceived by their friends above, for they came up with a dauntless bearing, as though accustomed to victory. Yet we held out copper armlets and long strings of shells to them, vociferously shouting out, "Sen-nen-neh," with appropriate and plausible gestures. They laughed at us; and one fellow, who had a mighty door-like shield painted black with soot, using his long spear as an index finger, asked us—if Katembo spoke correctly—if we thought we could disappoint them of so much meat by the presents of a few shells and a little copper.

Our canoes were lying broadside along the reedy island, and as soon as the first spears were thrown, the Wangwana received orders to reply to them with brass slugs, which created such a panic that a couple of shots from each man sufficed to drive them back in confusion. After a while they recovered, and from a distance began to fly their poisoned arrows; but the Sniders responded to them so effectually that they finally desisted, and we were again free from our meat-loving antagonists.

About 2 P.M. we dropped down river again a few miles, and at 4:30 P.M. halted to camp at an old clearing on the right bank. Had we dared, we might have continued our journey by night, but prudence forbade the attempt, as cataracts might have been more disastrous than cannibals.

Near sunset we were once more alarmed by finding arrows dropping into the camp. Of course there was a general rush to guns; but, upon noting the direction whence the arrows came, I ordered the people simply to go on about their duties as though nothing had occurred, while I sent twenty men in two canoes down the river with instructions to advance upon the enemy from behind, but by no means to fire unless they were overwhelmed in numbers.

Just at dark our canoe came back with three prisoners bound hand and foot. Except the poor dwarf at Ikondu upriver, I had not seen any human creatures so unlovable to look at. There was no one feature about them that even extravagant charity could indicate as elevating them into the category of noble savages. I do not think I was prejudiced; I examined their faces with eyes that up to that time had gazed into the eyes of over five hundred thousand black men. They were intolerably ugly. I would not disturb them, however, that evening, but releasing their feet, and relaxing the bonds on their arms, appointed Katembo and his friend to keep them company and feed them, and Wadi Rehani to stimulate the keepers to be hospitable.

By the morning they were sociable, and replied readily to our questions. They were of the Wanongi—in inland tribe—but they had a small fishing village about an hour's journey below our camp called Katumbi. A powerful tribe called the Mwana Ntaba occupied a country below Katumbi, near some falls, which they warned us would be our destruction. On the left side of the river, opposite the Mwana Ntaba, were the Wavinza, south of a large river called the Rumami or Lumami. The great river on which we had voyaged was known to them as the Lowwa.

As we stepped into our canoes we cut their bonds and permitted the unlovable and unsympathetic creatures to depart, a permission of which they availed themselves gladly.

The banks were from 10 to 30 feet high, of a grey-brown clay, and steep with old clearings, which were frequent at this part until below Katumbi. Half an hour afterwards we arrived at a channel which flowed in a sudden bend to the north-east, and following it, we found ourselves abreast of a most populous shore, close to which we glided. Presently several large canoes appeared from behind an island to our right, and seemed to be hesitating as to whether they should retreat or advance.

The "Open Sesame"—"Sen-nen-neh!"—was loudly uttered by Katembo with his usual pathetic, bleating accent and to our joy the word was repeated by over a hundred voices. "Sen-nen-neh! Sen-nen-neh! Sen-nen-neh!"—each voice apparently vying with the other in loudness. The river bore us down, and as they would not shorten the distance, we thought it better to keep this condition of things, lest the movement might be misconstrued, and we might be precipitated into hostilities.

For half an hour we glided down in this manner, keeping up a constant fire of smiling compliments and pathetic Sennennehs. Indeed, we were discovering that there was much virtue in a protracted and sentimental pronunciation of Sen-nen-neh! The men of the Expedition, who had previously ridiculed with mocking Ba-a-a-as, the absurd moan and plaintive accents of Sen-nen-neh, which Ketembo had employed, now admired him for his tact. The good natives with whom we were now exchanging these suave, bleating courtesies proved to us that the true shibboleth of peace was to prolong each word with a quavering moan and melancholic plaint.

We came to a banana grove, of a delicious and luxuriant greenness which the shadowy black green on the antique forest behind it, only made more agreeable and pleasant. Beyond this grove, the bank was lined by hundreds of men and women, standing or sitting down, their eyes directed towards our approaching flotilla.

"Sen-nen-neh!" was delivered with happy effect by one of our boat-boys. A chorus of Sen-nen-nehs, long-drawn, loud, and harmonious, quickly following the notes of the last syllable, burst from the large assembly, until both banks of the great river re-echoed it with all its indescribable and ludicrous pathos.

The accents were peaceful, the bearing of the people and the presence of the women were unmistakably pacific, so the word was given to drop anchor.

The natives in the canoes, who had hitherto preceded us, were invited to draw near, but they shrugged their shoulders, and declined the responsibility of beginning any intercourse with the strangers. We appealed to the concourse on the banks, for we were not a hundred feet from them. They burst out into a loud laughter, yet with nothing of scorn or contempt in it, for we had been so long accustomed to the subtle differences of passion that we were by this time adept in discovering the nicest shades of feeling which wild humanity is capable of expressing. We held out our hands to them with palms upturned, heads sentimentally leaning on one side, and, with a captivating earnestness of manner, begged them to regard us as friends, strangers far from their homes, who had lost their way, but were endeavouring to find it by going down the river.

The effect is manifest. A kind of convulsion of tenderness appears to animate the entire host. Expressions of pity break from them, and there is a quick interchange of sympathetic opinions.

"Ah," thought I, "how delighted Livingstone would have been had he been here to regard this scene! Assuredly he would have been enraptured, and become more firmly impressed than ever with the innocence and guilelessness of true aborigines," and I am forced to admit it is exceedingly pleasant, but—I wait.

We hold up long necklaces of beads of various colours to view; blue, red, white, yellow, and black.

"Ah-h-h," sigh a great many, admiringly, and heads bend toward heads in praise and delight of them.

"Come, my friends, let us talk. Bring one canoe here. These to those who dare approach us." There is a short moment of hesitation and then some forms disappear, and presently come out again bearing gourds, chickens, bananas, and vegetables, etc., which they place carefully in a small canoe. Two women step in and boldly paddle towards us, while a deathly silence prevails among my people as well as among the aborigines on the bank.

I observed one or two coquettish airs on the part of the two women, but though my arm was getting tired with holding out so long in one position those necklaces of glorious beads, I dared not withdraw them, lest the fascination might be broken. I felt myself a martyr in the cause of public peace, and the sentiment made me bear up stoically.

"Boy," I muttered in an undertone, to Mabruki, my gun-bearer, "when the canoe is alongside, seize it firmly and do not let it escape."

"Inshallah, my master."

Nearer the canoe came, and with its approach my blandness increased, and further I projected my arm with those beads of tempting colours.

At last the canoe was paddled alongside. Mabruki quietly grasped it. I then divided the beads into sets, talking the while to Katembo—who translated for me—of the happiness I felt at the sight of two such beautiful women coming out to see the white chief, who was so good, and who loved to talk to beautiful women. "There! These are for you—and these are for you," I said to the steerswoman and her mate.

They clapped their hands in glee, and each woman held out her presents in view of the shore people; and hearty hand-claps form all testified to their grateful feelings.

The women then presented me with the gourds of malofu—palm-wine—the chickens, bananas, potatoes, and cassava they had brought, which were received by the boat's crew and the interested members of the Expedition with such a hearty clapping of hands that it sent the shore people into convulsions of laughter. Mabruki was told now to withdraw his hand, as the women were clinging to the boats themselves, and peace was assured. Presently the great native canoes drew near and alongside the boat, forming dense walls of strange humanity on either side.

"Tell us, friends," we asked, "why it is you are so friendly, when those up the river are so wicked."

Then a chief said, "Because yesterday some of our fishermen were up the river on some islets near Kibombo Island, opposite the Amu-Nyam villages; and when we heard the war-drums of the Amu-Nyam we looked up, and saw your canoes coming down. You stopped at Kibombo Island, and we heard you speak to them, saying you were friends. But the Amu-Nyam are bad; they eat people, we don't. They fight with us frequently, and whomsoever they catch they eat. They fought with you, and while you were fighting our fishermen came down and told us that the Wajiwa (we) 'were coming;' but they said that they had heard the Wajiwa say that they came as friends and that they did not want to fight. Today we sent a canoe, with a woman and boy up the river, with plenty of provisions in it. If you had been bad people, you would have taken that canoe. We were behind the bushes of that island watching you; but you said 'Sen-nen-neh' to them, and passed into the channel between the island and our villages. Had you seized that canoe, our drums would have sounded for war and you would have had to fight us, as you fought the Amu-Nyam. We have left our spears on one of those islands. See, we have nothing."

It was true, as I had already seen, to my wonder and admiration. Here, then, I had opportunities for noting what thin barriers separated ferocity from amiability. Only a couple of leagues above lived the cannibals of Amu-Nyam, who had advanced towards us with evil and nauseous intentions; but next to them was a tribe which detested the unnatural custom of eating their own species, with whom we had readily formed a pact of peace and good will!

They said their country was called Kankoré, the chief of which was Sangarika, and that the village opposite to us was Maringa; and that three miles below was Simba-Simba; that their country was small, and only reached to the end of the islands; that after we had passed the islands we should come to the territory of the Mwana Ntaba, with whom we should have to fight; that the Mwana Ntaba people occupied the country as far as the falls; that below the falls were several islands inhabited by the Baswa, who were friends of the Mwana Ntaba. It would be impossible, they said, to go over the falls, as the river swept against a hill, and rolled over it, and tumbled down, down, down, with whirl and uproar, and we should inevitably get lost. It would be far better, they said, for us to return.

The strange disposition to rechristen the great river with the name of its last great affluent, was here again exemplified, for the Kankoré tribe called the river at the falls the Rumami, or Lumami, and it became known no more as the Lowwa.

Other information we received was that the Watwa and Waringa tribes lived on the other side of the Lumami. The dwarfs, called Wakwanga, were said to be in a south-west direction. The Wavinza occupied the tract between the Lumami and the Lowwa opposite to us. The Bukutzi, or Wakuti, live west across the Lumami, which agrees with Abed the guide's story. On the right bank are situated Kankura, Mpassi, and Mburri; the chief of the last-mentioned country being Mungamba. There is also a tribe called the Ba-ama, whose chief, Subiri, trades in dogs and shells. Dogs are considered by the Ba-ama as greater delicacies than sheep and goats. But we were specially instructed to beware of the Bakumu, a powerful tribe of light-complexioned cannibals, who came originally from the north-east, and who, armed with bows and arrows, had conquered a considerable section of Uregga, and had even crossed the great river. They would undoubtedly, we were told, seek us out and massacre us all.

The Kankoré men were similar in dress and tattooing to the Waregga, though whose forests we had passed. The women wore bits of carved wood and necklaces of the Achatina fossil shell around their necks, while iron rings, brightly polished, were worn as armlets and leg ornaments.

Having obtained so much information from the amiable Kankoré, we lifted our stone anchors and moved gently down stream. Before each village we passed groups of men and women seated on the banks, who gave a genial response to our peaceful greeting.

We were soon below the islands on our left, and from a course north by west the river gradually swerved to north by east, and the high banks on our right, which rose from 80 to 150 feet, towered above us, with grassy breaks here and there agreeably relieving the somber foliage of groves.

About 2 P.M., as we were proceeding quietly and listening with all our ears for the terrible falls of which we had been warned, our vessels being only about thirty yards from the right bank, eight men with shields darted into view from behind a bush-clump, and, shouting their war-cries, launched their wooden spears. Some of them struck and dinted the boat deeply, others flew over it. We shoved off instantly, and getting into mid-stream found that we had heedlessly exposed ourselves to the watchful tribe of Mwana Ntaba, who immediately sounded their great drums, and prepared their numerous canoes for battle.

Up to this time we had met with no canoes over 50 feet long, except that antique century-old vessel which we had repaired as a hospital for our small-pox patients; but those which now issued from the banks and the shelter of bends in the banks were monstrous. The natives were in full war-paint, one-half of their bodies being daubed white, the other half red, with broad black bars, the *tout ensemble* being unique and diabolical. There was a crocodilian aspect about these lengthy vessels which was far from assuring, while the fighting men, standing up alternately with the paddlers, appeared to be animated with a most ferocious cat-o'-mountain spirit. Horn-blasts which reverberated from bank to bank, lent a fierce éclat to the fight in which we were now about to be engaged.

We formed line, and having arranged all our shields as bulwarks for the non-combatants, awaited the first onset with apparent calmness. One of the largest canoes, which we afterwards found to be 85 feet 3 inches in length, rashly made the mistake of singling out the boat for its victim; but we reserved our fire until it was within 50 feet of us, and after pouring a volley into the crew, charged the canoe with the boat, and the crew, unable to turn her round sufficiently soon to escape, precipitated themselves into the river and swam to their friends, while we made ourselves masters of the *Great Eastern* of the Livingstone. We soon exchanged two of our smaller canoes and manned the monster with thirty men, and resumed our journey in line, the boat in front acting as a guide. This early disaster to the Mwana Ntaba caused them to hurry down river, blowing their horns, and alarming with their drums both shores of the river, until about forty canoes were seen furiously dashing down stream, no doubt bent on mischief.

At 4 P.M. we came opposite a river about 200 yards wide, which I have called the Leopold River, in honor of His Majesty Leopold II, King of the Belgians, and which the natives called either the Kankora, Mikonju, or Munduku. Perhaps, the natives were misleading me, or perhaps they really possessed a superfluity of names, but I think that whatever name they give it should be mentioned in connection with each stream.

Soon after passing by the confluence, the Livingstone, which above had been 2,500 yards wide, perceptibly contracted, and turned sharply to the east-north-east, because of a hill which rose on the left bank about 300 feet above the river. Close to the elbow of the bend on the right bank we passed by some white granite rocks, from one to six feet above the water, and just below these we heard the roar of the First Cataract of the Stanley Falls series.

But louder than the noise of the falls rose the piercing yells of the savage Mwana Ntaba from both sides of the great river. We now found ourselves confronted by the inevitable necessity of putting into practice the resolution which we had formed before setting out on this wild voyage—to conquer or die. What should we do? Shall we turn and face the fierce cannibals, who with hideous noise drown the solemn roar of the cataract, or shall we cry out "Mambu Kwa Mungu—"Our fate is in the hands of God"—and risk the cataract with its terrors!

Meanwhile, we are sliding smoothly to our destruction, and a decision must therefore be arrived at instantly. God knows, I and my fellows would rather have it not to do, because possibly it is only a choice of deaths, by cruel knives or drowning. If we do not choose the knives, which are already sharpened for our throats, death by drowning is certain. So finding ourselves face to face with the inevitable, we turn to the right bank upon the savages, who are in the woods and on the water. We drop our anchors and begin the fight, but after fifteen minutes of it find that we cannot force them away. We then pull up anchors and ascend stream again, until, arriving at the elbow above mentioned, we strike across the river and divide our forces. Manwa Sera is to take four canoes and to continue up stream a little distance, and, while we occupy the attention of the savages in front, is to lead his men through the woods and set upon them in rear. At 5:30 P.M. we make the attempt, and keep them in play for a few minutes, and on hearing a shot in the woods dash at the shore, and under a shower of spears and arrows effect a landing. From tree to tree the fight is continued until sunset, when, having finally driven the enemy off, we have earned peace for the night.

Until about 10 P.M. we are busy constructing an impenetrable stockade or boma of brushwood, and then at length, we lay our sorely fatigued bodies down to rest, without comforts of any kind and without fires, but (I speak for myself only) with a feeling of gratitude to Him who had watched over us in our trouble, and a humble prayer that His protection may be extended to us, for the terrible days that may yet be to come.

Land at Last

BY FRIDTJOF NANSEN

Norwegian-born polar explorer Dr. Fridtjof Nansen was one of the most celebrated adventurers of his day. His quest for the North Pole fell well short of its goal in 1895, but he reached a point roughly 160 miles farther north than any previous expedition, just 240 miles short of the pole. Nansen's pioneering methods led the way for later explorers to reach both poles, proving that dogs were the most efficient mode of travel and that survival in the desolate ice for long periods was difficult, but possible.

Earlier Arctic experience led him to believe that the drift of the polar ice would carry his ship, the *Fram*, close enough to have a shot at reaching the pole on foot over the ice. It worked to a degree, and when the ship began to drift in the wrong direction, Nansen set out with one companion, dog sleds, and kayaks, knowing that he would have to find his way back to land on his own. Tough terrain eventually forced the two men to make a course for Franz Josef Land, where they spent the winter living in a tiny shelter before making contact with another party the next summer.

The following excerpt from his book *Farthest North* picks up the story as Nansen and Hjalmar Johansen fight their way back to land. It is a great example of the roles that luck and fortitude play in any expedition.

★　★　★　★　★

"Wednesday, July 24th. At last the marvel has come to pass—land, land! And after we had almost given up our belief in it! After nearly two years, we again see something rising above that never-ending white line on the horizon yonder—a white line which for millennium after millennium has stretched over this sea, and which for millenniums to come shall stretch in the same way. We are leaving it, and leaving no trace behind us, for the track of our little caravan across the endless plains has long ago disappeared. A new life is beginning for us; for the ice it is ever the same.

"It has long haunted our dreams, this land, and now it comes like a vision, like fairy-land. Drift-white, it arches above the horizon like distant clouds, which one is afraid will disappear every minute. The most wonderful thing is that we have seen this land all the time without knowing it. I examined it several times with the telescope from 'Longing Camp' in the belief that it might be snow-fields, but always came to the conclusion that it was only clouds, as I could never discover any dark point. Then, too, it seemed to change form, which, I supposed, must be attributed to the mist which always lays over it; but it always came back again at the same place with its remarkable regular curves. I now remember that dark crag we saw east of us at the camp, and which I took to be an iceberg. It must certainly have been a little islet of some kind.

"The ice was worse and more broken than ever yesterday; it was, indeed, a labor to force one's way over pressure-ridges like veritable mountains, with valleys and clefts in between; but on we went in good spirits, and made some progress. At lanes where a crossing was difficult to find we did not hesitate to launch kayaks and sledges, and were soon over in this manner. Sometimes after a very bad bit we would come across some flat ice for a short distance, and over this we would go like wildfire, splashing through ponds and puddles. While I was on ahead at one time yesterday morning, Johansen went up on to a hummock to look at the ice, and remarked a curious black stripe over the horizon; but he supposed it to be only a cloud, he said, and I thought no more about the matter. When, some while later, I also ascended a hummock to look at the ice, I became aware of the same black stripe; it ran obliquely from the horizon up into what I supposed to be a white bank of clouds. The longer I looked at this bank and stripe the more unusual I thought them, until I was constrained to fetch the glass. No sooner had I fixed it on the black part than it struck me at once that this must be land, and that not far off. There was a large snow-field out of which black rocks projected. It was not long before Johansen had the glass to his eye, and convinced himself that we really had land before us. We both of us naturally became in the highest spirits. I then saw a similar white arching outline a little farther east; but it was for the most part covered with white mist, from which it could hardly be distinguished, and moreover, was continually changing form. It soon, however, came out entirely, and was considerably larger and higher than the former, but there was not a black speck to be seen on it. So this was what land looked like, now that we had come to it! I had imagined it in many forms, with high peaks and glittering glaciers, but never like this. There was nothing kindly about this, but it was indeed no less welcome; and on the whole we could not expect it to be otherwise than snow-covered, with all the snow which falls here.

"So then we pitched the tent and had a feast suited to the occasion: lobscouse made of potatoes (for the last time but one; we had saved them long for this occasion), pemmican, dried bear's and seal's flesh, and bear tongues, chopped up together. After this was a second course, consisting of bread-crumbs fried in bear's grease, also vril-food and butter, and a piece of chocolate to wind up."

We thought this land so near that it could not possibly take long to reach it, certainly not longer than till the next evening. Johansen was even certain that we should do it the same day, but nevertheless thirteen days were to elapse, occupied in the same monotonous drudgery over the drift-ice.

On July 25 I write: "When we stopped in the fog yesterday evening we had a feeling that we must have come well under land. This morning, when we turned out, the first thing Johansen did when he went to fetch some water for me to cook with was, of course, to climb up on the nearest hummock and look at the land. There it lay, considerably nearer than before, and he is quite certain that we shall reach it before night." I also discovered a new land to our west (S. 60° W. magnetic) that day; a regular, shield-like, arched outline, similar to the other land; and it was low above the horizon, and appeared to be a long way off.

We went on our way as fast as we could across lanes and rough ice, but did not get far in the day, and the land did not seem to be much nearer. In reality there was no difference to be seen, although we tried to imagine that it was steadily growing higher. On Saturday, July 27th, I seem to have a suspicion that in point of fact we were drifting away from land. I write: "The wind began to blow from the S.S.W. (magnetic) just as we were getting off yesterday, and increased as the day went on. It was easy to perceive by the atmosphere that the wind was driving the ice off the land, and land-lanes formed particularly on the east side of it. When I was up on a hummock yesterday evening I observed a black stripe on the horizon under land; I examined it with the glass, and, as I had surmised, there was an ice-edge or glacier stretching far in a westerly direction; and there was plainly a broad lane in front of it, to judge by the dark band of mist which lay there. It seems to me that land cannot be far off, and if the ice is tolerably passable we may reach it today.

"Tuesday, July 30th. We make incredibly slow progress; but we are pushing our way nearer land all the same. [In reality we were probably farther from it than before.] Every kind of hindrance seems to beset us: now I am uffering so much from my back (lumbago?) that yesterday it was only by exerting all my strength of will that I could drag myself along. In difficult places Johansen had to help me with my sledge. It began yesterday, and at the end of our march he had to go first and find the way. Yesterday I was much worse, and how I am today I do not know before I begin to walk; but I ought to be thankful that I can drag myself along at all, though it is with endless pain. We had to halt and camp on account of rain yesterday morning at three, after only having gone nine hours. The rain succeeded in making us wet before we had found a suitable place for the tent. Here we have been a whole day while it has been pouring down, and we have hardly become drier. There are puddles under us and the bag is soaked on the under-side. The wind has gone round to the west just now, and it has stopped raining, so we made some porridge for breakfast and think of going on again; but if it should begin to rain again we must stop, as it will not do to get wet through when we have no change of clothes. It is anything but pleasant as it is to lie with wet legs and feet that are like icicles, and not have a dry thread to put on. Full-grown Ross's gulls were seen singly four times today, and when Johansen was out to fetch water this morning he saw two.

"Thursday, August 1st. Ice with more obstacles than here—is it to be found, I wonder? But we are working slowly on, and that being the case, we ought, perhaps, to be satisfied. We have also had a change—a brilliantly fine day, but it seems to me the south wind we have had, and which opened the lanes, has put us a good way farther off land again. We have also drifted a long distance to the east, and no longer see the most westerly land with the black rocks, which we remarked at first. It would seem as if the Ross's gulls keep to land here; we see them daily.

"One thing, however, I am rejoicing over; my back is almost well, so that I shall not delay our progress any more. I have some idea now what it would be like if one of us became seriously ill. Our fate would then be sealed, I think.

"Saturday, August 3rd. Inconceivable toil. We never could go on with it were it not for the fact that we *must*. We have made wretchedly little progress, even if we have made any at all. We have had no food for the dogs the last few days except the ivory gulls and fulmars we have been able to shoot, and that has been a couple a day. Yesterday the dogs only had a little bit of blubber each.

"Monday, August 5th. We have never had worse ice than yesterday, but we managed to force our way on a little, nevertheless, and two happy incidents marked the day; the first was that Johansen was not eaten up by a bear, and the second, that we saw open water under the glacier edge ashore.

"We set off about 7 o'clock yesterday morning and got on to ice as bad as it could be. It was as if some giant had hurled down enormous blocks pell-mell, and had strewn wet snow in between them with water underneath; and into this we sank above our knees. There were also numbers of deep pools in between the blocks. It was like toiling over hill and dale, up and down over block after block and ridge after ridge, with deep clefts in between; not a clear space big enough to pitch a tent on even, and thus it went the whole time. To put a coping-stone to our misery, there was such a mist that we could not see a hundred yards in front of us. After an exhausting march we at last reached a lane where we had to ferry over in the kayaks. After having cleared the side of the lane from young ice and brash, I drew my sledge to the end of the ice, and was holding it to prevent it slipping in, when I heard a scuffle behind me, and Johansen, who had just turned round to pull his sledge flush with mine, cried, 'Take the gun!' I turned round and saw an enormous bear throwing itself on him, and Johansen on his back. I tried to seize my gun, which was in its case on the fore-deck, but at the same moment the kayak slipped into the water. My first thought was to throw myself into the water over the kayak and fire from there, but I recognized how risky it would be. I began to pull the kayak, with its heavy cargo, on to the high edge of the ice again as quickly as I could, and was on my knees pulling and tugging to get at my gun. I had no time to look round and see what was going on behind me, when I heard Johansen quietly say, 'You must look sharp if you want to be in time!'

"Look sharp! I should think so! At last I got hold of the butt-end, dragged the gun out, turned round in a sitting posture, and cocked the shot-barrel. The bear was standing not two yards off, ready to make an end to my dog, 'Kaifas.' There was no time to lose in cocking the other barrel, so I gave it a charge of shot behind the ear, and it fell down dead between us.

"The bear must have followed our track like a cat, and, covered by the ice-blocks, have slunk up while we were clearing the ice from the lane and had our backs to him. We could see by the trail how it had crept over a small ridge just behind us under cover of a mound by Johansen's kayak. While the latter, without suspecting anything or looking round, went back and stooped down to pick up the hauling-rope, he suddenly caught sight of an animal crouched up at the end of the kayak, but thought it was 'Suggen,' and before he had time to realize that it was so big he received a cuff on the ear which made him see fireworks, and then, as I mentioned before, over he went on his back. He tried to defend himself as best he could with his fists. With one hand he seized the throat of the animal, and held fast, clinching it with all his might. It was just as the bear was about to bite Johansen in the head that he uttered the memorable words, 'Look sharp!' The bear kept glancing at me continually, speculating, no doubt, as to what I was going to do; but then caught sight of the dog and turned towards it. Johansen let go as quick as thought, and wriggled himself away, while the bear gave 'Suggen' a cuff which made him howl lustily, just as he does when we thrash him. Then 'Kaifas' got a slap on the nose. Meanwhile Johansen had struggled to his legs, and when I fired had got his gun, which was sticking out of the kayak hole. The only harm done was that the bear had scraped some grime off Johansen's right cheek, so that he has a white stripe on it, and had given him a slight wound in one hand; 'Kaifas' had also got a scratch on his nose.

"Wednesday, August 7th. At last we are under land; at last the drift-ice lies behind us, and before us is open water—open, it is to be hoped, to the end. Yesterday was the day. When we came out of the tent the evening of the day before yesterday we both thought we must be nearer the edge of the glacier than ever, and with fresh courage, and in the faint hope of reaching land that day, we started on our journey. Yet we dared not think our life on the drift-ice was so nearly at an end. After wandering about on it for five months and suffering many disappointments, we were only too well prepared for a new defeat. We thought, however, that the ice looked more promising farther on, though before we had gone far we came to broad lanes full of slush and foul, uneven ice, with hills and dales, and deep snow and water, into which we sank up to our thighs. After a couple of lanes of this kind, matters improved a little, and we got on to some flat ice. After having gone over this for a while, it became apparent how much nearer we were to the edge of the glacier. It could not possibly be far off now. We eagerly harnessed ourselves to the sledges again, put on a spurt, and away we went through snow and water, over mounds and ridges. We went as hard as we could, and what did we care if we sank into water till far above our fur leggings, so that both they and our 'komager' filled and gurgled like a pump? What did it matter to us now, so long as we got on?

"We soon reached plains, and over them we went quicker and quicker. We waded through ponds where the spray flew up on all sides. Nearer and nearer we came, and by the dark water-sky before us, which continually rose higher, we could see how we were drawing near to open water. We did not even notice bears now. There seemed to be plenty about, tracks, both old and new, crossing and recrossing; one had even inspected the tent while we were asleep, and by the fresh trails we could see how it had come down wind in lee of us. We had no use for a bear now; we had food enough. We were soon able to see the open water under the wall of the glacier, and our steps lengthened even more.

"At last, at last, I stood by the edge of the ice. Before me lay the dark surface of the sea, with floating white floes; far away the glacier wall rose abruptly from the water; over the whole lay a sombre, foggy light. Joy welled up in our hearts at this sight, and we could not give it expression in words. Behind us lay all our troubles, before us the waterway home. I waved my hat to Johansen, who was a little way behind, and he waved his in answer and shouted, 'Hurrah!' Such an event had to be celebrated in some way, and we did it by having a piece of chocolate each.

"While we were standing there looking at the water the large head of a seal came up, and then disappeared silently; but soon more appeared. It is very reassuring to know that we can procure food at any minute we like.

"Now came the rigging of the kayaks for the voyage. Of course, the better way would have been to paddle singly, but, with the long, big sledges on the deck, this was not easy, and leave them behind I dared not; we might have good use for them yet. For the time being, therefore, there was nothing else to be done but to lash the two kayaks together side by side in our usual manner, stiffen them out with snowshoes under the straps, and place the sledges athwart them, one before and one behind.

"It was sad to think we could not take our two last dogs with us, but we should probably have no further use for them, and it would not have done to take them with us on the decks of our kayaks. We were sorry to part with them; we had become very fond of these two survivors. Faithful and enduring, they had followed us the whole journey through; and, now that better times had come, they must say farewell to life. Destroy them in the same way as the others we could not; we sacrificed a cartridge on each of them. I shot Johansen's and he shot mine.

"So then we were ready to set off. It was a real pleasure to let the kayaks dance over the water and hear the little waves splashing against the sides. For two years we had not seen such a surface of water before us. We had not gone far before we found that the wind was so good that we ought to make use of it, and so we rigged up a sail on our fleet. We glided easily before the wind in towards the land we had so longed for all these many months. What a change, after having forced one's way inch by inch and foot by foot on ice! The mist had hidden the land from us for a while, but now it parted, and we saw the glacier rising straight in front of us. At the same moment the sun burst forth, and a more beautiful morning I can hardly remember. We were soon underneath the glacier, and had to lower our sail and paddle westward along the wall of ice, which was from 50 to 60 feet in height, and on which a landing was impossible. It seemed as if there must be little movement in this glacier; the water had eaten its way deep underneath it at the foot, and there was no noise of falling fragments or the cracking of crevasses to be heard, as there generally is with large glaciers. It was also quite even on the top, and no crevasses were to be seen. Up the entire height of the wall there was stratification, which was unusually marked. We soon discovered that a tidal current was running westward along the wall of the glacier with great rapidity, and took advantage of it to make good progress. To find a camping-ground, however, was not easy, and at last we were reduced to taking up our abode on a drifting floe. It was glorious, though, to go to rest in the certainty that we should not wake to drudgery in the drift-ice.

"When we turned out today we found that the ice had packed around us, and I do not know yet how we shall get out of it, though there is open water not far off to our west.

"Thursday, August 8th. After hauling our *impedimenta* over some floes we got into open water yesterday without much difficulty. When we had reached the edge of the water we made a paddle each from our snow-shoe-staffs, to which we bound blades made of broken-off snow-shoes. They were a great improvement on the somewhat clumsy paddles, with canvas blades lashed to bamboo sticks. I was very much inclined to chop off our sledges, so that they would only be half as long as before; by so doing we could carry them on the after-deck of the kayaks, and could thus each paddle alone, and our advance would be much quicker than by paddling the twin kayaks. However, I thought, perhaps, it was unadvisable. The water looked promising enough on ahead, but there was mist, and we could not see far; we knew nothing of the country or the coast we had come to, and might yet have good use for the sledges. We therefore set off in our double kayak, as before, with the sledges athwart the deck fore and aft.

"The mist soon rose a little. It was then a dead calm; the surface of the water lay like a great mirror before us, with bits of ice and an occasional floe drifting on it. It was a marvellously beautiful sight, and it was indeed glorious to sit there in our light vessels and glide over the surface without any exertion. Suddenly a seal rose in front of us, and over us flew continually ivory gulls and fulmars and kittiwakes.

"Our course at first lay west to north (magnetic); but the land always trended more and more to the west and southwest; the expanse of water grew greater, and soon it widened out to a large sea, stretching in a southwesterly direction. A breeze sprang up from the north-northeast, and there was considerable motion, which was not pleasant, as in our double craft the seas continually washed up between the two and wetted us. We put in towards evening and pitched the tent on the shore-ice, and just as we did so it began to rain, so that it was high time to be under a roof.

"Friday, August 9th. Yesterday morning we had again to drag the sledges with the kayaks over some ice which had drifted in front of our camping-ground, and during this operation I managed to fall into the water and get wet. It was with difficulty we finally got through and out into open water. After a while we again found our way closed, and were obliged to take to hauling over some floes, but after this we had good open water the whole day. It was a northeasterly wind which had set the ice towards the land, and it was lucky we had got so far, as behind us, to judge by the atmosphere, the sea was much blocked. The mist hung over the land so that we saw little of it. According as we advanced we were able to hold a more southerly course, and, the wind being nearly on the quarter, we set sail about 1 o'clock, and continued sailing all day till we stopped yesterday evening. Our sail, however, was interrupted once when it was necessary to paddle round an ice-point north of where we are now; the contrary current was so strong that it was as much as we could do to make way against it, and it was only after considerable exertion that we succeeded in doubling the point. We had seen little of the land we are skirting up to this, on account of the mist; but as far as I can make out it consists of island. First there was a large island covered with an ice-sheet; then west of it smaller one, on which are the two crags of rock which first made us aware of the vicinity of land; next came a long fjord or sound, with massive shore-ice in it; and then a small, low headland, or rather an island, south of which we are now encamped.

"This land grows more of a problem, and I am more than ever at a loss to know where we are. It is very remarkable to me that the coast continually trends to the south instead of to the west. I could explain it all best by supposing ourselves to be on the west coast of the archipelago of Franz Josef Land, were it not that the variation, I think, is too great, and also for the number of Ross's gulls there still are. Not one has with certainty been seen in Spitzbergen, and if my supposition is right, this should not be far off. Yesterday we saw a number of them again; they are quite as common here as the other species of gull.

"Saturday, August 10th. We went up on to the little islet we had camped by. It was covered with a glacier, which curved over it in the shape of a shield; there were slopes to all sides; but so slight was the gradient that our snow-shoes would not even run of themselves on the crust of snow. From that ridge we had a fair view, and, as the mist lifted just then, we saw the land about us tolerably well. We now perceived plainly that what we had been skirting along was only islands. The first one was the biggest. The other land, with the two rocky crags, had, as we could see, a strip of bare land along the shore on the northwest side. Was it there, perhaps, the Ross's gulls congregated and had their breeding grounds? The island to our south also looked large; it appeared to be entirely covered by a glacier. [The first island I called "Eva's Island," the second "Liv's Island," and the little one we were then on "Adelaide's Island." The fourth island south of us had, perhaps, already been seen by Payer, and named by him "Freeden Island." The whole group of islands I named "Hvidtenland" (White Land).] Between the islands, and as far as we could perceive southeast and east, the sea was covered by perfectly flat fjord-ice, but no land was to be discerned in that direction. There were no icebergs here, though we saw some later in the day on the south side of the island lying to the south of us.

"About three in the afternoon we finally set off in open water and sailed till eight or so in the evening; the water was then closed, and we were compelled to haul the fleet over flat ice to open water on the other side. But here, too, our progress seemed blocked, and as the current was against us we pitched the tent."

On August 10th we were "compelled partly to haul our sledges over the ice, partly to row in open water in a southwesterly direction. When we reached navigable waters again, we passed a flock of walruses lying on a floe. It was a pleasure to see so much food collected at one spot, but we did not take any notice of them, as, for the time being, we have meat and blubber enough. After dinner we managed, in the mist, to wander down a long bay into the shore-ice, where there was no outlet; we had to turn back, and this delayed us considerably. We now kept a more westerly course, following the often massive and uneven edge of the ice; but the current was dead against us, and, in addition, young ice had been forming all day as we rowed along; the weather had been cold and still, with falling snow, and this began to be so thick that we could not make way against it any longer. We therefore went ashore on the ice, and hauled until ten in the evening.

"Bear-tracks, old and new, in all directions—both the single ones of old bachelors and those of she-bears with cubs. It looks as if they had had a general rendezvous or as if a flock of them had roamed backward and forward. I have never seen so many bear-tracks in one place in my life.

"We have certainly done 14 or 25 miles today; but still I think our progress is too slow if we are to reach Spitzbergen this year, and I am always wondering if we ought not to cut the ends off our sledges, so that each can paddle his own kayak. This young ice, however, which grows steadily worse, and the eleven degrees below freezing we now have, make me hold my hand. Perhaps winter is upon us, and then the sledges may be very necessary.

"It is a curious sensation to paddle in the mist, as we are doing, without being able to see a mile in front of us. The land we found we have left behind us. We are always in hopes of clear weather, in order to see where the land lies in front of us—for land there must be. This flat, unbroken ice must be attached to land of some kind; but clear weather we are not to have, it appears. Mist without ceasing; we must push on as it is."

After having hauled some distance farther over the ice we came to open water again the following day (August 11th) and paddled for four or five hours. While I was on a hummock inspecting the waters ahead, a huge monster of a walrus came up quite near us. It lay puffing and glaring at us on the surface of the water, but we took no notice of it, got into our kayaks, and went on. Suddenly it came up again by the side of us, raised itself high out of the water, snorted so that the air shook, and threatened to thrust its tusks into our frail craft. We seized our guns, but at the same moment it disappeared, and came up immediately afterwards on the other side, by Johansen's kayak, where it repeated the same manoeuvre. I said to him that if the animal showed signs of attacking us we must spend a cartridge on it. It came us several times and disappeared again; we could see it down in the water, passing rapidly on its side under our vessels, and afraid lest it should make a hole in the bottom with its tusks, we thrust our paddles down into the water and frightened it away; but suddenly it came up again right by Johansen's kayak, and more savage than ever. He sent it a charge straight in the eyes, it uttered a terrific bellow, rolled over, and disappeared, leaving a trail of blood on the water behind it. We paddled on as hard as we could, knowing that the shot might have dangerous consequences, but we were relieved when we heard the walrus come up far behind us at the place where it had disappeared.

We had paddled quietly on, and had long forgotten all about the walrus, when I suddenly saw Johansen jump into the air and felt his kayak receive a violent shock. I had no idea what it was, and looked round to see if some block of floating ice had capsized and struck the bottom of his kayak; but suddenly I saw another walrus rise up in the water beside us. I seized my gun, and as the animal would not turn its head so that I could aim at a spot behind the ear, where it is more easily wounded, I was constrained to put a ball in the middle of its forehead; there was no time to be lost. Happily this was enough, and it lay there dead and floating on the water. With great difficulty we managed to make a hole in the thick skin, and after cutting ourselves some strips of blubber and meat from the back we went on our way again.

At seven in the evening the tidal current turned and the channel closed. There was no more water to be found. Instead of taking to hauling over the ice, we determined to wait for the opening of the channel when the tide should turn next day, and meanwhile to cut off the ends of our sledges, as I had so long been thinking of doing, and make ourselves some good double paddles, so that we could put on greater pace, and, in our single kayaks, make the most of the channel during the time it was open. While we were occupied in doing this the mist cleared off at last, and there lay land stretched out in front of us, extending a long way south and west from S.E. right up to N.N.W. It appeared to be a chain of islands with sounds between them. They were chiefly covered with glaciers, only here and there were perpendicular black mountain-walls to be seen. It was a sight to make one rejoice to see so much land at one time. But where were we? This seemed a more difficult question to answer than ever. Could we, after all, have arrived at the east side of Franz Josef Land? It seemed very reasonable to suppose this to be the case. But then we must be very far east, and must expect a long voyage before we could reach Cape Fligely, on Crown Prince Rudolf Land.

"Wednesday, August 14th. We dragged our sledges and loads over a number of floes and ferried across lanes, arriving finally at a lane which ran westward, in which we could paddle; but it soon packed together again, and we were stopped. The ivory-gulls were very bold, and last night stole a piece of blubber lying close by the tent wall."

The following day we had to make our way as well as we could by paddling short distances in the lanes or hauling our loads over floes smaller or larger, as the case might be. The current, which was running like a mill-race, ground them together in its career. Our progress with our short, stumpy sledges was nothing very great, and of water suitable for paddling we found less and less. We stopped several times and waited for the ice to open at the turn of the tide, but it did not do so, and on the morning of August 15ᵗʰ we gave it up, turned inward, and took to the shore-ice for good. We set our course westward towards the sound we had seen for several days now, and had struggled so to reach. The surface of the ice was tolerably even and we got over the ground well. On the way we passed a frozen-in iceberg, which was the highest we saw in these parts—some 50 to 60 feet, I should say. [Icebergs of considerable size have been described as having been seen off Franz Josef Land, but I can only say with reference to this that during the whole of our voyage through this archipelago we saw nothing of the kind. The one mentioned here was the biggest of all those we came across, and they were, compared with the Greenland icebergs, quite insignificant masses of glacier-ice.] I wished to go up it to get a better view of our environment, but it was too steep, and we did not get higher than a third part up the side.

"In the evening we at last reached the islands we had been steering for for the last few days, and for the first time for two years had bare land under foot. The delight of the feeling of being able to jump from block to block of granite [I have called it granite in my diary, but it was in reality a very coarse-grained basalt. The specimens I took have unfortunately been lost] is indescribable, and the delight was not lessened when in a little sheltered corner among the stones we found moss and flowers, beautiful poppies (*Papaver nuudicaule*) *Saxifraga nivalis*, and a *Stellaria* (sp?). It goes without saying that the Norwegian flag had to wave over this, our first bare land, and a banquet was prepared. Our petroleum, meanwhile, had given out several days previously, and we had to contrive another lamp in which train-oil could be used. The smoking hot lobscouse, made of pemmican and the last of our potatoes, was delicious, and we sat inside the tent the kicked the bare grit under us to our heart's content.

"Where we are is becoming more and more incomprehensible. There appears to be a broad sound west of us, but what is it? The island ["Houen's Island"] we are now on, and where we have slept splendidly (this is written on the morning of August 16ᵗʰ) on dry land, with no melting of the ice in puddles underneath us, is a long moraine-like ridge running about north and south (magnetic), and consists almost exclusively of small and large—generally very large—blocks of stone, with, I should say, occasional stationary crags. The blocks are in a measure rounded off, but I have found no striation in them. The whole island barely rises above the snow-field in which it lies, and which slopes in a gradual decline down to the surrounding ice. On our west there is a bare island, somewhat higher, which we have seen for several days. Along the shore there is a decided strand-line (terrace). North of us are two small islets and a small rock or skerry.

"As I mentioned before I had at first supposed the sound on our west to be Rawlinson's Sound, but this now appeared impossible, as there was nothing to be seen of Dove Glacier, by which it is bounded on one side. If this was now our position, we must have traversed the glacier and Wilczek Land without noticing any trace of either; for we had travelled westward a good half degree south of Cape Buda-Pesth. The possibility that we could be in this region we consequently now held to be finally excluded. We must have come to a new land in the western part of Franz Josef Land or Archipelago, and so far west that we had seen nothing of the countries discovered by Payer. But so far west that we had not even seen anything of Oscar's Land, which ought to be situated in 82° N. and 52° E? This was indeed incomprehensible; but was there any other explanation?

"Saturday, August 17th. Yesterday was a good day. We are in open water on the west coast of Franz Josef Land, as far as I can make out, and may again hope to get home this year. About noon yesterday we walked across the ice from our moraine-islet to the higher island west of us.

"This island ['Torup's Island'] we came to seemed to me to be one of the most lovely spots on the face of the earth. A beautiful flat beach, an old strand-line with shells strewn about, a narrow belt of clear water along the shore, where snails and sea-urchins (*Echinus*) were visible at the bottom and amphipoda were swimming about. In the cliffs overhead were hundreds of screaming little auks, and beside us the snow-buntings fluttered from stone to stone with their cheerful twitter. Suddenly the sun burst forth through the light fleecy clouds, and the day seemed to be all sunshine. Here were life and bare land; we were no longer on the eternal drift-ice! At the bottom of the sea just beyond the beach I could see whole forests of seaweed (*Laminaria* and *Fucus*). Under the cliffs here and there were drifts of beautiful rose-colored snow. [This color is owing to a beautiful minute red alga, which grows on the snow (generally *Spaerella nivalis*). There were also some yellowish-green patches in this snow, which must certainly be attributed to another species of alga.]

"On the north side of the island we found the breeding-place of numbers of black-backed gulls; they were sitting with their young in ledges of the cliffs. Of course we had to climb up and secure a photograph of this un-usual scene of family life, and as we stood there high up on the cliff's side we could see the drift-ice whence we had come. It lay beneath us like a white plain, and disappeared far away on the horizon. Beyond this it was we had journeyed, and farther away still the *Fram* and our comrades were drifting yet.

"I had thought of going to the top of this island to get a better view, and perhaps come nearer solving the problem of our whereabouts. But when we were on the west side of it the mist came back and settled on the top; we had to content ourselves with only going a little way up the slope to look at our future course westward. Some way out we saw open water; it looked like the sea itself, but before one could get to it there was a good deal of ice. We came down again and started off. Along the land there was a channel running some distance farther, and we tried it, but it was covered everywhere with a thin layer of new ice, which we did not dare to break through in our kayaks, and risk cutting a hole in them; so, finally, a little way farther south we put in to drag up the kayaks and take to the ice again. While we were doing this one huge bearded seal after another stuck its head up by the side of the ice and gazed wonderingly at us with its great eyes; then, with a violent header, and splashing the water in all directions, it would disappear, to come up again soon afterwards on the other side.

"At last, after a good deal of exertion, we stood at the margin of the ice; the blue expanse of water lay before us as far as the eye could reach, and we thought that for the future we had to do with it alone. To the north [it proved later to be Crown Prince Rudolf's Land] there was land, the steep, black, basalt cliffs of which fell perpendicularly into the sea. We saw headland after headland standing out northward, and farthest off of all we could descry a bluish glacier. The interior was everywhere covered with an ice-sheet. Below the clouds, and over the land, was a strip of ruddy night sky, which was reflected in the melancholy, rocking sea.

"So we paddled on along the side of the glacier which covered the whole country south of us. We became more and more excited as we approached the headland to the west. Would the coast trend south here, and was there no more land westward? It was this we expected to decide our fate—decide whether we should reach home that year or be compelled to winter somewhere on land. Nearer and nearer we came to it along the edge of the perpendicular wall of ice. At least we reached the headland, and our hearts bounded with joy to see so much water—only water—westward, and the coast trending southwest. We also saw a bare mountain projecting from the ice-sheet a little way farther on; it was a curious high ridge, as sharp as a knife-blade. It was as steep and sharp as anything I have seen; it was all of dark, columnar basalt, and so jagged and peaked that it looked like a comb. In the middle of the mountain there was a gap or couloir, and there we crept up to inspect the sea-way southward. The wall of rock was anything but broad there, and fell away on the south side in a perpendicular drop of several hundred feet. A cutting wind was blowing in the couloir. While we were lying there, I suddenly heard a noise behind me, and on looking around I saw two foxes fighting over a little auk which they had just caught. They clawed and tugged and bit as hard as they could on the very edge of the chasm; then they suddenly caught sight of us, not twenty feet from them. They stopped fighting, looked up wonderingly, and began to run around and peep at us, first from one side, then from the other. Over us myriads of little auks flew backward and forward, screaming shrilly from the ledges in the mountain-side. So far as we could make out, there appeared to be open sea along the land to the westward. The wind was favorable, and although we were tired we decided to take advantage of the opportunity, have something to eat, rig up mast and sail on our canoes, and get afloat. We sailed till the morning, when the wind went down, and then we landed on the shore-ice again and camped. [off Brögger's Foreland.]

"I am happy as a child in the thought that we are now at last really on the west coast of Franz Josef Land, with open water before us, and independent of ice and currents.

"Wednesday, August 24th. The vicissitudes of this life will never come to an end. When I wrote last I was full of hope and courage; and here we are stopped by stress of weather for four days and three nights, with the ice packaged as tight as it can be against the coast. We see nothing but piled-up ridges, hummocks, and broken ice in all directions. Courage is still there, but hope—the hope of soon being home—that was relinquished a long time ago, and before us lies the certainty of a long, dark winter in these surroundings.

"It was at midnight between the 17th and 18th that we set off from our last camping-ground in splendid weather. Though it was cloudy and the sun invisible, there was along the horizon in the north the most glorious ruddy glow with golden sun-tipped clouds, and the sea lay shining and dreamy in the distance; a marvellous night. . . . On the surface of the sea, smooth as a mirror, without a block of ice as far as the eye could reach, glided the kayaks, the water purling off the paddles at every silent stroke. It was like being in a gondola on the Canale Grande. But there was something almost uncanny about all this stillness, and the barometer had gone down rapidly. Meanwhile, we sped towards the headland in the south-southwest, which I thought was

about 12 miles off [Clements Markham's Foreland]. After some hours we espied ice ahead, but both of us thought that it was only a loose chain of pieces
drifting with the current, and we paddled confidently on. But as we gradually
drew nearer we saw that the ice was fairly compact, and extended a greater
and greater distance; though from the low kayaks it was not easy to see the
exact extent of the pack. We accordingly disembarked and climbed up on a
hummock to find out our best route. The sight which met us was anything
but encouraging. Off the headland we were steering for were a number of
islets and rocks, extending some distance out to sea; it was they that were
locking the ice, which lay in every direction, between them and outside them.
Near us it was slack, but farther off it looked much worse, so that further advance by sea was altogether out of the question. Our only expedient was to
take to the edge of the shore-ice, and hope for the chance that a lane might
run along it some way farther on.

"As we were paddling along through some small bits of ice my kayak
suddenly received a violent shock from underneath. I looked round in amazement, as I had not noticed any large piece of ice hereabouts. There was nothing of the kind to be seen either, but worse enemies were about. No sooner
had I glanced down than I saw a huge walrus cleaving through the water
astern, and it suddenly came up, raised itself and stood on end just before Johansen, who was following in my wake. Afraid lest the animal should have its
tusks through the deck of his craft the next minute, he backed as hard as he
could and felt for his gun, which he had down in the kayak. I was not long either in pulling my gun out of its cover. The animal crashed snorting into the
water again, however, dived under Johansen's kayak, and came up just behind
him. Johansen, thinking he had had enough of such a neighbor, scrambled incontinently on to the floe nearest him. After having waited awhile, with my
gun ready for the walrus to come up close by me, I followed his example. I
very nearly came in for the cold bath which the walrus had omitted to give
me, for the edge of the ice gave way just as I set my foot on it, and the kayak
drifted off with me standing upright in it, and trying to balance it as best I
could, in order not to capsize. If the walrus had reappeared at that moment I
should certainly have received it in its own element. Finally, I succeeded in
getting up on to the ice, and for a long time afterwards the walrus swam
round and round our floe, where we made the best of the situation by having
dinner. It was a great ox-walrus. There is something remarkably fantastic and
prehistoric about these monsters. I could not help thinking of a merman, or
something of the kind, as it lay there just under the surface of the water,

blowing and snorting for quite a long while at a time, and glaring at us with its round glassy eyes.

"The lane along the shore-ice gave us little satisfaction, as it was completely covered with young ice and we could make no way. In addition to this, a wind from the S.S.W. sprang up, which drove the ice on to us, so there was nothing for it but to put in to the edge of the ice and wait until it should slacken again. We spread out the bag, folded the tent over us, and prepared for rest in the hope of soon being able to go on. But this was not to be; the wind freshened, the ice packed tighter and tighter, there was soon no open water to be seen in any direction, and even the open sea, whence we had come, disappeared; all our hopes of getting home that year sank at one blow.

Customs of the Fan Tribe

BY MARY KINGSLEY

Mary Kingsley really did not "discover" anything in particular when she traveled to West Africa in the 1890s. This area was reasonably well mapped by the time she reached it. But the descriptions of native life and traveling and trading in the interior she wrote in *Travels in West Africa* were so interesting that they remain in print a century later. Beyond the rarity of being a woman explorer in Victorian times, she showed a keen wit and writing ability in describing her travels.

This account of daily life and the ivory trade also pays homage to Paul Du Chaillu, the first white explorer to travel in this region, who was branded a liar for his fantastical but accurate descriptions 40 years earlier.

* * * * *

We will now enter into the reason that induces the bush man to collect stuff to sell among the Fans, which is the expensiveness of the ladies in the tribe. A bush Fan is bound to marry into his tribe, because over a great part of the territory occupied by them there is no other tribe handy to marry into; and a Fan residing in villages in touch with other tribes, has but little chance of getting a cheaper lady. For there is, in the Congo Français and the country adjacent to the north of it (Batanga), a regular style of aristocracy which may be summarized firstly thus: All the other tribes look down on the Fans, and the Fans look down on all the other tribes. This aristocracy has subdivisions, the M'pongwe of Gaboon are the upper circle tribe; next come the Benga of Corisco; then the Bapoka; then the Banaka. This system of aristocracy is kept up by the ladies. Thus a M'pongwe lady would not think of marrying into one of the lower tribes, so she is restricted, with many inner restrictions, to her own tribe. A Benga lady would marry a M'pongwe or a Benga, but not a Banaka, or Bapoka; and so on with the others; but not one of them would marry a Fan. As for the men, well of course they would marry any lady of any tribe, if she had a pretty face, or a good trading connection, if they were allowed to: that's just man's way. To the southeast the Fans are in touch with the Achille, Bakele, Dakele, practically one and the same tribe and a tribe that has much in common with the Fan, but who differ from them in getting on in a very friendly way with the little dwarf people, the Matimbas or Watwa, or Akkoa: people the Fans cannot abide. With these Achille the Fan can intermarry, but there is not much advantage in so doing, as the price is equally high, but still marry he must.

A young Fan man has to fend for himself, and has a scratchy kind of life of it, aided only by his mother until—if he be an enterprising youth—he is able to steal a runaway wife from a neighbouring village, or if he is a quiet and steady young man, until he has amassed sufficient money to buy a wife. This he does by collecting ivory and rubber and selling it to the men who have been allotted goods by the chief of the village, from the consignment brought up by the black trader. He supports himself meanwhile by, if the situation of his village permits, fishing and selling the fish, and hunting and killing game in the forest. He keeps steadily at it in his way, reserving his roisterings until he is settled in life. A truly careful young man does not go and buy a baby girl cheap, as soon as he has got a little money together; but works and saves on until he has got enough to buy a good, tough widow lady, who, although personally unattractive, is deeply versed in the lore of trade, and who knows exactly how much rubbish you can incorporate in a ball of India rubber, without the white trader or the black bush factory trader, instantly detecting it. The bush travelling trader has, in certain of the more savage districts, to take rubber without making an examination of it; that would hurt the sensitive feelings of his Fan friends. But then in these districts he carefully keeps the price low to allow for this. When the Fan young man has married his wife, in a legitimate way on the cash system, he takes her round to his relations, and shows her off; and they make little presents to help the pair set up housekeeping. But the young man cannot yet settle down, for his wife will not allow him to. She is not going to slave herself to death doing all the work of the house, etc., and so he goes on collecting, and she preparing, trade stuff, and he grows rich enough to buy other wives—some of them young children, others widows, no longer necessarily old. But it is not until he is well on in life that he gets sufficient wives, six or seven. For it takes a good time to get enough rubber to buy a lady, and he does not get a grip on the ivory trade until he has got a certain position in the village, and plantations of his own which the elephants can be discovered raiding, in which case a percentage of the ivory taken from the herd is allotted to him. Now and again he may come across a dead elephant, but that is of the nature of a windfall; and on rubber and ebony he has to depend during his early days. These he changes with the rich men of his village for a very peculiar and interesting form of coinage—bikei—little iron imitation axe-heads which are tied up in bundles called ntet, ten going to one bundle, for with bikei must the price of a wife be paid. You cannot do so with rubber or ivory, or goods. These bikei pass, however, as common currency among the Fans, for other articles of trade as well, but I do not think they will pass bikei out of the tribe. Possibly no one else will take this form of change. Thousands of these bekei, done up into ntets, go to the price of a wife. I was much interested in this coinage-equivalent, and found out all I could regarding it, but there is plenty more to be found out, and I hope the next voyager among the Fans will keep his eye on it. You do not find bikei close down to Libreville, among the Fans who are there in a semi-civilised state, or more properly speaking in a state of disintegrating culture. You must go for bush. I thought I saw in bikei a certain resemblance in underlying idea with the early Greek coins I have seen at Cambridge, make like the fore-parts of cattle; and I have little doubt that the articles of barter among the Fans before the introduction of the rubber, ebony, and ivory trades, which in their districts are comparatively recent, were iron implements. For the Fans are good workers in iron; and it would be in consonance with well-known instances among other savage races in the matter of stone implements, that these things, important of old, should survive, and be employed in the matter of such an old and important affair as marriage. They thus become ju-ju; and indeed all West African legitimate marriage, although appearing to the casual observer a mere matter of barter, is never solely such, but always has ju-ju in it.

We may as well here follow out the whole of the domestic life of the Fan, now we have got him married. His difficulty does not only consist in getting enough bikei together but in getting a lady he can marry. No amount of bikei can justify a man in marrying his first cousin, or his aunt; and as relationship among the Fans is recognised with both his father and his mother, not as among the Igalwa with the latter's blood relations only, there are an awful quantity of aunts and cousins about from whom he is debarred. But when he has surmounted his many difficulties, and dodged his relations, and married, he is seemingly a better husband than the man of a more cultured tribe. He will turn a hand to anything, that does not necessitate his putting down his gun outside his village gateway. He will help chop firewood, or goat's chop, or he will carry the baby with pleasure, while his good lady does these things; and in bush villages, he always escorts her so as to be on hand in case of leopards, or other local unpleasantnesses. When inside the village he will lay down his gun, within handy reach, and build the house, tease out fibre to make game nets with, and plait baskets, or make pottery with the ladies, cheerily chatting the while.

I must now speak briefly on the most important article with which the Fan deals, namely ivory. His methods of collecting this are several, and many a wild story the handles of your table knives could tell you, if their ivory has passed through Fan hands. For ivory is everywhere an evil thing before which the quest for gold sinks into a parlour game; and when its charms seize such a tribe as the Fans, "conclusions pass their careers." A very common way of collecting a tooth is to kill the person who owns one. Therefore in order to prevent this catastrophe happening to you yourself, when you have one, it is held advisable, unless you are a powerful person in your own village, to bury or sink the said tooth and say nothing about it until the trader comes to your district or you get a chance of smuggling it quietly down to him. Some of these private ivories are kept for yeas and years before they reach the trader's hands. And quite a third of the ivory you see coming on board a vessel to go to Europe is dark from this keeping: some teeth a lovely brown like a well-colored meerschaum, others quite black, and gnawed by that strange little creature—much heard of, and abused, yet little known in ivory ports—the ivory rat. This squirrel-like creature was first brought to Europe by Paul du Chaillu, and as far as I know no further specimen has been secured. I got two, but I am ashamed to say I lost them. Du Chaillu called it *Sciurus eborivorus*. Its main point, as may be imagined, is its teeth. The incisors in the upper jaw are long, and closely set together; those in the lower are still longer, and as they seem always to go in under the upper teeth, I wonder how the creature gets it mouth shut. The feet are hairless, and somewhat like those of a squirrel. The tail is long, and marked with transverse bars, and it is not carried over the back. Over the eyes, and on either side of the mouth, are very long stiff bristles. The mischief these little creatures play with buried ivory is immense, because, for some inscrutable reason, the seem to prefer the flavour of the points of the teeth, the most valuable part.

Ivory, however, that is obtained by murder is private ivory. The public ivory trade among the Fans is carried on in a way more in accordance with European ideas of a legitimate trade. The greater part of this ivory is obtained from dead elephants. There are in this region certain places where the elephants are said to go to die. A locality in one district pointed out to me as such a place, was a great swamp in the forest. A swamp that evidently was deep in the middle, for from out its dark waters no swamp plant, or tree grew, and evidently its shores sloped suddenly, for the band of swamp plants round its edge was narrow. It is just possible that during the rainy season when most of the surrounding country would be under water, elephants might stray into this natural trap and get drowned, and on the drying up of the waters be discovered, and the fact being known, be regularly sought for by the natives cognisant of this. I inquired carefully whether these places where the elephants came to die always had water in them, but they said no, and in one district spoke of a valley or round-shaped depression in among the mountains. But natives were naturally disinclined to take a stranger to these ivory mines, and a white person who has caught—as any one who has been in touch must catch—ivory fever, is naturally equally disinclined to give localities.

A certain percentage of ivory collected by the Fans is from live elephants, but I am bound to admit that their method of hunting elephants is disgracefully unsportsmanlike. A herd of elephants is discovered by rubber hunters or by depredations on plantations, and the whole village, men, women, children, babies, and dogs turn out into the forest and stalk the monsters into a suitable ravine, taking care not to scare them. When they have gradually edged the elephants on into a suitable place, they fell trees and wreathe them very roughly together with bush rope, all round an immense enclosure, still taking care not to scare the elephants into a rush. This fence is quite inadequate to stop any elephant in itself, but it is made effective by being smeared with certain things, the smell whereof the elephants detest so much that when they wander up to it, they turn back disgusted. I need hardly remark that this preparation is made by the witch doctors and its constituents a secret of theirs, and I was only able to find out some of them. Then poisoned plantains are placed within the enclosure, and the elephants eat these and grow drowsier and drowsier; if the water supply within the enclosure is a pool it is poisoned, but if it is a running stream this cannot be done. During this time the crowd of men and women spend their days round the enclosure, ready to turn back any elephant who may attempt to break out, going to and from the village for their food. Their nights they spend in little bough shelters by the enclosure, watching more vigilantly than by day, as the elephants are more active at night, it being their usual feeding time. During the whole time the witch doctor is hard at work making incantations and charms, with a view to finding out the proper time to attack the elephants. In my opinion, his decision fundamentally depends on his knowledge of the state of poisoning the animals are in, but his version is that he gets his information from the forest spirits. When, however, he has settled the day, the best hunters steal into the enclosure and take up safe positions, in trees, and the outer crowd set light to the ready-built fires, and make the greatest uproar possible, and fire upon the staggering, terrified elephants as they attempt to break out. The hunters in the trees fire down on them as they rush past, the fatal point at the back of the skull being well exposed to them.

When the animals are nearly exhausted, those men who do not possess guns dash into the enclosure, and the men who do, reload and join them, and the work is then completed. One elephant hunt I chanced upon at the final stage had taken two months' preparation, and although the plan sounds safe enough, there is really a good deal of danger left in it with all the drugging and ju-ju. There were eight elephants killed that day, but three burst through everything, sending energetic spectators flying, and squashing two men and a baby as flat as botanical specimens.

The subsequent proceedings were impressive. The whole of the people gorged themselves on the meat for days, and great chunks of it were smoked over the fires in all directions. A certain portion of the flesh of the hind leg was taken by the witch doctor for ju-ju, and was supposed to be put away by him, with certain suitable incantations in the recesses of the forest; his idea being apparently either to give rise to more elephants, or to induce the forest spirits to bring more elephants into the district. Meanwhile the carcasses were going bad, rapidly bad, and the smell for a mile round was strong enough to have taken the paint off a door. Moreover there were flies, most of the flies in West Africa, I imagine, and—but I will say no more. I thought before this experience that I had touched bottom in smells when once I spent the outside of a week in a village, on the sand bank in front of which a portly hippopotamus, which had been shot upriver, got stranded, and proceeded energetically to melt into its elemental gases; but that was a passing whiff to this.

Dr. Nassau tells me that the manner in which the ivory gained by one of these hunts is divided is as follows—"The witch doctor, the chiefs, and the family on whose ground the enclosure is built, and especially the household whose women first discovered the animals, decide in council as to the division of the tusks and the share of the flesh to be given to the crowd of outsiders. The next day the tusks are removed and each family represented in the assemblage cuts up and distributes the flesh." In the hunt I saw finished, the elephants had not been discovered, as in the case Dr. Nassau above speaks of, in a plantation by women, but by a party of rubber hunters in the forest some four or five miles from any village, and the ivory that would have been allotted to the plantation holder in the former case, went in this case to the young rubber hunters.

Of the method of catching game in traps I have already spoken. Such are the pursuits, sports, and pastimes of my friends the Fans. I have been considerably chaffed both by whites and blacks about my partiality for this tribe, but as I like Africans in my way—not *à la* Sierra Leone—and these Africans have more of the qualities I like than any other tribe I have met, it is but natural that I should prefer them. They are brave and so you can respect them, which is an essential element in a friendly feeling. They are on the whole a fine race, particularly those in the mountain districts of the Sierra del Cristal, where one continually sees magnificent specimens of human beings, both male and female. Their colour is light bronze, many of the men have beards, and albinoes are rare among them. The average height in the mountain districts is five feet six to five feet eight, the difference in stature between men and women not being great. Their countenances are very bright and expressive, and if once you have been among them, you can never mistake a Fan. But it is in the mental characteristics that their difference from the lethargic, dying-out coast tribes is most marked. The Fan is full of fire, temper, intelligence, and go; very teachable, rather difficult to manage, quick to take offence, and utterly indifferent to human life. I ought to say that other people, who should know him better than I, say he is a treacherous, thievish, murderous cannibal. I never found him treacherous; but then I never trusted him, remembering one of the aphorisms of my great teacher Captain Boler of Bonny, "It's not safe to go among bush tribes, but if you are such a fool as to go, you needn't go and be a bigger fool still, you've done enough." And Captain Boler's other great aphorism was: "Never be afraid of a black man." "What if I can't help it?" said I. "Don't show it," said he. To these precepts I humbly add another: "Never lose your head." My most favourite form of literature, I may remark, is accounts of mountaineering exploits, though I have never seen a glacier or a permanent snow mountain in my life. I do not care a row of pins how badly they may be written, and what form of bumble-puppy grammar and composition is employed, as long as the writer will walk along the edge of a precipice with a sheer fall of thousands of feet on one side and a sheer wall on the other; or better still crawl up an *arête* with a precipice on either. Nothing on earth would persuade me to do either of these things myself, but they remind me of bits of country I have been through where you walk along a narrow line of security with gulfs of murder looming on each side, and where in exactly the same way you are as safe as if you were in your easy chair at home, as long as you get sufficient holding ground; not on rock in the bush village inhabited by murderous cannibals, but on the ideas in those men's and women's minds; and these ideas, which I think I may say you will always find, give you safety.

It is not advisable to play with them, or to attempt to eradicate them, because you regard them as superstitious; and never, never shoot too soon. I have never had to shoot, and hope never to have to; because in such a situation, one white alone with no troops to back him means a clean finish. But this would not discourage me if I had to start, only it makes me more inclined to walk round the obstacle, than to become a mere blood splotch against it, if this can be done without losing your self-respect, which is the mainspring of your power in West Africa.

As for flourishing about a revolver and threatening to fire, I hold it utter idiocy. I have never tried it, however, so I speak from prejudice which arises from the feeling that there is something cowardly in it. Always have your revolver ready loaded in good order, and have your hand on it when things are getting warm, and in addition have an exceedingly good bowie knife, not a hinge knife, because with a hinge knife you have got to get it open—hard work in a country where all things go rusty in the joints—and hinge knives are liable to close on your own fingers. The best form of knife is the bowie, with a shallow half moon cut out of the back at the point end, and this depression sharpened to a cutting edge. A knife is essential, because after wading neck deep in a swamp your revolver is neither use nor ornament until you have had time to clean it. But the chances are you may go across Africa, or live years in it, and require neither. It is just the case of the gentleman who asked if one required a revolver in Carolina? and was answered, "You may be here one year and you may be here two and never want it; but when you do want it you'll want it very bad."

The cannibalism of the Fans, although a prevalent habit, is no danger, I think, to white people, except as regards the bother it gives one in preventing one's black companions from getting eaten. The Fan is not a cannibal from sacrificial motives like the negro. He does it in his common sense way. Man's flesh, he says, is good to eat, very good, and he wishes you would try it. Oh dear no, he never eats it himself, but the next door town does. He is always very much abused for eating his relations, but he really does not do this. He will eat his next door neighbour's relations and sell his own deceased to his next door neighbour in return; but he does not buy slaves and fatten them up for his table as some of the Middle Congo tribes I know of do. He has no slaves, no prisoners of war, no cemeteries, so you must draw your own conclusions. No, my friend, I will not tell you any cannibal stories. I have heard how good M. du Chaillu fared after telling you some beauties, and now you come away from the Fan village and down the Rembwé river.

The Labrador Wild

BY DILLON WALLACE

Dillon Wallace was a rank amateur among woodsmen when he left his law practice to set out with a friend and an Indian guide named George to explore a little-visited region of Labrador, Canada, in 1901. He managed to survive the inevitable disasters that befell the ill-prepared party, gaining experience and outdoor skills, and went on to write many popular books of adventure and woodcraft.

His companion, and the leader of that first trip, a man named Hubbard, was not so lucky. He perished on their harrowing retreat from Lake Michikamau as winter approached. Wallace told their story in *The Lure of the Labrador Wild*, which remains one of the most read books on the region to this day. Their retreat is a sad one and the trip probably one that never should have been taken, but the obvious friendship of the men and their loyalty to Hubbard even when he made the fateful decision that would end his own life and bring the others to the brink is touching.

$\star \quad \star \quad \star \quad \star \quad \star$

In our camp on the first little lake north of Lake Disappointment we ate on Monday morning (October 5) the last of the grouse we had killed on the previous day, and when we started forward we again were down to the precious little stock of pea meal. In a storm of snow and rain we floundered with the packs and canoe through a deep marsh, until once more we stood on the shore of the big lake where we had spent the weary days searching for a river—Lake Disappointment. We built a fire on the shore to dry our rags and warm ourselves; for we were soaked through and shivering with cold. Then we launched the canoe and paddled eastward.

Late in the afternoon we landed on an island that contained a semi-barren knoll, but which otherwise was wooded with small spruce. On the knoll we found an abundance of moss berries, and soon after we had devoured them we happened upon a supper in the form of two spruce grouse. George and Hubbard each shot one. The sun's journey across the sky was becoming noticeably shorter and shorter, and before we had realized that the day was spent, night began to close in upon us, and we pitched camp on the island.

In the morning (October 6) our breakfast flew right into camp. George crawled out early to build a fire, and a moment later stuck his head in the tent with the words, "Your pistol, Wallace." I handed it out to him, and almost immediately we heard a shot. Then George reappeared, holding up another spruce grouse.

"This grub came right to us," he said; "I knocked the beggar over close to the fire."

While we were eating the bird, Hubbard told us he had been dreaming during the night of home. Nearly every day now we heard that he had been dreaming the night before of his wife or his mother; they were always giving him good things to eat, or he was going to good dinners with them.

It had rained hard during the night, but with early morning there came again the mixture of rain and snow we had endured on the day before. When we put off in the canoe, we headed for the point where we expected to make the portage across the two-mile neck of land that separated Lake Disappointment from Lost Trail Lake; but soon we were caught by a terrific gale, and for half an hour we sat low in the canoe doing our best with the paddles to keep it headed to the wind and no one speaking a word. The foam dashed over the sides of our little craft, soaking us from head to foot. Tossed violently about by the big seas, we for a time expected that every moment would be our last. Had George been less expert with the stern paddle, we surely should have been swamped. As it was, we managed, after a desperate struggle, to gain the lee side of a small, rocky island, upon which we took refuge.

At length the wind abated and the lake became calmer, and venturing out once more, we made for the mainland some distance to the west of where we had intended to make our portage. There we stumbled upon a river of considerable size flowing in a southwesterly direction from Lake Disappointment into Lost Trail Lake. This river we had missed on the up trail and here had lost the old Indian trail to Michikamau. I volunteered to take my rifle and hunt across the neck of land separating the two lakes while Hubbard and George ran the rapids; but presently I heard them calling to me, and returning to the river, found them waiting on the bank.

"We'll camp just below here for the night," said Hubbard, "and finish the river in the morning. I couldn't manage my end of the canoe in a rapid we were shooting and we got on a rock. You'd better shoot the rapids with George after this."

I suppose Hubbard's weakness prevented him from turning the canoe quickly enough when occasion required, and he realized it.

All we had to eat that night was a little thin soup made from the pea meal, and an even smaller quantity had to serve us for breakfast. In the morning (October 7) we shot the rapids without incident down into Lost Trail Lake, and, turning to the eastward, were treated to a delightful view of the Kipling Mountains, now snow-capped and cold-looking, but appearing to us so much like old friends that it did our hearts good to see them. It was an ideal Indian summer day, the sun shining warmly down from a cloudless sky. Looking at the snow-capped peaks that bounded the horizon in front of me, I thought of the time when I had stood gazing at them from the other side, and of the eagerness I had felt to discover what lay hidden beyond.

> Something hidden. Go and find it. Go and look behind
> the Ranges—
> Something lost behind the Ranges. Lost and waiting for
> you. Go!

Well, we had gone. And we had found what lay hidden behind the ranges. But were we ever to get out to tell about it?

We stopped on the shore of Lost Trail Lake to eat some badly needed cranberries and mossberries. The mossberries, having been frozen, were fairly sweet, and they modified, to some extent, the acid of the cranberries, so that taken together they made a luncheon of which we, in our great need, were duly grateful. After eating as many of the berries as our stomachs would hold, we were able to pick a pan of them to take with us.

Paddling on, we passed through the strait connecting Lost Trail Lake with Lake Hope, and, recalling with grim smiles the enthusiastic cheers we had sent up there a few weeks before, sped rapidly across Lake Hope to the entrance of our old mountain pass, camping for the night on a ridge near the old sweat holes of the medicine men. Our supper consisted of a little more pea soup and half of the panful of berries.

While we were lying spoon-fashion under the blankets at night, it was the custom for a man who got tired of lying on one side to say "turn," which word would cause the others to flop over immediately, usually without waking. On this night, however, I said "turn over," and as we all flopped, Hubbard, who had been awake, remarked: "That makes me think of the turnovers and the spice rolls my mother used to make for me." And then he and I lay for an hour and talked of the baking days at the homes of our childhood. Under-the-blanket talks like this were not infrequent. "Are you awake, b'y?" Hubbard would ask. "Yes, b'y," I would reply, and so we would begin. If we happened to arouse George, which was not usual, Hubbard would insist on his describing over and over again the various Indian dishes he had prepared.

Weak as we were upon leaving Lake Hope (October 8), we did a heroic day's work. We portaged the entire six miles through the mountain pass, camping at night on the westernmost of the lakes that constitute the headwaters of the Beaver River, once more on the other side of the ranges. We did this on a breakfast of pea soup and the rest of our berries, and a luncheon of four little trout that Hubbard caught in the stream that flows through the pass. I shot a spruce grouse in the pass, and this bird we divided among us for supper. It was a terrible day. The struggle through the brush and up the steep inclines with the packs and the canoe so exhausted me that several times I seemed to be on the verge of a collapse, and I found it hard to conceal my condition. Once Hubbard said to me:

"Speak stronger, b'y. Put more force in your voice. It's so faint George'll surely notice it, and it may scare him."

That was always the way with Hubbard. Despite his own pitiable condition, he was always trying to help us get on and give us new courage. As a matter of fact, his own voice was getting so weak and low that we frequently had to ask him to repeat.

And the day ended in bitter disappointment. On our up trail we had had a good catch of trout at the place where the stream flowing out of the pass fell into the lake near our camp, and it was the hope of another good catch there that kept us struggling on to reach the end of the pass before night. But Hubbard whipped the pool at the foot of the fall in vain. Not a single fish rose. The day had been bright and sunshiny, but the temperature was low and the fish had gone to deeper waters.

It was a dismal camp. The single grouse we had for supper served only to increase our craving for food. And there we were, with less than two pounds of pea meal on hand and the fish deserting us, more than one hundred and fifty miles from the post at Northwest River. By the fire Hubbard again talked of home.

"I dreamed last night," he said, "that you and I, Wallace, were very weak and very hungry, and we came all at once upon the old farm in Michigan, and mother was there, and she made us a good supper of hot tea biscuits with maple syrup and honey to eat on them. And how we ate and ate!"

But George's customary grin as missing. In silence he took the tea leaves from the kettle and placed them on a flat stone close by the fire, and in silence he occasionally stirred them with a twig that he broke from a bush at his back. At length, the tea leaves having dried sufficiently, he filled his pipe from them, and I filled my pipe. We had not had any tobacco to smoke for many days.

The silence continued. On my right sat George, his cheeks sunken, his eyes deep down in their sockets, his long black hair falling over his ears— there he sat stiffly erect, puffing his tea leaves with little apparent satisfaction and gazing stoically into the fire. I could guess what was passing through his mind—the stories of the Indians who starved.

On my left was Hubbard. He had assumed the attitude that of late had become characteristic when he was dreaming of his wife and his mother and his faraway home. His elbows were resting on his knees, and his hands were supporting his head. His long hair hid his bony fingers and framed his poor, wan face. His sunken eyes, with their look of wistful longing, were fixed on the blazing logs.

The silence became so oppressive that I had to break it:

"George," I said, "were you never hungry before?"

"Never in my life was short of grub till now," he answered shortly.

At that Hubbard, aroused from his reverie, looked up.

"Well, I can tell you, George," he said, "there are worse places than Labrador to starve in."

"How's that?" grunted George.

"If you had been as hungry as I have been in New York City, you'd know what I mean," said Hubbard. "It's a heap worse to be hungry where there's lots of grub around you than in the bush where there's none. I remember that when I first went to New York, and was looking for work, I found myself one rainy night with only five cents in my pocket. It was all the money I had in the world, and I hadn't any friends in the city, and I didn't want to write home, because nearly all the people there had no faith in my venture. I was soaking wet and good and hungry; I hadn't been eating much for several days. Well, I went to a bakery and blew in my last nickel on stale rolls and crullers and took them to my room. Then I took off my wet clothes and got into bed to get warm and snug, and there I ate my rolls and crullers, and they were bully. Yes, I remember that although my room rent was overdue, and I didn't know where my breakfast was coming from, I was supremely happy; I sort of felt I was doing the best I could."

We went to bed that night feeling that our lives now depended on whether fish could be caught below.

More than anxious were we for the morrow, because then we should go to the first rapid on the Beaver River below the lakes, and there in the pool, where two fishings had yielded us more than 130 trout on the up trail, test our fortunes.

The morning (October 9) dawned crisp and wintry. The sun rose in a cloudless sky and set all the lake a-glinting. On the peaks of the Kipling Mountains the sunbeams kissed the snow, causing it to gleam and scintillate in brilliant contrast to the deep blue of the heavens above and the dark green of the forests below. Under normal circumstances we should have paused to drink in the beauty of it all; but as we in our faithful old canoe paddled quickly down over the lake I am afraid that none of us thought of anything save the outcome of the test we were to make of our fortunes at the rapid for which we were bound. It is difficult to be receptive to beauty when one has had only a little watered pea meal for breakfast after a long train of lean and hungry days. We were glad only that the sun was modifying the chill air of the dawn, thus increasing our chances of getting fish.

How friendly the narrow lake looked where we had seen the otter at play at sunset and where the loons had laughed at us so derisively. And the point where we had camped that August night and roasted our goose seemed very homelike. We stopped there for a moment to look for bones. There were a few charred ones where the fire had been. They crumbled without much pressure, and we ate them. No trout were jumping in the lake now—its mirror-like surface was unbroken. All was still, very still. To our somewhat feverish imagination it seemed as if all nature were bating its breath as if tensely waiting for the outcome at the fishing pool.

I can hardly say what we expected. I fear my own faith was weak, but I believe Hubbard's was strong—his was the optimistic temperament. How glad we were to feel the river current as it caught the canoe and hurried it on to the rapid! Suddenly, as we turned a point in the stream, the sound of the rushing waters came to us. A few moments more and we were there. Just above the rapid we ran the canoe ashore, and Hubbard with his rod hurried down to the pool and cast a fly upon the water.

Since the weather had become colder we always fished with bait, if any were available, and so, when after a few minutes a small trout took Hubbard's fly, he made his next cast with a fin cut from his first catch. Before he cast the fly, George and I ran the canoe through the rapid to a point just below the pool where we had decided to camp. Then, leaving George to finish the work of making camp, I took my rod and joined Hubbard. All day long, and until after dusk, we fished. We got sixty. But they were all tiny, not averaging more than six inches long.

The test of our fortunes was not encouraging. Hubbard especially was disappointed, as he had been cherishing the hope that we might catch enough to carry us well down the trail. And what were sixty little fish divided among three ravenous men! We ate fifteen of them for luncheon and eighteen for supper, and began to fear the worst. The pea meal was now down to one and a half pounds.

It was late when we gave up trying to get more fish, but we sat long by the fire considering the possibility of finding scraps at the camp down the Beaver where we had killed the caribou on August 12. The head, we remembered, had been left practically untouched, and besides the bones there were three hoofs lying about somewhere, if they had not been carried off by animals. We knew that these scraps had been rotting for two months, but we looked forward hopefully to reaching them on the morrow.

No lovelier morning ever dawned than that of Saturday (October 10), and until midday the weather was balmy and warm; but in the afternoon clouds began to gather attended by a raw west wind. While George and I shot the rapids, Hubbard fished them, catching in all seventeen little trout. Some of the rapids George and I went through in the canoe we should never, under ordinary conditions, have dreamed of shooting. But George expressed the sentiments of all of us when he said: "We may as well drown as starve, and it's a blamed sight quicker." Only when the river made actual falls did George and I resort to portaging. However, we did not make the progress we had hoped, and much disappointed that we could not reach Camp Caribou that night, we camped at the foot of the last fall above the lake expansion on the shore of which George and I had ascended a hill to be rewarded with a splendid view of the country and the Kipling Mountains. Our day's food consisted of three trout each at each of our three meals.

Sunday (October 11) was another perfect day. It was wintry, but we had become inured to the cold. We each had a pair of skin mittens, which although practically gone as to the palms, served to protect our hands from the winds. Before we started forward I read aloud John 17. Again in the morning we divided nine little trout among us, and the remaining eight we had for luncheon. The weather was now so cold that do what we would we never again could induce a trout, large or small, to take the bait or rise to the fly.

In the course of the day George took two long shots at ducks, and missed both times; it would have been phenomenal if he hadn't. There was one little fall that we could not shoot, and we landed on the bank to unload the canoe. All three of us tried to lift the canoe so as to carry it about thirty yards down to where we could again launch it, but we were unable to get it to our heads and it fell to the ground with a crash. Then we looked at one another and understood. No one spoke, but we all understood. Up to this time Hubbard and I had kept up the fiction that we were "not so weak," but now all of us knew that concealment no longer was possible, and the clear perception came to us that if we ever got out of the wilderness it would be only by the grace of God.

With difficulty we dragged the canoe to the launching place, and on the way found the cleaning rod Hubbard's father had made for him, which had been lost while we were portaging around the fall on our upward journey. Hubbard picked the rod up tenderly and put in into the canoe.

An hour before sunset we reached Camp Caribou, the place where we had broiled those luscious steaks that twelfth of August and had merrily talked and feasted far into the night. Having dragged the canoe up on the sandy shore, we did not wait to unload it, but at once staggered up the bank to begin our eager search for scraps. The head of the caribou, dried and worm-eaten, was where we had left it. The bones we had cut the meat from were there. The remnants of the stomach, partially washed away, were there. But we found only two hoofs. We had left three. Up and down and all around the camp we searched for the other hoof; but it was gone.

"Somebody's taken it," said George. "Somebody's taken it, sure—a marten or somebody."

When all the refuse we could find had been collected, and the tent had been pitched on the spot where it stood before, George got a fire going and prepared our banquet of bones and hoofs. The bit of hair that clung to the skin on the upper part of the hoofs he singed off by holding them a moment in the fire. Then, taking an axe, he chopped the hoofs and bones up together, and placed some of the mess in the kettle to boil. A really greasy, though very rancid, broth resulted. Some of the bones and particularly the hoofs were maggoty, but, as Hubbard said, the maggots seemed to make the broth the richer, and we drank it all. It tasted good. For some time we sat gnawing the gristle and scraps of decayed flesh that clung to the bones, and we were honestly thankful for our meal.

The bones from which we made our broth were not thrown away. On the contrary we carefully took them from the kettle and placed them with the other bones, to boil and reboil them until the last particle of grease had been extracted. There was little left on the head save the hide, but that was also placed with the pile of bones, as well as the antlers, which were in velvet, and what remained of the stomach and its contents.

After we had finished gnawing our bones, George sat very quiet as if brooding over some great problem. Finally he arose, brought his camp bag to the fire, and resuming his seat, went low into the recesses of the bag. Still holding his hand in the bag, he looked at me and grinned.

"Well?" said I.

"Sh-h-h," he replied, and slowly withdrawing his hand held up—an ounce package of cut plug tobacco!

I stared at the tobacco, and then again caught George's eye. Our smiles became beatific.

"I've been savin' this for when we needed it most," said George. "And I guess that time's come."

He handed me the package, and I filled my pipe, long unused to anything save leaves from the teapot and red willow bark. Then George filled his pipe.

From the fire we took brands and applied them to the tobacco. Deep, deep were our inhalations of the fragrant smoke.

"George," said I, "however in the world could you keep it so long?"

"Well," said George—puff, puff—"well, when we were getting' so short of grub"—puff—"thinks I"—puff—"the time's comin' "—puff, puff—"when we'll need cheerin' up—puff—"and, says I,"—puff—"I'll just sneak this away until that time comes."

"George," said I, lying back and watching the smoke curl upward in the light of the fire," you are not a half bad sort of a fellow."

"Wallace," said he, "we'll have a pipeful of this every night until it is gone."

"I'd try it, too," said Hubbard wistfully, "but I know it would make me sick, so I'll drink a little tea."

After he had had his tea, he read to us the First Psalm. These readings from the Bible brought with them a feeling of indescribable comfort, and I fancy we all went to our blankets that night content to know that whatever was, was for the best.

With the first signs of dawn we were up and had another pot of bone broth. Again the morning (October 12) was crisp and beautiful, and the continuance of the good weather gave us new courage. While the others broke camp, I went on down the river bank in the hope of finding game, but when, after I had walked a mile, they overtook me with the canoe I had seen nothing. While boiling bones at noon, we industriously employed ourselves in removing the velvet skin from the antlers and singeing the hair off. In the forenoon we encountered more rapids. Once Hubbard relieved me at the stern paddle, but he was too weak to act quickly, and we had a narrow escape from being overturned.

While making camp at night, George heard a whiskey jack calling, and he sneaked off into the brush and shot it. We reserved it as a dainty for breakfast. As we sat by the fire gnawing bones and chewing up scorched pieces of antlers, we again discussed the question as to whether we should stick to the canoe and run the river out to its mouth or abandon the canoe where we had entered the river. As usual George and I urged the former course.

"When you're in the bush stick to your canoe as long as you can," said George; "that's always a good plan."

But Hubbard was firm in the belief that we should take the route we knew, and renewed his argument about the possibility of getting windbound on Goose Bay, into which we thought the river flowed. Being windbound had for him especial terrors, due, I suppose, to his normally active nature. Another thing that inclined him towards taking the old trail was his strong faith that we should get trout in the outlet to Lake Elson where we had such a successful fishing on the inbound journey. He argued, furthermore, that along what we then thought was the Nascaupee River we should be able to recover the provisions we had abandoned soon after plunging into the wild.

"However," he said in closing," we'll see how we feel about it tomorrow. I'll sleep on it."

I remember I dreaded so much a return to the Susan Valley that I told Hubbard it seemed like suicide to leave the river we were on and abandon the canoe. I felt strongly on the subject and expressed my opinion freely. But it was a question of judgment about which one man's opinion was as likely to be right as another's and, recognizing this, we never permitted our discussions as to the best course to follow to create any ill-feeling.

On Tuesday (October 13) the weather continued to favor us. We shot the rapids without a mishap, and camped at night within three miles of where we had entered the river. But still the question about leaving it was unde-cided. The whiskey jack and a bit of pea meal helped our pot of bone broth at breakfast, and in addition to more broth we had in the evening some of the caribou stomach and its contents and a part of a moccasin that Hubbard had made from the caribou skin and had worn full of holes. Boiled in the kettle the skin swelled thick and was fairly palatable.

Clouds and a sprinkle of rain introduced the morning of Wednesday (October 14). While the bones were boiling for breakfast, George brought out the caribou skin that he had picked up on the shore of Lake Disap-pointment after we had abandoned it. Now as he put a piece of it in the kettle, we recalled his prophesy that some day we might want to eat it, and laughed. Into the pot also went one-sixth of a pound of pea meal together with a few lumps of flour that we carefully scraped from a bag we had thrown away in the summer and found near the camp. While we were eating this breakfast (and really enjoying it) we again considered the problem as to whether or not we should leave the river. In the course of the discussion George said quietly:

"I had a strange dream about that last night, fellus."

We urged him to tell us what it was.

"It was a strange dream," he repeated, and hesitated. Then: "Well, I dreamed the Lord stood before me, very beautiful and bright, and He had a mighty kind look on His face, and He said to me: 'George, don't leave this river—just stick to it and it will take you out to Grand Lake where you'll find Blake's cache with lots of grub, and then you'll be all right and safe. I can't spare you any more fish, George, and if you leave this river you won't get any more. Just stick to this river, and I'll take you out safe.'

"The Lord was all smiling and bright," continued George, "and He looked at me very pleasant. Then He went away, and I dreamed we went right down the river and came out in Grand Lake near where we had left it comin' up, and we found Blake there, and he fed us and gave us all the grub we wanted, and we had a fine time."

It was quite evident that George was greatly impressed by his dream. I give it here simply for what it is worth. At the same time I cannot help char-acterizing it as remarkable, not to say extraordinary; for none of us had had even a suspicion that the river we were on emptied into Grand Lake at all, much less that its mouth was near the point where we left the lake. But I my-self attached no importance to the dream at the time, whatever I may think now; I was chiefly influenced, I suppose, in my opposition to the abandon-ment of the river by the unspeakable dread I had felt all along of returning to the Susan Valley—was it premonition?—and no doubt it was only natural that Hubbard should disregard the dream.

"It surely was an unusual dream," he said to George: "but it isn't possible, as you know, for this river to empty into Grand Lake. We were talking about leaving the river until late last night, and you had it on your mind—that's what made you dream about it."

"Maybe it was," said George calmly: "but it was a mighty strange dream, and we'd better think about it before we leave the river. Stick to the canoe, Hubbard, that's what I say. Wallace and I'll shoot the rapids all right. They're sure to be not so bad as we've had, and I think they'll be a lot better. We can run 'em, can't we, Wallace?"

I added my opinion to George's that there would be more water to cover the rocks farther down, and said that however bad the rapids might be I should venture to take the stern paddle in every one that George dared to tackle. But Hubbard only said:

"I still think, boys, we should take the trail we know."

"That means suicide," I said for the second time, rather bitterly, I fear. "We'll surely leave our bones in that awful valley over there. We're too weak to accomplish that march."

Once more Hubbard marshalled his arguments in favor of the overland route, and George and I said no more that morning.

Soon after we relaunched the canoe something occurred to change the current of our thoughts. A little way ahead of us, swimming slowly down the river, George espied a duck. No one spoke while we landed him, rifle in hand, along the bank. Cautiously he stole down among the alders and willows that lined the shore, and then crawled on hands and knees through the marsh until the duck was opposite to him. It seemed a very small thing for a rifle target while it was moving, and as George put the rifle to his shoulder and carefully aimed, Hubbard and I watched him with nerves drawn to a tension. Once he lowered the rifle, changed his position slightly, and then again raised the weapon to his shoulder. He was deliberation personified. Would he never fire? But suddenly the stillness of the wilderness was broken by a loud, clear report. And Hubbard and I breathed again, breathed a prayer of gratitude, as we saw the duck turn over on its back. With his long black hair falling loosely over his ears, ragged, and dripping wet with the marsh water, George arose and returned to us. Stopping for a moment before entering the canoe, he looked heavenward and reverently said:

"The Lord surely guided that bullet."

It was still early in the morning when we arrived at the point where we had portaged into the river. George prepared the duck—small it was but very fat—for a delicious, glorious luncheon, and while it was cooking we had our last discussion as to whether or not we should leave the river.

"Well," I at length said to Hubbard, " a final decision can be deferred no longer. It's up to you, b'y—which route are we to take?"

"I firmly believe," said Hubbard, "that we should stick to our old trail."

George and I said no more. The question was settled. Hubbard was the leader. Immediately after luncheon we set to work preparing for the march overland. In addition to several minor articles of equipment, we decided to leave behind us the artificial horizon, the sextant box, and one of the axes. When our light packs had been prepared, we turned the canoe bottom up on the river bank. I hated to leave it. I turned once to pat and stroke the little craft that had carried us so far in safety. To me it was one of our party—a dear friend and comrade. It seemed cruel to abandon it there in the midst of the wilderness. In my abnormal state of mind I could scarcely restrain the tears.

But the best of friends must part, and so, shouldering our light packs, we bid the canoe a last farewell, and staggered forward to the horrors in store for us on the trail below.

Butting Blindly into the Storm

BY ROBERT DUNN

It would be hard to imagine a more entertaining book of exploration than Robert Dunn's *The Shameless Diary of an Explorer*. Dunn was selected as the geologist and second-in-command for Frederick Cook's 1903 expedition to reach the summit of Mt. McKinley in Alaska, the highest peak in North America. While this first expedition was a complete failure, Cook would claim to reach the summit on a later trip, in addition to claiming to have reached the North Pole just days before Peary. Both claims were proven ridiculous, but Cook clung to his assertions the rest of his life.

Dunn sarcastically refers to Cook in his narrative as "the Professor," and he pulls no punches in his cutting description of the poor leadership of the ill-conceived expedition or the petty bickering among its members. This book stands virtually alone among stories of exploration for its frank and funny look at aspects that seldom find their way into print.

Here, the group has made a base camp of sorts and is preparing a half-hearted assault on the mountain.

★ ★ ★ ★ ★

A ugust 16th—Not a wink all night. We divided the last caribou steak, and wrung water from our blankets to make tea, which Miller wouldn't drink as we had no sugar. But we felt cheerier. The raw dawn shifted weary glints on the dull blue glaciers of the front range. "What to do," thought I, "but go on zwie-backing?" I did. Miller cut wood. The baking over, we chased twenty caribou that had peeked at us, and hit back for the river. The flood hadn't fallen, but was spreading out into a hundred channels, so we waded it to camp. King crossed on Big Buck to get the wood, and it was very funny to see him buck in mid-stream with Fred on his back, too—the animated old wood-pile.

294

Simon was lazing by the fire, protected from the scud by a willow thatch importantly called a "Fuegian wind-break" by the Professor. He ran at me with all kinds of tales how we could get up some glacier—the one visible from here with the serac of dirty ice-blocks, under the highest point of the front range. The strange sacks of "mountain stuff" which seemed such a useless burden on the trail, were open, and weird Arctic clothing was passed around. I have drawn a pair of red stockings, with tassels, to pairs of Arctic socks (like mittens for the feet), hand mittens, a pair of grimy drawers, and one of the green eiderdown sleeping bags.

Now, we can't all wander about in the McKinley fogs. Some one of the five must stay to read the barometer at the base camp under the front range, whither we move tomorrow up this stream. The Shantung silk tent holds only four, and there aren't enough green sleeping bags—weighing just four pounds each unless wet—to go around. The Professor won't say who must stay behind, which seems to lie between Simon and Miller. I want Miller to climb, and told the Professor that it was a good deal to risk our lives with the kid, whose eyesight and hearing are defective, and is slower than old Ned. "Yes, Miller is more adaptable," was all he answered. Miller says he thinks that Simon has some previous agreement to be taken on the mountain; but I doubt that.

Now the Professor says that he expects "a man to volunteer to stay behind," which is the devil of a scheme. Yet vaguely he adds that whoever shows up worst on the first day's climb, goes back. Whew! How can such vacillation get our confidence? He's simply afraid, or unable, to decide anything beforehand. Of course, Simon has corralled a rucksack and a green sleeping-bag, and is importantly hammering the heads on the ice-axes. One he has already used to chop willows. Miller saw, and cursed him. I'm in the tent, mending those grimy drawers. The rest are out in that Fuegian wind-break. No one knows it's my birthday. What's the use?

August 17th—At bedtime last night the river was gouging away the bank so fast that Simon made a danger alarm by tying a rope to a log and hitching the end in the tent. We'd slept two hours, when the rope jerked. Outside, the stream was sweeping away that Fuegian business and splashing the grub. The Professor jumped up out of three inches of water (he's a sight when just awake, fingering his long, pale locks out of his eyes) and lugged the stuff dazedly into the brush. King wouldn't budge. "You can never tell with these glaysher streams," he drawled, and rolled over asleep. Miller turned in with me, and though I invited the Professor as well—perhaps too insistently—he wound himself up in his tent well out of the wet and in the morning was snoring there, like a big human chrysalis.

I chased and found the horses—King tracked them wrong for once—by the creek where we shot the last caribou, and we were packed and hiking up the south fork of our flooding stream by noon, as it rained again; the fifth incessant day, mind you.

Near the moraine of the glacier the Professor had explored—and little enough had he seen in the drizzle—the fog shut down tight. Instead of steering on by compass, we camped, though grass still struggled through the moss, and we could not go wrong in that narrow gorge. Having nothing but bowlders to tie the horses to as we unpacked, Little Buck ran amuck, scattering sacks right and left, and stampeding the whole bunch.

Thus we enter the fog to attack the virgin peak of Mt. McKinley, unknown and unexplored from all sides. Thus, without proper reconnoitering, we have jammed our heads into the 10,000-foot range which walls the main mountain mass. It seems to curve, and join the right-hand, or south haunch, of the main dome, whose face has appeared quite perpendicular. Below that face, between it, and our outer range, and at right angles to our direction, flows Peters' glacier (named by Brooks). We think that it heads into a curving wall, connecting front range and main mountain, by which we hope to reach an arête of the peak. But so reticulated with ridges and hung with glaciers are these heights, that I doubt if any one of us has a clear idea of just where we are going to hit; or will have, till clear weather comes. This is our base camp, and we're ready to make a ten or twelve days' attack on the old mountain without descending. Yet August is the Alaska rainy season, and it may drizzle on till the September frosts, which will mean checkmate by fresh snows on the mountain.

The outlook is cheerless; we're discouraged; the low clouds rain on, and on, and on. Grub-packs and pack-covers are saturated. A spirit of "Oh, let it go, it's wet anyhow," pervades the camp. The ground is littered with old boots, smelly sacks, unwashed dishes, and slabs of caribou which Fred has discarded after careful sniffs. Handfuls of fly-blows crust the meat bags.

Yet the Professor talks of pushing up the glacier anyhow, tomorrow. He has been out reconnoitering with King, and announces that he's found a way for horses across the moraine to the ice. I took a turn over the black hill, which splits the ice-foot in twain, and we call the "nunatak." Saw nothing, nothing, but crazy cataracts of mud water, in crazier gorges.

August 18th—Wetter drizzle. I was annoyed, because he had talked of moving, to find the Professor asleep in his tent with Miller, after breakfast over the stone fire-cairn I had built to economize wood; especially as he'd been trying to persuade King to go down the valley to hunt. King was in bed, too; so what for me but to turn in? We recited a few drummers' tales, and worked in a laugh over the querulous one beginning, "Father, pass the gentleman the butter;" when enter Simon, with a butter can full of roots, and spread his drying-frames all over our tent.

Fred and I cooked tea and meat outside alone. Simon says that the Professor was sore because we didn't call him to eat. "That was the first meal prepared on the whole trip," he had complained (but not to me), "to which we were not all called." Oh, dear! We're kept entirely in the dark about his plans; no one cares to make a suggestion or ask a question. But sometimes the manner of his silences lets the cat out of the bag. He has made no decisions yet, of any sort, whatsoever.

So here we lie abed soaked; listening to the roar of glacier streams, the rumble of snow avalanches, the sandy splutter of drizzle on the saturated tent. Now and then we peek out and make a great to-do if a bowlder more than ten yards off looms up. Then says Fred bitterly, "It's a-goin' ter clear. Yes, sir, she's a-goin' ter clear. See her, see her."

August 19th—And still rain. "Simon," said the Professor this morning through the drizzle, "go down to the stream and read the barometer" which meant that we were going to hit up the glacier. Nothing was said about who should stay behind; still no one dares ask the Professor his schemes. Fred, as we stumbled in the fog hunting horses, was very peevish over the shortness of grub, Simon as a companion on the mountain, and the Professor's indecision, especially as to who goes on the ascent. "Perhaps he thinks I ain't clean enough for his eidydown," he said. All but he have sleeping bags, yet he is treated as an essential for the climb.

At last we found and packed with rucksacks, small kerosene cans, Primus stove, etc.—and Simon's dunnage—Whiteface, Bridget, B horse, and the two Grays. We breakfasted on meat tainted from its mildewy sack and stewed in its absorbed water, and plunged upward into the fog toward the unknown ice. No one stayed behind. Each led a beast; crossed, re-crossed over sharp bowlders, down and up sheer, sliding talus, to stumble with feet and hoofs grueled by bowlders hurtled along under the brown foam of glacier streams. Finally over sharp moraine, like the Andes in miniature—to a luminous smooth lip of foggy ice.

We started up. It grew suddenly steep. Big Gray stumbled and fell, but was righted before rolling over. The ice whitened; leveled. The horses nosed a few lateral crevasses, nickered, jumped them with awkward care. Gradually, huge seracs (ice-falls) swam through the lightening mist, and a castellated black ridge struck down to bisect the glacier into two amphitheatres. The

Professor turned into the left hand and nearer one, against Fred's protest. From our futile talks, I had got too hazy ideas of where we were aiming to speak up. Between two upper seracs, fresh snow hid the crevasses, and the fog thinned. The Professor went ahead, sounding with his ice-axe. It was slow, ticklish work, winding back and forth over cracks that might, or might not, let you through to wait for the last trump—you couldn't tell till you tested them. The horses snorted; balked; leaned back, legs quivering, till we beat a terror-ized jump out of each. I had on sneakers, and was thinking what a testimonial could be made to the rubber company for wearing them to 7,000 feet on McKinley, when the Dark Gray bungled a leap, and lost his hind quarter down a crevasse. All hands unpacked him, and hauled him by saddle tie-ropes. Now and then the other beasts imitated him. Higher and higher we felt a way; piloting each horse in turn across each crevasse, quadrilling—at last over clean ice, netted with cracks—to a dome-like summit. Beyond, the glacier dipped down all around to vague ice-falls hanging upon paste-white walls banded with brown irony veins; and to the left and north, but not toward McKinley, a possible-to-climb talus slope flanked the dizzy ridge. The Profes-sor drew a brass aneroid from his money belt, and muttered, "Seventy-five hundred feet."

Fred, Miller, and I, cramped in the silk tent, are trying to fill the oil stove to give the beans another boil (Simon only half cooked them). We are talking weather, ice, and glacial erosion. Under us are wet blankets, wetter tarpaulins, wettest ice. It is suffocating hot; disordered food, clothing, instru-ments, all are steaming. Outside, some attempt has been made to sort the stuff, but it's rather hopeless; pounds have been added to the rucksacks, and the sugar is syrupy. The smell of meaty, mildewed cotton pervades the air. The Professor and Simon have gone out to reconnoitre the talus between the glaciers, following a route to shore (off the ice) explored by Fred and me, roped. . . .

At supper, he and I shivered outside the tent, as cups of tea and chunks of caribou were handed out from low voices within here. The zwieback was voted a success. The Professor is going to use it at the North Pole. Now and then—as the clouds parted overhead to let down a chill, silverish light, conceal the wavering edge of this snowy cistern, reveal shreds of sky too cold and lus-trous to be blue—Fred would say, "Yes, sir, a hundred and sixty acres more of heaven cleared off. She looks like the breakup of a hard winter."

We're all five to sleep here tonight, some one outside, as the tent, being meant for one man, holds only four. Just now, Simon took our breaths away by volunteering, and is rigging up a sort of couch out on the glacier, like a funeral pyre, of sacks, blankets, and boxes. The tent is guyed down with ice-axes. We have one teaspoon among us. Yes, it's the real Alpine thing, this. Good night.

August 20th—The Professor and Simon climbed the ridge to 8,100 feet last night, reporting the outlook ahead through fog "favorable" enough to try. All night I lay awake listening to avalanches, squeezed between Fred and the silk wall, mostly against the wall, which dribbled water till near morning, when everything froze stiff. Then the Professor struggled over on his stomach, fingered the pale locks out of his eyes, and started the stove at his head for tea, zwieback, and caribou. No one washed. Outside, Fred and I rubbed snow on our faces. No use. We had no soap. When I had suggested we take some, the Professor laughed at me. Then we drew in our frozen boots from the outside—they're never allowed to touch the tarpaulin under us, as they import snow—and put them on gymnastically, one by one, as the others lay cramped and still as cataleptics.

Without, it was absolutely clear. Never were such steep walls, such hanging glaciers jeering at the laws of gravity, such over-brilliance of sunlight and azure sky. Above our amphitheatre, snow slides had fingered straight converging paths down its mysterious east wall, upon the chaos of pale bowlders and yawning crevasses which surrounded us like a sea. Southwest, we looked out over sharp-angled black slate and rusty tuffa, clean-cut and glistening as if created yesterday, to the foothills fronting the hidden Foraker; and far below and away shone glacial ponds like diamonds strewn over the forbidden tundra. But clouds were gathering.

We were to climb the explored talus; curve around to its east wall; travel south, then east, around the headwall of the yet-unseen Peters glacier, to the south haunch of the main mountain. Slowly we packed our rucksacks, and double-tripped the outfit to "shore." Then each corraled what looked heaviest and was lightest, what according to suspicion as he read his neighbor's eyes overstated its weight—or understated it—as if he thought anything was to be gained by ostentatious heroism. When all had forty pounds anyway, we found that another trip would have to be made up the ridge with alcohol, tent, and stove. I had the two two-pound cheeses, ten cans of milk, pea soup, and my clothing. Simon had the little olive oil cans of kerosene, and Miller the two twenty-pound tins of pemmican, that there should be no doubt about *his* pack. At this moment it was vaguely bruited that Miller was to take the horses back to camp tonight, no matter how high we climbed today, and read the barometer below while we are on the mountain. How this came about, I don't know. On top the ridge Miller tried to tell me, but couldn't make it clear. I gathered that the Professor's procrastination sort of froze him into offering to sacrifice himself. "It's pretty hard after all we've been through to miss the main chance," he told me. "I only wish that the Professor had let me know beforehand I mightn't have a try at it." But Miller never kicked. Surely he hadn't "shown up worst," then. No one has had a chance, even yet. So the Simon infliction is a fact. Yet wouldn't Miller sooner than Simon shake hands with the danger devil before meeting him?

We began the ascent of Mt. McKinley.

Up shot the talus, straight as Jacob's ladder, into the clouds, and we hanging to it—Fred first, I last, and the rest strung in between. We kept now to rock-slide, to snow-slide, to glacier-edge. Heads bent to stomachs, sweating, gasping, we stopped to turn in silence every two hundred steps and view the poor horses, reduced to specks in their snowy purgatory, headed in on an island among crevasses—poor brutes that, twenty-four hours without food, had tried to find a way down to moss and lost their nerve. Fred kept tearing ahead, and made a point of always leaving a resting place just as Simon and the Professor stopped there. Once the Professor, carrying the tent pole, fell on a snow slope, and seemed nearly to roll to bottom. I caught Fred at the summit. He was leaning over an undercut snow cornice, dripping icy stalactites, God knows how many thousand feet, into the amphitheatre of glacier seven. A sickening look. We lay on our rucksacks, eating the last of the raisins, whose bag has sloughed away in the wet. The others grunted up to our side; Miller first.

Clouds had settled where the ridge mounted in the east. Thither the Professor, Fred, and I slabbed the talus, and sat down to wait for clearing—to wait, and wait, and wait. The base of the next rise lay across another cornice; to go down, then up to reach it, steps should be cut. I said that I'd follow anyone across, that way, or by the cornice. "No," said the Professor, "that won't be any use unless it clears. We must see where we are going." (Sic.) He went on to condemn the outlook into amphitheatre seven—"No possible slope from there, either," he said, " and even if we can get up this ridge to its peak, we are not sure of getting further." He did not see as far as this last night, he added. It seemed to me, that before butting up there we should have made sure of what lies behind this summit, if it took days; but I forbore to speak, and in such a place, that did not take much effort. Fred observed that horses properly shod could cross below the cornice. Still we waited. Behind, Simon in his poncho, like a fish-bone pen-wiper with his bow-legs, paced up and down like Napoleon before battle; and Miller, cold as usual, with his mackinaw collar turned up, was lying flat.

The Professor repeated, summarized, emphasized his objection to going on, and spoke of a return, but no move was made. And still no move. I suggested that we wait for it to clear until a certain moment, three o'clock say. It was so agreed, and on the moment we returned. The dilemma was restated to the others, who made no comment; and down the talus we slid, as the drizzle re-began, double-tripping the whole outfit across the crevasses, to where tea leaves, sodden in the ice, marked camp.

A catechism eked from the Professor that we should next try Fred's amphitheatre—the one to the east—which he had wanted to tackle. We saddled. Never were frozen hands so tortured on wetter, dripping cinches, galled in so inane defeat, on packs that were sponges. Back and down we have quadrilled over serac and softening snow-bridge, to camp on a quarter inch of gravel, covering water-flooded ice at the forks of the glacier. The horses savvied the crevasses better; nosed and jumped them by instinct, in pathetic impatience at release, and when unpacked, tore away through the scud, down the lower reaches of the ice, leaving Simon and Miller in the lurch. Both return also to the barometer camp, to bring up fresh beasts tomorrow, unless it still storms. For this order, as affecting Simon, many thanks. . . .

The sound of the horse-bell has just died. The drizzle is changing to snow. Again we're cramped in the tent on the sopping ice-gravel, playing detectives on ourselves and everything, to keep from touching the silk wall in the tiniest corner and making it leak. Under us, the sea-island cotton tarpaulin lets water through like tissue-paper. The Professor has just gone out to whirl a glass tube about his head—a thermometer, I think. He reports finer snowflakes. Every now and then we peek out under the flap, carefully lifting the soggy boots that keep it down and extend it. Of mountain ascents we don't say much. A snow slide roars down somewhere, and Fred observes, "Another lumber wagon." Every now and then the Professor clears his throat. Nothing is said of our rebuff, or of the future. . . .

Well, the caribou meat is stewed in the granite plate. The pea soup is slowly coming to a boil.

August 21st—Four inches of snow fell last night, and twice I unloaded the tent wall, which was pressing down and wetting us. I thought that the Professor would never grunt over and light the stove—but what was the use? You couldn't see the packsaddles in the fog ten feet from camp. Toward noon,

Fred and I felt our way northeast up the glacier, rounding the hill of dirty ice-blocks, visible from so far down the valley. The Professor went exploring south, along the ridge leading evenly to the highest point of the front range, but condemned for its length and indirectness as a route to the supposed head of Peters glacier.

Unroped in the driving snow, King and I wound among the sheer crevasses of the serac, where you could look down from four to four thousand feet. We poked with ice-axes, crawled from little ridge to ridge of hard snow. We gained the foot of a col joining the ridge that bisected the glacier. It looked possible to climb; at least, everything else was perpendicular. We started, when out from the white gloom below, and refracted to a spiritual nearness, tinkled a horse-bell. So Simon, afraid to be left behind, had brought up the horses despite the storm. We kept on harder; turning to the left around the spur, shinning the upper walls of crevasses where the glacier became almost hanging; higher, higher, till we topped the soiled snow-blocks, and steps had to be cut in the crevassed cliffs. More quadrilling to gain steep snow-bridges, and one huge crevasse where if you slipped you shot into the eternal like slush down a gable. I missed a jump on the first try, and slid back—a little. Towering ever above, swam the wall, now to waver to sheerness, now settling to a human angle, with the refractive trick of all snowy places even in clear weather in Alaska. So we plugged blindly on in the storm, where no foot had ever trod, up the scaffold of the highest peak on the continent.

Should we hit for the ridge's summit? Could more be proved from the top than from yesterday's height? Was this slope practicable for heavy packs? I was ardent, Fred apathetic. We kept on. The névé steepened, and we struck a rock gulley, lifting our bodies by our arms. Not a word spoke we. Vaguely we discerned the dark ice-blocks below, quivering deeper and deeper through the shaking flakes; vaguely the smooth slope, where the Professor had gone, arose and extended with us. Now treacherous, pasty granite pierced the snow. We'd stop to discuss if packs could be got up here. Now I was willing to return; but no, Fred had started, and must reach—somewhere. Two rock pinnacles, which had tantalized for an hour, neared in the likeness of those cliffs in Whymper's drawing of where old Humboldt met defeat on Chimborazo. We passed them. The coulée divided, and we came out upon a little nub of decaying granite. The storm seemed to thin. Light, like the first streak of winter dawn, settled upon the long ridge opposite. Suddenly, what we believed to be the top of our slope stretched itself a full thousand feet higher into the sky; and steeper, steeper. "Look, look!" I cried, and if the ridge had crumbled with us into the valley, we should have still stood staring.

That was enough for Fred. It was after four o'clock. Rock had ended. Sheer, hard névé, covered with six inches of fresh snow, down which balls were even now grooving trails, alone filled heaven. The aneroid said nine thousand feet. Fred crawled to the edge of the granite nub, to gaze straight down the most disturbing distance yet, into the abandoned amphitheatre of yesterday. When I look into such places, I have a feeling—not vertigo, not exactly fear, that worries me. I think too fast and too much, and of impulses which are not quite sane. So, down we slid, again defeated, Fred recklessly, I carefully bridging the crevasses; past the Humboldt cliffs, where the snow shut in denser than ever, and the long white ridge became a dark, magic line over the shadowy glacier.

Four horses were shivering on the gravel humps near camp. Miller was in the tent, making pea soup. From a distance, Simon and the Professor approached wearily. "We didn't think that you'd go so far," said the Professor, when we told that our ridge could be climbed, possibly with heavy packs. He paid little attention. "But you see," he discouraged, "even if it can, we don't know what's beyond. The problem is," etc. and he went on to tell how he and Simon had looked into a valley beyond the long ridge toward Mount Foraker, where the slopes were better, he said, and "we can get around to the main mountain on the divide between them"—(McKinley and Foraker, doubtless)—and where the rock was "much better, dark, apparently slate, and not that treacherous granite." Then he ordered to pack up and return the whole outfit down to the barometer camp!

Wondering how the weather could have allowed him to see so much in the next valley south, I protested mildly, "I hate to leave this place so soon and so suddenly." "So do I," he answered, "but what else is there to do?" And then recurred to me what I had left there in mid-air with Fred, that on a mountain of this size, unexplored, yet unseen in its entirety, it was foolish to stake all on a dash up on questionable pinnacle found blindly in a ten days' storm.

We started down to the valley—irony of ironies—as the snow clouds overhead boiled in the forgotten gold of sunset; and under a shreddy cloud edge draping the glacier, the forbidden tundra, far as the eye could reach, shone clean and rosy. . . .

Just now, after cleaning all the soggy food and stuff out of the large tent, and crawling into our steaming bags in the old comfortable way—feet on dunnage, heads on pants and sweater wrapped in poncho to extend the wall and get the drip—Simon made Fred and me very, very tired. "Well," said the kid, with most transparent bravado, "now I think that our chances for getting to the top of McKinley are brighter than ever. We'll get around to the south side of this glacier tomorrow, where the Professor explored, and we're practically certain of finding a good way to the summit of this front range."

Neither Fred nor I spoke. That sort of insincerity makes me boil. As if it would do any good in such a story-book, Arctic traveler-fashion, to *lie* in order to keep up our spirits. Pretty examples of courage men must be to rig up a fool's paradise around them to give them nerve. Victory lies first with who best faces the darkest side of the picture, and fights upward from the worst. Wonder if Simon wasn't parroting the Professor.

Did Peary Reach the North Pole?

BY DAVID ROBERTS

Robert Peary has long been credited as the first man to reach the North Pole. Certainly, no man worked harder to get there. His declaration of triumph in 1909 captivated the world, despite being marred briefly by fellow explorer Frederick Cook's claim to have reached it several days earlier. The controversy continued for some time, but Cook was eventually discredited. Peary's drive to the pole was remarkable on several fronts, not the least of which because it included an African-American, Matthew Henson.

Over the years, several attempts have been made to show that Peary, while close, probably did not actually reach the pole. Other studies have concluded that he almost certainly did. The truth will never be known. Peary was widely considered a man of great integrity, but he also must have felt the immense pressure to succeed with his polar quest after so many failures—and with so many other would-be explorers breathing down his neck.

The following examination of the Peary controversy is from *Great Exploration Hoaxes*, by David Roberts, a fascinating look at fake explorations through the centuries.

★　★　★　★　★

In 1908 the most coveted prizes in terrestrial exploration were the Poles. Antarctica had seen the dramatic rivalry of Scott and Shackleton and was to witness three years later Amundsen's clockwork success and the desperate retreat and deaths of Scott's polar party, an ordeal that still forms a canonic lesson in heroism and self-sacrifice for British schoolboys. There had been schemes for sailing to the North Pole as early as the Renaissance, but it was only after 1870 that explorers pursued the quest in earnest.

Seduced by the *a priori* idea of an "open polar sea," the first adventurers tried to push to the Pole by steamship from Spitsbergen, Greenland, and

Siberia. They met, of course, unrelenting and apparently permanent ice. The 1890s gave birth to two extraordinarily innovative attempts to reach the Pole. Between 1879 and 1881 the ill-fated De Long expedition's ship *Jeanette* had drifted, frozen inextricably in the ice, from near the Bering Strait to the New Siberian Islands. The crew abandoned her and reached the delta of the Lena River, but most of them died of starvation.

Three years later relics from the *Jeanette* were discovered on the southwest coast of Greenland. Thus was the existence of the remarkable drift of the polar ice pack discovered. A plucky Norwegian named Fridtjof Nansen decided to use this discovery to "hitchhike" toward the Pole. He had his ship, the *Fram*, designed specially to resist the ice by means of a hull shape that would cause it to be squeezed up on top of the floes rather than crushed between them. In 1893 he traversed the Northeast Passage to the New Siberian Islands, headed north, and deliberately let the Fram get frozen in. For a year and a half the ship drifted slowly northwest with the pack. When it began to trend southward again, Nansen and one companion set off on skis, with twenty-eight dogs, three sledges, and two kayaks for crossing open leads. They had no hope of rejoining the *Fram*, but planned to reach the Pole and make their way back to civilization unaided.

This brilliant and nervy scheme was defeated by the unexpected southerly drift of the ice the two men were walking on. They were, in effect, traveling in the wrong direction on a treadmill. They did reach 86° 13'6" N, the closest to the Pole any human beings had ever been. Their eventful return journey included a successful wintering over in Franz Josef Land, where one day in 1896 they were accidentally found by an English expedition, whose ship took the two explorers home. The *Fram*, under the able captainship of Otto Sverdrup, escaped the ice in the same spring and steamed home under its own power. Not a single life had been lost.

The next year a Swede named Salomon Andrée set in motion an equally bold scheme—to balloon to the North Pole. From Spitsbergen, with two companions, on July 11, 1897, Andree lifted off in the *Eagle*. His plan was to fly all the way across the Arctic Ocean to Alaska. A single homing pigeon launched from the balloon was captured on a Norwegian sealer. The three aviators disappeared.

Thirty-three years later, purely by chance, a scientific expedition came upon the trio's last camp on White Island. They found the remains of two of the men, the grave of the third, and numerous pieces of gear, notebooks, and diaries, all so well preserved that it was possible to reconstruct the fate of the *Eagle* in considerable detail. Film in the cameras had been kept so well by the cold that it was successfully developed after a third of a century!

The *Eagle* had lasted only three days in the air. What had caused it to come down was no miscalculation on Andrée's part, but the accumulation of ice on the top surface of the balloon. The three men had inadvertently discovered that future bane of fixed-wing planes, icing. Undaunted, the trio had set out southward over the ice and had reached White Island. Their diaries indicated that they were surviving well, with no shortage of game—but the entries stopped abruptly twelve days after the arrival on the island. Even today the cause of the three men's deaths remains a mystery. A leading theory hypothesizes that they were poisoned by an overdose of Vitamin D from eating polar bear liver.

It was becoming evident that the key to reaching the North Pole would have to involve dogsledging. The single man most responsible for adapting sledging to the polar effort, as well as the one who seemed most obsessed by that goal, was Robert E. Peary, who devoted twenty-four years of his life to reaching the northernmost point on earth.

In 1885, when he was twenty-nine, having been absorbed for years in the writings of Arctic explorers, Peary wrote himself a memorandum calling for "an entire change in the expeditionary organization of Arctic research parties." The next year he made his first trip to Greenland. Six subsequent expeditions between 1891 and 1906 took Peary north, as he probed the topography for the best route to the Pole and perfected his sledging technique. On the last expedition he reached 87° 6' to establish a new farthest north. By 1908 Peary was confident that he knew how to attain the Pole. His logistical attack depended on the coordination of several details, each of which gave him the maximum advantages; the establishment of a winter base at Cape Sheridan, on the north coast of Ellesmere Island, close to the northernmost land in the Western hemisphere; the use of Eskimo dogs and Eskimo drivers; and a pyramidal support system by which early parties would carry supplies successively farther north and retreat from predetermined latitudes, leaving the supplies to boost the final party safely to the Pole and back. It was analogous to the kind of pyramidal logistic effort that Scott was to utilize in reaching the South Pole, as well as that employed forty years later when the British at last climbed Everest.

The years of perfecting a system had taken their toll on Peary, however. He had lost all but two of his toes to frostbite in 1899, the amputations being performed in the field. By 1908 he was fifty-two years old, not nearly as strong as he had been when he first went to Greenland. The years of obsessive preoccupation had turned him, by some accounts, into a fanatically driven man who all too easily antagonized the very men on whose cooperation his success depended.

Peary's early years had given little evidence of the far-flung ambitions that flowered in his maturity; but there were hints. It is an eerie coincidence that, like his future polar adversary, Frederick Cook, Peary lost his father to pneumonia when very young (Peary at two, Cook at five); and like Cook, Peary suffered from a lisp which he struggled in adulthood to banish. As a child, "Bertie," as his mother called him, got into frequent fights with other boys who called him a sissy. Besides the lisp, he was to suffer all his life from the sense that he was a "poor relation," inferior by breeding to the socially graceful whose acceptance he longed for. Compensation for what he perceived as innate faults may have been the seminal cause for his driving ambition.

But Bertie's biggest problem was his mother. After his father's death she never considered remarriage, but turned her smothering attention to her only child. She brought the young lad up in some ways as if he were a girl, and seems to have projected her own hypochondriacal character onto her son. Relocating in her native Maine, she at first sent Peary away to a series of boarding schools, but was dissatisfied with each and pulled him out. When Robert went to high school in Portland, his mother lived with him in a two-story house in town. When the boy went off to Bowdoin, she insisted on moving to Brunswick—"I am going to college," she announced to dismayed relatives. Throughout his years at Bowdoin, Robert lived with his mother. Upon graduation, the pair moved to Fryeburg, where Robert hoped in vain for a modest career as a civil engineer. Only at the age of twenty-three, with a job in Washington, did he escape his mother's household.

Throughout Peary's adolescence he was tortured by her ailments and illnesses, which conjured up the intolerable prospect of losing her. John Edward Weems quotes a diary entry from the sixteen-year-old Peary:

> About nine o'clock as mother got up to go to bed she suddenly became very weak and cold on her left side so she could not walk. It scared me very much, but she laid on my bed and I chafed her hands and feet till she recovered and then I got the pistol in case of emergency.

The temptation to psychoanalyze Peary is hard to resist. Certainly the Oedipal confusion that he experienced must have been massive. According to a family tradition obviously innocent of its Freudian reverberations, Peary's most vivid memory from his first two years was of watching railroad trains disappear into a tunnel and being terrified they would not reemerge. For the student of his exploration, however, it suffices to wonder how Bertie ever did escape becoming a lifelong mama's boy, how he dared to leave home and get married, let alone run off to the Arctic year after year. In a direct sense his expeditions can be seen as a dogged and continuous effort to sever his mother's apron strings.

At Bowdoin, Peary was, understandably, a loner. He became a good athlete, although he preferred individual to team sports, and an assiduous solitary walker. An influential professor bent his interests toward civil engineering. But when he set up to do business in Fryeburg he had to resort to taxidermy to eke out a living. It was in the local post office that he noticed one day in 1878 a poster advertising drafting work with the Coast and Geodetic Survey in Washington.

Peary's biographer Weems does not record his mother's reaction to the desertion at twenty-three—only that, once ensconced in his job, he often brought her to the capital to visit. Peary's love of nature produced in the deskbound civil servant an increasing wanderlust. His first chance to gratify it came at the age of twenty-four, when the Survey proposed an expedition to study the proposed canal in Central America. He wrote his mother, asking permission. For two weeks she failed to write, and then when she did, she ignored his question. He pressed her again, and at last the answer came: no. Dutifully the son obeyed his mother's wishes, immersing himself instead in reveries about Cortéz and Balboa.

In 1881 he changed jobs, gaining a civil engineering post in the Navy. By managing to get himself "ordered" to participate in a Nicaraguan canal survey three years later, Peary finally, at age twenty-eight, still against his mother's wishes, got to go on an expedition. The Nicaraguan venture was followed in 1886 by a private jaunt to Greenland. For years Peary had been reading Arctic literature, and now, with the headstrong conviction that European explorers had not developed the proper system for travel in the north, he stormed off on the first of his six Arctic adventures. His mother stoutly opposed this trip too, but, curiously, lent him five hundred dollars for it.

At a dancing place in Washington, Peary in 1882 had met the charming and energetic Josephine Diebitsch, the daughter of a Smithsonian scholar. They courted for years, then married in 1888. On their honeymoon in a hotel in Seabright, New Jersey, they were accompanied by Peary's mother. Josephine joined him on two of his major expeditions, and when she gave birth to a daughter in Greenland in 1893, Peary proudly claimed that never in history had a white child been born in so northerly a latitude. The "Snow Baby," as she was nicknamed by the Eskimos, became part of the Peary legend.

All this time, in her self-pitying, guilt-laying letters, Peary's mother continued to oppose her wayward son's Arctic follies, even as he continued to seek her approval. An example, quoted by Weems:

> From my childhood, I was not strong, less so since your birth. In my weakness and loneliness I have tried hard and earnestly to do what I thought was best for you. . . . Now I cannot have your unhappiness laid at my door. Leave me entirely out of the question and do what you think will give you sunshine and happiness. The sudden though not unexpected announcement of your intentions wrung from me a cry of pain—it shall not happen again. All the clothes that you brought home I have put in as good order as my strength and ability would admit. You have only to say what else I can do to assist your preparations. If I have caused you the loss of a night's sleep you will forgive.
>
> Mother.

This meddlesome woman enlisted Peary's wife and child as fellow sufferers, writing him in the midst of one expedition: "I can imagine how much you suffered before you decided to stay another year in that dreary place. I would have borne it for you if I could. I have a mental photograph of you as you turned your face northward away from Jo and baby." Even on her deathbed she managed to transmit her messages of guilt, conveying to the explorer through his cousin that his mother has lost the will to live because he was in the Arctic. Peary's diary entries after her death reveal the extraordinary depth of his grief.

Peary was, it seems, devoted to Josephine. But his loyalty did not keep him from taking a fourteen-year-old Eskimo named Allakasingwah as a mistress, by whom he had at least one child. Greenland gossip suggests that "Ally" was not Peary's only dalliance. With the naïveté of the obsessive character he was becoming, he decorated one of his books with nude photos of Ally, aimed not at prurient minds but "to show physique and muscular development." In 1900, arriving unexpectedly by boat in northern Greenland to support her husband, Josephine ran into Ally, who ingenuously bragged of her relationship with the great explorer. Jo was deeply shocked, and contemplated a year's separation, but in the long run rallied to her husband's defense. "Life is slipping away so fast"—she wrote him shortly after learning about his affair— "pretty soon all will be over."

Over the years Peary's singleminded passion to get to the Pole, far from waning, continued to intensify. His drive can be deduced from that fact that within a month of suffering the amputation of his toes, he was out sledging again, although forced to ride at first or to walk with crutches.

From one expedition to the next Peary modified and perfected his system. One estimate suggests that in his lifetime the man sledged a total of thirteen thousand miles. But the Pole continued to elude him, as what he regarded as bad luck intervened again and again to frustrate his well-laid plans.

As skillful an explorer as he had become, Peary's strongest suit was his knack for drumming up institutional support. The frequent extended leaves form the Navy might have made a joke of his professional career, but by building up a network of influential backers he had made an alternative Arctic career for himself far beyond the dreams of the once-unemployed civil engineer.

By 1908, besides the strong support of the American Geographical Society, the American Museum of Natural History, and the National Geographic Society, Peary could rely on the "Peary Arctic Club" to provide a financial base, generate publicity, and lend an air of graybeard expertise to his upcoming eighth expedition. His well-chosen team included men who would become familiar names in Arctic exploration: George Borup and Donald MacMillan, for both of whom this was the first expedition; Matthew Henson; and Captain Bob Bartlett.

By this point in his life, Peary had begun to think of the region between northern Greenland and Ellesmere Island as his real estate. The route to the Pole was "his" route; even the inhabitants were "his" Eskimos. It was with considerable vexation, then, that in the middle of his preparations in 1907 he heard that Frederick Cook, who had been Peary's surgeon on the 1891–92 expedition, was planning an Arctic trip of his own. The vexation increased when Peary's party arrived at Etah, Greenland, to learn that Cook had been there and had left with two Eskimos on a sledging voyage, reportedly to try to reach the Pole. But no one in Peary's party was worried that Cook had a chance of succeeding: it was demonstrably impossible to travel such distances so light. Peary's wrath had much to do with the fear that Cook might have employed some of "his" native dogs, but was perhaps really grounded in the irrational proprietary obsession he now felt for the Smith Sound route to the Pole.

Peary was fairly confident that his eighth expedition was going to succeed. But he also knew that it was destined to be his last try: age, weariness, and the condition of his feet, which continued to be achingly sensitive to the cold, dictated as much.

The key man in his party was the Newfoundlander Bartlett, a brilliant and good-natured sledger who had proved his stuff on the 1905–6 expedition. Peary's plan put each of his principals in charge of a team of men and dogs with prearranged turnaround duties in support of his own polar party. Bartlett was to leave land first and break trail all the way to the last retreating point. There seems, however, to have been some confusion as to whether Bartlett would go on to the Pole himself.

Almost as important was Henson, Peary's oldest accomplice, a former manservant whom Peary had met in Washington and invited to Nicaragua. Henson, as that ultimate rarity, a Negro in the Arctic, has since been championed as a forgotten hero of exploration. It is interesting to look at Peary's view of the man, because he was to become the only non-Eskimo chosen to accompany the leader to the pole itself. In *The North Pole*, a book which, curiously, Peary had ghostwritten for him, but which consistently reflects his views, he indicated about Henson: "While faithful to me, and when with me more effective in covering distance with a sledge than any others, he had not, as a racial inheritance, the daring and initiative of Bartlett, or . . . MacMillan, or Borup."

Because of their "racial inheritance of ice technic," the Eskimos were regarded by Peary as more necessary in his final dash than any white men—but only in a subservient role. "Of course they could not lead, but they could follow and drive dogs better than any white man." What Peary never acknowledges is that his mind may have been influenced from the start by the knowledge that neither the Eskimos nor Henson knew how to take observations of latitude and longitude. And Bob Bartlett did.

On July 6, 1908, *The Roosevelt* steamed down the East River out of New York, shortly after the President himself had come on board and eagerly approved all the paraphernalia. The ship made an uneventful trip up through Smith Sound and delivered the men at Cape Sheridan on Ellesmere Island, where they spent the winter. The following spring, on February 28, Bartlett led the first party north across the ice from Cape Columbia, the island's northernmost point of land. Other contingents, with varying orders—some were to take out loads, drop them, and return for more supplies—set off within hours or days. In all the expedition comprised 24 men, 19 sledges, and 133 dogs.

On March 14 the first return party turned around at about 84° 30' N. MacMillan retreated the next day from a little farther north. The progress of most of the parties was smooth enough, but there were damnable open leads before which the men had to pause until enough "young ice" formed to support the sledges. The worst lead delayed Peary and Bartlett for more than a week, to the commander's infinite agitation. Borup returned on March 30, to be followed by Ross Marvin, a Cornell professor who was to die under mysterious circumstances on the way back. Before he headed for land on March 26, Marvin took a latitude observation and got 86° 38' N.

Now only Bartlett's and Peary's parties were still pushing north. The effort was beginning to show. Daily marches averaged between 10 and 17 miles, but some days saw dishearteningly meager progress. On April 1 Bartlett took an observation of 87° 46'49"N—a new farthest north, only 133 miles from the Pole. But the day before he had been told by his leader that he would have to return.

Bartlett's autobiography records a sanguine and magnanimous acceptance of the decision—while indicating that it came completely out of the blue. "Don't forget that Henson was a better dog driver than I. So I think Peary's reasoning was sound; and I have never held it against him." But a 1909 interview in the *New York Herald*, when Bartlett was fresh from the Arctic, reveals him "arguing, begging, almost quarrelling" with Peary to be allowed to go on.

> It was a bitter disappointment. I got up early the next morning while the rest were asleep and started north alone. I don't know, perhaps I cried a little. I guess perhaps I was just a little crazy then. I thought that perhaps I could walk on the rest of the way alone. I seemed so near. . . .
>
> I felt so strong I went along for five miles or so, and then I came to my senses and knew I must go back.
>
> They were up at camp and getting ready to start. Never mind whether there were any words or not . . . [Peary] said I must go; so I had to do it. But my mind had been set on it for so long I had rather die than give it up then. When I started on the back trail I couldn't believe it was really true at first, and I kind of went on in a daze.

"Peary's reasoning" has ever since puzzled students of the polar controversy. In *The North Pole* he suggests that besides the factor of Henson's superior sledging when with his commander, Peary was influenced by the reflection that "had I taken another member of the expedition also, he would have been a passenger, necessitating the carrying of extra rations and other impediments. It would have amounted to an additional load on the sledges, while the taking of Henson was in the interest of the economy of weight." This is murky thinking at best. Furthermore, Peary never indicates why the order to return came as such a shock to Bartlett. On other expeditions—notably Scott's to the South Pole and the British on Everest in 1953—the leader deferred deciding who would make up the "summit" party until the last moment, basing the decision on the relative performances of the men up to that point. But the men themselves understood and accepted this procedure. And if performance was the criterion for Peary, no one deserved to go to the Pole more than Bartlett.

The progress of the expedition, then, to 87° 46'N we have on the concurring testimony of Peary and Bartlett. There are some critics who feel that even Bartlett's last observation cannot be automatically swallowed. But the essential mystery of Peary's accomplishment in 1909 begins with Bartlett's turning south on April 1. The leader's last words to his departing lieutenant were, according to Bartlett, "Good-bye, Captain. . . . If we get there it will be the South Pole next and you as leader."

Bartlett had a close call on the way back when he fell through young ice and nearly drowned; his Eskimos saved him and restored him to health. On April 18 he reached Cape Columbia once again, and six days later was back aboard the *Roosevelt*. On his return he learned of the death of Marvin, apparently by drowning. (Years later Knud Rasmussen was to win from the Eskimos involved a confession that one of them had shot Marvin in a quarrel. Though it has no direct bearing on the polar controversy, Marvin's murder may reflect the intense psychological pressure all the returning parties felt.)

Peary himself, with Henson and the four Eskimos with whom he had continued north, regained the *Roosevelt* on April 26, only two days behind Bartlett. The latter recorded the reunion thus:

> I ran out on the ice to meet him. He looked haggard but not weak. He grasped my outstretched hand while I exclaimed: *"I congratulate you, sir, on the discovery of the Pole!"* "How did you guess it?" he asked, laughing at my excitement.

Peary's story of his triumph, as later told in *The North Pole*, was a straightforward one, on the surface. The day after Bartlett departed, April 2, the polar party headed north. At once they made better distances than they had been able to cover at any time so far. Peary wanted to guess thirty miles for the first day's sledging, but contented himself with a conservative twenty-five. He was able to keep up that average for the next four days as well, despite numerous small leads and pressure ridges.

> Many laymen have wondered why we were able to travel faster after the sending back of each of the supporting parties, especially the last one. To any man experienced in the handling of troops this will need no explanation. The larger the party and the greater the number of sledges, the greater is the chance of breakages or delay for one reason or another. A large party cannot be forced as rapidly as a small party.

On April 6 Peary took a latitude reading of 89° 57'. He was virtually on top of the Pole. To make sure, he set up camp, then made a short march until a second reading showed that he had passed beyond the Pole. He returned and set out on a zigzagging series of short marches to make sure he had got within a small margin of error of the Pole, and took thirteen separate sun altitudes over the thirty hours he lingered there. He wrote in his diary: "The Pole at last. The prize of three centuries. My dream and goal for twenty years. Mine at last! I cannot bring myself to realize it. It seems all so simple and commonplace."

Ceremonies at the Pole included the planting of five flags, one of which Josephine had given him fifteen years before and which he had carried wrapped around his body on every Arctic trip since. Another was the colors of Delta Kappa Epsilon, Peary's Bowdoin fraternity. Henson was ordered to lead "three rousing cheers," and the Eskimos "were childishly delighted with our success." Peary deposited records in a glass bottle commemorating "the last of the great adventure stories—a story the world had been waiting to hear for nearly four hundred years."

At 4:00 P.M. on April 7 they headed south. A little more than forty-eight hours later they were back at the 87° 47' camp, from which Bartlett had retreated. Peary had ordered double marches for fear of the coming spring tides, and all the way back to land the party covered, on the average, what had been five outward marches in three homeward ones. On April 23 they reached Cape Columbia; three days later they were on board the *Roosevelt*.

When the ice permitted they began their nautical voyage homeward. On August 8, Peary learned from natives that Cook had returned the previous spring with his two Eskimos, no sledges, and no dogs. Later, at the Greenland settlement of Etah, the party discovered that Cook was claiming he had reached the North Pole. In a fury Peary ordered his assistants to question the two Eskimos who had accompanied Cook. In Borup's recorded interview the Eskimos testified that Cook had never gone out of sight of land. Instead of heading toward the Pole, the trio had circled along the north shore of Ellesmere Island, rounded Alex Heiberg Island and headed south, cut north of Devon Island, wintered at Cape Sparbo, and returned via the southeastern shores of Ellesmere Island and Smith Sound to Annoatok, a little north of Etah. If so, it was an extraordinary journey in its own right—but nothing remotely connected with an attempt on the Pole.

Peary reached Indian Harbor in Labrador on September 6, 1909, and immediately wired the news of his success to the States. To his deep chagrin, Cook had scooped him by five days, announcing the attainment of the Pole from Lerwick in the Shetland Islands, where he had stopped en route to Copenhagen.

Thus began the great polar controversy. In its first stages Cook won all honors. He was given a tumultuous welcome in Copenhagen. Peary seemed to damage his case by viciously attacking Cook's claim, while Cook magnanimously offered Peary congratulations for also reaching the Pole. As mentioned in the previous chapter, an early poll of readers conducted by a Pittsburgh newspaper produced 73,238 supporters of Cook, only 2,814 supporters of Peary.

Cook's case began to crumble only when he was asked to produce the records of his observations. He delayed, maintaining that his instruments were still in Greenland. When he finally offered Copenhagen authorities only typewritten transcripts of alleged field notebooks, the examiners rejected his claim. But Peary, too, was refusing to produce records, on the ostensible grounds that he was afraid Cook might steal his observations.

The exceptionally bitter and prolonged battle between partisans of Cook and Peary is too complex and frankly, too tedious to summarize comprehensively here. Suffice it to say, in dealing with Cook's ultimately preposterous claim, that, despite modern "true believers," there is not even a shadow of a chance that he reached the Pole. The case against his claim rests on the probability that he did not know how to navigate out of sight of land; on the Eskimo testimony recorded by Borup; on the vagueness of Cook's own account; on the demonstrated hoax on Mount McKinley two years before; and on the logistical impossibility of reaching the Pole over four hundred miles of difficult ice, barren of game, without any help from supporting parties.

In the subsequent furor, as Cook began to be discredited, Peary was aided by a subconscious superstition on the part of the public; in such a dispute, it seemed to feel, one man had to be the charlatan, the other the honest man. If that assumption didn't hold, it was easier for most observers to entertain the possibility that both Cook and Peary had reached the Pole than to contemplate the idea that both had pretended to.

Eventually Peary submitted his records to a "subcommittee on research" appointed by the National Geographic Society. This three-man group made a rather casual investigation and certified Peary's achievement. The result was perhaps not unexpected, in view of the fact that the society was one of Peary's chief sponsors, and each of the three men was a personal friend of the explorer. Peary also hired two men from the Coast and Geodetic Survey to go over his data. They concluded that the commander had "probably passed within one and six-tenths geographic miles of the North Pole."

Encouraged by these pats on the back, in 1911 Peary supporters (and, *sub rosa*, Peary himself) lobbied to get through the House of Representatives a bill that would officially credit him with the Pole and retire him from the Navy as a rear admiral. The Senate had passed just such a bill already. But a small group of House members balked at rubber-stamping the achievement, and started asking some very close questions. Two in particular, Congressmen R. B. Macon of Arkansas and Ernest Roberts of Massachusetts, displayed a rare geographical acumen, and more than once had Peary squirming before their questions. When the vote came, however, the bill passed 154 to 34. Peary was made rear admiral and given a pension of $6,500 annually for life.

He retired with Josephine and his two children to Eagle Island, Maine, where he spent the last nine years of his life in relative tranquility. He dabbled during these years as a government adviser and champion of navigation. In 1917 he was stricken with pernicious anemia, the malady that took his life three years later. He died relatively secure in the knowledge that posterity had awarded him the palm; and in fact nearly all Americans who give the question a second thought today assume that Peary was the first to reach the North Pole.

It was not only the partisans of Cook, plugging away indefatigably for decades in their effort to restore their fallen hero, who were left uneasy by seeing Peary's claim cast in bronze. More than one explorer harbored private doubts about that final dash to the Pole; and a succession of students of the Arctic kept the controversy alive in print.

A Congressman from North Dakota, Henry Helgeson, who was originally dragged into a grass-roots pro-Cook movement, turned his scrutiny in 1916 to the loopholes in Peary's testimony. He found that five short years after the previous House investigation, he could hardly find a copy of its transcript. As he began poking into other spurious Peary discoveries, like the chimerical "Crocker Land" discovered on the 1905–6 expedition, he became convinced that Peary's 1909 claim was a fraud. He made himself a student of the journey, entering pages of informed analysis of the Peary record in the *Congressional Record*, and on August 2 introduced a bill to repeal the 1911 act that had given Peary his laurels and his pension. By now Helgeson was disenchanted with Cook, too, and dissociated himself from the forces trying to resuscitate the doctor's blasted fortunes.

Peary wrote out a court-martial threat against Helgeson, but was saved by an act of fate. The Representative died suddenly on April 10, 1917, and the budding Congressional interest in reopening hearings died with him.

Over the years some of the top Arctic explorers, like Roald Amundsen and Adolphus Greely, publicly expressed their disbelief in Peary's claim. Their demurrals were met with howls of indignation from the National Geographic Society and its brethren, for whom Peary had begun to seem a patriotic monument. Leaving aside the confusion and vagueness about just what kind of observations Peary had taken to ascertain where he was, students of the question were most skeptical about the astounding, sledging distances Peary claimed to cover once he had parted from Bartlett.

In 1929 a Britisher, J. Gordon Hayes, published what was to that date the best analysis of Peary's distances. From Cape Columbia outward to 87° 47', Bartlett's turnaround point, Peary averaged only 9.3 miles per day. His six best consecutive days yielded an average of 15.3. Suddenly, once there were no witnesses who could make observations, Peary made five days in a row to the Pole at an average, by his own reckoning of 26 miles per day.

Were this true, it would have been remarkable enough. But the most astounding feat of all was Peary's alleged return from the Pole to 87° 47'N— 133 miles at the very minimum—in 2¼ days. *The North Pole* disguises these unbelievable marches by making no mention of distances covered, but only of forced "double marches" on very little sleep. Yet the distances can be deduced easily from the text. Haye's step-by-step analysis reveals that, according to his own text, Peary traveled 429 miles to, around, and back from the Pole between April 2 and April 9, with "a few hours" of sleep mentioned only six times. In other words, according to Peary, six already deeply fatigued men, going on virtually no sleep, are supposed to have averaged more than 53 miles per day of difficult sledging.

In 1906 Peary had claimed the world's record for speed over the ice pack, around 30 miles per day. It hardly seems credible that, had he three years later consistently doubled and at times tripled that record, he would fail to mention it even in passing. As Hayes wrote, "Is not this a peculiar, not to say a suspicious, circumstance? Everyone knows that to hide his light under a bushel was not one of Peary's failings."

An average of 50 miles per day, Hayes goes on to point out, "is comparable only to the world's walking record, made in a few ounces of clothing." Certainly no one since has been able to approach Peary's apparent sledging times: one of the greatest Arctic explorers, Knud Rasmussen, averaged 36.6 miles per day in Greenland in 1912, which may be the legitimate all-time record. And the interior of Greenland is smooth icecap, unlike the polar pack with its constant pressure ridges and open leads.

If the impossible distances were not proof enough that Peary failed to reach the Pole, Hayes amassed a bookful of self-contradictions, navigational errors, and exaggerations that further discredited the claim. Hayes was confident that posterity would soon correct the record: "It is most improbable that Arctic history will be falsified." None of Peary's defenders ever began to answer the objections of Hayes and a half-dozen other critics. Yet such is the obstinacy of "heroism" or perhaps the power of institutions like geographical societies to sway public opinion, that as the decades passed the polar controversy receded like a bad memory, leaving a paradoxical confirmation of Peary's outlandish "dash" to the Pole.

Bob Bartlett seemed to have no trouble swallowing Peary's distances. In his autobiography this uncomplicated and honest man dismissed the controversy as so much sour grapes:

> There was no point falsifying his position even if he had been that sort of man. It was an easy jaunt to the Pole from where I left him, and conditions were improving right along. Anyway, the Eskimos never keep a secret. And they knew well in which direction he was going.

In the 1960s John Edward Weems was given access to Peary's personal papers in order to write a "definitive" biography. Weems took everything in *The North Pole* at face value, summarized the controversy as if it were merely a nasty conspiracy of pro-Cook forces, avoided the stickier questions (like the sledging distances) entirely, and dismissed scoffers with the kind of indignation one might expect from, say, close relatives of Robert Peary. Weems's popular book did much to teach a new generation of readers that Peary had undoubtedly reached the Pole.

In 1973 Dennis Rawlins published a book that must be regarded as the definitive analysis of the Peary controversy. His conclusion is unequivocal.

Peary may have gotten within 100 miles of the Pole, but he could not possibly have reached it. Besides reviving the qualms of Hayes and others about sledging times and sharpening the unanswered questions from the Congressional cross-examination, Rawlins, who was trained as an astronomer, made a devastating attack on Peary's "observations." The crux of this fairly technical matter is as follows: In the far North observations of latitude are fairly simple to make; they require only a record of the sun's altitude at local noon time. Even if one does not know what time noon is, a series of altitudes through the day will yield a highest one, which determines one's latitude. Because this observation is easy to make in the field, it is also quite easy to fake.

Where Peary's observations are most suspect is in the matter of direction-finding. All the explorers who have ever sledged across the Arctic ice pack have had a great deal of trouble keeping a straight line. There are, of course, no fixed landmarks to take position by; the pack itself is constantly drifting and the numerous detours forced by pressure ridges and leads defeat dead reckoning as a directional resource. In essence, a traveler in the Arctic is lost without regularly noting not only latitude and compass bearing, but also what is called transverse position, or deviation from the beeline between land and Pole. Yet Peary nowhere mentions the latter. Going by compass and dead reckoning alone, he claims to have struck a beeline from Cape Columbia to the Pole and back with an error of less than 0.6°. This "most superhuman aiming achievement in the entire history of Polar exploration," to quote Rawlins, would be the equivalent of "expect(ing) a rocket aimed from Cape Kennedy to hit the moon without any in-flight guidance system."

Some critics have entertained the possibility that Peary was the unwitting dupe of his own observational errors, that he genuinely believed he had reached the Pole even though he had not. Rawlins rejects this speculation on a number of grounds. For one thing, Peary's earlier writings make it clear he knew full well the failings of dead reckoning. He understood the need for observations of transverse position, but those were virtually impossible to fake. Sending back Bartlett, moreover, looks like the premeditated act of a man who knows that even his observations of latitude will not stand up to the checking of a single competent ally.

Peary's defenders have long maintained his innocence on the grounds of character as well as "fact." A man, they claim, who had never lied to anyone would not be the sort to pull off such a colossal hoax at the age of fifty-three. But, as Rawlins, Hayes, and even Representative Helgeson made clear, Peary's whole record as an explorer was checkered with spurious discoveries, exaggerations, and boasts. If we add to that unreliability the personality of a fanatically determined man who had devoted twenty-three years of his life to a goal that now seemed to be slipping away from him for good, we can perhaps understand why he decided to fake the last hundred miles or so to the Pole. His greatest virtue as an explorer was his obsessive will. As Hayes admiringly recalls, "He could stand any amount of physical pain, and stumped about for four weeks, after losing nearly all of his toes, with eight open wounds on his feet!" But the "*daimon*" that "drove him mercilessly" northward on eight successive expeditions must in the end have driven him into the refuge of a hoax.

An interesting question remains: was Matthew Henson privy to the fraud? Rawlins thinks not. Like the Eskimos, Henson had no independent way of knowing whether he was at the North Pole or not. He never directly confirmed the astounding sledging distances claimed by Peary; in fact his own account tends to emphasize that the final marches were only slightly more successful than those just before Bartlett turned back. Henson wrote an article for the *Boston-American* which Rawlins rediscovered after fifty years of neglect. It casts a fascinating light on Peary's behavior during the crucial days of April 6 and 7. According to Henson, as soon as Peary had made his observations from the last camp on April 6 (which he was to claim was situated only six miles from the Pole), he and two of the Eskimos "witnessed the disappointment" of their leader. "His face was long and serious." At first Peary would not speak to Henson.

> "Well, Mr Peary," I spoke up, cheerfully enough, "We are now at the Pole, are we not?"
>
> "I do not suppose that we can swear that we are exactly at the Pole," was his evasive answer.

Peary then spent some time deep in thought—while, we may imagine, he faced the fact that he would never reach the Pole, and pondered exactly what he would have to do to convince the world—and Matthew Henson—that he had done just that. Abruptly he confessed his surprise at being at 89° 57', "having fooled himself in the matter of distance." Henson shook off his glove to shake his leader's hand in congratulation.

> But a gust of wind blew something into his eye, or else the burning pain caused by his prolonged look at the reflection of the limb of the sun forced

him to turn aside; and with both hands covering his eyes, he gave us orders not to let him sleep for more than four hours.

And from that moment on Peary treated his assistant in a strange fashion:

From the time we knew we were at the Pole Commander Peary scarcely spoke to me . . . It nearly broke my heart on the return journey from the Pole that he would arise in the morning and slip away on the homeward trail without rapping on the ice for me, as was his established custom. . . . On board the ship he addressed me a very few times. When he left the ship (for good) he did not speak.

People of the Stone Age

BY VILHJALMUR STEFANSSON

Vilhjalmur Stefansson traveled extensively in the Arctic during the early 1900s. His books, particularly *The Friendly Arctic* and *My Life with the Eskimo*, did much to demystify the lives of Arctic people and their method of survival in the frozen wastes. He was probably best known for espousing the theory that certain tribes of so-called Copper Inuit were the result of a mixture of Norsemen and Inuit, leaving them with lighter skin, hair, and eye color. While few scientists and anthropologists believed this to be true, his "Blonde Eskimos" created quite a sensation at the time.

The following account of one of Stefansson's Arctic journeys from *My Life with the Eskimo* offers a good description of how he liked to travel and the nature of the natives he met.

★   ★   ★   ★   ★

On the 21st of April, 1910, we finally made the long-planned start from Langton Bay on our trip toward Coronation Gulf.

We were now fairly started for the unknown, but no one but myself was very enthusiastic over the enterprise. The reluctance of my people was due in part only (and in less part) to their fear of finding the unknown country gameless—they feared to find it inhabited by a barbarous and bloodthirsty race, of which the Baillie Islands Eskimos had been telling us grotesque tales. These dreaded people were the Nagyuktogmiut, the "People-of-the-Caribou-Antler," who lived far to the east, and who used to come in semi-hostile contact with the Baillie Islanders long ago.

"These people bear the name of the caribou antler," they had told us, "because of a peculiar custom. When a woman becomes of marriageable age her coming-out is announced several days in advance. At the appointed time she is made to take her place in an open space out of doors, and all the men

323

who want wives form a circle round her, each armed with the antler of a large bull caribou. The word is given, and they all rush at her, each trying to hook her toward him with the antler. Often the woman is killed in the scrimmage, but if some one succeeds in getting her alive from the others he takes her for wife. As strength and the skill which experience gives are the main requirements for success, some of the Nagyuktogmiut have a great many wives, while most of them have none. Because so many women are killed in this way there are twice as many men as women among them. We know many stories, of which this is one, to show what queer people these Easterners are. They also kill all strangers." That was the way all stories about the Easterners ended. Like Cato's *Delenda est Carthago*, "they kill all strangers" were the unvarying words that finished every discussion of the Nagyuktogmiut by the Baillie Islanders.

No matter how fabulous a story sounds there is usually a basis of fact; when we at last got to these Easterners we found that the kernel of truth consisted in the fewness of women as compared to men, but this had nothing to do with caribou antlers.

When we finally made our start for the east we were in many respects poorly equipped for spending a year away from any possible sources of supplies other than those which the Arctic lands themselves can furnish. When I had planned this undertaking in New York, I had counted on having good dogs, but the good dogs were now dead. I had counted on Dr. Anderson's company and cooperation, but necessity (chiefly the lack of ammunition for our rifles for the coming year) had dictated that he should go west for supplies, and that I should depend on Eskimo companions alone. I had counted on having a silk tent and other light equipment for summer use, and the lightest and most powerful rifles and high-power ammunition, but during one of our winter periods of shortage of food I had been compelled to abandon many of these things at a distance from which they could not now be fetched. Instead of the ten-pound silk tent, I therefore had to take a forty-pound canvas one, old and full of holes; I had only two hundred rounds for my Mannlicher-Schoenauer 6.5 mm. rifle, and had to piece out with far heavier and less powerful black-powder rifles and ammunition. In all, we had four rifles of different calibres, and a total of nine hundred and sixty rounds of three kinds of ammunition, when the right thing obviously is to have but one kind of rifle and ammunition. Had one of our rifles broken we should have had to throw away the ammunition suited to that gun.

What is right in theory cannot be wrong in practice. Still I fancy that there are few so sure of a theory that they are entirely free from nervousness when they come to stake their lives on its holding good. When our little party of three Eskimos and myself had finally started for the east, they felt, and expressed it, and I felt, but tried to refrain from expressing it, that we had embarked on a serious venture. At Cape Lyon, April 27th, we left behind the farthest point of the mainland upon which any of the American whalers were known to have landed, though some had cruised as far east as the western end of Dolphin and Union Straits in summer, standing well offshore, of course, and never seeing any people.

Cape Lyon is set down by Dr. John Richardson, who coasted this shore in the twenties and again in the forties of the last century, as the eastern limit of former occupation by the people who build permanent earth-and-wood houses, after the manner of the Mackenzie Eskimos, and as, coincidentally, the eastern limit of the bowhead whaling industry as carried on by the prehistoric Eskimos. We soon discovered to be a fact what we might have inferred, that it was Sir John's method of travelling—that of summer exploration by water, when the boats usually stood well off-shore—which had prevented his finding traces of permanent occupation. Following the coast as we did, we found every few miles the ruins of such permanent whaling villages as we had seen in Alaska and in the Mackenzie district. If these were not actually inhabited at the time of Sir John's coasting voyage in 1826, they must have been then but recently abandoned. The most easterly house ruin actually seen by us was near the mouth of Crocker River, though others farther east are almost certain to have escaped us, as the snow was deep on the ground.

Many ethnologists had considered that there was an area of isolation for two hundred or so miles east of Cape Parry, and that the Eskimos of the east and west had not had much or any contact with one another across this supposedly barren stretch; our work has shown that while this may be true for the last hundred years at the most, it was not true farther back. We saw no reason to think that a hundred years ago this coast was any less thickly populated than many other parts of the Arctic coast of America.

We had with us on starting from Langton Bay only about two weeks' supplies. From the outset, therefore, we tried to provide each day food for that day from the animals of the land. In carrying out such a program for a party of four, each had to do his share. My main reliance was the Alaskan man Natkusiak, and the woman Pannigabluk; the Mackenzie River boy Tannaumirk was cheerful and companionable, but without initiative and (like many of his countrymen nowadays) not in the best of health.

Our general plan was that the three Eskimos took care of the sledge, one, usually the woman, walking ahead to pick out a trail through the rough sea ice, and the other two steadying the load and pulling in harness at the same time to help the dogs. If they saw a seal or a bear one of them would go after him while the other two waited at the sledge, cooked a lunch if it was near midday, or made camp if night was approaching. If by camp time no game had yet been seen, Pannigabluk would stay by the camp to cook supper, while the two men went off in different directions to hunt.

That the two should go in different directions was wise, for it doubled the chances of seeing game, but it at times caused unnecessary waste of ammunition and the killing of more meat than was needed. The very first time that both men went out to hunt in this manner, for instance, Natkusiak killed two seven- or eight-hundred-pound bearded seals in one shot, and Tannaumirk a big, fat grizzly bear in four shots. This was meat enough for several weeks if we had (Eskimo fashion) stayed there to eat it up; travelling as we were, heavily loaded through rough ice, we could not take with us more than a hundred pounds of the meat.

Although the Eskimos frequently killed an animal or two if they happened upon them along the line of march, the chief responsibility of food providing was mine. Their main business was getting the sledge ahead as rapidly as convenient, which was seldom over fifteen miles in a working day averaging perhaps eight hours. We were in no hurry, for we had no particular distance to go and no reason to hasten back, but expected to spend the summer wherever it overtook us, and the winter similarly in its turn.

Caribou had been in some numbers on the Parry peninsula before we left home. (We called the Langton Bay district "home" for three years, for, no matter how many hundreds of miles of land and ice separated Dr. Anderson or me from it, we always had at least one Eskimo family there protecting what supplies we had and the scientific collections already made.) Crossing Darnley Bay on the ice we had, of course, seen no caribou; at Cape Lyon the Eskimos saw one yearling, but were unable to get it; and at Point Pierce, five days out from Langton Bay, we were stopped by an easterly blizzard without having yet secured any. The Eskimos, who had "known" all along that we were going into a gameless country, felt sure that the fawn they had seen at Lyon was the most easterly member of the species inhabiting the coast; it would therefore be wise to turn about now, they argued, before the journey back got too long and we got too weak from hunger—all this over huge troughs of boiled meat and raw blubber of the seals killed two days before, on which we were gorging ourselves, for much eating was always our chief pastime when delayed by a blizzard that the dogs would not face. As a matter of fact, what my Eskimos dreaded was not so much hunger, as the possibility of our success in the quest of what to me were the scientifically interesting "people who had never seen a white man," but to them were the dreaded Nagyuktogmiut.

Generally it is only in times of extreme need that one hunts caribou in a blizzard. Not that nine-tenths of the blizzards in the Arctic need keep a healthy man indoors, it is merely that the drifting snow (even when you can see as far as two hundred yards) diminishes may times over the chance you have of finding game. If you do find caribou, however, the stronger the gale the better your chance of close approach without being seen, for these animals, though they double their watchfulness in foggy weather, seem to relax it in a blizzard. In the present instance my reason for looking for caribou was that I wanted to kill a few for the moral effect it would have on my party; for in the midst of abundance they would be forced to fall back on their fear of the Nagyuktogmiut as the only argument for retreat, and this they were a bit ashamed of doing, even among themselves. It was therefore great luck that after a short hunt through the storm I ran into a band of seven cows and young bulls, about five miles inland, southwest from Point Pierce. I came upon them quite without cover, but saw them through the drifting snow at three hundred yards before they saw me—the human eye is a great deal keener than that of the caribou, wolf, or any other four-footed animal with which I have had experience, except the mountain sheep.

By stepping back a few paces till the drifting snow had hidden the caribou again, and then guardedly circling them to leeward, I found a slight ridge which allowed safe approach to within about two hundred yards of where they had been. The main thing in stalking caribou that are not moving is the ability to keep in mind their situation accurately, while you are circling and winding about so as to approach them from a new direction, behind cover of irregular hills and ridges that are of course unfamiliar to you. In this case my plans came suddenly to naught through the caribou appearing on the skyline two hundred yards off. I shot three of them, though we could not possibly use more than the meat of one. The moral effect on my Eskimos of having food to throw away would, I knew, be invaluable to me. Had I killed only one, they would not have believed it to be for any reason other than that I was unable to kill more. This was the only time in a period of fourteen months of continuous living off the country that I shot more animals than I thought we should need, although I often had to kill a single large animal, such as a polar bear or bearded seal, when I knew we should be unable to haul with us more than a small part of its meat.

On the journey eastward along the deserted coast beyond Point Pierce, the Eskimos handled the sledge, made camp and cooked, while I kept the job of food provider. On breaking camp in the morning, I used to get a start ahead of them by leaving when they were packing up and striking about five miles inland, then walking rapidly on my snowshoes parallel to the coast, keeping it and the sledge in sight as best I could.

There were not many adventures fortunately. An adventure is interesting enough in retrospect, especially to the person who didn't have it; at the time it happens it usually constitutes an exceedingly disagreeable experience. On May 2nd, near Point Deas Thompson, through incompetence of my own, I came near to having a serious one; that it did not end badly for me was due to the incompetence of a polar bear. After completely out-maneuvering me at the start, he allowed a fondness for grandstand play to lose him the game at the critical moment.

It happened in the afternoon. As usual, I was hunting caribou eastward along the sea front of the Melville Mountains that lie parallel to the coast a few miles inland. The sledge and the Eskimos were travelling more slowly along the coast and were several miles behind—for one thing, the load was heavy and the ice rough; for another, they used to stop an hour or so each day to cook a lunch. I had seen no caribou all day nor the day before, and our meat was low; therefore I stopped whenever I came to the top of a commanding hill to sweep the country carefully with my binoculars. For several days we had had small luck and food was running low. Ptarmigan there were, but they are uneconomical for a party of four that is to go a year on nine hundred and sixty rounds of ammunition; even the foxes were too small for our notice, though their meat is excellent; but a wolf that came within two hundred yards seldom got by, for a fat one weighs a hundred pounds, and all of us preferred them at this season to caribou—except Pannigabluk, who would not taste the meat because it is taboo to her tribe. This day the wolves did not come near, and the first hopeful sign was a yellow spot on the sea ice about three miles off. It was difficult to determine whether or not it was merely yellow ice. Had my party been abreast of me, or ahead, I should have given up and moved on, but as they were several miles behind I put in a half hour watching this thing that was a bit yellower than ice should be. Now and then I looked elsewhere, for a caribou or grizzly may at any time come out from behind a hill, a polar bear from behind a cake of ice, or a seal out of his hole. On perhaps the sixth or seventh sweep of the entire horizon with the field glasses, I missed the yellow spot. It had moved away and must therefore have been a polar bear that had been lying down; after sleeping too long in one position he had stood up and lain down again behind an ice-cake.

In a moment I was running as hard as I could in the direction of the bear, for there was no telling when he would start travelling or how fast he would go. As soon as I began to suspect what the yellow spot might be, I had taken careful note of the topography of the land with relation to the rough sea ice, for it is as difficult to keep a straight line toward an invisible object among pressure ridges as it is in a forest. I kept glancing back at the mountains as I ran and tried to guide myself towards the bear by their configuration. Every three or four hundred yards I would climb a high pressure ridge and have a look round with the glasses, but nothing was to be seen. I did not, in fact, expect to see anything, unless the bear had commended travelling, in which case he would perhaps expose himself by crossing a high ridge.

When at last I got to the neighborhood of where I thought the animal might be, I climbed an especially high ridge and spent a longer time than usual sweeping the surroundings with the glasses and studying individual ice-cakes and ridges, with the hope of recognizing some of those I had seen from the mountains. But everything looked different on near approach, and I failed to locate myself definitely. I decided to go a quarter of a mile or so farther before beginning to circle in quest of the bear's tracks. My rifle was buckled in its case slung across by back, and I was slowly and cautiously clambering down the far side of a pressure ridge, when I heard behind me a noise like the spitting of a cat or the hiss of any angry goose. I looked back and saw, about twenty feet away and almost above me, a polar bear.

Had he come the remaining twenty feet as quietly and quickly as a bear can, the literary value of the incident would have been lost forever. For, as the Greek fable points out, a lion does not write a book. From his eye and attitude, as well as the story his trail told afterward, there was no doubting his intentions; the hiss was merely his way of saying, "Watch me do it!" Or at least that is how I interpreted it; possibly the motive was chivalry, and the hiss was his way of saying "*Garde!*" Whichever it was, it was the fatal mistake in a game played well to that point. No animal on earth can afford to give warning to a man with a rifle. And why should he? Has a hunter every played fair with one of them?

Afterward the snow told plainly the short—and for one of the participants, tragic—story. I had overestimated the bear's distance from shore, and had passed the spot where he lay, going a hundred yards or two to windward. On scenting me he had come up the wind to my trail, and had then followed it, walking about ten paces to leeward apparently smelling my tracks from a distance. The reason I had not seen his approach was that it had not occurred to me to look back over my own trail. I was so used to hunting bears that the possibility of one of them assuming my own rôle and hunting me had been left out of consideration. A good hunter, like a good detective, should leave nothing out of consideration.

On May 9th, nineteen days out from Langton Bay, we came upon signs that made our hearts beat faster. It was at Point Wise, where the open sea begins to be narrowed into Dolphin and Union Straits by the near approach of the mountainous shores of Victoria Island. The beach was strewn with pieces of driftwood, on one of which we found the marks of recent choppings with a dull adze. A search of the beach for half a mile each way revealed numerous similar choppings. Evidently the men who had made them had been testing the pieces of wood to see if they were sound enough to become the materials for sledges or other things they had wished to fashion. Those pieces which had but one or two adze marks had been found unsound. In a few places piles of chips showed that a sound piece had been roughed down there to make it lighter to carry away.

Prepossessed by the idea that Victoria Island was probably inhabited because Rae had seen people on its southwest coast in 1851, and the mainland probably uninhabited because Richardson had failed to find any people on it in 1826 and again in 1848, I decided that the men whose traces we saw were probably Victoria Islanders who had with sledges crossed the frozen straits from the land whose mountains we could faintly see to the north, and had returned to its woodless shores with the drift timber they had picked up here. We learned later that this supposition was wrong; the people whose traces we found were mainland dwellers, and their ancestors must have been hunting inland to the south when Richardson twice passed without seeing them.

The night after this discovery we did not sleep much. The Eskimos were more excited than I was, and far into the morning they talked and speculated on the meaning of the signs. Had we come upon traces of the Nagyuktogmiut who "kill all strangers?"

Fortunately, my long entertained fear that traces of people would cause a panic in my party was not realized. In spite of all their talk, and in spite of being seriously afraid, the curiosity as to what these strange people would prove to be like—in fine, the spirit of adventure, which seldom crops out in an Eskimo—was far stronger than their fears. We were therefore up early the next morning and were soon on the road.

All that day we found along the beach comparatively fresh traces of people, chiefly wood-shavings and chips. None seen that day was of the present winter, though some seemed to be of the previous summer. But the next morning, just east of Point Young, we found at last human footprints in the crusted snow and sledge tracks that were not over three months old. That day at Cape Bexley we came upon a deserted village of over fifty snow-houses; their inhabitants had apparently left them about midwinter, and it was now the 12th of May.

The size of the deserted village took our breath away. Tannaumirk, the young man from the Mackenzie River, had never seen an inhabited village among his people of more than twelve or fifteen houses. All his old fears of the Nagyuktogmiut who "kill all strangers" now came to the surface afresh; all the stories that he knew of their peculiar ways and atrocious deeds were retold by him that evening for our common benefit.

A broad, but three months' untravelled, trail led north from this village site across the ice toward Victoria Island. My intentions were to continue east along the mainland into Coronation Gulf, but I decided nevertheless to stop here long enough to make an attempt to find the people at whose abandoned homes we were encamped. We would leave most of our gear on shore, with Pannigabluk to take care of it, while the two men and myself took the trail across the ice. This was according to Eskimo etiquette—on approach to the country of strange or distrusted people, non-combatants are left behind, and only the able men of the party advance to a cautious parley.

Tannaumirk was so thoroughly frightened by his own recital of the atrocities committed by the Nagyuktogmiut upon his ancestors long ago, that he let his pride go by the board and asked that he, too, might stay on shore at the camp. I told him he might, and Natkusiak and I prepared to start alone with a light sledge, but at the last moment he decided that he preferred to go with us, as the Nagyuktogmiut were likely in our absence to discover the camp, to surprise it by night, and to kill him while he slept. It would be safer, he thought, to go with us.

Pannigabluk was much the coolest of the three Eskimos; if she was afraid to be left alone on shore she did not show it; she merely said that she might get lonesome if we were gone more than three or four days. We left her cheerfully engaged in mending our worn footgear, and at 2:30 P.M., May 13th, 1910, we took the old but nevertheless plain trail northward into the rough sea ice.

It was only near shore that the ice was rough, and with a light sledge we made good progress. For the first time on the trip we did not have to pull at all in harness. Instead we not took turns riding, two sitting on the sledge at the same time and one running ahead to cheer the dogs on. We made about six miles per hour, which brought us in less than two hours to another deserted village, about a month more recent than the one at Cape Bexley.

As we understood dimly then and know definitely now, each village on the winter migration trail of a sealing people should be about ten miles from the one preceding, and about a month more recent.

The village of a people who hunt seal on level bay ice must not be on shore, for it is not convenient for a hunter to go more than five miles at the most from camp in search of seal holes, and naturally there are no seal holes on land. The inhabitants of a sea village can hunt through an entire circle whose radius is about five miles; the inhabitants of a shore village can hunt through only half a circle of the same radius.

When the frost overtakes the seals in the autumn, each of them, wherever he happens to be, gnaws several holes in the thin ice, one not far from the other, and rises to them whenever he needs to breathe. As the ice thickens he keeps the holes open by continuous gnawing, and for the whole of the winter that follows he is kept a prisoner in their neighborhood; for if he ever went to a considerable distance he would be unable to find a place to reach the air, and would die of suffocation. By the aid of their dogs the Eskimos find these breathing-holes of the seals underneath the snow that hides them in winter, and harpoon the animals as they rise for air. In a month or so the hunters of a single village will have killed all the seals within a radius of about five miles; they must then move camp about ten miles, so that a five-mile circle round their next camp shall be tangent to the five-mile circle about their last one; for if the circles overlapped there would be that much waste territory within the new circle of activities. If, then, you are following such a winter migration trail and come to a village about four months old, you will expect to find the people who made it not more than forty miles off.

In the present case our task was simplified, for the group we were following had been moving in a curve and had made their fourth camp west of the second. Standing on the roofs of the houses of the second camp, we could see three seal hunters a few miles to the west, each sitting on his block of snow by a seal hole waiting for a rise.

The seal hunters and their camp were up the wind, and our dogs scented them. As we bore swiftly down upon the nearest of the sealers the team showed enthusiasm and anticipation as keen as mine, keener by a great deal than did my Eskimos.

As the hunter was separated from each of his fellow-huntsmen by a full half-mile, I thought he would probably be frightened if all of us were to rush up to him at the top speed of our dogs. We therefore stopped our sledge several hundred yards away. Tannaumirk had become braver on near approach, for the lone stranger did not look formidable, sitting stooped forward on his block of snow beside the seal hole. He accordingly volunteered to act as our ambassador, saying that the Mackenzie dialect (his own) was probably nearer the stranger's tongue than Natkusiak's. This seemed likely, so we told him to go ahead. The sealer sat motionless as Tannaumirk approached him; I watched him through my glasses and saw that he held his face steadily as if watching the seal-hole, but that he raised his eyes every second or two to the strange figure of the man approaching. He was evidently tensely ready for action.

Tannaumirk had by now got over his fears completely, and would have walked right up to the sealer, but when five paces or so intervened between them the sealer suddenly jumped up, grasped a long copper-bladed knife that had lain on the snow beside him, and poised himself as if to receive an attack or to be ready to leap forward. This scared our man, who stopped abruptly and began excitedly and volubly to assure the sealer that he and all of us were men of excellent character and intentions.

I was, of course, too far away to hear, but Tannaumirk told me afterward that on the instant of jumping up the sealer began a monotonous noise, which is not a chant, nor is it words—it is merely an effort to ward off dumbness. For if a man who is in the presence of a spirit does not make at least one sound each time he draws his breath, he will be stricken permanently dumb. This is a belief common to the Alaskan and Coronation Gulf Eskimos. For several minutes Tannaumirk talked excitedly, and the sealer kept up the moaning noise, quite unable to realize, apparently, that he was being spoken to in human speech. It did not occur to him for a long time, he told us afterward, that we might be something other than spirits, for our dogs and dog harness, our sledges and clothes, were such as he had never seen in all his wanderings. Besides, we had not, on approaching, used the peace sign of his people, which is holding the hands out to show that one does not carry a knife.

After what may have been anything from five to fifteen minutes of talking and expostulation by Tannaumirk, the man finally began to listen and then to answer. The dialects proved to differ rather less than Norwegian does from Swedish, or Spanish from Portuguese. After Tannaumirk had made him understand that we were of good intent and character, and had indicated by lifting his own coat that he had no knife hidden, the sealer approached cautiously and felt of him, partly (as he told us later) to assure himself that he was not a spirit and partly to see if there were not a knife hidden somewhere under his clothes. After a careful examination and some further parley he told Tannaumirk to tell us that they two would precede us to the village, with Natkusiak and me following as far behind as we were now. When they got to the village we were to remain outside it till the people could be informed that we were visitors with friendly intentions.

As we proceeded toward the village other seal hunters gradually converged toward us from all over the neighboring four or five square miles of ice and joined Tannaumirk and his companion, who walked about two hundred yards ahead. As each of these was armed with a long knife and a seal harpoon, it may be imagined that the never very brave Tannaumirk was pretty thoroughly frightened—to which he owned up freely that night and the few days following, though he had forgotten the circumstance completely by next year, when we returned to his own people in the Mackenzie district, where he is now a drawing-room lion on the strength of his adventures in the remote east.

When we approached the village every man, woman, and child was outdoors waiting for us excitedly, for they could tell from afar that we were no ordinary visitors. The man whom we had first approached—who that day acquired a local prominence which still distinguishes him above his fellows—explained to an eagerly silent crowd that we were friends from a distance, who had come without evil intent, and immediately the whole crowd (about forty) came running toward us. As each came up he would say: "I am So-and-so. I am well disposed. I have no knife. Who are you?" After being told our names in return, and being assured that we were friendly, and that our knives were packed away in the sledge and not hidden under our clothing, each would express his satisfaction and stand aside for the next to present himself. Sometimes a man would present his wife or a woman her husband, according to who came up first. The women were in more hurry to be presented than were the men, for they must, they said, go right back to their houses to cook us something to eat.

After the women were gone the men asked whether we preferred to have our camp right in the village or a little outside it. On talking it over we agreed that it would be better to camp about two hundred yards from the other houses, so as to keep our dogs from fighting with theirs. When this was decided, half a dozen small boys were sent home to as many houses to get their fathers' snow-knives and house-building mittens.

We were not allowed to lend a hand to anything in camp-making, but stood idly by, surrounded continually by a crowd who used every means to show how friendly they felt and how welcome we were, while a few of the best house-builders set about erecting for us the house in which we were to live as long as we cared to stay with them. When it had been finished and furnished with the skins, lamp, and the other things that go to make a snow house the cosiest and most comfortable of camps, they told us they hoped we would occupy it at least till the last piece of meat in their storehouses had been eaten, and that as long as we stayed in the village no man would hunt seals or do any work until his children began to complain of hunger. It was to be a holiday, they said, for this was the first time their people had been visited by strangers from so great a distance that even their country was unknown.

These simple, well-bred, and hospitable people were the savages whom we had come so far to seek. That evening they saw for the first time the lighting of a sulphur match and the next day I showed them the marvels of my rifle.

Return from the Pole

BY ROBERT FALCON SCOTT

Robert Falcon Scott was the classic model of the English explorer: a gentleman with discipline, fortitude, and a strong sense of duty. Years of work went into his planned assault on the South Pole, but Robert Peary's claim to the North Pole led veteran explorer Roald Amundsen to make his own attempt on the South Pole. While Scott planned on using dogs, Siberian ponies, and motorcars to transport supplies, Amundsen had learned from previous expeditions—like Nansen's—that dogs and Nordic skis were the polar explorer's only friends. His approach was ruthless but effective—working the dogs until they wore out and then eating them, with carefully planned supply depots spaced out along the way. His plan was well executed and its success almost anti-climactic.

Scott, on the other hand, soon found that ponies weren't nearly as effective as dogs and his motorcars were rendered useless by the extreme conditions. Still, he pushed on, reaching the pole after much hardship—only to find Amundsen's Norwegian flag already planted in the ice. Amundsen reached the pole on December 21, 1911, Scott on January 4, 1912.

To fall just days short after years of work and immense suffering must have been a tremendous blow. Scott's retreat from the pole is one of the most riveting and tragic chronicles in exploration history, preserved in the journal next to his body that was found by a search party nearly a year later.

★　★　★　★　★

It is wonderful to think that two long marches would land us at the Pole. We left our depot today with nine days' provisions, so that it ought to be a certain thing now, and the only appalling possibility the sight of the Norwegian flap forestalling ours. Little Bowers continues his indefatigable efforts to get good sights, and it is wonderful how he works them up in his sleeping-bag in our congested tent. (Minimum for night -27.5°.) Only 27 miles from the Pole. We *ought* to do it now.

Tuesday, January 16. Camp 68. Height 9,760. T. -23.5°. The worst has happened, or nearly the worst. We marched well in the morning and covered 7½ miles. Noon sight showed us in Lat. 89° 42' S., and we started off in high spirits in the afternoon, feeling that tomorrow would see us at our destination. About the second hour of the march Bowers' sharp eyes detected what he thought was a cairn; he was uneasy about it, but argued that it must be a sastrugus. Half an hour later he detected a black speck ahead. Soon we knew that this could not be a natural snow feature. We marched on, found that it was a black flag tied to a sledge bearer; nearby the remains of a camp; sledge tracks and ski tracks going and coming and the clear trace of the dogs' paws—many dogs. This told us the whole story. The Norwegians have forestalled us and are first at the Pole. It is a terrible disappointment, and I am very sorry for my loyal companions. Many thoughts come and much discussion have we had. Tomorrow we must march on to the Pole and then hasten home with all the speed we can compass. All the day-dreams must go; it will be a wearisome return. Certainly we are descending in altitude—certainly also the Norwegians found an easy way up.

Wednesday, January 17. Camp 69. T. -22° at start. Night -21°. THE POLE. Yes, but under very different circumstances from those expected. We have had a horrible day—add to our disappointment a head wind four to five, with a temperature -22°, and companions labouring on with cold feet and hands.

We started at 7:30, none of us having slept much after the shock of our discovery. We followed the Norwegian sledge tracks for some way; as far as we make out there are only two men. In about three miles we passed two small cairns. Then the weather overcast, and the tracks being increasingly drifted up and obviously going too far to the west, we decided to make straight for the Pole according to our calculations. At 12:30 Evans had such cold hands we camped for lunch—an excellent "week-end one." We had marched 7.4 miles Lat. sight gave 89° 53'37". We started out and did 6½ miles due south. Tonight little Bowers is laying himself out to get sights in terribly difficult circumstances; the wind is blowing hard, T. -21°, and there is that curious damp, cold feeling in the air which chills one to the bone in no time. We have been descending again, I think, but there looks to be a rise ahead; otherwise there is very little that is different from the awful monotony of past days. Great God! This is an awful place and terrible enough for us to have laboured to it without the reward of priority. Well, it is something to have got here, and the wind may be our friend tomorrow. We have had a fat Polar hoosh in spite of our chagrin, and feel comfortable inside—added a small stick of chocolate and the queer taste of a cigarette brought by Wilson. Now for the run home and a desperate struggle. I wonder if we can do it.

Thursday morning, January 18. Decided after summing up all observations that we were 3.5 miles away from the Pole—one mile beyond it and three to the right. More or less in this direction Bowers saw a cairn or tent.

We have just arrived at this tent, two miles from our camp, therefore about 1½ miles from the Pole. In the tent we find a record of five Norwegians having been there, as follows:

> Roald Amundsen
> Olav Olavson Bjaaland
> Hilmer Hanssen
> Sverre H. Hassel
> Oscar Wisting
> 16 Dec 1911

The tent is fine—a small compact affair supported by a single bamboo. A note from Amundsen, which I keep, asks me to forward a letter to King Haakon!

The following articles have been left in the tent: three half bags of reindeer containing a miscellaneous assortment of mits and sleeping-socks, very various in description, a sextant, a Norwegian artificial horizon and a hypsometer without boiling-point thermometers, a sextant and hypsometer of English make.

Left a note to say I had visited the tent with companions. Bowers photographing and Wilson sketching. Since lunch we have marked 6.2 miles S.S.E. by compass (I.e. northwards). Sights at lunch gave us half to three-quarters of a mile from the Pole, so we called it the Pole Camp. (Temp. Lunch -21°.) We built a cairn, put up our poor slighted Union Jack, and photographed ourselves—mighty cold work all of it—less than half a mile south we saw stuck up an old underrunner of a sledge. This we commandeered as a yard for a floorcloth sail. I imagine it was intended to mark the exact spot of the Pole as near as the Norwegians could fix it (Height 9,500). A note attached talked of the tent as being two miles from the Pole. Wilson keeps the note. There is no doubt that our predecessors have made thoroughly sure of their mark and fully carried out their programme. I think the Pole is about 9,500 feet in height; this is remarkable, considering that in Lat. 88° we were about 10,500.

We carried the Union Jack about three-quarters of a mile north with us and left it on a piece of stick as near as we could fix it. I fancy the Norwegians arrived at the Pole on the 15th of Dec. and left on the 17th, ahead of a date quoted by me in London as ideal, viz Dec. 22. It looks as though the Norwegian party expected colder weather on the summit than they got; it could scarcely be otherwise from Shackleton's account. Well, we have turned our back now on the goal of our ambition and must face our 800 miles of solid dragging—and goodbye to most of the day-dreams!

Friday, January 19. Lunch 8.1 miles, T. -20.6°. Early in the march we picked up a Norwegian cairn and our outward tracks. We followed these to the ominous black flag which has first apprised us of our predecessors' success. We have picked this flag up, using the staff for our sail, and are now camped about 1½ miles further back on our tracks. So that is the last of the Norwegians for the present. The surface undulates considerably about this latitude; it was more evident today than when we were outward bound.

Night camp R 2 [A number preceded by R marks the camps on the return journey.] Height 9,700, T. -18.5°, Minimum -25.6°. Came along well this afternoon for three hours, then a rather dreary finish for the last 1½. Weather very curious, snow clouds, looking very dense and spoiling the light, pass overhead from the S., dropping very minute crystals; between showers the sun shows and the wind goes to the S.W. The fine crystals absolutely spoil the surface; we had heavy dragging during the last hour in spite of the light load and a full sail. Our old tracks are drifted up, deep in places and toothed sastrugi have formed over them. It looks as though this sandy snow was drifted about like sand from place to place. How account for the present state of our three-day-old tracks and the month-old ones of the Norwegians?

It is warmer and pleasanter marching with the wind, but I'm not sure we don't feel the cold more when we stop and camp than we did on the outward march. We pick up our cairns easily, and ought to do so right through, I think; but, of course, one will be a bit anxious till the Three Degree Depot is reached. [Still over 150 miles away. They had marched 7 miles on the homeward track the first afternoon, 18½ on the second day.] I'm afraid the return journey is going to be dreadfully tiring and monotonous.

Sunday February 18 R 32. Temp. -5.5°. At Shambles Camp. We gave ourselves five hours' sleep at the lower glacier depot after the horrible night, and came on at about three today to this camp, coming fairly easily over the divide. Here with plenty of horsemeat we have had a fine supper, to be followed by others such, and so continue a more plentiful era if we can keep good marches up. New life seems to come with greater food almost immediately, but I am anxious about the Barrier surfaces.

Monday, February 19 Lunch T. -16°. It was late (past noon) before we got away today, as I gave nearly eight hours sleep, and much camp work was done shifting sledges and fitting up new one with mast, etc., packing horsemeat and personal effects. [Sledges were left at the chief depots to replace damaged ones.] The surface was every bit as bad as I expected, the sun shining brightly on it and its covering of soft loose sandy snow. We have come out about 2' on the old tracks. Perhaps lucky to have a fine day for this and our camp work, but we shall want wind or change of sliding conditions to do anything on such a surface as we have got. I fear there will not be much change for the next three or four days.

R 33 Temp. -17°. We have struggled out 4.6 miles in a short day over a really terrible surface—it has been like pulling over desert sand, not the least glide in the world. If this goes on we shall have a bad time, but I sincerely trust it is only the result of this windless area close to the coast and that, as we are making steadily outwards, we shall shortly escape it. It is perhaps premature to be anxious about covering distance. In all other respects things are improving. We have our sleeping-bags spread on the sledge and they are drying out, but, above all, we have our full measure of food again. Tonight we had a sort of stew fry of pemmican and horseflesh, and voted it the best hoosh we had ever had on a sledge journey. The absence of poor Evans is a help to the commissariat, but if he had been here in a fit state we might have got along faster. I wonder what is in store for us, with some little alarm at the lateness of the season.

Monday, February 20 R 34. Lunch Temp. -13°, Supper Temp. -15°. Same terrible surface; four hours' hard plodding in morning brought us to our Desolation Camp, where we had the four-day blizzard. We looked for more pony meat, but found none. After lunch we took to ski with some improvement of comfort. Total mileage for day, seven—the ski tracks pretty plain and easily followed this afternoon. We have left another cairn behind. Terribly slow progress, but we hope for better things as we clear the land. There is a tendency to cloud over in the S.E. tonight, which may turn to our advantage. At present our sledge and ski leave deeply ploughed tracks which can be seen winding for miles behind. It is distressing, but as usual trials are forgotten when we camp, and good food is our lot. Pray God we get better travelling as we are not so fit as we were, and the season is advancing apace.

Tuesday, February 21 R 35. Lunch Temp. + 9½; Supper Temp. -11°. Gloomy and overcast when we started; a good deal warmer. The marching almost as bad as yesterday. Heavy toiling all day, inspiring gloomiest thoughts at times. Rays of comfort when we picked up tracks and cairns. At lunch we seemed to have missed the way, but an hour or two after we passed the last pony walls, and since, we struck a tent ring, ending the march actually on our old pony-tracks. There is a critical spot here with a long stretch between cairns. If we can tide that over we get on the regular cairn route, and with luck should stick to it; but everything depends on the weather. We never won a march of 8½ miles with greater difficulty, but we can't go on like this. We are drawing away from the land and perhaps may get better thing in a day or two. I devoutly hope so.

Wednesday, February 22 R 36. Supper Temp. -2°. There is little doubt we are in for a rotten critical time going home, and the lateness of the season may make it really serious. Shortly after starting today the wind grew very fresh from the S.E. with strong surface drift. We lost the faint track immediately, though covering ground fairly rapidly. Lunch came without sight of the cairn we had hoped to pass. In the afternoon, Bowers being sure we were too far to the west, steered out. Result, we have passed another pony camp without seeing it. Looking at the map tonight there is no doubt we are too far to the east. With clear weather we ought to be able to correct the mistake, but will the weather get clear? It's a gloomy position, more especially as one sees the same difficulty recurring even when we have corrected this error. The wind is dying down tonight and the sky is clearing in the south, which is hopeful. Meanwhile it is satisfactory to note that such untoward events fail to damp the spirit of the party. Tonight we had a pony hoosh so excellent and filling that one feels really strong and vigorous again.

Thursday, February 23 R 37. Lunch Temp. -9.8°, Supper Temp. -12°. Started in sunshine, wind almost dropped. Luckily Bowers took a round of angles and with help of the chart we fogged out that we must be inside rather than outside tracks. The data were so meagre that it seemed a great responsibility to march out and we were none too happy about it. But just as we decided to lunch, Bowers's wonderful sharp eyes detected an old double lunch cairn, the theodolite telescope confirmed it, and our spirits rose accordingly. This afternoon we marched on and picked up another cairn; then on and camped only 2½ miles from the depot. We cannot see it, but, given fine weather, we cannot miss it. We are, therefore, extraordinarily relieved. Covered 8.2 miles in seven hours, showing we can do 10 to 12 on this surface. Things are again looking up, as we are on the regular line of cairns, with no gaps right home, I hope.

Friday, February 24 Lunch. Beautiful day—too beautiful—an hour after starting loose ice crystals spoiling surface. Saw depot and reached it middle forenoon. Found store in order except shortage oil—shall have to be *very* saving with fuel—otherwise have ten full days' provision from tonight and shall have less than 70 miles to go. [Owing both to the severe conditions and to their disabilities, the Pole Party was now taking the full limit of time allowed for between depots. The oil tins had been opened by the return parties on their way back and the allowance for each man taken out. But the extremes of temperature had perished the leather washers round the stoppers of the tins and in the strong sunlight the oil had tended to evaporate through the stoppers, leaving the Pole Party short of oil at each depot.] Note from Meares who passed through December 15, saying surface bad; from Atkinson, after fine marching (2¼ days from pony depot), reporting Keohane better after sickness. Short note from Evans, not very cheerful, saying surface bad, temperature high. Think he must have been a little anxious. [He was already stricken with scurvy.] It is an immense relief to have picked up this depot and, for the time, anxieties are thrust aside. There is no doubt we have been rising steadily since leaving the Shambles Camp. The coastal Barrier descends except where glaciers press out. Undulation still, but flattening out. Surface soft on top, curiously hard below. Great difference now between night and day temperatures. Quite warm as I write in tent. We are on tracks with half-march cairn ahead; have covered 4½ miles. Poor Wilson had a fearful attack snow blindness consequent on yesterday's efforts. Wish we had more fuel.

Night Camp R 38. Temp. -17°. A little despondent again. We had a really terrible surface this afternoon and only covered 4 miles. We are on the track just beyond a lunch cairn. It really will be a bad business if we are to have this pulling all through. I don't know what to think, but the rapid closing of the season is ominous. It is great luck having the horsemeat to add to our ration. Tonight we have had a real fine hoosh. It is a race between the season and hard conditions and our fitness and good food.

Saturday, February 25 Lunch Temp. -12°. Managed just six miles this morning. Started somewhat despondent; not relieved when pulling seemed to show no improvement. Bit by bit surface grew better, less sastrugi, more glide, slight following wind for a time. Then we began to travel a little faster. But the pulling is still *very* hard; undulations disappearing but inequalities remain.

Camp 26 walls about two miles ahead, all tracks in sight—Evans's track very conspicuous. There is something in favour, but the pulling is tiring us, though we are getting into better ski drawing again. Bowers hasn't quite the trick and is a little hurt at my criticisms, but I never doubted his heart. Very much easier—write diary at lunch—excellent meal—now one pannikin very strong tea—four biscuits and butter.

Hope for better things this afternoon, but no improvement apparent. Oh! For a little wind—E. Evans evidently had plenty.

R 39 Temp. -20°. Better march in the afternoon. Day yields 11.4 miles—the first double figure of steady dragging for a long time, but it meant and will mean hard work if we can't get a wind to help us. Evans evidently had a strong wind here, S.E. I should think. The temperature goes very low at night now when the sky is clear as at present. As a matter of fact this is wonderfully fine weather—the only drawback the spoiling of the surface and absence of wind. We see all tracks very plain, but the pony walls have evidently been badly drifted up. Some kind people had substituted a cairn at last camp 27 The old cairns do not seem to have suffered much.

Sunday, February 26 Lunch Temp. -17°. Sky overcast at start, but able to see tracks and cairn distinct at long distance. Did a little better, 6½ miles to date. Bowers and Wilson now in front. Find great relief pulling behind with no necessity to keep attention on track. Very cold nights now and cold feet starting march, as day foot-gear doesn't dry at all. We are doing well on our food, but we ought to have yet more. I hope the next depot, now only 50 miles, will find us with enough surplus to open out. The fuel shortage still an anxiety.

R 40 Temp. -21°. Nine hours' solid marching has given us 11½ miles. Only 43 miles from the next depot. Wonderfully fine weather but cold, very cold. Nothing dries and we get our feet cold too often. We want more food yet and especially more fat. Fuel is woefully short. We can scarcely hope to get a better surface at this season, but I wish we could have some help from the wind, though it might shake us up badly if the temp. didn't rise.

Monday, February 27 Desperately cold last night: -33° when we got up, with -37° minimum. Some suffering from cold feet, but all got good rest.

We must open out on food soon. But we have done seven miles this morning and hope for some five this afternoon. Overcast sky and good surface till now, when sun shows again. It is good to be marching the cairns up, but there is still much to be anxious about. We talk of little but food, except after meals. Land disappearing in satisfactory manner. Pray God we have no further setbacks. We are naturally always discussing possibility of meeting dogs, where and when, etc. It is a critical position. We may find ourselves in safety at the next depot, but there is a horrid element of doubt.

Camp R 41 Temp. -32°. Still fine clear weather but very cold—absolutely calm tonight. We have got off an excellent march for these days (12.2) and are much earlier than usual in our bags. Thirty-one miles to depot, three days' fuel at a pinch, and six days' food. Things begin to look a little better; we can open out a little on food from tomorrow night, I think.

Very curious surface—soft recent sastrugi which sink underfoot, and between, a sort of flaky crust with large crystals beneath.

Tuesday, February 29 Lunch. Thermometer went below -40° last night; it was desperately cold for us, but we had a fair night. I decided to slightly increase food; the effect is undoubtedly good. Started marching in -32° with a slight north-westerly breeze—blighting. Many cold feet this morning; long time over foot-gear, but we are earlier. Shall camp earlier and get the chance of a good night, if not the reality. Things must be critical till we reach the depot, and the more I think of matters, the more I anticipate their remaining so after that event. Only 24½ miles from the depot. The sun shines brightly, but there is little warmth in it. There is no doubt the middle of the Barrier is a pretty awful locality.

Camp R 42. Splendid pony hoosh sent us to bed and sleep happily after a horrid day, wind continuing; did 11½ miles. Temp. not quite so low, but expect we are in for cold night (Temp. -27°).

Wednesday, February 29 Lunch. Cold night. Minimum Temp. -37.5°; -30° with north-west wind, force four, when we got up. Frightfully cold starting; luckily Bowers and Oates in their last new finnesko; keeping my old ones for present. Expected awful march and for first hour got it. Then things improved and we camped after 5½ hours marching close to lunch camp—22½. Next camp is our depot and it is exactly 13 miles. It ought not to take more than 1½ days; we pray for another fine one. The oil will just about spin out in that event, and we arrive three clear days' food in hand. The increase of ration has had an enormously beneficial result. Mountains now looking small. Wind still very light from west—cannot understand this wind.

Thursday, March 1 Lunch. Very cold last night—minimum -41.5°. Cold start to march, too, as usual now. Got away at eight and have marched within sight of depot; flag something under three miles away. We did 11½ yesterday and marched six this morning. Heavy dragging yesterday and very heavy this morning. Apart from sledging considerations the weather is wonderful. Cloudless days and nights and the wind trifling. Worse luck, the light airs come from the north and keep us horribly cold. For this lunch hour the exception has come. There is a bright and comparatively warm sun. All our gear is drying out.

Friday, March 2 Lunch. Misfortunes rarely come singly. We marched to the [Middle Barrier] depot fairly easily yesterday afternoon, and since that have suffered three distinct blows which have placed us in a bad position. First we found a shortage of oil; with most rigid economy it can scarce carry us to the next depot on this surface [71 miles away]. Second, Titus Oates disclosed his feet, the toes showing very bad indeed, evidently bitten by the late temperatures. The third blow came in the night, when the wind, which we had hailed with some joy, brought dark overcast weather. It fell below -40° in the night, and this morning it took 1½ hours to get our foot-gear on, but we got away before eight. We lost cairn and tracks together and made as steady as we could N. by W., but have seen nothing. Worse was to come—the surface is simply awful. In spite of strong wind and full sail we have only done 5½ miles. We are in a *very* queer street since there is no doubt we cannot do the extra marches and feel the cold horribly.

Saturday, March 3 Lunch. We picked up the track again yesterday, finding ourselves to the eastward. Did close on 10 miles and things looked a trifle better; but this morning the outlook is blacker than ever. Started well and with good breeze; for an hour made good headway; then the surface grew awful beyond words. The wind drew forward; every circumstance was against us. After 4¼ hours things so bad that we camped, having covered 4½ miles [R 46]. One cannot consider this a fault of our own—certainly we were pulling hard this morning—it was more than three parts surface which held us back—the wind at strongest, powerless to move the sledge. When the light is good it is easy to see the reason. The surface, lately a very good one, is coated with a thin layer of woolly crystals, formed by radiation no doubt. These are too firmly fixed to be removed by the wind and cause immediate friction on the runners. God help us, we can't keep up this pulling, that is certain. Amongst ourselves we are unendingly cheerful, but what each man feels in his heart I can only guess. Putting on foot-gear in the morning is getting slower and slower, therefore every day more dangerous.

Sunday, March 4 Lunch. Things looking *very* black indeed. As usual we forgot our trouble last night, got into our bags, slept splendidly on good hoosh, woke and had another, and started marching. Sun shining brightly, tracks clear, but surface covered with sandy frost-rime. All the morning we had to pull with all our strength, and in 4½ hours we covered 3½ miles. Last night it was overcast and thick, surface bad; this morning sun shining and surface as bad as ever. One has little to hope for except perhaps strong dry wind—an unlikely contingency this time of year. Under the immediate surface crystals is a hard sastrugi surface, which must have been excellent for pulling a week or two ago. We are about 42 miles from the next depot and have a week's food, but only about three to four days' fuel—we are as economical of the latter as one can possibly be, and we cannot afford to save food and pull as we are pulling. We are in a very tight place indeed, but none of us despondent *yet*, or at least we preserve every semblance of good cheer, but one's heart sinks as the sledge stops dead at some sastrugi behind which the surface sand lies thickly heaped. For the moment the temperature is on the -20°—an improvement which makes us much more comfortable, but a colder snap is bound to come again soon. I fear that Oates at least will weather such an event very poorly. Providence to our aid! We can expect little from man now except the possibility of extra food at the next depot. It will be real bad if we get there and find the same shortage of oil. Shall we get there? Such a short distance it would have appeared to us on the summit! I don't know what I should do if Wilson and Bowers weren't so determinedly cheerful over things.

Monday, March 5 Lunch. Regret to say going from bad to worse. We got a slant of wind yesterday afternoon, and going on five hours we converted our wretched morning run of three and a half miles into something over nine. We went to bed on a cup of cocoa and pemmican solid with the chill off. [R 47.] The result is telling on all, but mainly on Oates, whose feet are in a wretched condition. One swelled up tremendously last night, and he is very lame this morning. We started march on tea and pemmican as last night—we pretend to prefer the pemmican this way. Marched for five hours this morning over a slightly better surface covered with high moundy sastrugi. Sledge capsized twice; we pulled on foot, covering about 5½ miles. We are two pony marches and four miles about from our depot. Our fuel dreadfully low and the poor Soldier nearly done. It is pathetic enough because we can do nothing for him; more hot food might do a little, but only a little, I fear. We none of us expected these terribly low temperatures, and of the rest of us Wilson is feeling them most; mainly, I fear, from his self-sacrificing devotion in doctoring Oates's feet. We cannot help each other, each has enough to do to take care of himself. We get cold on the march when the trudging is heavy, and the wind pierces our warm garments. The others, all of them, are unendingly cheerful when in the tent. We mean to see the game through with a proper spirit, but it's tough work to be pulling harder than we ever pulled in our lives for long hours, and to feel that the progress is so slow. One can only say, "God help us!" and plod on our weary way, cold and very miserable, though outwardly cheerful. We talk of all sorts of subjects in the tent, not much of food now, since we decided to take the risk of running a full ration. We simply couldn't go hungry at this time.

Tuesday, March 6 Lunch. We did a little better with help of wind yesterday afternoon, finishing 9½ miles for the day, and 27 miles from depot. [R 48.] But this morning things have been awful. It was warm in the night and for the first time during the journey I overslept by more than an hour; then we were slow with foot-gear; then, pulling with all our might (for our lives) we could scarcely advance at rate of a mile an hour; then it grew thick and three times we had to get out of harness to search for tracks. The result is something less than 3½ miles for the forenoon. The sun is shining now and the wind gone. Poor Oates is unable to pull, sits on the sledge when we are track-searching—he is wonderfully plucky, as his feet must be giving him great pain. He makes no complaint, but his spirits only come up in spurts now, and he grows more silent in the tent. We are making a spirit lamp to try and replace the primus when our oil is exhausted. It will be a very poor substitute and we've not got much spirit. If we could have kept up our nine-mile days we might have got within reasonable distance of the depot before running out, but nothing but a strong wind and good surface can help us now, and though we had quite a good breeze this morning, the sledge came as heavy as lead. If we were all fit I should have hopes of getting through, but the poor Soldier has become a terrible hindrance, though he does his utmost and suffers much I fear.

Wednesday, March 7. A little worse I fear. One of Oates' feet very bad this morning; he is wonderfully brave. We still talk of what we will do together at home.

We only made 6½ miles yesterday. [R 49]. This morning in 4½ hours we did just over four miles. We are 16 from our depot. If we only find the correct proportion of food there and this surface continues, we may get to the next depot [Mt. Hooper, 72 miles farther] but not to One Ton Camp. We hope against hope that the dogs have been to Mt. Hooper; then we might pull through. If there is a shortage of oil again we can have little hope. One feels that for poor Oates the crisis is near, but none of us is improving, though we are wonderfully fit considering the really excessive work we are doing. We are only kept going by good food. No wind this morning till a chill northerly air came ahead. Sun bright and cairns showing up well. I should like to keep the track to the end.

Thursday, March 8 Lunch. Worse and worse in morning; poor Oates' left foot can never last out, and time over foot-gear something awful. Have to wait in night foot-gear for nearly an hour before I start changing, and then am generally first to be ready. Wilson's feet giving trouble now, but this mainly because he gives so much help to others. We did 4½ miles this morning and are now 8½ miles from the depot—a ridiculously small distance to feel in difficulties, yet on this surface we know we cannot equal half our old marches, and that for that effort we expend nearly double the energy. The great question is: What shall we find at the depot? If the dogs have visited it we may get along a good distance, but if there is another short allowance of fuel, God help us indeed. We are in a very bad way, I fear, in any case.

Saturday, March 10. Things steadily downhill. Oates' foot worse. He has rare pluck and must know that he can never get through. He asked Wilson if he had a chance this morning, and of course Bill had to say he didn't know. In point of fact he has none. Apart from him, if he went under now, I doubt whether we could get through. With great care we might have a dog's chance, but no more. The weather conditions are awful, and our gear gets steadily more icy and difficult to manage. At the same time of course poor Titus is the greatest handicap. He keeps us waiting in the morning until we have partly lost the warming effect of our good breakfast, when the only wise policy is to be up and away at once; again at lunch. Poor chap! It is too pathetic to watch him; one cannot but try to cheer him up.

Yesterday we marched up the depot, Mt. Hooper. Cold comfort. Shortage on our allowance all round. I don't know that anyone is to blame. The dogs which would have been our salvation have evidently failed. [For the last six days the dogs had been waiting at One Ton Camp under Cherry-Garrard and Demetri. The supporting party had come out as arranged on the chance of hurrying the Pole travellers back over the last stages of their journey in time to catch the ship. Scott had dated his probable return to Hut Point anywhere between mid-March and early April. Calculating from the speed of the other return parties, Atkinson expected him to reach One Ton Camp between March 3 and 10. Here Cherry-Garrard met four days of blizzard; then there remained little more than enough dog food to bring the teams home. He could either push south one more march and back, at imminent risk of missing Scott on the way, or stay another two days at the camp where Scott was bound to come. He decided to stay, but on March 10, at the limit of the dog food, turned homeward, believing there to be enough supplies in the depots further south to bring the Pole Party to the camp.] Meares had a bad trip home, I suppose.

This morning it was calm when we breakfasted, but the wind came from the W.N.W. as we broke camp. It rapidly grew in strength. After travelling for half an hour I saw that none of us could go on facing such conditions. We were forced to camp and are spending the rest of the day in a comfortless blizzard camp, wind quite foul. [R 52.]

Sunday, March 11. Titus Oates is very near the end, one feels. What we or he will do, God only knows. We discussed the matter after breakfast; he is a brave fine fellow and understands the situation, but he practically asked for advice. Nothing could be said but to urge him to march as long as he could. One satisfactory result to the discussion; I practically ordered Wilson to hand over the means of ending our troubles to us, so that any one of us may know how to do so. Wilson had no choice between doing so and our ransacking the medicine case. We have 30 opium tabloids apiece and he is left with a tube of morphine. So far the tragical side of our story. [R 53.]

The sky completely overcast when we started this morning. We could see nothing, lost the tracks, and doubtless have been swaying a good deal since—3.1 miles for the forenoon—terribly heavy dragging—expected it. Know that six miles is about the limit of our endurance now, if we get no help from wind or surfaces. We have seven days' food and should be about 55 miles from One Ton Camp tonight, 6 x 7 = 42, leaving us 13 miles short of our distance, even if things get no worse. Meanwhile the season rapidly advances.

Monday, March 12. We did 6.9 miles yesterday, under our necessary average. Things are left much the same, Oates not pulling much, and now with hands as well as feet pretty well useless. We did four miles this morning in 4 hours 20 min—we may hope for three this afternoon, 7 x 6 = 42. We shall be 47 miles from the depot. I doubt if we can possibly do it. The surface remains awful, the cold intense, and our physical condition running down. God help us! Not a breath of favourable wind for more than a week, and apparently liable to head winds at any moment.

Wednesday, March 14. No doubt about the going downhill, but everything going wrong for us. Yesterday we woke to a strong northerly wind with temp. -37°. Couldn't face it, so remained in camp [R 54] till two, then did 5¼ miles. Wanted to march later, but party feeling the cold badly as the breeze (N.) never took off entirely, and as the sun sank the temp. fell. Long time getting supper in dark. [R 55.]

This morning started with southerly breeze, set sail, and passed another cairn at good speed; halfway, however, the wind shifted to W. by S. or W.S.W., blew through our wind clothes and into our mits. Poor Wilson horribly cold, could [not] get off ski for some time. Bowers and I practically made camp, and when we got in the tent at last we were all deadly cold. Then temp. now midday down -43° and the wind strong. We *must* go on, but now the making of every camp must be more difficult and dangerous. It must be near the end, but a pretty merciful end. Poor Oates got it again in the foot. I shudder to think what it will be like tomorrow. It is only with greatest pains rest of us to keep off frostbites. No idea there cold be temperatures like this at this time of year with such winds. Truly awful outside the tent. Must fight it out to the last biscuit, but can't reduce rations.

Friday, March 16 or Saturday 17. Lost track of dates, but think the last correct. Tragedy all along the line. At lunch, the day before yesterday, poor Titus Oates said he couldn't go on; he proposed we should leave him in his sleeping-bag. That we could not do, and we induced him to come on, on the afternoon march. In spite of its awful nature for him he struggled on and we made a few miles. At night he was worse and we knew the end had come.

Should this be found I want these facts recorded. Oates' last thoughts were of his mother, but immediately before he took pride in thinking that his regiment would be pleased with the bold way in which he met his death. We can testify to his bravery. He had borne intense suffering for weeks without complaint, and to the very last was able and willing to discuss outside subjects. He did not—would not—give up hope till the very end. He was a brave soul. This was the end. He slept through the night before last, hoping not to wake; but he woke in the morning—yesterday. It was blowing a blizzard. He said, "I am just going outside and may be some time." He went out into the blizzard and we have not seen him since. [Oates' body was never found.]

I take this opportunity of saying that we have stuck to our sick companions to the last. In case of Edgar Evans, when absolutely out of food and he lay insensible, the safety of the remainder seemed to demand his abandonment, but Providence mercifully removed him at this critical moment. He died a natural death, and we did not leave him till two hours after his death. We knew that poor Oates was walking to his death, but though we tried to dissuade him, we knew it was the act of a brave man and an English gentleman. We all hope to meet the end with a similar spirit, and assuredly the end is not far.

I can only write at lunch and then occasionally. The cold is intense, -40° at midday. My companions are unendingly cheerful, but we are all on the verge of serious frostbites, and though we constantly talk of fetching through I don't think any of us believes it in his heart.

We are cold on the march now, and at all times except meals. Yesterday we had to lay up for a blizzard and today we move dreadfully slowly. We are at No. 14 pony camp, only two pony marches from One Ton Depot. We leave here our theodolite, a camera, and Oates' sleeping-bags. Diaries, etc., and geological specimens carried at Wilson's special request, will be found with us or on our sledge.

Sunday, March 18. Today, lunch, we are 21 miles from the depot. Ill fortune presses, but better may come. We have had more wind and drift from ahead yesterday, had to stop marching; wind N.W., force four, temp. -35°. No human being could face it, and we are worn out *nearly.*

My right foot has gone, nearly all the toes—two days ago I was proud possessor of best feet. Those are the steps of my downfall. Like an ass I mixed a small spoonful of curry powder with my melted pemmican—it gave me violent indigestion. I lay awake and in pain all night; work and felt done on the march; foot went and I didn't know it. A very small measure of neglect and have a foot which is not pleasant to contemplate. Bowers takes first place in condition, but there is not much to choose after all. The others are still confident of getting through—or pretend to be—I don't know! We have the last *half* fill of oil in our primus and a very small quantity of spirit—this alone between us and thirst. The wind is fair for the moment, and that is perhaps a fact to help. The mileage would have seemed ridiculously small on our outward journey.

Monday, March 19 Lunch. We camped with difficulty last night, and were dreadfully cold till after our supper of cold pemmican and biscuit and a half a pannikin of cocoa cooked over the spirit. Then, contrary to expectation, we got warm and all slept well. Today we started in the usual dragging manner. Sledge dreadfully heavy. We are 15½ miles from the depot and ought to get there in three days. What progress! We have two days' food but barely a day's fuel. All our feet are getting bad—Wilson's best, my right foot worst, left all right. There is no chance to nurse one's feet till we can get hot food into us. Amputation is the least I can hope for now, but will the trouble spread? That is the serious question. The weather doesn't give us a chance—the wind from N. to N.W. and -40° temp. today.

Wednesday, March 21. Got within 11 miles of depot Monday night; had to lay up all yesterday in severe blizzard. [R 60.] Today forlorn hope, Wilson and Bowers going to depot for fuel.

Thursday March 22 and 23. Blizzard bad as ever—Wilson and Bowers unable to start—tomorrow last chance—no fuel and only one or two of food left—must be near the end. Have decided it shall be natural—we shall march for the depot with or without our effects and die in our tracks.

Thursday, March 29. Since the 21st we have had a continuous gale from W.S.W. and S.W. We had fuel to make two cups of tea apiece and bare food for two days on the 20th. Every day we have been ready to start for our depot *11 miles away*, but outside the door of the tent it remains a scene of whirling drift. I do not think we can hope for any better things now. We shall stick it out to the end, but we are getting weaker, of course, and the end cannot be far.

It seems a pity, but I do not think I can write more.

R. Scott

Last entry.

For God's sake look after our people.

Message to the Public

The causes of the disaster are not due to faulty organization, but to misfortune in all risks which had to be undertaken.

1. The loss of pony transport in March 1911 obliged me to start later than I had intended, and obliged the limits of stuff transported to be narrowed.
2. The weather throughout the outward journey, and especially the long gale in 83° S. stopped us.
3. The soft snow in lower reaches of glacier again reduced pace.

We fought these untoward events with a will and conquered, but it cut into our provision reserve.

Every detail of our food supplies, clothing and depots made on the interior ice-sheet and over that long stretch of 700 miles to the Pole and back, worked out to perfection. The advance party would have returned to the glacier in fine form and with surplus of food, but for the astonishing failure of the man whom we had least expected to fail. Edgar Evans was thought the strongest man of the party.

The Beardmore Glacier is not difficult in fine weather, but on our return we did not get a single completely fine day; this with a sick companion enormously increased our anxieties.

As I have said elsewhere, we got into frightfully rough ice and Edgar Evans received a concussion of the brain—he died a natural death, but left us a shaken party with the season unduly advanced.

But all the facts above enumerated were as nothing to the surprise which awaited us on the Barrier. I maintain that our arrangements for returning were quite adequate, and that no one in the world would have expected the temperatures and surfaces which we encountered at this time of the year. On the summit in lat. 85°/86° we had -20°, -3-°. On the Barrier in lat. 82°, 10,000 feet lower, we had -30° in the day, -47° at night pretty regularly, with continuous head wind during our day marches. It is clear that these circumstances come on very suddenly, and our wreck is certainly due to this sudden advent of severe weather, which does not seem to have any satisfactory cause. I do not think human beings ever came through such a month as we have come through, and we should have got through in spite of the weather but for the sickening of a second companion, Captain Oates, and a shortage of fuel in our depots for which I cannot account, and finally, but for the storm which has fallen on us within 11 miles of the depot at which we hoped to secure our final supplies. Surely misfortune could scarcely have exceeded this last blow. We arrived within 11 miles of our old One Ton Camp with fuel for one hot meal and food for two days. For four days we have been unable to leave the tent—the gale is howling about us. We are weak, writing is difficult, but for my own sake I do not regret this journey, which has shown that Englishmen can endure hardships, help one another, and meet death with as great a fortitude as ever in the past. We took risks, we knew we took them; things have come out against us, and therefore we have no cause for complaint, but bow to the will of Providence, determined still to do our best to the last. But if we have been willing to give our lives to this enterprise, which is for the honour of our country, I appeal to our countrymen to see that those who depend on us are properly cared for.

Had we lived, I should have had a tale to tell of the hardihood, endurance, and courage of my companions which would have stirred the heart of every Englishman. These rough notes and our dead bodies must tell the tale, but surely, surely, a great rich country like ours will see that those who are dependent on us are properly provided for.

R. Scott

The Ends of the Earth

BY ROY CHAPMAN ANDREWS

There is very little across the face of the earth that Roy Chapman Andrews did not see in his relentless travels for the Museum of Natural History. He studied whales and saltwater fish species from Alaska to Borneo before turning his attention to land-based explorations, primarily in central Asia. He would eventually spend a great deal of time in the Gobi Desert, searching for signs of the earliest existence of mammals and making large contributions to the world's knowledge of this remote area—one of the last places on earth to be explored extensively.

Andrews was more interested in scientific discovery than adventure, but the early days of the twentieth century provided plenty of both. While he was often working in areas that had been previously explored, his keen observations shed light on a way of life that few in the western world could even imagine at the time.

The following story of his first foray into the steppes of Mongolia is taken from his autobiography, *Ends of the Earth*.

★   ★   ★   ★   ★

Never again will I have such a feeling as Mongolia gave me. The broad sweeps of dun gravel merging into a vague horizon; the ancient trails once traveled by Genghiz Khan's wild raiders; the violent contrast of motor cars beside majestic camels fresh from the marching sands of the western Gobi! All this thrilled me to the core. I had found my country. The one I had been born to know and love. Somewhere in the depths of that vast, silent desert lay those records of the past that I had come to seek.

We had two cars. One of them carried Mr. and Mrs. Ted MacCallie, who were to manage Coltman's trading station in Urga; we occupied the other. It was to be a leisurely trip with stops to shoot antelopes and wolves along the way. We had lots of fun with the gazelle. Nothing on four legs can equal them in speed. Like all plains animals they cannot resist a motor car. It was a fatal fascination which draws them like a magnet from hundreds of yards on either side. They just have to cross in front of it or their lives are ruined.

At first a gazelle will lope along at twenty or twenty-five miles an hour, head up, sometimes leaping into the air as though on springs drawing always closer to the car. Then with a sudden rush he tries to cross in front. He goes just fast enough to keep well away from the motor. One might think he was running at full speed. But just drop a bullet near him and see what happens. He seems to flatten out, his legs are only a blur like the wings of an electric fan, and he really begins to run. After many tests we have put the maximum speed for the first dash at sixty miles an hour. This is a conservative estimate. He cannot maintain a mile-a-minute pace for more than half a mile; then he drops to forty miles an hour at which he can continue for a long distance.

Once while we were following a herd of gazelle we ran over a sharp rise and down the long slope of a wide valley. A wolf, lying asleep behind a rock, suddenly leaped out in front of us. There were a dozen antelope on either side but he was not interested. Neither were they. Then a fat yellow marmot joined the procession, rushed along for a few yards and frantically ducked underground. We seemed to be driving a whole zoological garden. Coltman stepped on the gas but a sand-spit intervened and the fleeing menagerie scattered to the four winds of heaven.

There was a portable Delco electric light plant, destined for the Living Buddha of Urga, packed in the back of MacCallie's car. One of our camps was near a Mongol village. That night Mac rigged a great arc light on a pole for we wanted to give the Mongols a real celebration. To our surprise not one came near us. Next morning when we stepped out of the tent, the village was gone. I rubbed my eyes and looked again. It had been there last night right enough; a dozen *yurts* and perhaps five hundred sheep. Now the place was bare. The Mongols had been so frightened by the strange ball of light suddenly appearing in the desert that they had packed their yurts and left with every man, woman, and sheep!

Superstition is a Mongol's middle name. Anything that he does not understand is attributed to supernatural agency. By this means the lamas (priests) keep their power over the laymen.

Sometimes this superstition becomes most annoying. Last year, in a part of the desert where we were working, there had been no rain for some time. Shortly after we left, torrential downpours swept away half a dozen yurts pitched at the bottom of a steep bluff. The priests had to have an alibi for such a calamity. We were it. Because those foreigners dug bones there, said they, the Gods are angry and produced the floods!

Again rinder-pest had taken a dreadful toll of cattle near one of our fossil deposits. The lamas blamed it all on us. They refused to let us continue work there. But I persuaded the high priest to visit our camp. After three drinks of brandy I showed him twenty-five dollars and asked if he didn't think the Gods could be appeased. He pocketed the money and agreed that it might be done. But he particularly stated that it must be a secret between us two. The Gods would be annoyed, said he, if I mentioned it to any of the other lamas!

Urga, the city of the Living Buddha, is one of the most interesting places I have ever seen. Coltman left us there to return to Kalgan. At that time (1919) it was as free as air. We could come and go without restriction as though we were on the open plains. Today, it is a far different place. Since the Russian Soviet took Outer Mongolia under its "protection" Urga has become a city of suspicion. It is difficult enough to enter, Heaven knows, but to get out is even worse. Every person, stranger or resident, is a potential spy and is watched accordingly.

Both my wife and I were fascinated with the bizarre, medieval life of Urga. It was like a pageant on the stage of the Hippodrome. When a dozen wild nomads in flaming red, yellow or purple dashed at full speed down the main street it seemed that we must be present at some special celebration; that this barbaric spectacle could not be the life of every day.

At that time Urga numbered about twenty-five thousand inhabitants but fully fifteen thousand were lamas. The Living Buddha, who ranked only after the Dalai and Tashi Lamas of Tibet, was the actual head of both church and state. Now he is dead and I saw his mummified body in a very sacred temple which I had entered by a ruse. Then he was old and blind but he had been a gay bird in his day. The stories of his revels with a few chosen spirits were the talk of Urga.

I visited him in his palace beside the Tola River. An amazing place it was, filled with Western inventions gleaned from mail order catalogues of America. The Living Buddha ordered a motor car to be brought from Peking. He seldom rode in it but had much amusement by attaching a wire to the batteries and giving worshiping pilgrims an electric shock. They thought that they had been especially blessed by the Living God!

My wife and I pitched our tent on a beautiful green lawn beside the river. It would have been a charming spot except for the dogs which swarmed like ants about the city. Thousands of them maintained a continual roar around us all through the night and day. Huge black mastiffs they were, savage as wolves and always starving. It was worth one's life to pass through the meat market at night. We never ventured away from camp without a club or pistol.

The Mongols do not bury their dead but throw them out to be devoured by the dogs, wolves, and birds. Almost every day some corpse was dragged down by the river from the lama city. One was left within a hundred yards of our tent. It took just seven minutes for a pack of dogs to tear it into a dozen pieces. It was not a nice sight.

My wife nearly met a horrible death from these same dogs when returning from Mongolia. We were camped for the night at Turin, a great mass of jagged rocks not far from a desert monastery. It was a starlight night and we did not bother to pitch a tent. Our sleeping bags were spread side by side near the car. I had placed two rifles between us on the ground. One was my 6.5 mm Mannlicher; the other a tiny .22 cal. repeater I had used for killing birds. The usual chorus of barking dogs sounded faintly from the monastery but I thought nothing of it. During the night my wife was restless and at two o'clock sat up suddenly, wide awake. In the moonlight she saw a pack of fourteen huge dogs stealthily circling about our camp. As they closed in she screamed. Half awake, I grasped the first rifle my hands touched and fired blindly. It happened to be the .22 Winchester. The tiny bullet caught the huge leader in some vital spot for he sank in his tracks stone dead. As the pack swept by I fired twice more hitting two other dogs. Instantly there was a blood-curdling chorus of yelps, and growls as the wounded animals were devoured by their ravenous comrades.

I never knew where the bullet struck the leader. I dragged him far beyond our camp and the next morning all the remained of his carcass were a few bits of bloody hair. Had my wife not waked at that very second we would never had lived to see another day.

Every family and every caravan owns a dog. They are encouraged to be savage. God help the person that comes near a Mongol *yurt* unannounced. Often a particularly vicious dog is kept in a wooden cage and only allowed free at night to range the compound.

I have had six or eight very narrow escapes from being killed by dogs during my ten years in Mongolia. One night as I rode into Urga on horseback four dogs attacked me. One leaped for my stirrup leather, another for the pony's tail and third caught him by the fetlock. As I reached to draw my rifle from the scabbard the pony kicked wildly rolling over one of the hounds. Instantly the others were on their injured companion tearing him to bits.

From Urga my wife and I went southward into the grasslands. Our equipment was carried in three carts; we, ourselves, rode ponies. For weeks we camped from place to place trapping small mammals, collecting birds and antelope.

Shooting gazelle from motor cars is butchery. Hunting them on horseback is sport. We would ride over the plains scanning the country from every rise, until antelope were sighted. Then ride quietly toward them, gradually edging nearer until they began to run. Almost always they would try to cross in front. With a yell I would be off at full speed, standing in the stirrups, rifle free. Jumping ditches, among treacherous marmot holes, down into valleys and out again, wild with excitement. Then suddenly checking the pony I would throw myself off and begin to shoot. That was real sport. The marmot holes made it exceedingly dangerous and the antelope had much the advantage. They could run twice as fast as the best pony. All I had was a high power rifle.

My pony Kublai Khan loved the sport. He was just like a shooting dog. Often he would see gazelle before we did and would toss his head restlessly, wild to be off. I could shoot from the saddle or right under his nose while he stood quietly. When we came up to the dead antelope, he would nozzle it proudly as though he had done it all himself.

It is not easy at first to shoot a gazelle going fifty to sixty miles an hour at three hundred yards. But it comes with practice. Suddenly you will get the knack, learn just how much to lead the animals and the rest is easy. For the first fortnight I averaged one antelope to ten cartridges. By the end of the season I had cut it down to one in two.

My wife and I lived much on game. Sand grouse and bustard varied the diet of the antelope; sometimes we could buy a sheep from the nomad Mongols. It was free and healthy life and we were happy. I was learning the country and its ways, talking with wandering Mongols about the far western desert, studying the physical problems of transport and maintenance in the arid reaches of the Gobi. All I learned made me more certain that this was the chosen spot for the new conquest of Central Asia; the place where I could stake all to lose or win on a single play.

We were seldom far from the main Kalgan-Urga trail in the northern grasslands. With our carts and ponies it would have been impossible to go into the desert. There was neither enough feed nor water. Camels alone could be used there. But that made little difference for we were gathering a superb collection of mammals and I was getting the "feel of the country."

Early in July of that year we wandered back to Urga and from there went north into the great larch forests. In less than twenty miles from the city we were out of the plains fauna into the Siberian life zone. A wilderness of virgin forest swept over the mountains inhabited only by moose, elk, roedeer, bear, wild boar, and lynx. Capercaille, black grouse, hazel hens, and ptarmigan were abundant in almost every parklike opening of the forest. In contrast to what we had left, it might have been another world.

Far up in the wilderness, in a secluded river valley, we found a Mongol village and a strange old hunter. Tserin Dorchy was his name. I bore a message to him from a Mongol duke, but that would have made precious little difference had he not liked us. Of all human beings I have ever met he was the most independent. His word was law in the village. But our mutual love for sport soon put us on a friendly basis and we were accepted as welcome additions to the valley's community.

Our main camp was a mile above the village and always some of the Mongols were at the tents.

Immediately I had to assume my usual role of doctor. All sorts of diseases were brought to me for treatment. Tserin Dorchy's wife presented a baby with a case of eczema and before the month was out I had the kiddie well on the road to health. A wandering lama had ridden into the village shortly before our arrival. He had been saying prayers for all the community invalids but none of them was better for it. When my treatments began to have beneficial effects, he stole all my glory. I think most of the Mongols were convinced that the foreign medicines really did the work but they were too superstitious to admit the fact openly. Anyway, whenever one of my patients showed signs of recovery the lama collected a fee. He was a rich man as lamas go, in the way of sheep, boots and clothing before we left the valley. He never offered to split fifty-fifty with me either. But you couldn't have dragged him away as long as we remained.

He settled himself comfortably in the village. A preemptory demand got him the finest *yurt* that the community boasted. Then he looked over the feminine members and selected one of Tserin Dorchy's eighteen year old daughters to share his temporary prosperity. I don't think she liked it much for she was enamoured of one of my Chinese assistants, but disinclination did not get her anywhere. Even the independent old Tserin Dorchy was too superstitious to offend the lama. He was afraid of the curses which the priestly visitor might place upon him and all his flocks. Still the lama did not seem to mind greatly when his temporary wife rode out at night to keep a tryst in the moonlight with my taxidermist!

Chastity is hardly a virtue in a Mongol's scheme of life. It isn't considered important. The Mongols are simply immoral according to Western standards. They have definite marriage customs, of course, and I think that few of them have more than one wife, but that is merely a matter of economics. A harem would be too expensive either to acquire or maintain.

The lamas are forbidden to marry but I have known only one or two who took their vows seriously enough to let them interfere with the pleasures of feminine society. As a result of such promiscuity considerably more than half the entire population of the country is infected with devastating diseases. Naturally such a condition plays havoc with healthy offspring and the race is rapidly disappearing. Those children that do live are as hard as nails. Certainly they are the survival of the fittest if there ever was such a thing. The poor kiddies simply don't have a chance. Filth surrounds them from the day they are born. The ordinary *yurt* is not only a stable for young sheep, goats, and calves but a playground for the babies. Unsanitary isn't the word. As Mark Twain said about the Ganges River:

"It is so filthy that germs can't live in it."

An ordinary Mongol never takes a bath from the time he is born until he dies unless it be by accident. There are certain extenuating circumstances for water is scarce and during most of the year the bitter cold makes bathing disagreeable. Also about as soon as one is clean a sand storm nullifies all the good work. I must confess that I myself once went for nearly a month without a bath during a period of continual sand storms. The effort just did not seem worth while, with a temperature below freezing and a yellow haze filling the tent.

One thing saves the lives of many Mongols and that is sunlight. They live out of doors most of the day and the thin population, even in the grasslands, breeds few germs. When the interior of a *yurt* becomes too dirty even for them, they simply shift it a few yards to another spot.

This is for summer. Winter is the time when trouble comes. Then it is too cold to stay outside and usually a wall of dung is constructed about the *yurt* to act not only as a store of fuel but as a wind break. The house is seldom shifted in the winter. The children become incredibly hardy. I have seen three- or four-year-old babies stark naked playing about in a bitter wind when I was shivering in a fur coat. The kiddies are taught to ride when they are hardly able to walk. Often they are tied on horseback. If by chance they fall off such an accident evokes no sympathy. At five or six years they are herding sheep or camels and doing it amazingly well.

I believe that the present day Mongol is equal in endurance or very nearly so to those of Genghiz Khan's time. The weak have not survived. Of course there are not as many of them but the hardship and privation which they can endure upon occasion is little short of superhuman.

With all their faults they are distinctly a likeable people. Good sportsmen, ready to try anything once, brave, strong, self-reliant, excellent fighters, magnificent horsemen. They possess so many of the characteristics which Anglo-Saxons admire that we have many points of contact. Most of all, the Mongols have a sense of humor. They are able even to appreciate a joke upon themselves which is more than many of our own people can boast.

Independence is perhaps their most distinctive characteristic. Their way of life upon the plains has made them supremely self-reliant and to acknowledge a master, either individually or as a nation, is abhorrent. Witness the political changes of the last two decades when they have become affiliated first with China, then with Russia and back again. Each change was brought about because the greater power had become intolerably domineering. They hoped that by switching to the other neighbor, relief might come.

I was continually impressed by the similarity in the customs of the Mongols and those of our own great West during the early days. Like conditions bred like habits. Hospitality is a law of the land. Time after time I have ridden up to a *yurt*, hobbled my pony and gone inside. A place about the fire was made for me as a matter of course. Taking out my little wooden food bowl I dipped into the common pot and was given tea. Always they spread my blankets in the best sleeping place farthest from the door. In the morning there was no thought of payment. I have done the same thing for dozens of Mongols at my own camp.

Our ponies often slipped their hobbles and strayed during the night. Many time they were brought back by natives who had found them miles away. They would expect as much from us. It is a law of the land to inform every traveller if a well or spring is dry. To be caught without water may mean death.

Horse stealing is as great a crime as murder. Death is the only punishment. The few Mongol soldiers in Urga were kept to enforce such laws. If a man reported the theft of a pony the soldiers took up the trail following it for days or weeks if need be and seldom returned without their man.

In those days (1919) the Mongols were still using one of the most horrible forms of punishment of which I know. A prisoner was placed in a heavy wooden coffin about four and one-half feet long by three feet wide and as many high. He could neither lie down nor sit erect. In this cramped position he might stay for days or weeks or even years according to his sentence. Though a round hole six inches wide in the side of the box food was passed—when the jailers did not forget it! In the prison I saw a dozen coffins and all were occupied.

One of the inmates told me that he had been there five years; his was a life sentence. At first he used to be taken out every week for a little exercise but soon his arms and legs had atrophied and he could no longer walk. Still he lived. Many coffins on the street corners contained men who had committed minor crimes. They would remain inside for perhaps a week or two and could be given food by any one who wished. I saw one poor fellow in a box whose legs and hands were tightly manacled as well. Fortunately this punishment was abolished in 1920. The last time I visited the jail in Urga I saw a pile of old coffins in a corner of the yard and none in use.

Our days in the northern forests passed all too quickly for they were very happy days. It was a paradise for small mammals and I caught dozens of new and little known species of voles, shrews, woodmice, rats, picas, squirrels, and hares. Moose, roedeer, wapiti, bear, and wild boar were among our larger game. We lived like veritable children of the woods, shooting in the morning and late afternoon, eating and sleeping when we would, careless of the weeks that passed.

On August the fourteenth there came the first touch of frost. Valleys and forests had been bright with masses of blue-bells, forget-me-nots, jensens and dozens of other wild flowers but then they quickly began to droop and wither. Blueberries and currants were ripe. By September first it was freezing hard each night. Still we lingered on, loath to leave that wild free life. Snow drove us out in mid-September and we crossed the plains again to Kalgan. Coltman's house was the first we had been in for many weeks and that night we could not sleep. The walls oppressed us; we missed the kiss of the night wind on our faces. Unrolling our fur bags we carried them to a grass spot in the courtyard and there slept happily till morning.

Harry Caldwell, the tiger-shooting missionary, with whom I had hunted in South China, was waiting in Peking. Almost immediately he and I started northward for the rugged mountains of the Sino-Mongolian frontier for the bighorn sheep and wapiti. Eight magnificent *argali*, including a world's record head, four wapiti, six goral, ten roedeer and two wolves and scores of pheasants, partridges, quail, ducks and geese were our bag for eighteen days of actual shooting.

We were the first foreigners to visit the region for six years because it was infested with bandits and the Chinese authorities would give us no passports. Our base camp for sheep hunting was only five miles from the ancient Mongol city of Kwei-hua-cheng. When the governor found that Harry and I were actually shooting in the mountains he was frantic with fear that we might be killed or captured. He sent an officer to pray us to go away. We categorically refused for there were no bandits.

Then he said he must send soldiers to accompany us into the mountains every day. That was not so good but there was nothing to do. The governor must "save his face." Four of them arrived in full uniform carrying a flag and bugle. We announced that they must be ready to go before daylight. Hardship number one, for Chinese are late sleepers! Our first morning out Harry and I set a terrific pace to the foothills. After going a thousand feet straight up in the roughest part of the mountains, the soldiers were absolutely exhausted. They simply could not go on. I suggested that they descend to a tiny temple at the base of the peak and await us there. Then we could return together at night and no one would be the wiser. The idea was a life-saver. Down they went to spend the day sleeping peacefully in the sunshine while we did our shooting. At night we picked them up and returned to the village with the flag flying and the bugle blowing. This farce went on every day during the time we hunted in that vicinity. The governor's "face was saved," the soldiers had a fine rest and we got good shooting. One soon finds out that in China there is a way of getting around almost everything. They are the greatest "compromisers" in the world. If the outward form is observed and no one loses face you can get away with murder.

When we returned to Peking in mid-November I took account of stock. The seven months work had brought a collection of fifteen hundred mammals, all from a region that was virtually new to science. That was important as a tangible result to the Museum authorities and my friends who had helped finance the trip. But the really vital thing was the knowledge I had gained of Mongolia as a theater of work for the great expedition of my dreams.

Journey to Lhasa

BY ALEXANDRA DAVID-NEEL

Tibet and the city of Lhasa proved a compelling yet unattainable goal for many explorers. Foreign visitors were usually expelled before getting very far into the country, and all outsiders were most unwelcome. Alexandra David-Neel was among those told that she could not enter, but her extensive study of Eastern philosophy and mysticism and of the languages and customs of the region left her ready to make her way to the forbidden city despite the obstacles. Linking up with a young Buddhist named Yongden, who would accompany her on many journeys, she eventually managed to slip into Lhasa in disguise in 1924.

The account of her trip, *My Journey to Lhasa*, is more adventure than exploration, but it still provides some wonderful insights into what was then one of the most mysterious cultures in the world. This episode from their trip deals with the infamous bandits of Tibet, with whom virtually every traveler in the region had to contend.

★   ★   ★   ★   ★

Until then our journey through the Po country had been perfectly peaceful, and I began to think that there must be much exaggeration in the stories which are current about the Popas.

Popas—so Thibetans say—are born robbers. Each year gangs, sometimes to the number of a hundred, fall unexpectedly on their neighbors of the Kong-bu or Dainshi provinces and loot their villages. Beside these organized expeditions, most Popas—traders, pilgrims, or mere villagers—find it difficult to let any traveller they may happen to meet on their way pass without trying to levy an undue tax on his baggage, however miserable it may be. A few handfuls of barley flour, a worn-out blanket, two or three copper coins—all is good to them. But if, as a rule, they let the poor folk who meekly submit to their demands go unmolested, they are quick to turn murderers when resistance is offered or a valuable booty expected.

Truly, no wealthy travellers venture to go through the forests of Po. Only the poorest of the poor—the beggar pilgrims made bold by the fact of their utter destitution—are to be met along the tracks which cross the Popas' hill.

As for us, we had not met any outsider, either rich or poor, on our way. The few people whom we had seen on the solitary roads were all natives of the country or settlers who had practically become Popas.

Events were now to take another turn, and that gay New Year marked the end of a period of quietness.

The very afternoon after we had left the hospitable house where such good cakes were baked, we passed by an isolated farm just as a number of people were emerging from it. The New Year festivities were still going on; some of the men who had enjoyed themselves were decidedly drunk, and the remainder were not very sober. All of them carried guns across their shoulders, and some made a pretence of shooting at us. As for us, we proceeded as if we had noticed nothing.

In the evening I discovered a roomy cave in which we slept comfortably. We slept much too long, and delayed still further over some soup at breakfast. As we did so, a man appeared and asked us if we had nothing to sell. He regarded the contents of our bags, which were still open.

Our two common spoons especially attracted his attention. Then he seated himself, and taking a piece of dried, fermented cheese out of his dress he began to eat it.

That kind of cheese is very much like French Roquefort. Thinking it would improve our menus, Yongden asked the man if he had some to sell. He answered in the affirmative; he had some at home, not far from the cave, and would barter one against needles, if we had any. We had a few which we had carried for this purpose. So the man when to fetch his cheese.

We had not yet finished our packing when he came back with a cheese and followed by another man. The newcomer was much bolder than the first with whom we had dealt. He fingered the cloth of our tent and told us he would purchase it. He then took our spoons and examined them, while his companion cast glances in the direction from which they had come, as if expecting other arrivals.

We had no doubt about the intentions of the two Popas. The bolder one had already put the two coveted spoons in his *amphag* and refused to give them back, while the other one endeavoured to take the tent out of the lama's hands.

I realized that others had been summoned and were to assist in the robbery.

The matter would soon become serious. We must frighten these two away and start in haste. Perhaps we would be able to reach the next village, and the thieves would not dare to follow us.

I endeavoured to appeal to the good feelings of the men, but it was of no avail. Time was of importance; we must put an end to this business, and show the others that we were not timid and defenceless folk.

"Let that tent alone at once!" I commanded, "And give the spoons back!"

In the meantime I had my revolver in readiness under my dress. The boldest of the thieves only laughed and, turning his back on me, he bent to pick up some other object. I shot, from close behind him, turning my revolver away from him. But his companion saw me, and being too terrified to warn his friend, he could do nothing but stare wildly at me. Whether or not the other fellow saw him, I cannot tell, but he threw himself backwards just as I shot, and the bullet passed close to his head, grazing his hair.

Flinging the spoons and the tent on the ground, the two ran like hunted hares across the thicket.

The situation was not entirely pleasant. The ruffians might have gone to fetch some of their kindred, the men whom they seemed to expect. I told Yongden to tie the loads in haste and be off as quickly as possible.

What would have happened, had we remained alone, I cannot say, for a party of about thirty pilgrims—the first foreign travellers we met in Po *yul*, and the only ones we were ever to meet—suddenly appeared. They had heard the shot, and inquired as to its cause.

It was annoying to be identified as carrying a revolver, for only chiefs and rich traders own these. Of course they thought that it was Yongden who had fired; and later on when they asked to see the weapon, we produced an old-pattern small one, instead of the automatic pistol that had nearly sent the Popa on to another world.

We joined the party, and perhaps we owe our lives to this most unexpected meeting.

We learned from our new companions that the Popas truly deserved their bad name, and we were soon to confirm this from our own experience.

The party which we had joined was mostly composed of people from Zogong in the Nu valley, the place that we had avoided by crossing the river and cutting through several ranges.

The very day after we arrived at the *dokpas'* camp where we had taken a guide and a horse to climb to the Aigni *la*, they had reached another cowmen's encampment at the foot of the pass leading into the Nagong valley.

Before crossing the mountains a number of the *trapas* wished to sew new soles on their boots, and so the larger part of the band decided to remain one day more near the *dokpas'* encampment to get this done. A few laymen and nearly all the women preferred to ascend the pass slowly, instead of lingering at the *dokpas'* place. They set out and slept somewhere under the trees, lower down on the other side of the range. At daybreak a number of Popas appeared, proceeding, with loaded yaks, toward the Daishin province to exchange dried apricots, chillies, etc., for barley. When they saw the poor pilgrims they rushed at them and took away all their blankets and the few coins they had hidden under their clothes. Then, learning that others were expected, they ordered them to proceed, without loitering on the road. They unloaded their yaks, drove them on the hills, and seating themselves near the top of the pass waited for the remainder of the party to appear.

The *trapas* found them there, on the watch, like demoniacal spirits of the mountains, ready to prey upon travellers. The Popas asked them for some present, which is a polite way common to robbers of China and of Thibet. But many of the monks were armed with spear or sword, and preferred to do battle. The Popas had swords, too, but the pilgrims were more numerous, and the valiant sons of Po *yul* were defeated. The lamas joined their unfortunate vanguard the following day.

Some of these, acting as guides to their companions, had already travelled to Po *yul* through the Gotza *la*. When they heard that we had been able to force our way through the ranges, they very much regretted that fear of the snow had prevented them from following the summer road across the solitudes, where we had a hard time but avoided robbers. Of the three passes on that side, they knew only the Gotza *la*.

Like most Kampus of the Nu and upper Giamo nu chu valleys, these people were exceedingly pleasant. We greatly enjoyed their company, and accompanied them for several days. But then, in order to make up the time they had lost in the highlands of Po, they began to race with such speed that I left them to their sport, and fall back.

On the second day that we spent with that gay party we left the banks of the Po lung river, which we had followed from its source in the snow-buried highlands. It was now a beautiful, large, blue stream, about to lose itself in the Yeru Tsangpo. But before this merging of its personality it had still to receive a tributary as big as itself, the Yigong Tsangpo. We had to cross this river in the same way as we crossed the Giamo nu chu, and before it the Mekong, that is to say, by hanging to a rope and being hauled from the opposite side.

Our good luck had again brought us companions at that moment when they were so sorely needed. The *tupas* [ferrymen] who make a trade of hauling the travellers across would never have taken the trouble for two lone beggars. We should, perhaps, have waited for days, camped on the bank of the river, until a number of passengers had collected.

An insolent lot they seemed, these ferrymen whose ferry was a woefully sagging leather cable spanning a river at least twice as wide as the Giamo nu chu where we had crossed it. Their chief seemed to be an old grandmother, who looked like a witch. She received the money paid for the passage and directed operations.

At first the Popas told us to wait until the morning, but after repeated entreaties, and because we were a large party, they condescended to do the work that afternoon. Truly it was a difficult business. The *tupas* were at least a dozen strong. To begin with, some of them passed the towing rope across— a real acrobatic feat that requires an uncommon strength in the wrists and a complete absence of giddiness. These men were not towed, as we, the passengers, would be. They scrambled unaided over that sagging and swaying rope at a considerable distance above the rushing waters. When they had reached the opposite bank, the passage of the luggage began, during which the old woman required from us all three needles or a little money as a supplement to the price already paid. Needles are in great demand in the interior of Thibet, and are very difficult to get. The mother *tupa* certainly made a profitable trade with those she exacted from the travellers.

Most of the men in our party belonged to the lamaist order and to the great state monasteries of Lhasa: Sera, Depung, or Galden. The old woman did not show any regard for them, but she approached Yongden and asked him to make *mos*, telling him a quantity of things about her private concerns. She also let us go without any needle tax. My turn to cross came long before that of the lama. Passengers were sent two together, and I was tied at the hook with a woman in exactly the same way as at the Salween. No accident happened this time, but on account of the greater length of the cable the jolting over the river was much more lively and unpleasant. From the middle of the river the wonderful snowy peak of the Gyalwa Pal Ri (the victorious and noble mountain) [Which is also styled, "the victorious lotus mountain,"

Gyalwa Ped Ri] appeared in all its splendour. Enclosed in the narrow frame of the river gorge, it had a peculiarly mysterious beauty which I had never seen in the wide snowy ranges.

I hastened to find a shelter for the night, and came across a cave amongst the huge rocks which form the river banks.

When Yongden arrived, I had already collected the necessary fuel. We had our food and went to sleep. The temperature was mild, and it was hard to realise that we were in the middle of winter.

In the morning light the Gyalwa Pal Ri appeared still more glorious than on the day before. It was a perfect jewel; one might have fancied it to be the immaculate abode of some radiant god, feeding upon pure light. Our companions, who thought much more of the gifts which the Lhasa government grants to the monks of the three state monasteries who attend the solemn New Year gathering, than of any God, were now in a great hurry to reach the capital, and did not lose any time in contemplating the "victorious" peak. When we started they had already gone, and we found the large cave in which they had slept quite empty. This looked like an annoying complication, for the right trail to follow was hard to find in the dense jungle which now reminded me of the lower slopes of the Himalayas. I noticed a large number of plants and creepers which I was accustomed to find in the Sikkin forest between 3,000 and 4,000 feet level. The air had also entirely lost that peculiarly strong and invigorating savour of the dry tablelands. It never freezes in that region. The ground was muddy, the sky cloudy, and the people on the other bank of the river Ygong had told us that we must expect rain.

A number of trails crossed near the river. One led north toward the upper country of Potöd where it joined tracks that allowed one to reach the grassy northern solitudes. Another went down toward the Brahmaputra, and third one led to the Kongbu province.

We started off correctly on the Kongbu track, but hesitated when it branched into a short cut and a main path. We decided in favour of the former, following mere intuition, without suspecting that the two would join later one. This short trail was a true masterpiece of the "Public Works" engineers of Po *yul*. It was cut by perpendicular rocks against which ladders of a peculiar pattern had been placed to enable one to climb up and down. At other places it ran like a balcony on branches thrust horizontally into the ground, and the whole device was built for tall Popas, with much longer legs than ours. Our feet were left waving in the air on the primitive staircases, whose steps were shaky stones or the notched trunks of trees. What we could not do with our feet we had to perform with the help of our hands, hanging in the air until we touched a point of support, and relying on our strength to raise ourselves when climbing. Had we not carried baggage on our backs, we should have enjoyed the sport, but we were heavily laden. Knowing that no food would be available on our way, which lay through uninhabited forests, we had provided ourselves with a full supply of *tsampa*, which weighed heavily on our backs and put our acrobatic feats of equilibrium in jeopardy.

But worst of all, we feared missing our road. Such a trail might lead to some forest village, but it could scarcely be the main highway from Kongbu to Po *yul*, followed, as we knew by loaded horses and mules. We also failed to discover any trace of the party of pilgrims. Thirty men would have left the imprint of their feet in the soft mud. It was most certain that our former companions had not passed this way. Yet, as we were proceeding in the right direction, I ventured to continue. After all, we were again alone. We had no gift to expect from the Lhasa government, nor was our presence requested to read the Scriptures. It would be enough for our own enjoyment if we reached the Lamaist Rome in time to witness the various New Year festivities. We therefore had time to loiter over the country. Fresh meetings with robbers were the only serious annoyance we had to fear. The Popas villagers themselves had told us to be careful on this forest track, which they call the Po southern road (*Po lho lam*), for robbers haunted it and people ventured on this side only in large parties. But as we were now in that ill-famed region, being willingly or unwillingly compelled to cross it, it was useless to torment ourselves with the possibility of future danger, which could not be averted.

This most uneven trail, on which we had expended so much exertion, ended near a beautiful, huge tree dedicated to some sylvan deity. And here, also, it joined the main track. Happily, we had not missed our way.

This spot broke the monotony of the jungle in a pleasant way. The giant tree, from the lowest branches of which hung countless tiny paper flags bearing spells meant to protect travellers, appeared to be a mighty guardian against the dangers that lie in the gloomy forest. Around it spread that queer psychic atmosphere peculiar to places consecrated to Nature's gods, which tells of times long past when mankind's heart was still young and naive.

Our progress became more rapid now that we were treading a tolerably good path, and I regretted having taken the difficult short cut. I ought rather to have blessed the very friendly sylvan deity of that road who had perhaps suggested the choice to me.

A little farther on I found in the middle of the road a long shoot of wild orchids in full bloom and quite fresh, as if it had just been plucked. I relate the fact because, as we were then in January, it shows that the whole of Thibet is far from being an icy-cold, bleak country, like the region which extends from the south of Lhasa to the Himalayas.

At the end of the afternoon we overtook a party of pilgrims, who were camped in a pretty clearing near the junction of the Po river and one of its tributaries.

Our arrival caused some commotion, and our new friends rushed toward us to ask if we had met any robbers. We were astonished, and replied that we had not seen a single human being on our road. They could not understand how this could be, for they had met a gang of about thirty men who had tried to extract some presents from them. As they refused to give the least thing, a fight followed in which the robbers had been defeated and some of them wounded. Two of the travellers had been wounded with swords and had lost a quantity of blood. Another, who had been pushed violently and had fallen on a rock, complained of internal pains.

At last, when we had explained that we had come by the narrow short cut, our new friends congratulated us on having escaped the robbers on the main path. For, angered as they must have been after their defeat, they would certainly have stripped us of all our belongings.

After having heard this news I ceased completely to regret my tiring exertion on the short cut. Once more I had been uncommonly lucky.

Encounters with brigands are common enough in Thibet, and fail to impress travellers deeply, unless they are extraordinarily bloody. In spite of the three who lay suffering near a fire, the others did not feel in the least sorrowful or depressed. On the contrary, it seemed as if this little adventure had relieved the monotony of their journey, and had joyfully excited them! We spent a very pleasant evening. The Lhasa *trapas* related a lot of stories told in the capital, and the latest gossip about the lamaist court, the high officials, and the *philings* rulers of India. We heard, also, interesting details about the economic situation of the country and the political opinions of the clergy. Lastly, they took us into their confidence as to a number of private affairs in which some of their companions were concerned. Thanks to them, my store of observation was further enriched.

The big fires which the party had lit, and the noise made in the forest by cutting wood, attracted the notice of a few Popas villagers living on the bank of the river. Several men, who did not look perfectly sober, came, inspected our camp, and chatted with some of us. I suspected that they were scouting to ascertain our strength and would inform their friends of the chance they might have of successfully looting us.

They came to Yongden and asked him to remain one day with them to bless their houses and properties. The lama, of course, declined the invitation, mentioning the necessity of making haste in order to reach Lhasa in time for the great New Year *mönlam*. [The gathering to send good wishes, including the festivals taking place at that time.] They understood his excuse and did not press him, but added that they would send him their wives and children to be blessed the next morning.

In spite of these soft speeches, watchmen were posted at night around our camp, but the hours passed peacefully—so calmly and silently, indeed, that, having pitched our tent apart from the others, we did not hear our companions starting. I then insisted on drinking our early hot tea, a custom that I seldom neglected and which, I am certain, had much to do with the good health that not only myself, but Yongden and all our servants during previous journeys, have always enjoyed; whereas so many Thibetan travellers whose habit it is to start before dawn without any breakfast, even during the winter and in the coldest regions, often suffer from severe attacks of fever and other ailments.

But this most excellent and agreeable custom detained us, and Yongden felt very uneasy at remaining behind in that unsafe country. We were finishing our packing and I was bending over some pieces of luggage when he suddenly announced the arrival of robbers. I glanced in the direction he pointed out, and saw a number of people coming toward us; but when they arrived we discovered that they were women and children.

In spite of the spirits they had drunk, our visitors of the previous evening had not forgotten to send their womenfolk and youngsters to be blessed. The latter brought with them a very acceptable present of chillies, which are a valuable article of exchange at Lhasa, and also some butter and dried fruits. So the dreaded robbers became in fact our benefactors. The ceremony of blessing, packing our gifts, and some unavoidable gossip delayed us still further, and when we started we had but little hope left of being able to rejoin our companions.

It was wonderful indeed to have escaped so many dangers of various kinds and to be there, just as I had planned it, in Po *yul*, *en route* for Lhasa. Nevertheless, it is always presumptuous to rejoice too soon about one's good luck or success. I had not finished with the Popas. But they, too, were to see more of the first foreign woman who walked through their beautiful country, and while their acts were to be quite commonplace and not in the least surprising, mine will probably live long in the memory of those who witnessed them. Maybe a legend will arise out of it all; and who knows if, in the future, a learned student of folklore will not offer some interesting commentary on the story, being far from suspecting the truth of it.

At dusk that every evening, weary after a long tramp and having definitely abandoned the hope of joining the travellers, at least that same night, we were following the rising course of the Tongyuk river which, hidden by the thick foliage, roared far beneath our narrow trail. I was walking ahead, looking for a camping place, when I saw seven men coming toward me. A sudden foreboding seized me. I did not expect any good from this meeting. Nevertheless, as *sang froid* is the best of weapons, and as many years' experience of adventurous life had accustomed me to situations of this kind, I continued to walk calmly, with the indifferent air of a tired woman pilgrim. One of the band stood in the middle of the narrow track and asked me where I was coming from and where I was going to. I muttered the names of some holy places, and passed between him and the bushes. He did not attempt to stop me. I was already rejoicing inwardly at the thought that this time, once more, nothing would happen, when looking back, I saw that my "son" had stopped and was leaning against a rock and speaking with the men. However, the talk seemed friendly and the voices did not rise above the normal pitch. But I could not hear what was said.

Then I noticed that one of the tall fellows was taking something from the handkerchief of the lama. I knew that he had a few coins in it. But I did not realize what was happening, and I thought that the Popas were selling us something.

I only understood the truth when Yongden shouted to me, "They have taken my two rupees!"

The amount was not worth a thought, but I saw that some of the robbers had laid their hands on the load he carried on his back and were about to open it.

The situation was growing serious. Fighting was out of the question. Had I shot one of the men, the others would have immediately stabbed my defenceless companion with the long swords they carried thrust in their belts.

On the other hand, to let them examine the contents of our bags would be dangerous. In them were a few foreign objects, unfamiliar to these savages, that would have appeared strange in the possession of ragged pilgrims and would have awakened suspicion as to our identity. And once on the track, the robbers might perhaps search us and discover the gold hidden under our clothes. What would follow? They might kill us on the spot, or take us before one of their chiefs, who would inform the nearest Lhasa government official if I confessed to be a foreigner in disguise, or would treat us as thieves if I persisted in my incognito. In a word, he would appropriate our gold and beat us both mercilessly.

Most of all, I feared being recognised, and thus prevented from proceeding. At any rate, the robbers must be left with the quickly forgotten impression that they had but met a poor lama pilgrim with his aged and beggar mother.

In much less time than I have taken to write it, all these thoughts passed through my mind. I found the plot of the drama to be played on that rustic stage and I began my part.

Screaming at the top of my voice, howling in utter despair, with tears rolling on my cheeks, I lamented the loss of the two rupees; the *only*, *only* money we had got. What was to become of us? How could we feed ourselves during the long trip to Lhasa? . . .

And these two rupees were sacred money indeed, the offering of a pious householder whose father had died and for whom my son, the lama, had performed the funeral rites, dispatching him to the "Land of Bliss, the Western Paradise." Now these miscreants had dared to steal it! But revenge would come!. . . .

Here I ceased to weep and rose to imprecation. The task was not very difficult, well acquinted as I am with the various deities of the Thibetan pantheon.

I called upon the most dreaded ones, uttering their most terrible names and titles.

There was Palden Dorjee Lhamo, who rides a wild horse on a saddle made of a bloody human skin; there were the Angry Ones who devour the flesh of men and feast on the fresh brains served in their skulls; and the giant Frightful Ones, companions of the King of Death, crowned with bones and dancing on corpses. I conjured them all and implored them to avenge us.

Verily, I was the initiated and ordained wife of a black *nag spa*. His tutelar demons would not fail to avenge the harm done to his innocent son, who had taken to the pure saintly path of the *gelong*.

I am a tiny woman with nothing dramatic in my appearance; but at that moment I felt myself rising to the height of a powerful tragedienne.

The forest had become darker and a light breeze had arisen which caused a distant murmur to run under the foliage. Lugubrious and mysterious voices seemed to spring out of the unseen torrent below, climbing toward us and filling the air with threatening words in an unknown language.

I was cool and did not fear the thieves—I had seen more than seven together on other occasions—yet I could not suppress a thrill born of the occult atmosphere I myself had created.

I was not alone in this. The seven robbers looked petrified, some standing in one line against a rock behind my son, and others lower down on the path—an awe-struck group which tempted my photographic inclinations. But the hour was not ripe for snapshots.

Then one of the Popas cautiously moved toward me and from a little distance uttered words of peace:

"Do not be angry, old mother. Here are your two rupees. Do not weep. Do not curse us any more! We only want to go peacefully back to our village."

So I allowed my anger and my despair to be cooled, and I took the two coins with the air of one who recovers a unique treasure.

My young companion had rejoined me. The thieves reverently requested his blessing, which he gave them, adding some good wishes. We then parted.

There was no fear that this same band would retrace its steps to rob us. But this new adventure was a warning, not to be overlooked, to leave that specially dangerous area as soon as possible.

That night we made a prolonged march in the forest, which seemed still alive with the phantoms of the deities I had summoned.

A slow rain, mixed with half-melted snow, began to fall, and a melancholy waning moon rose late amongst the clouds. About two o'clock in the morning we came to a place near the river where there was a small level clearing. We were too tired to proceed farther, and discussed the question of how to camp there. Would we dare to pitch our miserable tent, or did prudence command that we should sleep unsheltered on the wet moss, hidden under the trees?

Supper was, once more, not to be thought of, although we had neither eaten nor drunk since early morning, nearly twenty-four hours before. No dry fuel could be found to boil our Thibetan tea, and the dim light was not sufficient to find a place amongst the rocks where we could safely fetch water from the foaming torrent.

I thought we could at least give ourselves the comfort of a shelter. It was very doubtful that anybody would be traveling at night in that bad weather. We therefore pitched the small tent, and lay down in our wet damp clothes and muddy boots on the damp ground.

The moon, which appeared and disappeared between the clouds, cast fantastic moving shadows of branches and rocks on the white cloth above our heads. The river talked loudly with the many voices of a crowd. Invisible beings seemed to surround us. I was thinking of those I had invoked . . . and, after all, I did not altogether disbelieve in that mysterious world that is so near to those who have lived long in the wilds. My heavy head resting on a small bag of *tsampa*, I smiled to unknown friends, and departed for dreamland.

It was not the first time, in the course of my peregrinations in Thibet, that sham magic and robbers combined in the same adventure. I may perhaps be allowed to relate here a rather amusing incident which happened in the Desert of Grass some eighteen months before my meeting with the Popas brigands.

I had lingered that day far behind my men to collect plants which I meant to send to the Botanical Society of France. It was the rainy season. The grassy desert had become a sea of mud. Under a dull sky low clouds rolled heavily, hiding the summits, filling the valleys, and wrapping the steppes in a grayish, melancholy shroud. I did not recognize the luminous solitudes, the scenes of so many of my joyful rides some years before, and I should easily have been overpowered by the depressing influence of that region of dampness, rain and fog across which we had wandered, shivering and feverish, for weeks, had I not had many reasons to prevent me from giving way to lassitude and discouragement.

My present party numbered seven, including myself. The six were Yongden, three servants, and a Chinese Musselman soldier, going back to his country with his Thibetan wife and their little boy, whom I do not reckon in the number.

Yongden and the woman had remained with me, helping me to gather the plants, and the other men were far ahead of us. The weather had now cleared. One could see, between the clouds, the sun almost setting. It was time to proceed to the camp, so we set out, riding slowly in full enjoyment of the peaceful evening.

We had left the plain, and having turned the spur of a range, entered a narrow valley, when I saw on my left three men carrying guns slung over their shoulders, who silently disappeared in a recess of the mountains. Who they were was clear enough. Thibetan travellers, in that country, never fail to salute one another with the customary greeting: "*Oghiai! Oghiai.*" [This means, "You have undergone hardship," and the answer is: "*Lags, ma Kaa; kiai la oghiai!* I have suffered no hardship but you have had a hard time!"] Then they habitually exchange questions about the country whence they came and toward which they go. The silence of these men looked very suspicious, not to mention the fact that they hid themselves, instead of walking along the trail.

I went my way, pretending to pay no attention to them, but feeling under my dress to see if my revolver was handy. I whispered to the woman who rode near me, "Did you see them?" "Yes," she answered. "They are robbers. Perhaps they are the scouts of a gang."

I looked at a flower that grew on a rock, as if deeply interested in it, and pointing it out to Yongden, I called him to me. To show any sign of agitation which the brigands, who were perhaps watching us, might interpret as fear, would endanger our lives. The members of the special Order of Lamas, whose dress I wore, are believed to be fearless and to possess occult powers, and this was our best safeguard.

"Have you seen the men in the ravine?" I asked my young companion. "No."

"Three men carrying guns—thieves, no doubt. The woman has seen them. Have your revolver ready. As soon as we reach the turning of the trail, and are out of sight, we will ride on fast. We must reach the camp quickly and inform the servants." As I had spoken in English, I did not fear being overheard.

We had good beasts, and proceeded quickly. But what was this? We heard a shot in the direction of our people. We rode faster and soon discovered our four tents pitched in the high grass near a stream.

"Have you seen three men on your road?" I immediately asked the servants who came to hold our horses. No, nobody had seen any human being for the last ten days.

"I heard a shot."

They all hung their heads. "I have killed a hare," confessed the soldier. "We have no more meat, and my wife feels weak."

I always strictly forbid my servants to hunt, but the soldier was not my servant. I dropped the subject.

"This woman and I have seen three armed men who appeared to hide from us," I said. "We must take special precautions tonight for the safety of the camp. It may be that these three have companions in the vicinity."

"There they are!" exclaimed my head servant, Tsering, pointing out two men who stood on the crest of the hill above the camp.

I looked at them with my glasses. They were the very men whom we had seen on our way. Where was the third one? Had he been dispatched to call still other ruffians in order to attack us? The two remained watching us.

"Let us take no more notice of them," I said. "We will devise a plan while drinking tea. Put the guns and revolvers in such places that they may be seen by the robbers, if there are any besides these two. It is good to let them know that we are able to defend ourselves."

The tea was ready. One of the servants dipped a ladle into the cauldron and threw a few drops of the liquid toward the six quarters (including zenith and nadir), shouting "Drink tea, O Gods!" Then our bowls were filled, and, seated around the fire, we began to discuss the situation.

The servants suggested that they might climb the neighbouring hills and from there try to discover if any gang was in the vicinity. I did not like this idea. The robbers might arrive while they were roaming far from the camp, taking that opportunity to steal some beasts or other things. Yongden and I alone would have a hard time to defend our belongings, even if the three men whom we had seen, and who had good guns, were the only ones to attack us.

"I know a better way," said the soldier. "Let night come, and when darkness hides us, I and two of the men will ambush ourselves separately outside the camp at three different points. Another will remain here as watchman, and he will, according to the Chinese custom, beat a drum or make some such noise all night. The robbers will think that we are all in our tents, and if they appear, one or another of those who are hidden outside the camp will see them and shoot at them when they are between him and the tents. They will thus be surprised and fired upon from behind and in front at the same time!"

This appeared to be the best plan for a small party like ours, and I decided to follow it. We tied the beasts as fast as we could, for when they do not dare to fight openly, Thibetan brigands fire volleys at short range to frighten the animals. If some of these break their cords and escape, they chase them away and seldom miss capturing a few.

Yongden insisted on erecting a barricade with the bags and boxes containing our provisions. He meant it, of course, as a shelter for us, but, as distinguished a *literatus* as my adopted son might be, his knowledge does not extend to the art of war. As it was built, it appeared to me that we should rather protect the barricade with our bodies than be protected by it, but I am myself far from being an expert in these matters, and no great general happened to be there to enlighten us.

Seldom have I spent such a delightful night as that one, when at each minute we expected an attack! But it was not this prospect which lent charm to my vigil.

Seated at the entrance of his tent, bowl of tea near him, Tsering sang ballads of the land of Kham, thousands of years old. He marked the cadence by striking with a small rod on a Thibetan cauldron in which we boiled tea or soup over our camp fire. The songs extol the high deeds of rustic knights and the primeval forests in which arise shining peaks clad with eternal snows. Robbers these heroes are, like those whose presence in our neighbourhood compelled us to keep a watch, like the watchman himself, who—I was aware—had played his part in more than one hot encounter, like the three others who are now acting as sentinels, like everyone in that land of primitive braves who know of no other field in which to show their prowess other than the trails followed by rich caravans.

Tsering had a fine voice. His accents were now heroic, now mystic. The songs told not only of warriors, but of merciful goddesses and holy lamas. Some of the stanzas finished with ardent aspirations toward the spiritual awakening that puts an end to fear and all sorrow. The vulgar cauldron itself had risen to the level of that poetry; its metal sounded solemn as a bell. Tsering was indefatigable; he went on with his bewitching recital until dawn.

The sentinels came back benumbed by their prolonged stay on the damp grass, and ran to revive the fire and make tea. Tsering's song had ceased, and the harmonious cauldron, fallen back to its utilitarian role, stood already filled with water, among the flames. As for Yongden, he was fast asleep with his head resting against his barricade.

The robbers had not dared to attack us, but they had spent the night near our camp. As we were finishing eating our breakfast the three men appeared, each one leading a horse. My boys leaped to their feet and ran to them.

"Who are you?" they asked. "We saw you yesterday. What are you doing here?"

"We are hunters," answered the newcomers.

"Indeed! That is good luck for us. We have no meat left. We will buy some game from you."

The self-styled hunters looked embarrassed. "We have not yet killed anything," they said.

My servants did not need to hear more.

"Do you know," asked Tsering of the three Thibetans, "who is the noble, reverend lady who travels with such a beautiful tent and wears a *toga* (kind of vest worn by lamas) of golden brocade?"

"Would she be the *philing* Jetsunma who lived in Jakyendo? We have heard about her."

"Yes, she is. And you understand that she does not fear robbers any more than the wild beasts or any other thing. One who stole the least of her belongings would immediately be discovered and caught.

"In that case, she has only to look in a bowl full of water, and at once she sees in it the likeness of the thief, together with the stolen articles and the place where both are to be found."

"So it is really true," said the men. "All the *dokpas* say white foreigners have this power."

"Nothing is more certain." confirmed my head servant.

Tsering was well acquinted with the story which was repeated among the cowmen, and he had cleverly taken advantage of it to frighten the robbers and to dissuade them from going to bring their friends to rob us a few days later.

About ten days after that incident, we stopped for the night in front of an encampment of *dokpas*. I retired to my tent before night had fallen, and I heard many visitors in the camp. They were bringing presents of milk and butter, and Yongden told them that the lama lady had shut herself up for religious meditation and could not be disturbed, but that she would see them the following morning. Then some whispering took place, and a servant having called the *dokpas* to drink tea near the kitchen fire, they all moved away and I heard no more of what was said.

At dawn Yongden asked permission to enter my tent.

"I must," he said, "inform you, before the *dokpas* call again, about the request they made yesterday. They say that some of their horses have been stolen, they do not know by whom, and they wish you to look in a bowl of water in order to describe to them the thieves and the place where they are keeping the stolen animals."

"What did you tell them?" I asked.

"I think," answered Yongden, "that maybe these men have bad intentions. Perhaps they have not suffered any loss and they only wish to know if what is said about that bowl of water and the magic power of the 'white foreigner' is really true or not. Who knows whether they have not an eye on our fine Chinese mules and would not be delighted to steal them if they were convinced that you could not trace the thieves, especially if the robbery happened at a few days' march from their own encampment, at a place where the tribe to which the brigands belong could not be located? If you tell them that you have seen their horses, and that none have been stolen, they will be convinced that you have not been able to detect their lie, and that, therefore, as you are powerless in magic, they may loot us with impunity. I accordingly explained to them that you could indeed see all that they want to know in a bowl of water, but that the water needed is somewhat different from the ordinary water just drawn from the stream. This water must be prepared by ceremonies and the recitation of a ritual that lasts for three days. They understood this at once. I then said that it was doubtful if you would stay here three days, because you were called to Amdo for an important meeting with a great lama. Also, as I know how much they shrink from the idea of killing in cold blood a man who has only stolen property, I added that as soon as you had discovered the thieves you would hand them over to the Chinese magistrate to be put to death. It would be, I said, in the power of no one to spare their lives. The *Towo* [Wrathful Deity] by whose power this divinatory rite is performed would claim them as victims and, if they were not sacrificed, he would turn his anger against those who had requested the rite to be performed, and he would take their lives instead.

"On hearing this, they all became terrified. They declared that they feared to irritate the *Towo*, and preferred to look after their horses in their own way, trying to get a good compensation from the thieves."

I smiled at his ruse, and when the *dokpas* came with some more presents, I repeated to them the very things Yongden had told them the day before, so that they definitely gave up all idea of requesting the celebration of the too tragic rite.

The head servant, Tsering, had traveled in his early youth as far as Tachienlu, and had been in the service of foreigners. As a result of these associations he had acquired a skepticism which he liked to display before his more credulous companions. During the next few days, he did not cease making the incident a subject of his jokes, and laughing at the simpletons who had been so easily fooled.

By that time we had reached the shore of the large blue lake, the most holy Koko-nor, worshipped by thousands of Thibetans and Mongolians. The rains were over. I could see that wonderful inland sea, bathed in bright sunshine, and its rocky islands, the largest of which has been for centuries the dwelling of a few anchorites.

Once when I was coming back to the camp after having bathed in the lake, I saw Tsering leaving Yongden's tent and hastily putting something in his breast pocket. He looked a little agitated and proceeded quickly toward the kitchen place without noticing me. The same evening Yongden told me that, having been called away on some business while counting money, he had left his purse on a box in his tent and had forgotten about it. When he returned, three rupees were missing.

I did not tell him about Tsering. I only scolded him for his carelessness, and the thing ended there.

Three days later I arranged on my camp table a few blades of grass and some rice. I lighted several incense sticks, and in the middle I placed a bowl full of water. Then I waited until I knew that the servants were in their tent, undressed and lying down, if not yet asleep. At that time, according to their custom, all their most precious belongings, and especially their money, would be hidden beneath whatever they used as a pillow.

For a while I rang the small bell and beat the tambourine used by lamas in their religious ceremonies. Then I called Tsering.

"Tsering," I said with a stern voice, when he appeared, "three rupees are missing from Lama Yongden's purse. I have seen them under your head when you were lying down. Go and fetch them!"

The skeptic dropped his manner of sneering incredulity. He turned pale, his teeth were chattering. He bowed down three times at my feet and without a word went to the servants' tent and brought back the money.

"*Jetsun Kusho rimpoche*," he asked, trembling, "will the *Towo* kill me?"

"No," I answered, gravely. "I shall do what is needed to spare your life."

He bowed down again and went away.

Then, alone in my small tent, open to the silent desert and the bright starry sky, I took once more the lamaist bell and the drum of mystic rites and, led by their archaic music, I meditated on the strength of ancestral faiths in the human mind and on the deep and mysterious side of the farce that had just been enacted.

The Empty Quarter

BY WILFRED THESIGER

Wilfred Thesiger was a reluctant chronicler of his explorations through the Empty Quarter of Arabia in the years following World War II. He lived with the Bedouin, learned their dialect, and immersed himself in their traditional and fast-disappearing way of life. While his job, ostensibly, was to assess the migration patterns of the hugely destructive locusts that plagued the entire region, his real love was exploring the desolate wastes that had been left virtually untouched by the progress of civilized man.

Thesiger made several crossings of the Empty Quarter, more from personal interest than to fill in spots on a map. The book he eventually authored, *Arabian Sands*, is one of the best adventure and exploration stories ever written. The very fact that he did not really want to write it, and did not care for personal recognition as an explorer, makes it far more interesting than those penned for fame and glory. This excerpt is from one of his earliest journeys and the descriptions it contains of the Bedouin lifestyle are fascinating.

★　　★　　★　　★　　★

This first journey on the fringes of the Empty Quarter was only important to me as my probation for the far longer and more difficult journeys that were to follow. During the next five months I learned to adapt myself to Bedu ways and to the rhythm of their life.

My companions were always awake and moving about as soon as it was light. I think the cold prevented them from sleeping, except in snatches, for they had little to cover them other than the clothes they wore, and during those winter nights there was often a ground frost. Still half asleep, I would hear them rousing the camels from their couching places. The camels roared and gurgled as they were moved, and the Arabs shouted to each other in their harsh, far-carrying voices. The camels would shuffle past, their forelegs hobbled to prevent them straying, their breath white on the cold air. A boy would drive them towards the nearest bushes. Then someone would give the call to prayer:

> God is most great.
> I testify that there is no god but God.
> I testify that Muhammad is the Prophet of God.
> Come to prayer!
> Come to salvation!
> Prayer is better than sleep.
> God is most great.
> There is no god but God.

Each line except the last was repeated twice. The lingering music of the words, strangely compelling even to me who did not share their faith, hung over the silent camp. I would watch old Tamtaim, who slept near me, washing before he prayed. Every act had to be performed exactly and in order. He washed his face, hands, and feet, sucked water into his nostrils, put wet fingers in his ears, and passed wet hands over the top of his head. The Bait Kathir prayed singly, each man in his own place and in his own time, whereas the Rashid, with whom I later travelled, prayed together and in line. Tamtaim swept the ground before him, placed his rifle in front of him, and then prayed facing towards Mecca. He stood upright, bend forward with his hands on his knees, knelt, and then bowed down till his forehead touched the ground. Several times he performed these ritual movements, slowly and impressively, while he recited the formal prayer. Sometimes, after he had finished his prayers, he intoned long passages from the Koran, and the very sound of the words had the quality of great poetry. Many of these Bedu knew only the opening verse of the Koran:

> In the name of God, the Compassionate, the Merciful.
> Praise be to God, Lord of the worlds!
> The Compassionate, the Merciful!
> King on the day of reckoning!
> Thee *only* do we worship and to Thee do we cry for help.
> Guide us on the straight path.
> The path of those to whom Thou hast been gracious;
> With whom Thou art not angry, and who go not astray.

This verse they repeated several times as they prayed. Muslims should pray at dawn, at noon, in the afternoon, at sunset, and after dark. The Bait Kathir prayed at dawn and sunset, but most of them neglected the other prayers.

A little later I would hear bell-like notes as someone pounded coffee in a brass mortar, varying his stroke to produce the semblance of a tune. I would get up. In the desert we slept in our clothes so that all I had to do was adjust my head-cloth, pour a little water over my hands, splash it over my face, and then go over to the fire and greet the Arabs who were sitting round it: "Salam Alaikum" (Peace be on you), and they would stand up and answer "Akaikum as Salam" (On you be peace). Bedu always rise to return a salutation. If we were not in a hurry we would bake bread for breakfast, otherwise we would eat scraps set aside from our meal the night before. We would drink tea, sweet and black, and then coffee, which was bitter, black, and very strong. The coffee-drinking was a formal business, not to be hurried. The server stood as he poured a few drops into a small china cup, little bigger than an egg cup, which he handed to each of us in turn, bowing as he did. Each person was served until he shook the cup slightly as he handed it back, signifying that he had had enough. It was not customary to take more than three cups.

The camels were now rounded up and brought in to be saddled and loaded. Sultan went over to fetch Umbrausha, the camel I was riding. She was a magnificent animal, a famous thoroughbred from Oman. The other camels seemed to me to be very small, judged by Sudanese standards, and all of them were in poor condition. Sultan had told me that there had been no proper rain in the desert for the last three years, and that their animals were weak from hunger.

The camels which these Bedu rode were females. In the Sudan I had always ridden on bulls, since both there and in those parts of the Sahara where I had travelled the females are kept for milk and never ridden. Throughout Arabia, however, females are ridden from choice. The tribes which carry goods for hire use the bulls as pack animals, but the Bait Kathir slaughter nearly all the male calves at birth. They live largely on camels' milk, and have no desire to squander food on animals which can make no return, since there is no carrying trade in this desert. Bull camels to act as sires are consequently very rare. Later, when I travelled to the Hadhramaut, I was accompanied by a man who rode one. We were continuously pursued by tribesmen with females to be served. We had a long journey in front us and this constant exercise was visibly exhausting my companion's mount but he could not protest. Custom demanded that this camel should be allowed to serve as many females as were produced. No one even asked the owner's permission. They just brought up a camel, had it served, and took it away.

Loading the camels was a noisy business, for most of them roared and snarled whenever they were approached, and especially when the loads were placed on their backs. I asked Sultan how they managed on raids when silence was important, and he told me that they then tied the camels' mouths. The noise which our camels were making would have been heard two miles away or even farther in the desert stillness. Sultan had brought Umbrausha over to the place where I had slept, leading her by her head-rope. He now jerked downwards on it, saying "Khrr, khrr," and she dropped to her knees; she then swayed backwards, and after settling her hind legs under her, sank down on to her hocks; she then shuffled her knees forward until she was comfortably settled on the ground, her chest resting on the horny pad between her forelegs. Sultan tied one of her forelegs with the end of the head-rope to prevent her rising while he was loading her. Umbrausha was properly trained and this was not necessary, but an Arab near us was having a lot of trouble with a young animal. She struggled back to her feet after he had couched her, and even after he had tied her knees she half rose and then pivoted round among the loads which he had been trying to put on her back. She snarled and gurgled, spewing half-chewed green cud over his shirt. "May raiders get you," he shouted at her in exasperation. She looked as if she would bite his head off at any moment, but female camels are really very gentle and do not bite. Male camels will bite, especially when they are rutting, and they inflict appalling injuries. I had treated a man in the Sudan who had been bitten in the arm and the bone was splintered to fragments.

The southern Bedu ride on the small Omani saddle instead of on the double-poled saddle of northern Arabia to which I was accustomed. Sultan picked up my saddle, which was shaped like a small double wooden vice, fitted over palm-fibre pads, and girthed it tightly over Umbrausha's withers just in front of the hump. This wooden vice was really the tree on which he now built the saddle. He next took a crescent-shaped fibre pad which rose in a peak at the back and, after fitting it round the back and sides of the camel's hump, attached it with a loop of string to this tree. He then put a blanket over the pad, and folded my rug over this, placed my saddle-bags over the rug, and finally put a black sheepskin on top of the saddle-bags. He had already looped a woollen cord under the camel's stomach so that it passed over the rear pad, and he now took one end of this cord past the tree and back along the other side of the saddle to the original loop. When he drew the cord tight it held everything firmly in place. He had now built a platform over the camel's hump and the fibre pad which was behind it. Sitting on this, the rider was much farther back on the camel than he would have been if riding on the northern saddle, which is set over the camel's withers.

My saddle-bags were heavy with money and spare ammunition, and the small medicine-chest which I took with me. Most of the other riding camels carried forty or fifty pounds of rice or flour; all of them would be heavily laden when we were travelling long distances between wells and all our goatskins would be filled with water. I had hired four baggage camels, and these carried between a hundred and fifty and two hundred pounds.

When all was ready we set off on foot. We always walked for the first two or three hours While we were still in the mountains each of us led his camel, or tied her by the head-rope to the tail of the one in front. Later, when we were on gravel plains or in the sands, we turned them loose to find whatever food they could as they drifted along. We would walk behind them with our rifles on our shoulders, held by the muzzle. This is the way Bedu always carry their rifles. At first I found it disconcerting, for I knew that all the rifles were loaded. Then I got used to it and did the same myself. When at length the sun grew hot we rode. The Bedu never bothered to stop their mounts and make them kneel before they got up, but pulled down their heads, put a foot on their necks, and were lifted up to within easy reach of the saddle. At first they insisted on couching my camel when I wished to mount. This was meant as a kindness. So it was when they begged me to ride instead of walking as we started out in the morning, and when they frequently offered me a drink, but I found this constant attention irksome, because I was only anxious for them to treat me as one of themselves.

A Bedu who is going to mount a couched camel stands behind her tail. He then leans forward and catches the wooden tree with his left hand as he places his left knee in the saddle. Immediately the camel feels his weight she starts to rise, lifting her hindquarters off the ground, and he swings his right leg over the saddle. The camel then rises to her knees and with another jerk is on her feet. The Bedu either sit with a leg on either side of the hump, or kneel in the saddle, sitting on the upturned soles of their feet, in which case they are riding entirely by balance. They prefer to ride kneeling, especially if they mean to gallop. It is an extraordinary feat of balance, for riding a galloping camel, especially over rough ground is like sitting on a bucking horse. A Bedu usually carries his rifle slung under his arm and parallel with the ground, which must add greatly to the difficulty of balancing. I could not ride kneeling; it was too uncomfortable and too precarious even at a walk. I had therefore to sit continuously in one position, which became very tiring on a long march. The first time I rode a camel in the Sudan I was so stiff next day I could scarcely move. This had not happened to me again, but I was afraid that it might when I started on this journey, for it was seven years since I had last ridden any distance. It would have been humiliating, for I had claimed that I was already an experienced rider.

In Darfur I had fed my camels on grain and had trotted them. A good camel travelling at about five or six miles an hour is very comfortable, but when walking even the best throw a continuous and severe strain on the rider's back. In southern Arabia the Bedu never trot when they are on a journey, for their camels eat only what they can find, which is generally very little, and have to travel long distances between wells. I had already learnt on the journeys to Bir Natrun and to Tibesti not to press a camel beyond its normal walking pace when travelling in the desert. I was soon to discover how considerate the Bedu were of their camels, always ready to suffer hardship themselves in order to spare their animals. Several times while travelling with them and approaching a well, I have expected them to push on and fill the water-skins, as our water was finished, but they have insisted on halting for the night short of the well, saying that farther on there was no grazing.

Whenever we passed any bushes we let our camels dawdle to strip mouthfuls of leaves and thorns, and whenever we came to richer grazing we halted to let them graze at will. I was making a time-and-compass traverse of our route and these constant halts were frustrating, making it difficult to estimate the distance which we had covered. On good going, where there was no feeding to delay us, we averaged three miles an hour, but in the Sands, where the dunes were steep and difficult, we might only do one mile an hour.

It often seemed incredible to me, especially when I was on foot and conscious of the steps I was taking, that we could cover such enormous distances going at this pace. Sometimes I counted my footsteps to a bush or some other mark, and this number seemed but a trifle deducted from the sum that lay ahead of us. Yet I had no desire to travel faster. In this way there was time to notice things—a grasshopper under a bush, a dead swallow on the ground, the tracks of a hare, a bird's nest, the shape and colour of ripples in the sand, the bloom of tiny seedlings pushing through the soil. There was time to collect a plant or to look at a rock. The very slowness of our march diminished its monotony. I thought how terribly boring it would be to rush about this country in a car.

We drifted along, our movements governed by an indefinable common consent. There was seldom much discussion; we either halted or we went on. Sometimes we would start in the morning, expecting to do a long march, come unexpectedly on grazing soon after we started, and halt for the day. At other times we planned to stop somewhere, but finding when we got to our destination that there was no grazing, we would push on without a halt till dark or even later. If we stopped in the middle of the day we would hurriedly unload the camels, hobble them, and turn them loose to graze. Then we might cook break or porridge, but more often we ate dates. Always we drank coffee, which my companions craved for as a drug. Some of them smoked, and this was their only other indulgence. No one ever smoked without sharing his pipe with the others; they would squat round while one sifted a few grains of tobacco from the dust in the bottom of a small leather bag which he carried inside his shirt next to his skin. He would stuff this tobacco into a small stemless piple cut out of soft stone, or into an old cartridge case open at both ends, light it with a flint and steel, take two or three deep puffs and hand it to the next person. If we were travelling when they wished to smoke, they stopped, got off, squatted down, smoked, and then climbed back into their saddles.

We always camped crowded together. All around us was endless space, and yet in our camps there was scarcely room to move, especially when the camels had been brought in for the night and couched around the fires. When we started on this journey we had divided ourselves into messes of five or six people, who each carried their own food. I fed with old Tamtaim, Sultan, and three others. One was Mabkhaut, a slightly built man of middle age; he was good-humoured and considerate, but he seldom spoke, which was unusual among these garrulous Bedu. Another was Musallim bin Tafl, who had been pointed out to me by the Wali as a skillful hunter. He was avaricious even by Bedu standards, quick-witted, and hard-working. He was often in Salala, hanging about the palace, and had had in consequence the unusual experience of some contact with the outside world. He volunteered to do the cooking for our party.

When we had enough water he would cook rice, but generally he made bread for our evening meal. He would scoop out three or four pounds of flour from one of the goatskin bags in which we carried our supplies, and would then damp this, add a little salt and mix it into a thick paste. He would divide the dough into six equal-sized lumps, pat each lump between his hands until it had become a disc about half an inch thick, and would then put it down on a rug while he shaped the others. Someone else would have lighted the fire, sometimes with matches but generally with flint and steel. There was plenty of flint in the desert and the blade of a dagger to use as steel. They would tear small strips off their shirts or head-cloths for tinder, with the result that each day their clothes became more tattered in appearance. Musallim would rake some embers out of the fire to make a glowing bed, and then drop the cakes of dough on to it. The heat having sealed the outside of the cakes, he would turn them over almost immediately, and then, scooping a hollow in the sand under the embers, would bury them and spread the hot sand and embers over them. I would watch bubbles breaking through this layer of sand and ashes as the bread cooked. Later he would uncover the cakes, brush off the sand and ashes and put them aside to cool. When we wished to feed he would give one to each of us, and we would sit in a circle and, in turn, dip pieces of this bread into a small bowl containing melted butter, or soup if we happened to have anything from which to make it. The bread was brick hard or soggy, according to how long it had been cooked, and always tasted as if it had been made from sawdust. Sometimes Musallim shot a gazelle or an oryx, and only then did we feed well. After we had eaten we would sit round the fire and talk. Bedu always shout at each other, even if they are only a few feet apart. Everyone could therefore hear what was being said by everyone else in the camp, and anyone who was interested in a conversation round another fire could join in from where he was sitting.

Soon after dinner I would spread out my rug and sheepskin and, putting my dagger and cartridge belt under the saddle-bags which I used as a pillow, lie down beneath three blankets with my rifle beside me. While I was among the Arabs I was anxious to behave as they did, so that they would accept me to some extent as one of themselves. I had therefore to sit as they did, and I found this very trying, for my muscles were not accustomed to this position. I was glad when it was night and I could lie down and be at ease. I had sat on the ground before, but then I had been travelling with men whom I knew well, and with them I could relax and lie about. Now I would get off my camel after a long march and have to sit formally as Arabs sit. It took me a long time to get used to this. For the same reason I went barefooted as they did, and at first this was torture. Eventually the soles of my feet became hardened, but even after five years they were soft compared with theirs.

It hardly occurred to the Bedu that there could be other ways of doing things than those to which they were accustomed. When they fetched me from the R.A.F. camp at Salala they had seen an airman urinating. Next day they asked me what physical deformity he suffered from which prevented him from squatting as they did. In the mountains it was easy to go behind a rock to relieve myself. Later, on the open plains, I walked off to a distance and squatted as they did, with my cloak over my head to form a tent. Except when we were at a well, we used sand to scrub our faces after we had fed, and to clean ourselves after we had defecated. Bedu are always careful not to relieve themselves near a path. In the trackless sands Arabs who stopped behind to urinate turned instinctively aside from the tracks which we ourselves had made before they squatted.

Muslims are usually very prudish and are careful to avoid exposing themselves. My companions always kept their loin-cloths on even when they washed at the wells. At first I found it difficult to wear a loin-cloth with decency when sitting on the ground. Bedu say to anyone whose parts are showing, "Your nose!" I had this said to me once or twice before I learnt to be more careful. The first time I wiped my nose thinking that there was a drip on the end of it, for the weather was very cold.

At first I found living with the Bedu very trying, and during the years that I was with them I always found the mental strain greater than the physical. It was as difficult for me to adapt myself to their way of life, and especially to their outlook, as it was for them to accept what they regarded as my eccentricities. I had been used to privacy, and here I had none. If I wanted to talk privately to someone it was difficult. Even if we went a little apart, others would be intrigued and immediately come to find out what we were talking about and join in the conversation. Every word I said was overheard, and every move I made was watched. At first I felt very isolated among them. I knew they thought that I had unlimited money, and I suspected that they were trying to exploit me. I was exasperated by their avarice, and wearied by their importunities. Whenever during these early days one of them approached me, I thought, "Now what is he going to ask for?" and I would be irritated by the childish flattery with which they invariably prefaced their requests. I had yet to learn that no Bedu thinks it shameful to beg, and that often he will look at the gift which he has received and say, "Is this all that you are going to give me?" I was seeing the worst side of their character, and was disillusioned and resentful, and irritated by their assumption of superiority. In consequence I was assertive and unreasonable.

Some rain had fallen three months earlier on the northern slopes of the Qarra mountains, and there was a little green grazing in some of the valley-bottoms where freshets had run down. The Bedu were loath to leave this grazing and push on into the empty wastes which they knew lay ahead. They dawdled along doing one hour's marching one day, and perhaps two the next, while my exasperation mounted. Whenever we came to a patch of grazing they vowed that it was the last and insisted on stopping; and then next day we would find more grazing and stop again. Anyway, most of this grazing did not seem to me to be worth stopping for. Usually it was only a few green shrubs. I did not yet realize how rare any fresh vegetation was in this desert. I still thought in terms of so many marching hours a day, which had been easy to do in the Sudan where we hand-fed our camels. I fretted at the constant delays, counting the wasted days instead of revelling in this leisurely travel Unfairly, I suspected that the Arabs were trying to lengthen our journey in order to collect more money from me. When in the evenings I would protest and insist that we must do proper marches, Sultan and the others would add to my exasperation by saying that I knew nothing about camels, which was true. I would, however, explain indignantly what a lot of experience I had had with them in the Sudan. I found it difficult to understand what they were saying and this added to my frustration.

Bedu, attracted from afar by the fresh grazing, were herding camels and goats into the valleys through which we passed. They were hungry, as Bedu always are, and they collected each evening in our camp to feed at our expense. Everyone had heard that the Christian had great quantities of food with him. These unwanted guests never waited for an invitation before sitting down with us to feed. They just joined and shared whatever we had for as long as they were with us. Many of them followed us, turning up evening after evening. My companions accepted their presence with equanimity, since they would have done the same; and anyway, not Bedu will turn a guest away unfed. But I was irritated by their assumption that we should feed them, and disturbed by their numbers. I realized that we had not brought enough food with us and that we were going to be short before we returned to Salala. In my more bitter moments I thought that Bedu life was one long round of cadging and being cadged from.

It was three months before I returned to Salala. They were hard months of constant travel during which I learnt to admire my companions and to appreciate their skill. I soon found these tribesmen far easier to consort with than the more progressive town Arabs who, after discarding their own customs and traditions, have adopted something of our ways. I myself infinitely preferred the Bedu's arrogant self-assurance to the Effendi's easily wounded susceptibilities. I was beginning to see the desert as the Bedu saw it, and to judge men as they judged them. I had come here looking for more than locusts, and was finding the life for which I sought.

Two memories in particular remain with me of this journey. I had turned aside into the sands of Ghanim with a dozen Arabs, while the others when on to Mughshin. It was eight days since we had left the well at Shisur and our water had been finished for twenty-four hours. We were near Bir Halu, or "the sweet well," when we came on clumps of yellow-flowering tribulus, growing where a shower had fallen a few months before. We grazed our camels for a while, and I then suggested going on to the well, for I was thirsty. Eventually Tamtaim, Sultan, and Musallim came with me; the others said they would join us later after feeding the camels. We arrived at the well, unsaddled our camels, watered them, and then sat down near the well. No one had yet drunk. I was anxious not to appear impatient, but eventually I suggested we should so so. Sultan handed me a bowl of water. I offered it to old Tamtaim but he told me to drink, saying that he would wait till the others came, adding that as they were his travelling companions it would be unseemly for him to drink till they arrived. I had already learnt that Bedu will never take advantage over a companion by feeding while he is absent, but this restraint seemed to me exaggerated. The others did not arrive until five hours later, by which time I was thoroughly exasperated and very thirsty. Though the water looked deliciously cold and clear, it tasted like a strong dose of Epsom salts; I took a long draught and involuntarily spat it out. It was my first experience of water in the Sands.

A few days later we passed some tracks. I was not even certain that they were made by camels, for they were much blurred by the wind. Sultan turned to a grey-bearded man who was noted as a tracker and asked him whose tracks these were, and the man turned aside and followed them for a short distance. He then jumped off his camel, looked at the tracks where they crossed some hard ground, broke some camel-droppings between his fingers and rode back to join us. Sultan asked, "Who are they?" and the man answered, "They were Awamir. There are six of them. They have raided the Junuba on the southern coast and taken three of their camels. They have come here from Sahma and watered at Mughshin. They passed here ten days ago." We had seen no Arabs for seventeen days and we saw none for a further twenty-seven. On our return we met some Bait Kathir near Jabal Qarra and, when we exchanged our news, they told us that six Awamir had raided the Junuba, killed three of them, and taken three of their camels. The only thing we did not already know was that they had killed anyone.

Here every man knew the individual tracks of his own camels, and some of them could remember the tracks of nearly every camel they had seen. They could tell at a glance from the depth of the footprints whether a camel was ridden or free, and whether it was in calf. By studying strange tracks they could tell the area from which the camel came. Camels from the Sands, for instance, have soft soles to their feet, marked with tattered strips of loose skin, whereas if they come from the gravel plains their feet are polished smooth. Bedu could tell the tribe to which a camel belonged, for the different tribes have different breeds of camel, all of which can be distinguished by their tracks. From looking at their droppings they could often deduce where a camel had been grazing, and they could certainly tell when it had last been watered, and from their knowledge of the country they could probably tell where. Bedu are always well informed about the politics of the desert. They know the alliances and enmities of the tribes and can guess which tribes would raid each other. No Bedu will ever miss a chance of exchanging news with anyone he meets, and he will ride far out of his way to get fresh news.

As a result of this journey I found that the country round Mughshin was suffering from many years of drought. If there had been grazing we would have found Arabs with their herds, but we had just travelled for forty-four days without seeing anyone. I asked my companions about floods and they told me that no water had reached Mughshin from the Qarra mountains since the great floods twenty-five years before. It was obviously not an "outbreak centre" for desert locusts. I now decided to travel westwards to the Hadhramaut along the southern edge of the Sands, where I would be able to find out if floods ever reached these sands from the high Mahra mountains along the coast. No European had yet travelled in the country between Dhaufar and the Hadhramaut.

I had met with one of the Rashid sheikhs, called Musallim bin al Kamam, on my way to Mughshin, and had taken an immediate liking to him. I had asked him to meet me with some of his tribe in Salala in January, and to go with me to the Hadhramaut. I found bin al Kamam and some thirty Rashid waiting for me when I arrived in Salala on January 7th. I decided to keep Sultan and Musallim bin Tafl with me from the Bait Kathir and agreed to pay for fifteen Rashid, but bin al Kamam said that thirty men would come with us and share this pay. He explained that the country through which we should pass was frequently raided by the Yemen tribes. He had news that more than two hundred Dahm were even then raiding the Manahil on the steppes to the east of the Hadhramaut.

The Rashid were kinsmen and allies of the Bait Kathir, both tribes belonging to the Al Kathir. They were dressed in long Arab shirts and head-cloths, which had been dyed a soft russet-brown with the juice of a desert shrub. They wore their clothes with distinction, even when they were in rags. They were small deft men, alert and watchful. Their bodies were lean and hard, trained to incredible endurance. Looking at them, I realized that they were very much alive, tense with nervous energy, vigorously controlled. They had been bred from the purest race in the world, and lived under conditions where only the hardiest and best could possibly survive. They were as fine-drawn and highly strung as thoroughbreds. Beside them the Bait Kathir seemed uncouth and assertive, lacking the final polish of the inner desert.

The Rashid and the Awamir were tribes in southern Arabia who had adapted themselves to life in the Sands. Some of their sections lived in the central sands, the only place in the Empty Quarter with wells; others had moved right across the Sands to the Trucial Coast. The homelands of both the Rashid and the Amawir were on the steppes to the north-east and to the north of the Hadhramaut. The Bait Imani section of the Rashid still lived there, and we should pass through their territory on our way to the Hadhra-maut. The Manahil lived farther to the west, between there and the Awamir. Beyond the Awamir were the Saar, bitter enemies of the Rashid. The Mahra, divided into many sections, lived in the mountains and on the plateau along the coast; beyond them were the Humum to the north of Mukalla.

The Bedu tribes of southern Arabia were insignificant in numbers compared with those of central and northern Arabia, where the tents of a sin-gle tribe might number thousands. In Syria I had seen the Shammar migrat-ing, a whole people on the move, covering the desert with their herds, and had visited the summer camp of the Rualla, a city of black tents. In northern Arabia the desert merges into the sown and there is a gradual transition from Bedu to shepherds and cultivators. Damascus, Aleppo, Mosul, and Baghdad exert their influence on the desert. They are visited by Bedu, who see in their bazaars men of different races, cultures, and faiths. Even in the Najd the Bedu have occasional contact with towns and town life. But here scattered families moved over great distances seeking pasturage for a dozen camels. These Rashid, who roamed form the borders of the Hadhramaut to the Persian Gulf, numbered only three hundred men, while the Bait Kathir were about six hundred. But these Arabs were among the most authentic of the Bedu, the least affected by the outside world. In the south the desert runs down into the sea, continues into the kindlier deserts of the north, or ends against the black barren foothills of the Yemen or Oman. There were few towns within reach of the southern Bedu, and these they rarely visited.

My ambition was to cross the Empty Quarter. I had hoped that I might be able to do so with these Rashid after we had reached the Hadhramaut, but I realized when I talked with them that by then it would be too hot. I was resolved to return, and was content to regard this first year as training for later journeys. I knew that among the Rashid I had found the Arabs for whom I was looking.

Permissions Acknowledgments

Alexandra David-Neel, "Journey to Lhasa" from *My Journey to Lhasa*. Copyright © 1927 by Harper & Row, Publishers, Inc. Renewed 1955 by Alexandra David-Neel. Reprinted with the permission of HarperCollins Publishers Inc.

David Roberts, "Did Peary Reach the Pole?" from *Great Exploration Hoaxes*, pp. 107–124. Copyright © 1982 by Dave Roberts. Originally published by Sierra Club Books, San Francisco. Reprinted New York: Modern Library, 2001. Reprinted here with permission from Dave Roberts.

Fergus Fleming, "John Franklin: The Man Who Ate His Boots" from *Barrow's Boys*. Copyright © 1998 by Fergus Fleming. Used by permission of Grove/Atlantic, Inc. and Gillon Aitken Associates, Ltd.

Roy Chapman Andrews, "Ends of the Earth" from *Ends of the Earth*. Copyright © 1929 by the Curtis Publishing Company. Originally published by G.P. Putnam's Sons, New York/London. Reprinted with permission by George B. Andrews.

Wilfred Thesiger, "The Empty Quarter" from *Arabian Sands*. Copyright © 1959 by Sir Wilfred Thesiger. Originally published by E.P. Dutton and Company, Inc. Acknowledge Curtis Brown on behalf of Sir Wilfred Thesiger.

910.9   1
Greates

**The Greatest Exploration
Stories Ever Told.**